Praise for the novels of Paula Treick DeBoard

"In Paula Treick DeBoard's latest breathtaking thriller, she paints a stark and chillingly real portrayal of a family torn apart by teenage transgressions. Gritty and inauspicious from the start, *The Drowning Girls* left me awestruck, revealing DeBoard's true brilliance as an author. Spellbinding."
—Mary Kubica, *New York Times* bestselling author of *The Good Girl*

"*The Drowning Girls* by Paula Treick DeBoard is cleverly plotted, full of twists and turns and so well-written that it pulls you in from page one. Genuinely suspenseful, Treick DeBoard delivers a disturbing, multilayered, provocative novel that is impossible to put down."
—Heather Gudenkauf, *New York Times* bestselling author of *The Weight of Silence*

"A heart-pounding look at what lies behind the deceptively placid veneer of the well-to-do suburbs. The kaleidoscopic view of innocence, danger, and malice shifts and twists as it races to a shattering conclusion."
—Sophie Littlefield, bestselling author of *The Guilty One*, on *The Drowning Girls*

"In *The Drowning Girls*, DeBoard pulls you right into her world and holds you in her grip until the book's final twist. Fans of *The Good Girl* and *The Luckiest Girl Alive*, and really anyone who enjoys great suspense, have found their next must-read. Sure to be the book everyone is talking about in 2016, I could not put it down."
—Catherine McKenzie, bestselling author of *Hidden* and *Smoke*

"*The Drowning Girls* casts a spell as brilliant and alluring as the gated community of its setting. Paula Treick DeBoard maps this world of privilege and secrets with a deft hand, and from the novel's terrifying opening pages reveals a family's tragic unraveling. These characters long for love and happiness, but the trail of duplicity that ultimately ensnares them creates a suspenseful and compelling page-turner I couldn't put down."
—Karen Brown, author of *The Longings of Wayward Girls*

"A coming-of-age tale about a family in crisis expertly told by Ms. DeBoard. *The Fragile World* examines how profound loss changes all who are forced to come to terms with it. Touching and compelling, it will move you."
—Lesley Kagen, *New York Times* bestselling author of *Whistling in the Dark* and *The Resurrection of Tess Blessing*

"Assured storytelling propels DeBoard's first novel."
—*Publishers Weekly* on *The Mourning Hours*

"Rich and evocative...compelling."
—*RT Book Reviews* on *The Mourning Hours*

"Tautly written and beautifully evocative, *The Mourning Hours* is a gripping portrayal of a family straining against extraordinary pressure, and a powerful tale of loyalty, betrayal and forgiveness."
—*Bookreporter.com*

Also by Paula Treick DeBoard

THE FRAGILE WORLD
THE MOURNING HOURS

THE DROWNING GIRLS

PAULA TREICK DeBOARD

MIRA®

ISBN-13: 978-0-7783-1837-8

The Drowning Girls

Copyright © 2016 by Paula Treick DeBoard

Recycling programs
for this product may
not exist in your area.

For questions and comments about the quality of this book, please contact us at
CustomerService@Harlequin.com.

www.MIRABooks.com

Printed in U.S.A.

First printing: May 2016
10 9 8 7 6 5 4 3 2 1

For Will, for always.

THE DROWNING GIRLS

"One day you will do things for me that you hate. That is what it means to be family."

—Jonathan Safran Foer
Everything is Illuminated

JUNE 19, 2015

5:40 P.M.

LIZ

Someone was screaming.

For a moment, with the ceiling fan whirring quietly over my head, I allowed myself to believe it was a benign sound—the kids next door on their play structure, maybe, sliding and swinging and climbing, their voices carrying on a breeze.

I propped myself up on my elbows, blinking myself awake. How long had I been sleeping? Twenty minutes, an hour? The tank top I was wearing was streaked with dust and damp with sweat. Dizzy, I focused on my bare feet, where chipped red polish dotted my toes. On the dresser was a nearly empty bottle of Riesling, a slick ring of condensation bubbling on the wood.

I reached a hand onto Phil's side of the bed, groping and coming up empty. Of course. Phil was gone, and he'd taken everything with him—armfuls of shirts and pants, suit coats and blazers, slippery mounds of ties and belts, even the dry cleaning in its plastic sheeting. Shoes, too: wing tips, loafers, sneakers, the pair of black Converse I'd never once seen him wear. He'd taken the neatly folded stacks of T-shirts and boxers, the lumps of paired socks, the heavy woolen sweater that smelled like a Greek fishing village—or at least, how I'd imagined a Greek fishing village would smell, briny and deep-down damp.

After he left, I'd searched the floor for a button, a collar stay, a lonely sock, as if I could keep that one discarded thing as evidence of our life together. For a long time, I'd wanted to go back, to pin our relationship to a wall and study it, like a specimen, from every angle. I wanted to be able to say: *Here*. This is where it all went wrong. This was the point at which the inevitable was still evitable.

But that was a long time ago. Months now.

I shook my head, chasing away the thoughts, and heard the screams again, over a relentless pounding of bass. Was the television on downstairs? That was the simple explanation, and for a moment, I allowed myself to be reassured by the thought of actors following a script, raising their voices on cue.

And then I remembered: the girls.

The pool.

The screams were coming from outside, distorted by the triple-paned windows, as if they were being filtered through a kaleidoscope, splitting and fracturing.

I swung my legs over the side of the bed and moved toward the door. My head pounded, an angry thing.

Danielle.

My baby.

No—not a baby. Fifteen and so angry we'd barely exchanged more than a sentence in a month.

I stumbled on the stairs, catching myself with a hand on the rail. *Steady, Liz.* I had to navigate around the stacks of boxes in the foyer marked Towels and Office and, helpfully, Stuff.

Closer now, the screams became words, and the words became language, mixed with the thumping of the stereo, the music that had been playing all afternoon.

Help!

Mom!

Ohmygodno!

I yanked open the sliding door, catching my foot on the frame in my hurry. A bright bloom of pain flowered in my vision. After the interior darkness, the outside was a trick of sunlight, bright against the water, a shimmering, endless blue. I squinted into the glare, trying to understand what I was seeing.

It looked at first like a game of tug-of-war, a three-headed, six-armed monster writhing in the water.

But of course, it wasn't a game.

It was another inevitable, a thing that had been coming and coming, a thing I'd let come. There were three girls in the water and one of them was limp, her head flopped forward, blond hair plastered over her face.

Still the shouts came, an unrelenting swirl of voices. In that half second while my mind puzzled, before my body could snap into action, I realized that the loudest voice, the one that couldn't stop screaming, belonged to me.

JUNE 2014
LIZ

The Mesbahs' house was only a block away, but it was a long block, outsize the way everything else was at The Palms—half-acre lots, semicircular driveways, the occasional six-foot frond dropped from one of the signature palm trees like the feather of an exotic, towering bird. Next to me, Phil had his hands in his pockets, his legs shooting forward in confident strides. I kept my eyes on my feet, sure that one of my heels would snag in a sidewalk crack.

"It's the Spanish Revival, right around the corner from you," Myriam Mesbah had said during our sole conversation the week before, when I'd called to RSVP for the party. I'd scribbled *Spanish revival?* on the back of a receipt so I'd remember to look it up on Google later. "The *whole neighborhood* will be there," she'd said. "You can't miss it."

Her words always carried that sense of emphasis—as if they needed italics, air quotes, long deliberate stresses. *What I have to say is important.*

Spanish Revival meant curves and arches, white stucco and terra-cotta tile and ornamental ironwork. It meant courtyards and balconies and quiet little nooks. For the Mesbahs and everyone else in The Palms, it meant a minimum of four thousand square feet and a resale value that was climbing—an asset they could list in a portfolio along with the apartment on the Upper East Side, the villa in Tuscany, the time-shares in Bali and Saint Thomas and little islands with names I couldn't pronounce or locate on a map.

To me, it was just intimidating.

As we passed through the ornamental gate and entered the courtyard, Phil squeezed my hand, already damp and tacky with sweat. His grin belied a fierce kind of optimism.

We were three weeks into our new life, our boxes mostly unpacked, the strong leathery smell beginning to wear off the couches, fingerprints already smearing our stainless appliances. Still, I hadn't been able to shake the feeling that it was an experiment, like one of Danielle's science projects on trifold cardboard: hypothesis, observation, data, conclusion.

Hypothesis: the McGinnises will never fit in with these people.

The observations were in progress, the data accumulating.

But I figured it was a foregone conclusion: we didn't belong.

The Mesbahs' house was humming with energy—outside the ten-foot mahogany doors, we heard the low pulse of music, a woman's high-pitched laugh over the other voices. It was seven twenty, late enough to avoid the awkwardness of being too early, of having to stand around and explain ourselves, the new people. I'd taken my time in the bathroom, selecting a pair of earrings, spraying my hair repeatedly, dabbing the dregs of an old perfume bottle on my wrists— anything to avoid this moment, to prolong the inevitable.

Phil made a minuscule adjustment to his collar and

breathed a short huff into his cupped palm, checking his breath. "Ready?"

I caught his fist halfway to the knock, imagining them all standing just inside the door, turning to look at us. "No."

"*Liz…*"

"I know. Just give me…" I bent down and began to fiddle with the straps on my sandals. They'd been a last-minute purchase only this afternoon, after I'd rejected every single thing in my closet as being wrong for this kind of event. The trouble was that I didn't understand the event. It wasn't a barbecue; it was no one's birthday. The invitation had read *An instruction on wine and cheese pairing,* as if we were meant to come armed with spiral notebooks and expect an exam at the end. In the dressing room at Macy's, I'd felt good enough about the silky black pants to put them on my credit card; now, bent nearly double in the Mesbahs' courtyard, I noticed that the fabric across my thighs was creased horizontally with hash marks. I loosened the skinny strap on one shoe and rebuckled it into the next hole before shifting my attention to the other foot.

"Come on," Phil breathed.

Sure—I was stalling. Every minute spent on the Mesbahs' porch was a minute I wouldn't have to spend inside their house. In our previous lives, Phil and I had lived in a three-bedroom rental a few blocks off the freeway. When friends invited us over, we stopped by Trader Joe's for a bottle of wine or a six-pack of microbrew. That was a social convention I understood. On the bottom of this invitation had been printed, in delicate scroll: *Donations will be accepted for Shriners Hospital, Sacramento.*

"So this is a thing?" I'd asked Phil, showing him the invitation. "Come to our house, bring your checkbook and we'll teach you about wine?"

He'd shrugged. "It's just an excuse to get together. It sounds fun."

"We're going?"

"Why wouldn't we?"

I'd been saying it in a hundred ways, and he hadn't heard me yet. *Because these aren't our kind of people. Because we don't belong.* It was all a mistake, beginning with Phil's new job and our move to The Palms, and ending with me standing in front of the Mesbahs' front door in these silly pants and uncomfortable shoes.

"All right," Phil said now in the voice he sometimes used with Danielle, when she took too long in the bathroom or kept him waiting in the car. I secured the second buckle and straightened, spotting the outline of the folded envelope in his breast pocket. Two hundred dollars, payable to the Shriners Hospital of Sacramento, the going rate of admission into the social world of The Palms. It was both more than we could afford and ridiculously cheap, considering the heavy door knocker and the immaculate tile work.

"We wouldn't want to miss any instruction," I said, trying to bring back a note of levity, of shared camaraderie and let's-make-the-best-of-it. But Phil was looking away from me, the door was opening and the joke was lost.

Victor Mesbah stood in the doorway, a glass of wine in one hand. In the golden light from the wall sconces, it looked like blood sloshing in his glass. "Here they are!" he boomed in a voice that echoed off the floors. "Just when we were beginning to think you wouldn't show."

Phil met his aggressive handshake. "Wouldn't think of it."

I extended a hand, too, but Victor threw his free arm

around my shoulder. "It's so nice to meet you," I said, but his neck smothered my words.

"Liz, *finally*," Myriam said, and I disentangled myself from Victor's half hug. She was slender and severely beautiful, with a nose that would have been too much on another woman. She hooked me by the arm and led me through a wide foyer to an open great room, our heels clattering on the mahogany floors. "Our new neighbors, the McGinnises," she announced to the room at large, where at least a dozen couples were gathered in polite clusters. Everyone turned, chorusing their hellos. They looked so smooth and shiny, as if they'd all arrived, en masse, from appointments at the salon. Overhead, an enormous ceiling fan moved like a sluggish insect.

"Of course, most of us have met Phil by now. But you've been so *elusive*. I've wondered about you, alone in that house all day," Myriam continued.

"Not alone, exactly. My daughter, Danielle...we've been unpacking, getting things in order," I said. This was only half-true. Danielle was gone for the week, and after a few days of diligent unpacking, I'd stacked the rest of the boxes in the living room, with vague plans to tackle one a day for the rest of the summer.

Next to me, I could feel Myriam's interest waning, her eyes roving the room. "Come on," she said, her hand still at my elbow. "Let me get you something to drink and I'll make some introductions."

I glanced over my shoulder at Phil, who had already forgotten his promise to stay by my side. That was one of the benefits of being a couple, after all—in new situations, we could share the little anecdotes about each other that we wouldn't have mentioned about ourselves, play off each other like a straight man and a comic. But already a few of the men had stepped forward to talk to Phil, and Victor had a possessive arm clapped to his back.

I smiled at Myriam. "That would be wonderful." She released my arm and left me standing alone, in front of the frank stares of my neighbors. It was the adult equivalent of a naked-at-school nightmare. I felt the blush rising up my neck, settling in rosy splotches on my cheeks. It was funny—back in our old lives, I never gave much thought to who my neighbors were or what they thought of me. But The Palms was so exclusive, so tightly knit, it was like living in a fishbowl.

"So, you're in the Rameys' house," someone said, the voice rising disembodied from a corner. "Thank goodness. That place was empty for what...eight months?"

I shrugged. "I'm not sure."

"Oh, it was more than eight months," someone else answered. "Don't you remember how the lawn just about died out?"

"Well, however long it was, I'm so glad someone finally bought the place."

"Actually, we—" I began, then stopped. Didn't everyone know? The house had come with Phil's job, a package deal. Parker-Lane covered our lease and $1,495 in monthly HOA fees, or room and board, as I'd come to think of it, with a salary that left us house-rich, cash-poor. In practical terms, this meant that the people who were fawning over us now were also paying dearly for the right to hit tennis balls and jog along the community trail, while we could do those things for free. I tried again, feeling the need to set the record straight. "My husband, Phil, is..."

But my husband, at that moment, let out a hearty laugh from somewhere behind me. He was telling a story, his accent strong despite two decades away from Melbourne. Men and women alike were drawn to that accent—imagining, I supposed, a swashbuckling hero in the outback. Heads turned to look in his direction, and in the swirl of voices, my words were lost.

"Oh, no, no, no," Myriam said, stepping in to clarify. She handed me a glass, saying, "Cabernet." Then to the room at large, she announced, "Phil is our new community relations specialist, but they'll be living right here, on-site. Isn't that fantastic?"

I nodded, ducking my head as if to study the wine more closely. Maybe she thought of us as charity cases, worthy of a fund-raiser. *Donations will be accepted on behalf of the McGinnises, who have only been able to furnish half of their four thousand square feet.*

"Let's see," Myriam said. "Where should we start? I suppose you've met the Sieverts."

"I haven't really met anyone," I confessed. "What with all the unpacking..."

"Well, then, here we go," Myriam said, taking a swallow from her own glass, as if to fortify herself.

For the past three weeks, I'd been watching my neighbors from the safety of my front porch with a morning cup of coffee, like an anthropologist afraid to actually encounter the natives. I'd seen them entering and exiting the community trail in their jogging clothes, the men with their long shinbones, the women with their tight ponytails. Our greetings had never gone beyond a raised hand of solidarity, a brisk *Hello!* Who were these people? I'd wondered. What did they do, how could they afford such extravagant lives? The answers were in a stack of file boxes temporarily relocated to our dining room while Phil's office was being repainted. I knew it was wrong, or at least *wrongish*, as my sister,

Allie, and I used to say, to sneak these clandestine peeks into strangers' lives, but from the moment I opened the first manila folder, I lacked all willpower to stop. I pawed through housing applications, ogled the lists of assets (three thousand acres in Montana! The yacht, the wine collection, the jewelry!) and raised an eyebrow at the alphabet soup that trailed their names—CEO, CFO, MBA, MD. Someone in Phase 2 had paid $750,000 for a *racehorse*, and I still had four years of payments on my student loan.

I'd emailed Allie in Chicago: One of my neighbors has an actual Picasso.

She replied, I have a set of four Picasso coasters. I'd fit right in.

Being at the Mesbahs' party was like playing a real-life game of Memory—matching the faces of the people in front of me with the snippets of information I already knew.

The Sieverts were our closest neighbors across the street. Rich owned a string of fast-food restaurants in the Bay Area; Deanna (only twenty-four, I remembered from their file), was his second wife. It was Rich's son, Mac, from his first marriage, who drove the monster truck that blasted to life several times a day and was often parked crookedly in their four-car driveway.

"Don't you just love living in The Palms?" Deanna asked. She shimmered next to me in a strapless green pantsuit, her question punctuated by the grip of her glittery fingernails on my forearm. Up close, her hair was a brassy, yellowish blond.

"I do," I said, and then with more emphasis, as if I were performing for a lie detector test, "It's really great."

"Moving on," Myriam murmured, her hand at my elbow.

The Berglands owned the colonial farmhouse closest to the clubhouse; they passed by our house a few times each day in a burgundy Suburban loaded with kids. Carly Bergland was so petite, her baby bump stood out like a ledge, perfectly positioned to hold a glass of mineral water. "You'd think we'd learn," she said, rubbing her belly. "This is number six. But babies are our business, I guess you could say."

"Carly and Jeremy *own* Nah-Nah Foods," Myriam explained.

I remembered this from their files—Nah-Nah Foods was an organic baby food business. "That's fantastic," I said.

Carly smiled. "Have you seen our displays in Whole Foods? We mostly do formula, but we've been venturing into the world of purees."

The one time I'd gone into Whole Foods, I'd left with a twelve-dollar carton of blueberries and vowed never to return. "I'll have to look for it," I said.

Carly took a sip of her water. "I have a mommy blog, too. Between the two ventures, we've been very successful." There was no trace of modesty in her voice, none of the sarcasm or self-deprecation that was my staple. In his first weeks, Phil had received a number of complaints about the Berglands—kids' toys on the lawn, bikes left at the curb. I wondered if she knew that.

"My oldest must be about the age of your daughter," Carly continued. "Hannah. She's fifteen."

I smiled. "Danielle's fourteen. Just starting high school. Where does Hannah go?"

Carly blinked. "Oh, no. She's homeschooled. We won't even *dream* of it anymore, with the state of public education—"

Myriam steered me away, her grip insistent. This was her task as a hostess, I realized, an obligation she was determined to fulfill so she could be done with me.

I recognized Trevor and Marja Browers as the couple who

walked past my house each morning at sunrise, their two white heads bobbing in sync, their hands raised in benevolent hellos. I'd come to think of them as the grandparents of the community. Trevor was a laser specialist, officially retired from Lawrence-Livermore Labs, although he still consulted part-time. "He has *top-level* security clearance," Myriam said. "And Marja, *dear* Marja…"

"It's very secluded here, *ja*?" Marja asked, her Dutch accent strong. Her face was soft and friendly, accented with a slash of red lipstick.

I stopped myself, but only barely, from agreeing with a *ja* in return.

She smiled, revealing teeth that were charmingly crooked. "Sometimes too secluded, if you know what I mean?"

I did.

Oh, I did.

We were only a few feet away when Myriam whispered, "We call those *socialist teeth*," with a wicked laugh at her own joke. I realized it was the same laugh she would utter when I left. *We call those sales-rack shoes.*

I decided right there that I hated her—that I hated all of them—as we worked our way through the room: the Roche-Edwardses, the Navarres, the Coffeys. They blended together, along with their details: the Mediterranean with the blue mosaic inlay, the husband in finance, the daughter who had been homecoming queen. I nodded along, my feet aching in my heels. Was it too early to leave, to grab Phil's arm and make a run for it, claiming exhaustion or food poisoning or cramps? When I got home, I promised myself, I would toss these sandals into the depths of our walk-in closet, which was large enough to guarantee I wouldn't have to see them again, ever. I would avoid all other parties, all fund-raisers and wine-and-cheese pairings. Where was the cheese, anyway? It was a horrible trick of advertising.

Victor passed, touching my shoulder. "Are you having a good time?"

In a mirror over the fireplace, I saw my own wine-stained smile reflected back at me.

Myriam pointed out Janet Neimeyer, who was anywhere between forty and sixty, her body toned and deeply tanned next to her white dress, skin stretched tight across her cheekbones. "She got the house in the divorce settlement," Myriam said casually. "She likes her men, but if she settles down, she'll have to kiss this place goodbye."

"Oh," I said, not sure how I was supposed to react. I looked mournfully at the half inch of wine in my glass, wondering where the rest had gone.

"And that's Helen Zhang," Myriam continued. I sorted through my mental file, remembering that Helen and her husband were both dermatologists, parents of twin boys. Helen had short, almost boyish hair that somehow framed her face perfectly.

"Oh, sure. I've seen her walking a dog around the neighborhood."

"Yes," Myriam said, her mouth tight. "Isn't he the most *darling* thing?"

Too late, I remembered something else Phil had told me—that the Mesbahs had filed various complaints against the Zhangs, whose darling dog had a tendency to bark at inconvenient hours.

And then there was Daisy Asbill, former Google employee turned wife of a Google executive. She was young and slim-hipped in a gray silk dress. "Does your daughter babysit?"

she asked me. "I've got twins, and sometimes it's about impossible to find someone…"

I hedged, recalling that Danielle's sole babysitting effort for a neighbor down the street in Livermore had been a semidisaster.

"Oh, I don't mean all the time," Daisy qualified, sensing my hesitation. "Only when the nanny has the day off."

"Of course," I said, savoring this one: *only when the nanny has the day off*. Allie would get a kick out of that.

Over and over I said *It's so nice to meet you* and *We're loving it out here* and took miniscule sips of cabernet, trying to make it last as long as possible. My mouth ached from incessant smiling. At one point, Helen asked if Myriam's closet was finished, and half the crowd trooped down the hallway to see the improvements. I spotted Phil next to Rich Sievert, a fresh glass in his hand. He smiled at me, and I took a relieved step toward him.

"Oh, *here* they are," Deanna called, stepping between us. At the front door, Victor was fussing over another couple, so tall and blond and perfectly paired, they might have been a set of Barbies.

"So sorry we're late," the woman said, giving cheek kisses as she moved through the entryway. Her hair was so blond it was almost colorless, her eyes a piercing blue. As she came closer, I realized that she was an older version of a girl I'd seen walking through the neighborhood, her head bent, thumbs tapping the screen of her cell phone. "Oh, hello." She smiled at me. "I don't think we've met. I'm Sonia Jorgensen."

"Liz McGinnis," I said, shifting my glass so we could shake hands. Sonia's nails were pale silver, her skin buttery soft.

"Liz's husband is the one with the yummy British accent," Deanna put in, suddenly at my side.

"Australian," I corrected.

"Don't you just love British accents? It's like those episodes of, what's it called? On Netflix?" Deanna wrinkled her nose, thinking. "Oh! *Downton Abbey*!"

Sonia Jorgensen smiled at me, the sort of smile that made us coconspirators. *Isn't she ridiculous?* She half turned toward me, her shoulders subtly angling Deanna out of the conversation. "We're your neighbors right around the corner, I think. The two-story Grecian—"

"Oh, with the columns," I said. When we'd first passed the house, Danielle had gaped. "Who lives *there*?" And I'd answered, "A dead president."

"Yes! Tim—that's my husband—said he wasn't sure about them, but when I saw the designs, I just *knew*."

"It's a beautiful house."

"Sonia's a party planner," Deanna said, edging back into the conversation. "She flies all over the world, just putting on parties. Can you imagine?"

"Corporate events, mostly," Sonia explained. "I try to stay as far from weddings as possible."

Deanna shook her head. "I'm so jealous it makes me sick. I try to get Rich to go somewhere, and he looks at me like I've got three heads."

Sonia looked at her pointedly. "You just got back from Hawaii."

"Right, but it was just Hawaii. We go there all the time," Deanna pouted. Her effusiveness was both familiar and uncomfortable—a slightly more polished version of a high school student. "You've been to— Where did you just get back from?"

"Corpus Christi," Sonia said. "Hardly exotic."

"Still," Deanna whined.

Sonia turned to me, her eyes crinkling in a smile. "Liz. Is that short for Elizabeth?"

There was something engaging about her, something that made me lower my guard, my mouth relaxing into its first genuine smile of the night. "No, just Liz. I always wanted to be an Elizabeth, though. I used to sign my name that way on my papers in elementary school."

Sonia's laugh showed teeth so straight and white, they might have belonged to a dental hygienist. "What did your parents think about that?"

"Oh, you know, typical kid stuff." I took a careful sip of wine. Of course she didn't know; it wasn't the sort of situation a person could guess. My mom was fully blind by the time I was in elementary school, so she never saw my name on any work sheets or permission slips or report cards. And my dad wouldn't have noticed—he was too busy seeing everything else. *Elizabeth* had been my own private rebellion.

"So, *Liz*, then. What do you do?"

I finished the last drop of wine in my glass. Funny—but after all the introductions tonight, Sonia was the first person to ask about me. "I'm a high school counselor," I said. "Miles Landers High School, in Livermore."

Sonia's eyes widened, and I braced myself for the cocked head, the subtle up-and-down assessment. Was she calculating my salary, my overall net worth? Was she recalling the sudden appearance of my seven-year-old Camry in the neighborhood, remembering that most of our clothes had been packed in black plastic garbage bags, toted from my trunk to the house? But she surprised me by grabbing my arm. "Oh, my God. That's wonderful."

"Well…" *Wonderful* was overstating it a bit, although I did love my job. In seven years, I'd never had the same day twice. "This year will be interesting, because my daughter will be there, too. She's going to be a freshman."

"Oh, this is fantastic. You don't understand… My daughter, Kelsey, is starting there in the fall. She'll be a sophomore. She used to go to Ashbury Prep, but…well, that's a story for another time. It turns out those other kids were such bad influences. But this is such a fantastic coincidence. It'll be so nice for Kelsey to have some friendly faces at Miles Landers, not to mention another responsible adult in her life."

Her touch was warm, as if we'd known each other for years. I recognized it as the *mom connection*, a bond that had always been elusive for me. I'd been a single mom for most of Danielle's life, those early years spent shuttling between her day care and my internships, and later between the carpool lane at her elementary school and the counseling office. There had never been time to get to know the other moms, and I'd envied their chummy closeness at back-to-school nights and honor-roll assemblies.

"That will be nice," I agreed, allowing myself to get sucked into the moment. Of course, there was no guarantee that our daughters would be friends. Danielle spent most of her days with her nose in a book. Kelsey, from what I'd observed, was years ahead of her socially. I remembered her walking past in her microshorts and tank tops, her bra straps winking like a dirty secret.

"So, would it be weird…" Sonia began. "I'm just thinking out loud here, and you can feel free to say no. But maybe we could plan some kind of get-together for them?"

I grinned. "Like…a playdate?"

Sonia laughed. "Well—I don't know. Is that silly? It could just be a little thing. I'd be happy to host."

Deanna returned, as if she'd been listening in from just

over my shoulder. "What a great idea! We could invite all the teenagers at The Palms. Let's see—there's Mac, the Zhang boys, Hannah Bergland..."

Sonia's gaze crossed mine, tolerant and amused. How did she do it? How did she keep her composure, keep herself from laughing or rolling her eyes? Pay attention, I ordered myself, as if I were watching for clues on how to be a woman, on what to wear, on when to speak.

"Are you sure Mac would be interested?" she asked.

Deanna rolled her eyes. "Oh, please. He just hangs around the house all day doing nothing, driving me insane."

And then I made the connection between the driver of the massive yellow truck and the name I'd heard often enough at school over the past three years. Mac Sievert, the chronic underachiever; Mac Sievert, the big man on campus. "I just realized Mac goes to Miles Landers. He's a senior?"

Deanna laughed, taking an exaggerated sip of her wine. "Oh, poor you. I was waiting for you to figure that out. Just remember, when he fails Econ, the phone call goes to his dad, not to me. One of the benefits of being the stepmother," she added with a wink.

"Noted," I said.

"This is a great idea," Deanna gushed. "I'll go tell Helen."

We watched her walk away, heels clacking on the hardwood.

Sonia cleared her throat. "Well, I guess I'm hosting the neighborhood. What about Saturday night? Would that work with Danielle's schedule?"

"She gets back from science camp tomorrow, so—I'm sure that's fine."

Sonia mock-swooned, latching onto my sleeve. I was sure this was the most my arm had been touched, ever, and I had a blind mother. "*Science camp.* I love it. Hang on to that phase while you can. Kelsey's into boys and clothes and drama. Fifteen going on thirty."

I smiled. Danielle hadn't yet discovered those things, but I knew it was coming. At the beginning of her eighth grade year, I'd had to hide her favorite pair of camo pants, purchased from the army surplus store, when she insisted on wearing them three days in a row. But for her graduation last month, we'd spent hours combing the mall for a dress. I commented, "Sometimes I think Danielle is still fourteen going on twelve."

Victor breezed past, swapping out my empty glass for a full one, and Sonia and I smiled at each other. Wordlessly, we touched our glasses together, and they produced an inharmonious *clink*.

There was a burst of chatter as Myriam and the rest of the women filed back into the room, having exhausted the virtues of the remodeled closet. Janet Neimeyer just couldn't get over the lighting; Helen Zhang was noting the name of the contractor.

I felt a hand on my back, a warm hand, the thumb running over the ridge of my spine. I glanced over my shoulder and Phil gave me a happy, sloppy grin, his cheeks flushed.

Halfway home, I propped myself against Phil and wiggled out of my shoes, not able to tolerate them for another step. I tipped to one side, laughing, and he caught me. Were the neighbors watching from their windows, behind their custom drapes, the slats of their plantation blinds? Somehow it didn't matter as much anymore.

"So we survived," Phil said. "It wasn't the horror show we imagined."

"I suppose it could have been worse."

He pulled me close and I leaned against him, warm and light-headed. His breath smelled like the wine Victor had foisted on us, refilling our glasses until I'd lost count.

Ahead of us, our house loomed, a towering behemoth. I'd begun to think of it as a chameleon—neutral beige in the morning, so dark just after sunset that it became almost invisible. Despite several attempts with the manual, neither of us had figured out the automated lighting system, so the front porch was rendered a dark alcove, hidden in the sloped overhang of the Tudor roofline. While Phil fumbled with the house key, I tugged his shirt from his waistband, pressing my hand against the flat of his back.

He threw open the door, grinning. "I like where this is going."

"I'm a horrible drunk," I confessed, backing into the house, dropping my sandals onto the tile entry. With one hand, I undid the buttons of my blouse.

"That's what I love about you," Phil said, letting the door click shut behind him. My blouse fell open and he whistled. "Anyway, define *horrible*."

It was too hard to talk. My words felt slurred, my tongue thick. It was easier to kiss him, to show rather than tell.

We were good at this; I'd come to realize that we were maybe best at this. It had been there from the beginning—a playful physical attraction, the foresight that our bodies would be good together. We'd met at a Sharks game, neither of us particularly hockey fans, both of us accompanying friends with extra tickets. Phil, seated behind me, had spilled beer on my sweatshirt and spent the rest of the night apologizing over my shoulder, then flirting, charming me with that accent. I'd had a few beers, too, which was the only way I could explain the kiss I gave him in the parking lot after the game, one that was long and ripe and full of promise, as if I didn't have a child at home, an early morning ahead of me. On the train back to Livermore, I'd laughed at myself, so stupid for thinking that a kiss with a stranger was anything more than a kiss with a stranger. And then twelve hours later, he'd walked into the counseling office at Miles Landers, a bouquet of daisies in one hand.

That was five years ago.

We pulled apart now, and I sloughed off my blouse, the fabric fluttering to the floor. Phil's hands were on my bra, struggling with the back clasp, his breath hot in my ear. "Danielle should go away more often. One of those summer-long camps."

"Mmm."

"Or a study-abroad program. Foreign exchange, whatever you call it. An entire semester, maybe."

"Early college," I murmured. "Send her off at sixteen."

He groaned, nudging me toward the stairs, our king-size bed beckoning. We'd had it for three weeks now, relegating our queen-size mattress to a spare bedroom, and it still felt spacious, as if we were splurging on an expensive hotel every night.

Maybe it was the wine; maybe it was the feeling that had been coming over me slowly since our move to The Palms, the realization that I didn't have to be *me* anymore. I'd left the old Liz Haney behind—pregnant in college, dependent on financial aid and a half-dozen part-time jobs and Section 8 housing until I landed my counseling position, but still struggling with the rent when I met Phil. Now she was a ghost, wisp-thin and floating away, that old Liz. Because look at us. Here we were, hobnobbing with the rich and the very rich, and almost blending in.

"I have a better idea," I told him.

"I'm all ears."

"Follow me," I said, and he did—past the living room stacked with boxes, the unfurnished dining room, the gleaming granite of the kitchen. I opened the sliding door off the den, and the Other Woman, the electronic narrator of our lives, warned, "Back door open."

But once I was through the door, I hesitated. The backyard was almost too bright, with tasteful landscaping lights aimed at the potted topiaries, the dripping strands of crepe myrtle. Overhead, the moon was a crescent sliver, its gleam reflected on the surface of the pool, where an invisible hand pulled the water gradually toward the infinity edge. Beyond the pool, the yard sloped downward and beyond that was the flat, seamless green of the fairway.

I faced Phil and undid the button on my waistband slowly, watching him watch me. I hooked my thumbs in my underwear and let them shimmy down my thighs.

Phil was motionless in the doorway.

I must have been drunk; my body felt good in the moonlight, strong and sexy, like Eve in the Garden of Eden, before that pesky snake. "Aren't you going to join me?"

Phil grinned. "I was just appreciating the view." He worked his way out of his dress shoes and toed them off in separate directions. One sailed onto the grass, landing upside down with a soft thud.

I turned, breaking the surface of the water with one foot, then another. We had neighbors on either side, but these were one-acre lots, and they might have been miles away. *Too secluded*, Marja Browers had said. I took a few tentative strokes in the water and flipped onto my back, wetting my hair. Phil was undressing clumsily, struggling with his socks. My breasts rose above the ripples of the water, and I closed my eyes. Maybe this was what a house at The Palms could give you—a sense of owning something, of deserving the license that came with it.

When I looked up, Phil was standing at the edge of the pool, his clothes shed in untidy piles at his feet. From the water, he looked larger than life—on the scale of Michelangelo's *David*, rather than a mere human. He lowered one foot in the water.

"No, wait a second," I said. "It's my turn to appreciate the view."

He gave me a mock pose, muscles flexed. I laughed and kicked water in his direction.

"That's it," he said, splashing into the water. We reached for each other.

The neighbors, I thought.

And then: *forget the neighbors*.

Afterward, we let our bodies drift, float, slide next to and over each other, pulled by the current of gravity, the slow drift toward the infinity edge. It was an illusion, of course— but with my eyes closed, it felt as if I could float past the lawn, out to the golf course, where it was green and green and green forever.

Sometimes, dangling my feet over the edge of the pool, a book in one hand, I'd heard sounds from the golf course— the *thwack* that sent a ball soaring, the occasional raised voice. From the neighborhood, I'd heard cars starting, engines revving and disappearing; I'd caught snatches of conversation, carried on a breeze. But mostly, I'd grown used to the quiet of The Palms, beginning with the empty rooms in our house, so well carpeted and insulated that I could hear my own breath. This week, with Danielle gone and Phil moving into his office in the clubhouse, I'd found myself singing along with the radio, testing out my voice in the emptiness just to hear another sound.

Now the quiet was peaceful, calming, broken only by the occasional ripple in the water when our bodies broke the surface.

But then there was a clanging sound, the rattle of metal on metal, the sound I recognized as the latch and hook of our back gate.

I looked over at Phil, floating with his chest and shoulders above water, a blissed-out smile on his face. "Someone's out there," I hissed.

He shook his head. "Probably just sound carrying."

But then I heard someone laughing.

Instinctively, I shrank into the water, my eyes scanning the dark pockets of the backyard. The euphoria was gone, the feeling of freedom and invincibility and entitlement. Or maybe I was just sobering, fast. Now I was a flabby, naked woman with a potential audience. "Phil—"

He worked his way toward the shallow end, his chest and shoulders bright in the moonlight. "Probably someone in their backyard."

"What if there's someone out on the golf course?"

"I don't think anyone could see us, anyway."

But I'd spotted the occasional heads of joggers and walkers bobbing past, the quick, colorful blurs of polo shirts and checkered pants. There was no way to gauge how close this laugh had been, whether someone was standing twenty feet away or all the way at the clubhouse. "I'm going inside," I said, swimming for the steps.

"Oh, come on." Phil laughed. "Really?"

But the moment was broken, the fantasy evaporating fast. The Liz who could float naked and free beneath the stars was gone, a once-in-a-lifetime flash of a comet, an anomaly. My clothes were scattered on the deck and inside the house, but I could make a run for it, heading straight for the downstairs laundry room, where a load of towels was waiting in the dryer.

"*Liz.*"

I sloshed up the pool steps, not realizing until I hit the concrete that I wasn't entirely sober. My feet were heavy, uncooperative. And then I heard the laugh again, echoing off the tile surround, bouncing off the stucco exterior of our house. I turned, half expecting to spot someone in our bushes. Instead, I caught a flash in the distance, out on the walking trail—the tiny, bright screen of a cell phone. I bent double, clutching at my breasts with one hand.

In the water, Phil was laughing. "It was just someone walking by. Get back in here. Come on. I'll plant a hedge out there. I'll plant a goddamned forest, if that's what you want."

But I was already moving toward my reflection in the sliding door—a pale, lumpy mass of flesh, hair dripping, mascara streaked across my face. I'd felt so weightless, sliding into the water. Now I saw the sag of my breasts, the width of my hips, the fourteen-year-old flap of skin hanging low on my belly.

I was still the old Liz, after all.

Danielle was waiting for me at the BART station the following afternoon, considerably dirtier than when I'd dropped her off on Monday. Her feet were crammed into her old hiking books, laces flopping. She waved and ran around to the driver's side to kiss me through the window.

I pulled back, feigning disgust. "You smell like nature."

"I actually showered this year, not that it made much difference," she said, tossing her backpack into the backseat. Her shoulders were sunburned, her cheeks dotted with new freckles. Red welts of mosquito bites pockmarked her legs.

"So? Tell me everything."

We eased into traffic, and she did: the wasp nest in her cabin, the nature hikes, the bonfires, the visiting botanist from UC Davis. It was her last year as a camper; next summer, when she was fifteen, she could apply as a counselor.

"The rest of the summer is going to suck in comparison," she announced, digging into her pocket until she came up, triumphant, with a pack of trail mix. She split the plastic and a stray peanut went flying into the console.

"You could always babysit, earn some spending money. I met a family with twins in The Palms—"

"Are you kidding? It was a disaster that time I babysat for the Lees, and that was only one kid. Remember how I had to call you fifteen times?" She held up the remainder of the bag of trail mix, letting the last sunflower seeds and raisins trickle directly into her mouth.

"Let's not lead with that line on your résumé."

She laughed through her mouthful.

"Phil and I went to that party last night, that wine-and-cheese thing—"

"That's right. Was it fun?"

I hesitated. This morning, fighting a hangover headache, I'd dashed off a message to Allie, telling her about Janet, who could barely stretch her mouth into a smile and Deanna, with her too-large and too-perky breasts. I'd told her about the drama of Myriam's remodeled closet, about Daisy Asbill's reference to her nanny. But to Danielle I said only, "Sure. It was fun."

Keeping my tone casual, I told her about Sonia's invitation, the pool party planned for seven tomorrow night.

Danielle had been bending over, freeing her feet from her hiking shoes and a dirt-rimmed pair of socks, but when my words sank in, she looked up at me wild-eyed. "Tomorrow night? Are you kidding?"

"I didn't realize you have plans."

"I don't have plans, *per se*," she fumed. "I had plans to *not* be at a party with people I don't know. I had plans to read a book or watch a movie. Those were my plans."

"So now you'll be swimming and playing games and eating junk food and making new friends. I suppose there are worse things."

"Who are we talking about? Not that blonde girl."

"Kelsey," I said. "You've met her?"

"No, but I've seen her hanging around the clubhouse. Mom, she's like…"

"Like what?"

But Danielle only glared out the window, arms folded across her chest. We'd exited 580, thick with traffic even on a Saturday, and were winding our way through twelve miles of twists and turns on the sole access road to The Palms. The road mimicked the switchbacks of the encroaching Diablo Range. In the distance, the mountains rose brown and bare, dotted with the occasional thirsty-looking clumps of cows beneath a thatch of trees. Up close the ranch land was so dry, its fissures were deep as fault lines.

"Hey," I said, giving Danielle a nudge with my elbow. "It would be good for you to know some people in the area. And she might be nice."

She grunted.

"What?"

"You said swimming. It's a pool party, Mom. How am I supposed to wear my swimsuit in front of people I don't even know?"

"Didn't you do that all week at camp?"

"But those were just *kids*. These are..."

"They're kids, too," I said, forcing a note of conviction into my voice. I knew what Danielle was thinking. Somehow, they weren't just kids—they were miniature reflections of their parents, with designer clothes and disposable income. They'd inherited all the best that life could offer without the struggle, without even the stories that came with triumph and success.

"What if they hate me?" Her voice was small. "What if they make fun of me?"

I swallowed hard. It was one of those parent-fail moments, listening to my daughter rehash my own fears, the same lines from the mental argument I'd had on the Mesbahs' front porch. *That never stops, honey*, I wanted to tell her. There will always be those people. The difference is that at some point—a point I hadn't quite reached myself—their opinions stopped mattering.

We were approaching the final bend on the access road, where the pavement suddenly smoothed out and the scrubby ranch land was replaced with towering, evenly spaced palm trees. Ahead of us the road forked before the wrought-iron ingress and egress gates, flanking the sign that announced our arrival: THE PALMS AT ALTAMONT RIDGE. It still struck me as pompous, and I'd lived in apartment complexes that had a genuine need to inflate themselves: Willow Glen and Stony Brook, where there had been no glens or brooks in sight. This sign announced wealth and privilege, something worth protecting, something with a high cost of admission.

Recognizing my car's tracking device, the entrance gate rolled slowly open, then closed behind us. Janet Neimeyer's Italianate villa loomed ahead, its terra-cotta roof flaming under the sun. As we coasted forward, I turned to Danielle. "Listen to me. You look fantastic in that swimsuit. Just be yourself—smart, outgoing, funny. How could anyone not love you?"

She shook her head, but one corner of her mouth twitched in a smile. "Okay. But what if I hate them?"

"If you want to leave, you can. It's right around the corner. Just say, adios, goodbye, I'm heading home to watch C-SPAN with my mom."

Behind us there was a sharp *beep*, and a little green Mini swerved around my Camry and zoomed past.

Danielle rolled her eyes. "That'll firmly cement my coolness."

Saturday night, she left in cutoff jeans and a shapeless T-shirt that read *It's elementary, dear Watson* next to a fading graphic of the periodic table. The blue halter straps of her swimsuit flopped at her neck. It was the first time in years I'd been able to cajole her into a two-piece, and she did look great in it, taller than last summer, limbs longer, her body lean with the merest suggestion of curves. I watched from the front porch as she rounded the turn at the end of our street. Until she disappeared from sight, I wasn't sure she was going to go through with it.

All night, I watched the clock while Phil watched the Giants game. I snuggled close to his T-shirt–clad chest, inhaling the smell of aftershave and laundry detergent. Outside the sliding door, the pool glimmered darkly, a reminder of my failed romantic overture last night. Eventually I nodded off, my face warm against his torso, only waking when the game was over, the players being interviewed. Phil had muted the sound. He didn't like this part, the explanations and excuses.

My gaze drifted back to the clock. "It's ten fifteen. Maybe I'll just walk down there and check."

"You'll ruin any hope she has of being cool if you do," Phil warned. "And believe me, there's a kid who needs all the help she can get."

I mock-swatted him. He wasn't kidding, but he wasn't being malicious, either. It was amazing how well he and Danielle understood each other, how well they'd adapted to each other's presence. "You can call me Phil," he'd said when they'd first met, and she'd told him solemnly, "You can call me Danielle." In the beginning, they had bonded over shows on Animal Planet, made visits to the Bass Pro Shops on weekends, regaled each other with trivia about geology and astronomy and anatomy. She'd outgrown some of this, but what was left between them was an easy sort of comfort, a mutual respect.

The room flashed between blue and black as Phil flipped through silent channels, not lingering long on any particular image.

I knew that Danielle wasn't a typical fourteen-year-old, and that was part of my worry. Over the years, I'd counseled hundreds of teenage girls over breakups and arguments with their parents and spats with their best friends. I was the only female counselor on staff, and girls seemed to feel more comfortable sharing their troubles with me. It was a running joke that the bulk of the school's tissue budget went to my office. So far, Danielle had avoided those messy entanglements of adolescence—the sole perk of being nerdy. Her weekends weren't spent at parties; they were spent at the kitchen table, where she zipped through extra-credit assignments.

Only a month ago, amidst the craziness of our impending move to The Palms, she'd delivered the salutatorian address at her middle school graduation. I had barely recognized her behind the microphone; she'd been so witty and confident, her jokes delivered with the spot-on timing of a comic.

I hopped to my feet when she came in at a quarter to eleven, her hair slicked back postswim and drying stiffly on her shoulders. Upstairs, she changed into pajamas and gave me the play-by-play as we lounged on her bed, goose bumps forming on our arms beneath the whirr of the ceiling fan. She smelled faintly of chlorine, and her fingers retained the telltale orange residue of Cheetos.

"The Jorgensens have this massive pool. Olympic-sized," she said.

"Really?"

"Well, *huge*, anyway. And you should see their pool house. Our old house could practically fit in there. It has this massive TV and all these couches."

"Sounds nice. So what did you do—watch a movie?"

Danielle rolled her eyes. "It was kind of lame. The guys—Mac from across the street and then Alex and Eric Zhang—played video games the whole time. I guess they expected the rest of us to watch them, like that would be any fun."

I smiled. "So you went swimming?"

"Yeah. Kelsey and Hannah and me."

"What are the girls like?"

She yawned, pulling the comforter halfway over us. "Hannah was kind of clingy. She kept hanging on to my arm like we were best friends already. But, I don't know—she's okay.

And Kelsey's really pretty, like the kind of pretty you see on magazines. She's nice, though. Oh—" She sat up halfway, propping her head on her hand. "Is it okay if she comes over tomorrow to swim?"

"Of course. Are you going to invite Hannah, too?"

She grimaced. "Do I have to? I don't think they get along very well."

"Kelsey and Hannah? Why not?"

Danielle shrugged.

I raked my fingers through her hair, separating clumps that had dried together. "Wouldn't Hannah feel left out?"

Danielle groaned. "I guess."

We were quiet for a while, listening to the sounds of Phil getting ready for bed—his feet plodding on the stairs, the water running in the bathroom.

"What about the boys?" I asked.

"Are you kidding? No way am I inviting the boys."

I laughed. "No, I meant—what are they like?"

"Oh, um—besides their video game skills? Alex and Eric are really smart and kind of quiet. Kelsey told me they're both going to be doctors, like their parents. They go to the school she used to go to, Ass Bury."

"*Ash*bury."

"And then Mac...he's kind of an idiot. But he's funny, I guess."

"Thank goodness for that," I said, smiling. Maybe this would be the beginning of something—of friends in and out of our house, breathing life into our empty spaces. "So it was fun overall?"

But Danielle had closed her eyes and was already drifting off to sleep.

★ ★ ★

In the morning, I made a trip into Livermore for groceries, lingering for a long time in front of the aisle of chips. What did teenage girls eat? Flavored chips, diet soda? Was it possible to make a wrong choice and completely blow my daughter's chance at a social life?

I put Danielle to work straightening the house, which mostly consisted of hauling unpacked boxes from the living room to the garage. It was junk, all of it, but junk I couldn't bear to throw away—an old spaghetti pot with the enamel worn thin, binders and outdated college textbooks.

Hannah arrived twenty minutes early—shy, answering my questions with polite monosyllables. Unlike her mother, she was plump, fat puddling at her armpits. She was awkward in her racerback tank suit, and I decided I liked her.

Kelsey was twenty minutes late, her face dwarfed by an oversize pair of sunglasses. Danielle was right. In her black bikini, with a sarong tied casually across her hips, Kelsey might have been a model for an advertisement in a men's magazine. "It's so nice to meet you," she said, holding out a confident hand, as if she were the adult, welcoming me to her home. "I hear that you work at Miles Landers."

"Right, I've been there for seven years now. I think you'll like it."

She pushed the sunglasses to the top of her head, revealing eyes that were the same pale blue as her mother's, but somehow colder and flatter. "Anything would be better than Ass Bury."

All together, they were an odd trio, thrown together by circumstance rather than similarity. Throughout the afternoon I caught odd snatches of their conversation and glimpses of them from various windows of the house. Danielle blew up the beach ball I'd bought at the Dollar Store and the three of them smacked it back and forth across the surface of the water, sometimes viciously, sometimes idly, until it popped.

At one point Danielle came inside to use the bathroom and I intercepted her with a kiss on the forehead. At my insistence, she'd slathered herself with sunscreen, and her skin gleamed pink and raw from the previous week's burn. "I'm glad you're making friends."

"Well, we haven't taken a blood oath or anything yet, so don't get too excited," she said, hurrying past.

When Phil came home, he found me browning beef for enchiladas and wrapped his arms around my waist, swaying gently with me cheek to cheek.

"You're in a good mood," he observed.

"Why wouldn't I be?"

"So how did it go? The great swim party of 2014?"

"Still going." I jerked my head in the direction of the backyard, where the girls had been taking turns on the diving board. Hannah was there now, pumping her legs, her large breasts jiggling with the vertical motion. She took a clumsy leap and hit the water with a splash. I saw Kelsey and Danielle exchange smirks and felt suddenly, inexpressively sad. "I invited the girls to stay for dinner."

Phil straightened, releasing me. We stood next to each other, watching out the window as the three of them bobbed in the pool.

"It seems to be working out," I said. "And here Danielle didn't think she had anything in common with them."

And then Kelsey emerged from the water, one long leg following the other. *Oh, to be so young*, I thought. *To be so lovely.* She made her way to the diving board, water droplets glistening on her body, blond hair slicked back.

We watched transfixed as she hooked her thumbs into her bikini top, carefully adjusting her breasts within the two black triangles. She called something that sounded like "Geronimo!" and did a perfect swan dive into the water below. When she surfaced, her bikini top was twisted, revealing a perfectly round nipple.

"I bet the Jorgensens could afford a little more fabric," I commented lightly.

Phil only said, "Shit," and turned away.

PHIL

A question: What's the difference between a pedophile and an innocent person accused of pedophilia? What about a rapist and a person accused of rape? Practically speaking—nothing. They're the same. One might as well be the other. It doesn't matter if you're innocent, because the accusation plants the suggestion, and from there the guilt grows. The innocent are the most vulnerable, really. They've got the most to lose—those with wives and kids who aren't looking for something on the side.

On my first official day of work at The Palms, she was there. The office had been repainted for me, and plastic sheeting still covered my desk when I'd arrived. I'd been sorting through files in the cabinet when I heard the door close. By the time I looked up, she was sitting in one of the club chairs. Her skirt was so short that it nearly disappeared when she crossed her legs.

I smiled. "Can I help you?"

"I hope so. I have a complaint."

I'd spent the previous week getting to know the residents, schmoozing with the men and flattering the ladies, fielding complaints about the wattage of lightbulbs and the leaky faucet in the women's locker room and a slight hump near the service line on one of the tennis courts. I'd written it all down, made the appropriate phone calls. There had been other complaints, too—private ones—made by residents who stopped me on the sidewalk, always prefacing their thoughts with *You didn't hear it from me, but...* and ending them with some variation of the same theme. *Of course, I wouldn't complain just for myself, but I'm thinking about the good of the community.* Myriam Mesbah hated Helen Zhang's dog, which barked constantly. Rich Sievert's view was spoiled by the excavator that was digging out a pool in one of the backyards in Phase 3. The trees on the edge of the Asbills' property dropped leaves into Janet Neimeyer's backyard, and her gardener was forever having to blow the debris, which in turn disturbed the Asbills' twins, who needed a midmorning nap.

But I'd smiled through it all, because this wasn't real hustling, like selling had been—courting buyers and talking clients down from unrealistic asking prices, running from open house to open house on weeknights and weekends, waiting for above-asking-price offers that might never come. This job meant regular hours and a steady paycheck, not to mention a house Liz and I would never have been able to afford on our own.

"Buyers in these communities tend to be high-maintenance," Jeff Parker had told me, after we'd shaken hands a second time, and the job was officially mine. He was a vice president at Parker-Lane, and eventually he would inherit his dad's job. "The thing is to soothe them, to kiss a few asses here and there, to deal with what you can immediately and pass the buck upward for the rest. Above all—they like the quiet, the security, the exclusivity. They like to feel like they're the most important people in the world when you're talking to them."

At that point I was still trying to wrap my mind around the day-to-day expectations of the job. "So essentially my job is to..."

"Bottom line, McGinnis? Keep them happy."

It hadn't seemed like a difficult task. How could people live here and not be happy? They had minimansions with up to six garages, golf and yoga and walking trails and all the amenities of a resort, year-round. There was enough room to spread out, to really breathe. Liz and Danielle and I had been crawling on top of each other like cockroaches in that crappy rental, sharing a single bath and a kitchen so narrow I could stand in the middle and touch the walls on either side. Here we had all the room we needed, plus some to spare.

I was surprised how much convincing it had taken to get Liz on board, when I'd jumped in feetfirst.

"Are we raiding an orphanage or something?" she had asked, counting the upstairs bedrooms.

"We could make one into a home gym," I said.

"There's a gym in the clubhouse. Plus golf, tennis..."

"Okay, a sewing room, a music room. Whatever you want."

Liz laughed. "Just what every girl in the 1800s wants," she'd murmured, but this didn't deter me.

It was a chance at the good life. So what if we didn't need so many bedrooms, if the job requirement was to kiss a few asses here and there?

So when Kelsey Jorgensen came into my office unannounced, when she plopped into my chair and pouted, I only said, "You've come to the right place, then. What can I do for you?"

She yawned in response, stretching her limbs like a cat sunning itself on the pavement. I tried not to look directly at her body, focusing instead on the tips of her fingers, the pink wink of her toes. I heard it already then, that little warning bell in the back of my mind, but I pushed it to the side.

"What you can do," she said, dragging out the syllables, "is keep me from being so bored."

Most days, she wandered through the clubhouse with her limbs on display in tiny dresses that fluttered in the air-conditioning, or halter tops and shorts that ended at her crotch. "I just wanted to say hello," she would say, lingering in my doorway. "So, hello, Mr. McGinnis." In her mouth a simple greeting sounded full of suggestion.

At first, for all of five minutes, it was entertaining. I figured it was the charm she turned on every man, equally—neighbors and groundskeepers, the college kid who maintained the play area, even, yes, the thirty-seven-year-old community relations specialist. That first day I figured, where's the harm? This was how most of the women at The Palms acted around me, and playing along seemed to be required by the job. Deanna Sievert couldn't talk without flirting, and Janet Neimeyer couldn't keep her hands off me—there was always a collar to be straightened or an invisible crumb to be picked from my chin.

But I loved Liz, and I wasn't looking.

Sure, it was flattering. It made me feel young again, like the Phil I'd been in my twenties, after my parents died and my brother, Zeke, and I pooled their assets and moved to Corfu, where we opened a bar that catered to college kids on holiday and gap years. There had always been a girl—a German tourist, or Swedish or Czech—who didn't leave at closing time, who hinted that she needed a place to stay before her boat left the next morning. When I shook her awake, she would snuggle closer and say she could catch the next one, the next time. But I'd come to California, in part, to leave that Phil behind. I'd had too many fuzzy mornings when I cleared the condensation in the mirror and didn't like what I saw. I wanted more out of life than a rented room, a bank account that emptied month to month, women who moved out, moved on.

When I met Liz, I knew she was the real deal—funny and sexy and so damned smart, someone who had met life on its terms. For the first time, I was the one in pursuit; she had too much riding on her life to hang around waiting for my call. She'd been the one who was hesitant to commit, who introduced me, for months, as a "friend." She hinted that a relationship wasn't possible until Danielle went off to college—at that point, nine years away. When I'd proposed to her at the lighthouse on a lonely stretch of Highway 1, it had been like preparing for a debate—laying out my reasons, providing evidence, anticipating the rebuttal. *We're a good team, we'll have a great life together, and I cannot wait for you one more minute.*

Sometimes, when we fought, I cursed myself for the empty years, the ones before Liz and Danielle. If only our paths had crossed sooner, we would have figured it out by now. We would have built up more trust in each other. We'd know each other's little quirks, which buttons were the wrong ones to push. I was jealous of the older, long-married couples, who'd committed early and could spend a full life together, like the Browerses. When it came to Liz, I wanted more time, not less.

So I wasn't looking for Kelsey Jorgensen, not at all.

She claimed boredom, a symptom of the same problem everyone had at The Palms. There were too many options and too few challenges. I knew I was exciting simply because I was someone different. So I laughed it off at first. I didn't take it seriously. I smiled back at her. I played along.

She stopped by my office on the day of the Mesbahs' party, and I asked if I would be seeing her that night.

She smiled. "Would you like that?"

I swallowed. It had been a fine line we'd been walking, but it was gone now. She'd practically pole-vaulted over it. "I'm looking forward to meeting your parents," I answered, and she'd fixed me with those steely eyes. It was the right answer, but the wrong one, too.

Although Parker-Lane encouraged an open-door policy, I began closing mine, trying to avoid her. She opened it anyway, poking her head around the corner, followed by a bare shoulder, a thigh.

I feigned busyness when she arrived, replying to emails that weren't at all urgent, taking imaginary phone calls. "I'm sorry, Kelsey. This is very important," I would say, but she was persistent. She called my bluff, waiting patiently through one-sided conversations until I turned my attention to her. And while she waited, she coiled and uncoiled a long strand of blond hair around a finger, smiling.

It was too late to go back to that first day, but I wished I could. I would have told her I was busy, asked her to leave. I would have put her in her place as nothing more than a silly, spoiled fifteen-year-old girl. It wasn't funny or flattering anymore; it wasn't the sort of thing I could laugh about after a few beers. She was young and lovely, but mostly young.

Still, I tried. "Isn't there something else you want to do today, Kelsey? Play tennis, maybe?"

She shrugged.

"It's just that I have work to do," I told her.

She raised an eyebrow. "You're a community relations specialist, and I'm part of the community. So by definition, isn't it your job to have relations with me?"

I found it was best not to be in my office at all—to have long lunches with Liz in the clubhouse, to chat with Rich Sievert at the bar, to try out the putting green with the Zhang boys or check on the progress of the homes in Phase 3. Still, hardly a day went by without her crossing my field of vision, blindsiding me with a wave, a wink.

And then one afternoon she was in my backyard, on my diving board, adjusting her bikini. She couldn't have known I was there, watching her through the kitchen window with Liz standing next to me. And yet it was almost choreographed—the languid walk, the stretching, the perfect swan dive, the bathing suit top that slipped off, revealing her firm breast. I closed my eyes, swallowing hard. My palms went clammy, my heart hammered in my chest. Upstairs, I stripped off my shirt and sat on the edge of the bed, wondering what the hell I was going to do.

JUNE 19, 2015
5:43 P.M.

LIZ

By the time I reached them, Danielle had hoisted herself over the edge. "Mom, help me!" she screamed.

In the pool, Hannah was pushing clumsily against the limp mass of Kelsey's body.

Kelsey.

But I'd known that, hadn't I, from the first scream that penetrated my sleep?

Her head flopped backward at a strange angle, like a marionette with no one pulling her strings. A red stain flowered on the back of her head. She was wearing the clothes I'd seen her in earlier, cutoff shorts and a T-shirt that billowed around her in the water. At the bottom of the pool, something magenta shimmered—her cell phone.

I asked the question even as I hooked an arm through Kelsey's, even as the three of us pushed and heaved and Kelsey's body emerged from the pool, followed by her dangling legs, scraping the concrete surround. She was wearing one sandal. "What is she doing here?"

"I don't know! We were inside and I saw her floating," Danielle panted.

"She was just out here all of a sudden," Hannah sobbed.

Kelsey's face stared up at me, her blue eyes unnervingly open. I pressed my hand over the cut on the back of her head, a gash several inches long, gaping wide. "Kelsey, can you hear me?" I slapped lightly against her cheeks, giving her shoulders a shake as if she were merely sleeping, as if this were the scene of a late-afternoon nap. My mind was a wild thing, racing backward and forward. I remembered Kelsey in my driveway earlier that afternoon, remembered shouting at her as the door closed.

Think, Liz. Think. I could picture the flip chart near the door of the counseling office—In Case of Emergency, with a dozen color-coded tabs for every conceivable situation.

And then something kicked in—a hyperfocus, the world narrowing to a single element, a sole requirement. My mother instinct, dormant over these past hard months, came out of the cave now, roaring. I snapped into action, ordering Danielle to turn off the music that pulsed in the background and call 911, and Hannah to run over to the Jorgensens' house to see if Kelsey's parents were home. Danielle, teeth chattering, ran inside and returned with her cell phone. Hannah's footsteps thundered through the house and disappeared.

Airway, Breathing, Circulation. How long since I'd taken a CPR class? The procedure had changed, but how, to what? I felt along Kelsey's neck for a pulse. Just one beat. Anything.

I heard Danielle's voice, but dimly, as if it were a sound track dubbed in to the background. "Hello? Hello? There's been an accident. 4017 Fairview. My friend—I don't know. She was in the pool. She's not responding."

I tilted Kelsey's head back—*Airway*—my cheek to her face, hoping for a whisper of breath. *Say something. Wake up and tell me to get the hell away from you.* I watched her chest, alert for a single, small rise, a slight fall, but it was still, her sodden T-shirt cold. My fingers, unsure, found the notch beneath Kelsey's ribs, just beneath the clasp of her bra. I steadied myself, remembering those long-ago lessons with Annie the plastic dummy, her synthetic lips reeking of hydrogen peroxide. Annie's torso had been smooth and pliable, her face a plastic, colorless mask.

But this was Kelsey, not a life-size doll.

This was an all-too-real nightmare.

JULY 2014
LIZ

With school done for the summer, my days fell into a pattern: wake late, meet Phil for lunch in the clubhouse, swim in the afternoons, have dinner in front of the television, drink a glass or two of wine in the evenings. Anything more required an energy I didn't have. My previous life and the things I used to do in it were only half an hour away, but somehow elusive now—the library, the farmers' market, the public swimming pool where I'd spent hours on a blanket in a shady corner with a novel, looking up occasionally to spot Danielle's head bobbing in the water.

"Aren't we going anywhere on vacation?" Danielle asked once, almost waking me from the dream fugue of The Palms. But why would we go anywhere when we were practically living in a resort, down to the marble floors in our very own bathrooms?

Lunch at the clubhouse was Phil's idea, his way of solidifying our place in the community. Danielle came sometimes, but mostly it was just Phil and me, ordering the overpriced panini of the day. "It's all schmoozing and boozing here," he told me. "Not bad for a day's work." From our table looking over the driving range, we nodded to Rich Sievert and Victor Mesbah as they made their way to the bar; we traded hellos with Daisy Asbill and her nanny, Ana, always a few feet behind, pushing the double-wide stroller that held the twins. Myriam stopped by to drop hints about the fund-raiser she was hosting for the Leukemia & Lymphoma Society; Janet Neimeyer wondered if I would join her book club, a rival of the book club started by Helen Zhang. Deanna Sievert, effusive as always, dangled her cleavage over our soup and sandwiches. She'd spent her summer trying to convince Rich to take a cruise in the fall, and for some reason she'd taken to soliciting my advice. A stop in Bermuda? Skip Antigua altogether?

"Oh, no, you'll definitely want to see Antigua," I gushed. Phil kicked me under the table, and I managed not to laugh until she was safely out of the room.

I wrote to Allie, trying to capture what I couldn't say out loud, not even to Phil. *There's a garden club, but they don't actually get their hands dirty. They just vote on what annuals the gardeners should plant in the public areas.* It didn't take me long to realize that just about everything was outsourced at The Palms—child care and housekeeping and cooking, the running into town to grab something from Target. Deanna's hair stylist came to her house before parties; Janet once referred to a personal shopper who bought her clothes for the entire season with one swipe of the debit card.

These women, I thought, amazed again at every turn. They were like modern-day fairy-tale princesses.

Phil was busy overseeing the final phase of construction at The Palms, sixteen luxury homes overlooking the foothills of the Altamont with its famous giant wind turbines. The community trail had been slightly rerouted to loop around the new construction, and a green area with a gazebo and outdoor kitchen was being added, so there were plans to approve and contractors to supervise. Phil was in his element, rushing between projects, keeping things on course. I joked with Allie that he was a politician on the campaign trail, shaking hands and trading good-natured hellos with anything that moved.

For their part, our neighbors treated him like a benevolent god, as if he could simply wave a hand and cause things to appear—new sprinkler heads, new bulbs in the carriage lights that lined The Palms' cul-de-sacs. The women worshipped him; more than once, Janet laid a hand on my arm, saying, "He's just an absolute doll, isn't he?"

Phil grimaced when I repeated this to him. "That's a compliment? A *doll*?"

"Well, they adore you, anyway."

He shook this off, as if the attention were merely annoying. "They adore bossing me around. They like having me at their beck and call. It's not exactly the same thing."

Still—I noted it. Heads turned as he walked through the clubhouse; women touched him on the arm, the shoulder, the back; they laughed loudly at everything he said; they swooned over his accent. Even the dining room employees said *g'day*; asked if they could get him a *draught* or a burger with *the lot*. Phil treated all of them to the same generous dispensation of his time, the same friendly smile and listening ear. Maybe at times I was a bit jealous, or even a bit possessive, but I didn't say anything to Phil. That would have given the issue more attention than it deserved.

It's the accent, Allie speculated over email.

No, it's the fact that he jumps to their every whim. He pays more attention to them than their husbands do.

How much attention? Allie asked, and then followed up about ten seconds later with a smiling emoticon, so I would know the question was a joke. When I didn't reply, she wrote, Hey—you know I'm an idiot, right?

Of course, I replied.

I wouldn't have minded so much, but they were so beautiful, so shiny and healthy and smooth. And once the suggestion was there, I had a hard time shaking it. Allie's comment had touched a nerve, opened an old wound. When I was eleven and Allie was fourteen, my father had an affair. I never knew any specifics or learned how my mother found out, but I remembered their argument late one night, the house reverberating with her question: *Who is she?* Then he'd slammed the door and driven away in his truck, and I'd climbed into Allie's bed and we'd cried ourselves to sleep. The following night Dad was back, joining us at the table in his PG&E uniform. I'd never heard them mention it again.

Sometimes as an adult, I thought I understood the affair. My mother had been beautiful—was, still—but blindness had robbed her confidence. Terrified of mismatching her clothes, she only wore black—shirts, pants, shoes. Even in the house, she wore her dark glasses. One of my earliest memories was of watching her get ready for a party, not long before her diagnosis—a red dress, lipstick, her hair in giant curlers. Blind, she was uncomfortable leaving the house, and my father had to coax her to visit friends, to try a new restaurant. Over the years I wondered who his other woman had been, what she was like—exciting and adventurous, scared of nothing? Had she worn bright colors, high heels? Or had it simply been the allure of the outside world, someone who would have a drink with him after work, someone who would dance in the middle of a crowded bar and not care who saw her or what she looked like?

Let it go, I told myself when Deanna strutted past in her shorts and heels, when Janet winked at him from across the room. *Being friendly is just part of the job.* Besides, as the summer passed, the languid days blending together, I had another worry, from a problem I'd created myself. Kelsey had taken my first invitation to dinner as a standing offer, arriving at our house late every afternoon for a swim with Danielle. Afterward, they lounged next to the pool, ruining their appetites with chips and Popsicles, their bodies fueled by mysterious teenage metabolism. We grilled burgers or mixed taco salads for a late dinner, and then there was always something on TV, even if it was a rerun of an episode they'd seen a dozen times. When it grew late, and I started yawning and dropping hints, Danielle would ask, "Is it okay if Kelsey spends the night?"

Later, when their giggles woke me, I wondered how we had become Kelsey's unofficial caretakers without so much as a word from her parents. Tim was some kind of attorney, and on the rare occasions when I bumped into Sonia, she was either just back from a trip or packing for her next one.

In the mornings, Kelsey was still there, appearing on the stairs in a skimpy tank top and a pair of men's boxers, her hair tousled. When she stretched, her tank top rode up, revealing the same flat, tanned stomach that was on display every afternoon but somehow looked obscene before my morning cup of coffee.

"Morning, Mrs. McGinnis, Mr. McGinnis," she yawned, stepping past us on her way to grab a carton of juice from the refrigerator.

At least Danielle was happy. She'd never had a friend like this, a *bestie*. Her middle school friends were self-described nerds, shrieking number-themed jokes at each other on our way to once-a-month Saturday math meets. What about that girl Gabby? I wanted to ask her. What about Estrella?

The truth was, I missed the old Danielle, the one who would play epic games of Battleship with me, who would read upside down on the couch, her legs draped over the back, occasionally calling out passages. *Mom, did you know that...?* Now her interests were the same as Kelsey's—sharing YouTube videos, snooping on other people's Facebook pages, ogling *Glamour* and *TMZ*. Almost overnight, what I'd feared most had happened. She'd grown up.

Oh, to be young, Allie said.

But I don't think I'd ever been that kind of young.

Sometimes, just to escape the house, I took walks after dinner, when the sky was turning from blue to purple to black, the white windmills on the horizon fading to a ghostly gray before disappearing altogether. I met the Browerses regularly and nodded at Trevor's complaints about water usage at The Palms; didn't anyone care that California was in a drought? I agreed with him, of course, but it was hard to get too excited. We weren't in California; we were on our own island. It was easy to believe that what happened elsewhere didn't concern us at The Palms. One night I heard giggling around a corner and spotted Janet Neimeyer and her boyfriend, both barefoot and taking swigs out of a bottle of champagne. Another time, the house stuffy and stifling even at midnight, I expected to be the only one on the streets and was surprised when I heard the slap of tennis shoes behind me.

"Oh, hello. I didn't mean to scare you." A woman emerged from the darkness, her hair a wild tangle of curls escaping a bun at the nape of her neck. Her face, where it wasn't freckled, was a pinkish pale. She was pushing a boy in a wheelchair.

"I don't think we've met yet. I'm Liz McGinnis. I live over—" I pointed behind me.

"Oh, I know where you live. I'm Fran Blevins, your next-door neighbor. We don't get out too much, except late at night. Sometimes Elijah has a hard time settling down, and a walk calms him." She gestured, and I bent lower, smiling. He wasn't a boy at all, but a man in his midtwenties with a scruffy beard, his limbs pulled tightly to one side. "Elijah," Fran said, her voice loud and cheerful. "This is Liz."

"Hello, Elijah. It's nice to meet you."

His eyes regarded me, unblinking. I'd only heard the Blevins referenced occasionally—Doug (Dan?) was a commercial airline pilot with a San Francisco to Tokyo route; their son, Deanna had told me with a hand over her heart, had cerebral palsy.

Fran said, "I've been meaning to stop by to welcome you to The Palms." While we talked, she rocked Elijah's wheelchair slowly forward and back, the way I used to rock Danielle when we stood in line at the grocery store or the DMV. "We have a daytime caretaker, but she takes her vacation during the summer, so I've been on twenty-four-hour duty."

"It's good to meet you. I feel like I've been adequately welcomed, though. Everyone's been so nice."

Fran smiled at me, her head cocked to one side. "Have they?"

I laughed.

"I don't find people here to be particularly nice, myself.

But for the most part, it's quiet, and they leave us alone." Her voice wasn't malicious or bitter, just matter-of-fact, as if we were talking about the weather. She bent over Elijah, dabbing a finger at the corner of his mouth, where a thin line of drool had appeared. When she straightened, she said, "I admit, I was a bit curious about your house, about how it all came out."

"Oh, we haven't done anything much to it," I said, thinking of the three empty bedrooms, the dining room with its folding card table from Costco. I'd covered it with a tablecloth, but its general flimsiness was undeniable. "The house was pretty much move-in-ready."

"No, I meant the repairs. From before you moved in."

I stared at her. "I'm not sure what you mean."

"Really? I figured you knew. Well, that house has had its share of bad luck. It was foreclosed on, and the owners had to be evicted. When they finally went, they'd stripped the house of everything—the fixtures, the plumbing, even the doorknobs."

"Wow—that's horrible." Incidents like those had been common on the news when the housing bubble burst, but it was surprising to hear in connection with The Palms.

"That wasn't even the worst of it. After they left, someone broke in, kicked holes in the walls, spray-painted obscenities, even scratched up the granite. The last I heard, everything had to be replaced."

I shuddered. "I had no idea…"

"I suppose it's the sort of thing Parker-Lane wouldn't want to advertise. There was a big stink about it around here, as you can imagine. Myriam and her cronies insisted it was someone from outside the community, as if juvenile delinquents from Livermore drive all the way out here to scale the fences and wreak havoc." She shook her head, freeing a few more wild strands of hair. "Look, I've lived here long enough to know that this place is a hotbox of discontent. The gates might be there to keep out the riffraff, but they don't protect us from each other."

"You think that—" But my words were lost in a sudden choking sound from Elijah. His eyes blinked wildly, and he thrust his head back.

"Oh, dear." Fran bent down, tipping his head to one side, settling him. "We'd better keep going. He likes the constant motion. Well, it was so nice to meet you, Liz. We'll have to bump into each other again like this."

I called a goodbye and watched as she disappeared into a pocket of darkness between carriage lights, the soft slurring of Elijah's wheels fading to nothing. I continued on to the entrance to the trail, which began and ended in front of the clubhouse, Fran's words ringing in my ears. Someone had kicked holes in our walls, scratched the countertops. I didn't know what was more unsettling, the idea of a vandal wielding a can of spray paint, or how easily it had been covered up, leaving no trace of the damage.

I paused along the trail when I reached the back of our Tudor. It was almost unrecognizable from this angle, as if the experience of living there was completely disconnected from what I was seeing now. There was the lawn and the pool, the patio with its topiaries in gigantic terra-cotta pots. Next to the door rose the hump of a forgotten beach towel. Darkness seeped from the windows.

I live here.

It not only didn't seem real, it suddenly didn't seem like a great idea.

That night my dreams were dogged with images of the

vandalism I'd never seen, a reverse version of the shows I watched on HGTV, where the beautiful home was smashed apart by strong-armed men swinging willy-nilly with sledge-hammers, leaving gaping holes in their wake.

And when I woke, the house didn't feel the same. It wasn't as solid and impenetrable, despite the security system, despite the Other Woman telling me when I was entering and ex-iting, what was locked and unlocked. That house had been a fantasy. It had existed in a dreamlike fugue, and now that was gone.

Eager to escape the stasis of The Palms, I went back to school a week early, before the office was filled with parents and students, new registrants and those pleading for a last-minute schedule change, the line five-deep out the door. It was nice to work without the distraction of an endless stream of Reply-All emails, the vaguely threatening administrative memos, the standard litany of complaints about the amount of homework in AP courses.

For now, I locked the door to the counseling office behind me and blasted the radio, sorting papers and settling unfin-ished business from the end of the past school year.

It was good to be back.

It would be good for Danielle, too. I'd been too lenient over the summer, lax on chores and responsibilities. School would mean essays and projects and speeches; it would mean clubs and activities and friends who weren't Kelsey.

Deep down, I knew that was the trouble, the real trouble, with Kelsey: she was going to break my daughter's heart. Sure, they were friends at The Palms, but what would hap-pen when Kelsey had more options to choose from, when she decoded the social strata at Miles Landers and infiltrated the popular crowd? She wouldn't hesitate to ditch my sweet, naive, awkward daughter who'd once spent a summer memorizing the periodic table *just for fun*. No, Danielle had been good for staving off boredom. She was a mere placeholder until Kelsey found her place among the jocks and mean girls of Miles Landers.

"Just tell her not to hang around Kelsey," Phil said one night, while we watched the end of the Giants game in bed. Down the hall, a deep quiet emanated from Danielle's room, punctuated by occasional shrill bursts of laughter.

I laughed. "You were never a teenage girl."

"What tipped you off?" He shifted and I moved closer to him, my head in the crook of his neck.

"If I tell her not to hang around Kelsey, she'll just want to hang around Kelsey more. That's the first rule of being a teenager." I yawned, pulling a sheet up to my chin. "Maybe they'll have some kind of fight, some big blowup, and things will cool off for a bit."

Over the roar of the crowd and the notes of the pipe organ, I heard Phil say, "We should be so lucky."

No matter the amount of preplanning, the carefully posted directional signs, the color-coordinated packets, registration was always a zoo. I'd come to expect parents who ignored directions, the horde of unattended children, the inevitable air-conditioner malfunction. Basically, it was a three-day circus in a stuffy gymnasium.

I worked side by side with Aaron Harrigfeld, my colleague and closest friend at Miles Landers. In seven years, we'd formed a bond based on sarcastic insights about our coworkers and a mutual quest for interesting lunches within driving distance of campus. When there was a lull, we caught up on our summers: he'd broken up with Lauren, the girl he'd been dating since January, during a five-day cruise to Mexico.

"During?" I repeated.

He closed his eyes, as if to block out the memory. "During."

"What happened? Not the hot-girl effect again?"

"Sadly, yes."

I rolled my eyes, even though I was the one who coined the term years earlier to describe Aaron's tendency to date stunning women in their early to midtwenties. I'd seen a whole parade of Laurens at this point—either he grew tired of them, or they moved on to bigger and better.

"And by the way," he said, cracking open a water bottle the next time the line died down, "I'm still waiting for my dinner invitation."

"It's coming. Once we get a dining room table."

He laughed. "All summer, I thought of you. Poor Liz, suffering with all that tennis and golf and swimming."

"It was pretty rough," I admitted.

"And now you're back here, slumming with the rest of the working world," he mused.

I gave him a friendly kick beneath the table. "Don't worry, I haven't forgotten the little people." Just that morning, in fact, I'd taken a detour past our old house in Livermore—tiny, run-down, the lawn a patchwork of weeds, the street choked with cars. I was expecting to feel a rush of nostalgia, but from my drive-by perspective, it was hard to imagine we'd ever been happy there.

Aaron mock-bowed at the waist. "On behalf of the little people, I thank you. So, when do I get to see Danielle, anyway? Is Phil bringing her through?"

I hesitated. Danielle was supposed to be there with me now, helping with the registration table. I'd planned to take her around to the various stations when the line was low, reintroducing her to staff members she'd met over the years. But last night Sonia had called, offering to take the girls to the mall for back-to-school shopping in the morning, then to registration in the afternoon. "It's the least I can do," she gushed. "You've been so generous with Kelsey all summer, and now that she'll be carpooling with you…"

She was right. It was the least she could do. I'd planned to offer occasional rides to Kelsey, figuring I left too early each morning to make that an attractive offer. But Sonia had embraced the idea enthusiastically. It wasn't until later that I wondered if she saw me as part of her support staff, one of the sprawling, faceless army of people who performed her menial tasks.

I brushed off this thought and told Aaron, "Danielle's coming with a friend. One of the girls in our neighborhood is starting here, too."

"This place is getting overrun with millionaires," he quipped.

All afternoon, I found myself scanning the cafeteria for a sight of them, two leggy blonde models and my own knock-kneed, dark-haired daughter, trailing behind in her Converse. When they did arrive, I spotted Kelsey first—a sheaf of white-blond hair, cutoffs so short the pockets hung below the hem. Sonia was next to her, tall in a pair of heels that dented the floor varnish. But even then, it took me a minute to recognize Danielle next to them.

"What the…" I stood, craning to get a better look, and Danielle spotted me at the same time. Her cheeks were red.

"Don't be mad," she blurted, coming toward me. "There was this place in the mall—"

"Your *hair*," I breathed. Since kindergarten, she'd worn

it long—ponytails, a braid, a dark waterfall down the middle of her back. I'd shampooed it for her, picked carefully through the wet knots, brushed it in the mornings, snapped it into place with an elastic band. Sure, she hadn't needed that help for years—but now that her hair was gone, I was sharply nostalgic for those mother-daughter tasks. Danielle's hair hadn't just been cut, it was cropped short, ending above her ears, fitting her head like a dark skullcap.

Next to me, Aaron whistled. "You know who you look like? Mia Farrow in *Rosemary's Baby*."

Danielle laughed. "Is that good?"

"Absolutely," he said, leaning across the table to give her a quick hug. "Ready for high school?"

She shrugged. "Yeah, I guess. Do you like it, Mom?"

I touched her hair tentatively, trying to find a piece long enough to tuck behind her ears. She looked lovely, striking—but in a surreal way, as if this wasn't my fourteen-year-old daughter in front of me, but a grown, postcollege version of herself, home for a visit. I tried to keep my tone light, tried not to let the hurt seep through. "You didn't tell me you wanted a haircut."

"Well, Kelsey was getting hers cut anyway, and Mrs. Jorgensen offered…"

"Kelsey's mom paid for this?"

"I know. I told her I had money, but she insisted…"

"How much are we talking?"

Danielle bit her lip. "Seventy-eight dollars."

"Seventy-eight dollars!" I hissed.

Next to me, Aaron whistled.

Then Sonia was there, oohing and aahing over the cut, offering a faux apology as if she simply couldn't help herself. "I mean, with these cheekbones," she gushed, "she was practically a diamond in the rough."

She was a diamond already, I seethed.

"You know what we should do tonight?" Kelsey asked. "We should try on all our clothes, and I could do your makeup."

Danielle laughed. "I don't know. I look funny with makeup."

"Seriously, I'll give you a whole new look."

I had a sick feeling, as if I were on a roller coaster and the momentum was building and building, and the whole thing might just go off the tracks.

"Let me get you girls your class schedules," Aaron said, bustling behind me, saving me from whatever ugly thing was going to come out of my mouth. He found Danielle's schedule under the *M*'s, and then hesitated, looking at Kelsey. "What's your last name?"

"Jorgensen," Sonia said. "Kelsey."

Aaron thumbed through a stack and handed Kelsey her schedule. She glanced at it, then asked, "So which of you is going to be my counselor?"

"Oh," I said, realizing. "You'll be mine. I have *H* through *M*."

She smiled. "Cool."

Danielle held up both papers, looking back and forth between them. I couldn't stop staring at her, as if she were some kind of mythical creature, half girl, half woman. "Hey," she said. "We have a class together! Geometry."

"Oh, my God, you *would* be in advanced math," Kelsey teased, and Danielle blushed.

Sonia glanced at her cell phone, noting the time. "What's next here? Why don't we get in line for ID photos while we can."

Danielle gave me an uncertain wave. "Bye."

"Yes, bye," Kelsey chorused.

I slumped back into the plastic cafeteria chair, watching them walk away from me. The crowd seemed to part at Sonia's approach, and more than a few heads turned. They were looking at Danielle, too, I realized.

Aaron helped the next people in line and then took a seat beside me. "She does look great, you know."

"Of course she does," I breathed.

"But that friend. *Whew.*" He shook his head. "I'm glad she's one of yours. She looks like a pack of trouble."

"She might have asked me," I huffed to Phil that night. "I have a phone. Would it have been too difficult for her to call me, to at least mention the idea? *Oh, by the way, Liz, we're going to stop by a salon. Would you mind if I had Danielle's hair hacked all the way back to her scalp?*"

"You did say you liked it."

I sighed. "That's not the point."

The girls were upstairs, in the beginning stages of what promised to be a marathon clothes-trying-on session. They were using the mirror in our walk-in closet, so Phil and I were banished to the back deck, where we were slowly working our way through a forty-four-dollar bottle of wine from Victor Mesbah, a just-because gift he'd dropped by the office. I was slowly burning through my anger, too.

Phil sighed. "It's hair, Liz. It's not like it's a neck tattoo. And she does look cute."

"Of course she looks cute," I bristled. "She couldn't not look cute." But she'd been cute before, when she'd been so patently herself.

Phil's voice was calm, his words nearly lapped up by the pool. "You're probably going to have to let this go." He was distancing himself, I thought, playing the role of the disengaged stepfather.

Earlier, driving home, the blades of the wind generators on the Altamont rotated so slowly, they might have been giant house fans, barely displacing the warm air. Now the grass by the fourteenth hole was fading into a purplish blue, and sunset had brought with it a slight chill. I pulled my knees to my chest. "She's becoming one of them."

Phil laughed. "Who?"

"You know. The pretty girls."

He leaned over, emptying the bottle between our glasses. "What pretty girls?"

"Please. Don't tell me you haven't noticed. Look at Deanna Sievert. Look at Sonia Jorgensen. Look at Kelsey, for goodness' sake. *Those* pretty girls, the ones the world smiles on, the ones who get everything they want without even trying for it."

"I haven't noticed, particularly." But his voice was distant, his gaze far away.

Liar. I took a large gulp, savoring the slow trickle of wine down my throat, and set the half-empty glass at my feet.

The night had been so quiet that the sound of a car starting still registered a few minutes later, an echoic memory. Out of the darkness came another sound, a strangled cry.

"What was that?" I sat up, thinking the worst—the girls upstairs, Fran Blevins home alone with Elijah.

He held up a hand, shushing me. We waited, and the sound came again—clearly a scream this time, its shrill edge piercing the night. Phil didn't have to think, he was on his feet, heading for the door. I stood, toppling my glass, which shattered on the concrete.

"Shit." I stooped to gather the shards.

"Leave it," Phil called over his shoulder. "We'll get it later."

Inside, Danielle and Kelsey were at the top of the stairs, looking down on us. From this angle I could see straight up Danielle's skirt, a tiny white thing that was a waste of money, no matter what she'd spent.

Phil charged through the kitchen to the garage.

"What's going on?" Danielle demanded.

The garage door slammed and Phil was back, flicking a flashlight on-off, on-off to test the battery.

"We heard a noise," I told them. "Just stay put. We'll check it out."

But Danielle had started down the steps, Kelsey trailing her in a skimpy baby-doll dress. "I'm coming, too," Danielle said. "I want to go with you."

"Right? That's always how it is in horror movies. The killer comes upstairs, and there's nowhere left to go at that point," Kelsey put in.

"I'm sure there's no—"

"Absolutely not," Phil snapped. "You're staying here. And put some clothes on, both of you."

Danielle looked down at her legs, as if she were seeing them for the first time. Kelsey only smiled.

"Stay," I ordered, as if they were disobedient pets. I followed Phil as he barreled down the front walkway, the beam of his flashlight bringing into stark relief the rounded humps of our landscaping rocks. I saw a dark figure standing in the middle of the road, and he spotted me, moving into the yellow glow of an overhead carriage light. He was tall, gray hair cropped close to his head, a button-down shirt tucked firmly into his waistband.

"Everything all right at your house?" he called.

"We're fine. I guess you heard that, too?"

"Sounded like a scream." He extended a hand. "I'm Doug Blevins."

"Liz—Liz McGinnis. That's my husband, Phil," I gestured to Phil's retreating form, a dark shadow preceded by the beam of his flashlight. "I've met your wife and son a few times."

"That's what I hear. Fran said it was nice to have another normal person around."

I laughed. "I feel the same way."

Again, the scream came. It was louder this time, and definitely female. I whirled around, trying to get a sense of its origin.

"That's it," Doug said, digging in his pocket. "Woman screaming? I'm calling the police."

Phil was coming back from the clubhouse, his flashlight zigzagging toward us.

Doug took a step away, speaking into his phone. "Yes, I'm calling from The Palms. Alameda County, outside Livermore."

"It's not coming from the clubhouse," Phil panted. "Everything's shut up for the night." He frowned at Doug Blevins, overhearing part of his conversation.

The scream became a breathy wail, carried by someone coming off the trail at a sprint. Footsteps pounded closer, and Phil stepped in front of me. "Who's out there?" he called.

The running figure became first a woman, then Deanna Sievert in a fitted running tank and shorts, hair escaping her ponytail. Seeing us, she cried out again, more sob than scream this time.

"Deanna? What happened?" I called.

She stopped short in front of us, nearly collapsing. Phil caught her by the arm. "Are you okay? Are you hurt?"

Her breath came in ragged gasps, and when she straightened up, her face was blotchy with tears. "There was—something—" she wheezed. "On the golf course. These two glowing eyes—"

"You saw someone out there?" I asked.

"No, some*thing*. At first—I thought it was someone's dog. But the way it moved—it was *feline*, just massive—" She doubled over again, hands on her knees. Phil still had her by the arm, as if he were propping her up. "It disappeared when I screamed, and then I ran like hell."

Doug joined us, phone in hand. "Police are sending out a patrol. I'm supposed to call back to update them. What did you see, exactly?"

Deanna repeated her story, only this time the predator seemed larger, stronger, faster, like the great fish that got away. She seemed less scared now, enjoying her position as the center of attention. I focused on Phil's thumb, which was rotating in a circle on Deanna's twenty-four-year-old shoulder.

Doug nodded knowingly. "Sounds like a mountain lion. We've had those before, off and on. The drought brings them out here to the golf course. They see all that green and think they've got a better chance of finding food."

Headlights rounded the curve at the end of the block, blinding us with sudden light in the middle of the street. We didn't move. It was a dark sedan, but it couldn't have been the police, especially if they were coming down the winding access road from Livermore.

"Hey! It's the Mesbahs." Deanna waved to them, and Victor rolled down the window. He was wearing a tuxedo, a bow tie unclasped at his neck.

Myriam leaned across his body, alarmed. "What's going on?"

Deanna called into the sedan, "I just saw a mountain lion on the trail!"

"My God." Victor shifted the car into Park. Heat radiated from the engine.

"Well, we don't actually know—" Phil tried.

Doug said, "The police are on their way. Actually, I need to call them back, give them an update." He took a few steps away, redialing.

Myriam stepped out of the car, holding up the hem of a midnight blue dress, its fabric pooling near her ankles. "You must be so *terrified*," she said. Deanna collapsed immediately against her shoulder.

"You don't want to mess around with mountain lions," Victor boomed in his too-loud voice, as if he were educating all of us, everyone in The Palms. "Have you ever seen a mountain lion going after something? They're just stupendous creatures."

"My God, *yes*," Myriam said, patting Deanna's head. "They can just tear something from limb to limb."

No one seemed to be listening to Phil, but he kept talking. "We need to keep cool heads here. Deanna's not sure what she saw, exactly."

"Who's that?" Deanna sniffed, pointing down the street.

It was the Jorgensens, dressed in dark jeans and white shirts. The hard soles of Sonia's sandals smacked the asphalt. "Is everyone okay?" she called.

"Sonia! It was horrible, you wouldn't believe—" Deanna began.

"So *horrible*," Myriam echoed, as if she had been on the trail, too, taking a lap in her evening gown.

Tim Jorgensen shook hands with Victor and Phil and nodded at me. Deanna repeated her story, trembling when she got to the glowing eyes.

Doug was back, sliding his cell phone into his pocket.

"They're going to send out some kind of wild animal team in the morning."

"In the *morning*!" Myriam scoffed. "What good will that do?"

"I don't suppose there's much they can do out there in the middle of the night," Doug said. "And we hardly want them driving out on the golf course."

Tim looked shocked. "No, of course not. They could do a lot of damage out there."

"But we need to let people know," Deanna protested. "I mean, think of all the people who jog first thing in the morning. The Browerses, for one. Sometimes Daisy's out there, too. And then there's the Berglands, with all those kids. You don't think a mountain lion could hop one of those fences along the course, do you?"

"I don't see why not," Victor said. He clapped Phil on the shoulder. "What do you say, mate? I've got a handgun. If you give me a minute to change out of this monkey suit, we could head out there in my cart and chase down some mountain lions."

I could feel Phil's annoyance. He hated the *Crocodile Dundee* act, the assumption that all Australians were swashbuckling men in dungarees and a hat rimmed with jagged teeth. "Let's keep a cool head here," he repeated.

"But we want to be sure," Victor said. "It's about keeping our women safe, right?"

"A *handgun*, Victor? You're not serious." Myriam shook her head. "And I don't think the cart is charged, even. When's the last time you went golfing?"

"Rich has a .22," Deanna offered. "He's in the city tonight, but you could take it. And I know our cart is charged. Mac was on it earlier today. He's too lazy to walk anywhere."

"We could make some phone calls," Myriam said. "I have the HOA directory."

"What do you say?" Victor said. "Give me ten minutes?"

Phil's eyes met mine, a swift glance that told me everything he was thinking—that this was a ridiculous idea and these were ridiculous people, but it was his job to cater to them even at their most ridiculous. He nodded slowly. "Okay, then. We'll just take a look around. But watch that trigger finger, Victor."

Victor guffawed, slapping him on the shoulder. Myriam picked her way back to the car in her heels, and a moment later their sedan passed us, the taillights winking around the curve and disappearing. "Well, good night, all," Doug called over his shoulder.

"Mom?"

I whirled around. Danielle was on the lawn, dressed in the cargo shorts and T-shirt she'd been wearing earlier that day. Again, it took me a moment to recognize this version of her, the adult version with the cropped hair. Kelsey was behind her on the lawn, barefoot in her baby-doll dress. One of her spaghetti straps trailed down her arm.

"Did you get your hair cut?" Deanna squealed, her previous terror forgotten.

Danielle came forward, grinning, and Deanna ruffled fingers through her hair, first mussing it and then rearranging it before pronouncing it "smashing."

"Kelsey, come on," Tim said. "You're walking home with us."

"Why?"

"Because there's a mountain lion out there, and I don't want you walking home by yourself. That's why."

Kelsey dropped her sandals to the ground one by one and wiggled her feet into them.

"Faster," Tim barked.

"We have things to do, Kelsey," Sonia warned.

I watched as the three of them set off down the street, Kelsey trudging ten feet behind, as if she weren't part of their group. I felt sorry for her, understanding suddenly why she preferred to be at our house.

"Doesn't she look so grown up now?" Deanna was cooing. "You'll have to beat off the boys with a stick."

Danielle blushed.

Phil had loosened up a bit, maybe accepting the reality of the night ride with Victor. "Believe me, I have a big stick at the ready," he said. There was a moment of embarrassed silence. "That came out wrong. I meant—"

But it was too late. Deanna had doubled over, laughing. "I bet you do. I bet you do..."

Later, I grabbed a broom and dustpan from the outdoor utility closet and swept up the remnants of my broken wineglass. Nothing bounded past me in the backyard, nothing bared its teeth, but I didn't take any chances. It may have been nothing—I wouldn't have put it past Deanna to exaggerate a house cat into a mountain lion—but I felt uneasy on our patio, as if I were being watched.

Upstairs, I puzzled over the mess on the floor of the master suite—jeans and skirts and complicated, sparkly tops—before remembering that Danielle and Kelsey had used the room for its full-length mirror. I scooped up the clothes and tossed them onto the floor of Danielle's room. She was sitting cross-legged on her bed, thumbs tapping her phone's keypad.

"Oh, sorry," she said. "I forgot about those."

"I'm not your maid," I said, kicking at the clothes I'd just dropped, which already blended in with the other clothes on the floor.

She looked up. "I never said you were my maid."

"Well, this place is a mess," I said, stalking through the room. "Half of these clothes are Kelsey's, and there are wet beach towels…"

"I know. I'm going to clean it up, don't worry."

I nudged a pair of shoes to the side of the room with my bare foot. "Tonight, before you go to bed."

"It's almost eleven o'clock. I'll do it in the morning."

"Tonight," I repeated, and something in my tone caused Danielle to finally put her phone down.

"What's wrong?" she asked, bewildered. "Are you mad at me for something? Is it still the haircut?"

I didn't know how to answer that. Everything, suddenly, felt wrong. Things were feeling more and more wrong from one moment to the next. "Just do what I said," I told her— that parental cop-out, that all-purpose directive I'd hated when my parents used it on me.

I ran a bath and soaked in it, lights out, until the water ran cold. What was wrong with me? I closed my eyes, but I could still picture Phil's hand on Deanna's shoulder, the slow circling of his thumb. I wondered if there was a way I could turn it around, make a joke out of it. *Poor Deanna. Thank goodness she had you to comfort her.* No—it wasn't even funny. Besides, Phil would be annoyed about his ride with Victor; he would be grumpy when he came upstairs. I waited until my skin was wrinkled and soft before toweling off and sliding, still damp, into my pajamas. I tossed the pile of throw pillows out of the way—a silly splurge, since neither of us could be bothered to make the bed properly in the morning—and that's when I saw it: a tiny black strip of fabric, tucked along the bed skirt on Phil's side. I stared at it for a long time before touching it with my toe, spreading it out to see what it was.

A thong.

Not mine. Not Danielle's—unless she'd spent her back-to-school money on silky black underwear.

There was a brief, horrible moment where I could picture Deanna Sievert in our bedroom, shedding one thin layer, then another. It was possible, of course—Danielle and I had been out of the house, and Rich had been out of town. And then I laughed out loud, shocked at how easily that image came to mind.

Of course not.

The thong was Kelsey's—she'd been changing clothes in here; she was exactly the sort of teenager who wore a black silk thong. Why she felt the need to strip down altogether when trying on a few skirts, I had no idea.

I shook my head, remembering her standing on the front lawn in her short baby-doll dress, then casually following her parents down the street, apparently *au natural*. Apparently not worried about sudden gusts of wind.

I thought about flinging the underwear into Danielle's room, one more item for her to clean off the floor. She would express disgust, and I would say, "Tell Kelsey to keep her panties on next time." But it wasn't worth the mention. Instead, I pinched the thong between two fingers and airlifted it to the wastebasket in the bathroom, where I shoved it deep beneath crumpled tissues and an empty bottle of shampoo.

PHIL

I didn't say anything to Liz about Kelsey in the beginning, and then suddenly, it was too late. Liz was already suspicious of Deanna, who had nothing better to do than chat for half an hour here, an hour there. I could have said something about Kelsey, but it would have been more grist for the mill, more fodder for Liz's jokes about The Palms. And that was when it was a mindless flirtation, a situation that I figured would blow over and be gone, like a bit of dandelion fluff.

Later, mentioning it would have given it too much weight in our lives. Even saying her name would have been dropping clues about an affair I wasn't having. I tried it out in my head, worked on the phrasing. *There's this girl who has a bit of a fixation on me. It's probably just a little crush. I haven't done anything—much—to encourage it. It's nothing.* But it wouldn't be nothing to Liz. She wouldn't have been able to let it go. I knew how she was, how at her core was a kernel of insecurity, dormant until we'd moved to The Palms. She'd never been especially concerned with her own appearance before. She'd never obsessed about exercise. Her wardrobe had been a steady rotation of black pants and button-down

shirts, the occasional jacket. In the mornings, every morning of our lives before moving to The Palms, she simply ran
her fingers through her wet hair, added a bit of lip gloss, and
was ready to go.

I'd loved that about her.

Now, she weighed herself each morning, frowned at her
face an inch from the mirror. She bought expensive clothes
that hung in our closet, receipts dangling, while she made
a final decision.

"You look sexy," I'd murmur in her ear, nuzzling along
her neck, and she would frown, not buying it.

"I love you," I said.

She wrinkled her nose. "You just said that ten minutes
ago."

"It's still true."

I thought that Kelsey's friendship with Danielle would
be a good thing, that she would drop the flirtation when
those worlds intersected. What kind of fifteen-year-old girl
was interested in her friend's stepfather? But overnight, she
wormed her way into our lives. I hadn't figured on the lo-
gistics of Kelsey in my home, coming out of the bathroom
late at night when I climbed the stairs, eating a bowl of cereal
in the morning, her nipples outlined against the thin fabric
of her tank top. In the afternoons, she paraded through our
house in her bikini, letting the strap slip over her shoulder
until the top of her breast was exposed. She'd already caught
me looking. One night at dinner she brushed her leg against
mine under the table and I jumped up, saying that I wanted
to catch the end of the game.

I tried, in a general way, to get rid of her. I joked: *she's eating all our food*. I complained: *they're too loud at night, and I'm*

not getting enough sleep. I coaxed: *I wish we could just be alone, the two of us, without the girls always in our hair.*

I wanted Liz to see it, without me having to say it.

It was a mess, but I told myself I could ride it out. What other choice did I have? Kelsey Jorgensen would outgrow me eventually. School would start, and she would find a real boyfriend, someone her own age. She would look at me and see thinning hair, wrinkles around my eyes. If I didn't encourage her, she would wander off—like a stray dog.

The morning after the mountain lion sighting—the "alleged" mountain lion sighting, I told Jeff Parker, checking in—Deanna came by my office to make copies. In giant, bold font, her flier said WARNING: PROTECT YOUR FAMILIES AND YOURSELVES, with a picture of a mountain lion, jaws bared, feline haunches rolling. She offered to walk the fliers door-to-door herself, no doubt planning to relive the experience for anyone unlucky enough to be at home. When Deanna left, clutching an armful of thick orange card stock, Marja Browers stopped by, wondering if I could draw up some kind of schedule for "running buddies." I was fumbling my way through a spreadsheet when Kelsey came into my office, draping herself across the chair in front of me. I was already in a foul mood, not to mention exhausted from spending half the night on the golf course with Victor Mesbah, who'd been so full of bloodlust I was afraid he would shoot himself in the foot. Or worse, shoot me. Liz had already been asleep when I came in, and she'd been frosty this morning, as if I'd been out for a night on the town without her.

"I'm very busy, Kelsey," I said, stabbing at a few keys to emphasize the point.

She leaned forward, centering my nameplate on my desk. She lifted the framed photo of Liz and me at a friend's wedding in Napa, studying us closely.

"Kelsey, I'm serious. Did you need something?"

"I was just wondering if you found what I left for you." She was close enough for me to smell her lotion, both nutty and sweet at the same time.

I looked around the room slowly, as if I were scanning for a booby trap or a car bomb.

She placed her palms on my desk and leaned forward, giving me a straight shot down her shirt. "Not here. In your bedroom, silly."

I pushed back my chair, wanting to stand. My legs felt as substantial as jelly. "What do you mean?"

When she straightened, she flung her hair over her shoulder in a dramatic arc. It was a calculated move. Everything she did was calculated, designed for attention. Had she learned about life from reading men's magazines, from watching porn on her laptop? She smiled at me. "If I told you what it was, that would take away all the fun."

I watched her leave, trying to stay calm. I wanted to race out of the office, tear through the clubhouse, across the parking lot, down the street. Count to a hundred, I ordered myself. I didn't make it past ten.

She wasn't in the hall or the dining room, although I expected her around every corner, stretching out a hand and inviting me to follow her, like the White Rabbit, down, down, down. I took deliberate steps, one foot in front of the other. I said hello to a waitress emerging from the dining room with three plates balanced on her arms. I passed Myriam and told her I'd be back in my office in just a few minutes. I clapped Rich on the back and declined his offer of a Bloody Mary.

"I hear you were out there keeping us safe," he said. "I bet we're out of danger now."

Not at all, I thought. Not a bit.

It was bright outside, a deceptively cold East Bay morning. I let myself in through the front door and took the stairs two at a time. Danielle met me on the landing, surprised. My mind had been reeling with worst-case scenarios, and I'd simply forgotten about her.

"Why are you here?" Danielle asked.

"I live here. Why are you here?"

"Very funny."

"I'm not feeling so great. I need a private bathroom."

"Ewwwww..." she groaned, waving me past.

I locked the bedroom doors behind me and surveyed the scene. My clothes were draped over a chair, where I'd left them last night. Liz's pajamas were balled next to them. I'd made the bed haphazardly this morning, and the duvet hung low on my side. Nothing looked out of place, nothing looked as if it didn't belong. But I wasn't the most observant guy under the best of circumstances. I was the wrong person for this sick little game.

I pulled back the sheets, running my hand under the pillows and along the foot of the mattress, gingerly, as though I was away at summer camp, feeling in my sleeping bag for a snake. I opened my nightstand drawer, then Liz's, rifling through the junk that had accumulated there in only a couple of months. I was beginning to feel queasy, imagining Kelsey in our room, touching our sheets, holding the tube of K-Y Jelly in Liz's nightstand. I bent to the floor, lifting the bed skirt. Nothing. I rifled through my dresser, upsetting the folded stacks of boxers, the balled pairs of socks. Nothing. I was more careful with Liz's dresser. If she came in the room right now, or Danielle did, how would I explain myself?

But there was nothing.

Fuck.

Maybe it was there, but I just didn't know what I was supposed to find. What would an obsessed teenager leave in the bedroom of a man three times her age? A folded love letter, a heart drawn in lipstick on the vanity mirror?

She was sick—that was it. She was a sick person, this was a sick joke. And somehow I was the punch line. I'd fallen right into it.

I flushed the toilet twice before leaving the master suite, and called, "All better now," as I passed Danielle's room.

She was lying on her bed, reading a book, and she grimaced at me. "Seriously? TMI."

I didn't see Kelsey again that day, but I jumped every time someone passed in the hallway. In the dining room, I chose a seat with my back to the corner, like a character in a gangster movie. I wasn't going to be surprised by her again.

That night in bed, Liz ran her hand down my back in a quiet invitation, and I rolled over to face her. I slid my hands beneath her top, helped her wriggle out of the bottoms. But I wasn't able to shut out the image of Kelsey in this very room, invading what had been a sacred space. Eyes closed, I could picture her in detail—the long line of her legs, the pink scar on her kneecap. When I opened my eyes, I had a vision of her standing just over Liz's shoulder, smiling that teasing smile.

"Hey," Liz said, sliding off me, her skin clammy with sweat. "What's wrong?"

I claimed exhaustion, which was true. I'd hardly slept the night before, and my mind had been racing, endlessly, around the same track. I'd pawed through our room like a cat burglar sniffing out a dirty secret.

"You're sure that's it?" she asked, and when I glanced at her, she'd gone still, as if she were holding her breath, waiting for my reply.

Tell her.

But I didn't. I couldn't.

From that point on, I resolved not to look at Kelsey, not to talk to her, not to give her the slightest acknowledgment. School started, which meant that five days a week, she was out of sight until four thirty. After that, I locked my office door, citing a call to make, business that couldn't be interrupted.

What I'm trying to say is that I tried. *I tried.*

Days went by without so much as a glimpse of her. But she was still there, if only in my thoughts—like the black widow Liz had spotted in our house in Livermore. Once she knew it was there, she claimed she couldn't rest easy.

I knew Kelsey was still there, lurking in the shadows, unpredictable and therefore dangerous. I was busy with the construction on Phase 3, walking through homes at various stages of completion, chatting with contractors. The progress had little to do with me—the homes had been planned before I took the job with Parker-Lane, the contractors chosen, subcontractors hired. But it felt good to be out there in a hard hat and boots, stopping to lunch with the crew next to the temporary construction trailer.

One afternoon near the end of September, I logged on to my email after a morning at the site. Half my emails were from Parker-Lane—press releases about a planned expansion over the Altamont in the Central Valley, interdepartmental memos. There was one from Myriam, complaining about the cement mixer that had arrived at seven thirty this morning. Farther down, sent at 10:37 a.m., was an email from kelseybelle98@gmail.com. The subject line read: Phil McGinnis, this is for you. I clicked on the message, hoping it was spam, hoping I was wrong about the name in the address.

A photo was embedded in the email, and even as it filled my screen, I wasn't sure exactly what I was seeing. It was a woman's body, shot from an angle somewhere near her neck—the pale skin of her chest exposed, breasts meeting, a dark V gaping between them. She was wearing a white shirt, buttons undone to her navel. One arm was visible, the sleeve rolled to her elbow. Below that was the hem of a miniskirt, thighs and knees. It was the angle more than anything that made me curious—it was too strange and tame to be pornography. It looked more like a shot from an art magazine, a play on perspective. In the background, the floor loomed large, pale gray industrial-sized tiles outlined by thick black grout. I zoomed in, noticing two things at once. At the edge of the frame was a piece of curved plastic and below it hung the feathered edge of a piece of toilet paper. This was a picture of someone sitting on a toilet.

And not just *someone*—I recognized that knee with its shiny sickle-shaped scar. It was Kelsey Jorgensen, sitting on a school toilet.

Sweat bloomed in my armpits. I punched keys frantically. *Delete*—delete again from my deleted mail. But was it still there, somewhere? I emptied the computer's trash, shut down and rebooted. I couldn't find it when I looked again, but I imagined it getting caught by Parker-Lane in some kind of employee-email scan. *Phil, you want to explain this photo for us?* In the bathroom next to the men's locker room, I splashed water on my face and blotted myself dry with a paper towel.

Shit.

What was she thinking?

I came home early that night and found Kelsey perched on the edge of the love seat in the den, watching TV with Danielle. She didn't look up as I passed, but her appearance confirmed what I already knew. Denim miniskirt, white shirt, sleeves rolled up to the elbow, fully buttoned now. Liz called something about me starting the grill, and I told her I'd be right there.

I waited in the upstairs hallway, and Kelsey met me a minute later. She gave me that bedroom smile—soft eyes, pouty lips. She worked the top button of her shirt back and forth between two fingers.

"Did you like the picture?" she asked.

I grabbed her arm just above the elbow, hard enough so that she gasped. "You will leave me alone," I seethed in her ear. "You will stop these stupid games right now. Do you understand?" She didn't say anything, but her eyes were wide, her irises a startling blue. And then I released her with a little backward shove.

In our bedroom, I leaned against the door, half expecting her to rattle the handle, to come after me like the ax murderer who had chased me to the most secluded point of the house, from which there could be no escape.

Fuck.

Fuck.

JUNE 19, 2015
5:56 P.M.

LIZ

The day was still hot, the sun beating on my neck. I puffed twice into Kelsey's airway, locking my lips over her mouth. When her father had told me to stay away from his daughter, was this what he'd meant? Once Kelsey had sat on a stool in my kitchen and laughed so hard orange juice snorted out her nose. Once she'd come to my office and almost convinced me not to trust my own daughter.

Her skin was clammy beneath my touch, her chest yielding as I began compressions, counting out loud. "One, two—" Was I pressing too hard, not hard enough? I tried not to think of cracked ribs, punctured lungs. Danielle was sobbing into the phone, water dripping from her suit. With each compression, Kelsey's body jerked and settled back, unresponsive.

Seven, eight, nine—

I tried to picture the life-size poster of a human heart on the wall in my doctor's office—the valves, the veins and arteries, the chambers, the blood.

I caught snatches of Danielle's sentences:

I don't know how long.

There was blood…her head.

My mom is doing CPR.

And then to me: "Is she breathing? Is there a pulse?"

No. *No.*

Two breaths, fifteen compressions, check for pulse, repeat.

I gasped, out of breath, "Tell me what happened. Tell me what you did."

But Danielle only shook her head, tears leaking down her face.

Miles overhead, a plane passed en route to Oakland or San Jose. The passengers couldn't see us, of course, but I had a dizzying thought that maybe they were looking down, framing through their rectangular windows our small, particular tragedy.

"Why aren't you coming?" Danielle shrieked into the phone.

But I knew the answer to that, even though time had slipped away along with all the other rules of the universe. Twelve miles down a dusty access road, full of twists and turns. It would be twenty minutes at least, and then there were the winding avenues, the dead-end cul-de-sacs. *It's so far away,* I'd protested to Phil. *It's practically in the middle of nowhere.* He'd grinned. That was the selling point, after all.

I pressed on, dizzy, sick. Kelsey was lifeless underneath me, her body only rising and falling with the compressions, a trick of nature. It was like manipulating a corpse. My arms had begun to feel like jelly, and my mind was wandering. *What had they done while I was sleeping? What had she done, to end up floating in my pool, with her clothes still on?* I lost count of compressions and started over.

Breathe, damn it, I pleaded.

After the mess she'd created, it was the least she could do.

The beginning of the school year was always a mess for the counseling office, no matter how much we preplanned—a blur of students and parents, late registrants and scheduling complaints. Somehow, I'd figured that this year it would be different because Danielle would be on campus. I'd imagined her in my office before class began and after the last bell, chatting with Aaron or Jenn, the administrative assistant, thumbing through old yearbooks, volunteering to straighten the fliers on the table or replenish the pamphlets in the rotating case. I'd imagined the talks we would have to and from school (the only perk to having a longer commute from The Palms, I'd reasoned in May)—her witty observations about classmates and teachers, the advice I would give about clubs and cliques and boys. I'd imagined mother-daughter bonding, the deep insights we would gain into each other's lives.

Instead, Kelsey was always there, waiting in her driveway at 6:45 a.m. each morning, wearing a short skirt or tight jeans, as if she only owned clothes that challenged the dress code. While I played the role of chauffeur, a necessary but unwanted presence in the front seat, she adjusted Danielle's makeup—glittery shadow, sparkly lip gloss.

Sometimes I caught a glimpse of the two of them passing the counseling office on the way to the cafeteria, and I was hit hard by nostalgia for the girl Danielle used to be, the one with the camo pants and the rotation of graphic T-shirts that said things like Reunite Pangaea or My Other Car is a Flying Saucer. Now, with her shorn hair and glittery eye shadow, she might have been an exotic bird, some rare and endangered species.

I waited for the inevitable breakup, the messy fallout when Kelsey realized that Danielle wasn't her ticket to cool. I'd been bracing myself for it, like a long fall through the air with the ground looming. But somehow—it didn't come. Within weeks, they were part of the in crowd, "friending" juniors and seniors on Facebook, lunching with a sprawling, noisy group at two pulled-together tables in the cafeteria. I regretted that I'd ever encouraged the friendship, as if they might never have glommed on to each other without that fateful pool party. Kelsey was too sophisticated for Danielle, interested in things I didn't want Danielle to care about. What was it Sonia had said? *Fifteen going on thirty.*

Maybe it would be better if we weren't at the same school, I thought—if I didn't see Danielle walking by with an upperclassman's arm draped over her shoulders, or catch her exchanging a full-body hug with a boy she hadn't seen in half a day. Maybe it was better not to know.

I tried to embrace the changes, to be friendly and encouraging, to understand just how another person had come to inhabit my daughter's skin, but it was hard to say goodbye to the girl I used to know. One night when it was just the two of us in the kitchen, forming hamburger patties, I asked

Danielle if she ever ran into Devon, one of her old middle school friends.

She looked puzzled, as if the name had already slipped out of her working memory. "Devon from math meets? I don't know. Why?"

I shrugged. "I saw her in the counseling office today, and I remembered how you used to be such good friends." Devon had been picking up information for the PSAT, more than a year away. I'd almost swooned over her geekiness, her quirky glasses and threadbare Toms. "Maybe you could invite her over here sometime."

Danielle was quiet for a long moment, the only sound the smack-smack of her hands, shaping a patty. "I don't know, Mom. We're so different now. I'm not sure we'd have that much to talk about."

Another time, on our drive home, I listened to Danielle laugh when Kelsey talked about a kid in her PE class who was so fat, she hadn't been able to run a single lap around the track.

I cleared my throat and said, "Girls, that's not nice." My words hung in the air, and in the embarrassed silence, I realized they had forgotten I was there, as if there were an invisible wall separating us. At the last stoplight, I studied Danielle in the rearview mirror, looking for clues. Who was she now? How had she become this new person?

"What?" she asked finally, meeting my glance.

I shook my head.

Nothing.

Everything.

On the last Friday of September, Danielle asked if she could spend the night at Kelsey's, and Phil took me out for an impromptu dinner date. We didn't have reservations, and the first three restaurants we visited had waits of up to an hour. Eventually, we ended up at a Pizza Hut, filling our plates at the buffet. A dozen kids were crammed into the arcade, their shrieks drowning out the radio.

"If this is a date, I'm letting you off easy," I said, wiping greasy fingers on a stack of single-ply napkins.

Phil rubbed a circle on my wrist with his thumb. "I thought about renting a helicopter for the night and taking you on a tour of the bay, but it turns out you have to book those months in advance."

"I'm sure we could have borrowed one from a neighbor."

"Damn. Next time."

We grinned at each other. Five weeks in, we'd fallen into the rhythm of the school year—the frozen entrées, the leftovers stretched to a third day, the unfolded laundry heaped on the floor of an empty bedroom. I'd been waiting for things to settle into some kind of normal, but it hadn't happened yet. Maybe there was no normal at The Palms.

There hadn't been another mountain lion sighting, although it was still the talk of The Palms, as real as if we'd all witnessed it ourselves. Deanna had achieved a sort of celebrity status in the neighborhood from an appearance on the local ABC affiliate, where she'd been interviewed about her "brush with danger." Phil and I had watched the clip so many times, I'd memorized each word said in Deanna's trembling voice, each curl of her blond hair in the sunlight. Next to her, with his receding hairline and rounded paunch, Rich might have been her lecherous uncle. It had been Phil's job to repeat Parker-Lane's party line to whoever called, needing a sound bite. *We're taking the situation very seriously and doing everything to ensure the safety of our residents at The Palms.* Just about every resident had approached him with a concern, including the people who had bought into Phase 3. I could always tell when he was on one of those phone calls; his voice changed, became deferential and solicitous in a way that grated on my ears.

Phil ran a finger along the condensation from his beer. "Oh, Liz," he sighed.

I sat back hard against the wooden booth, bracing myself for the delivery of bad news, whatever it was. "What's wrong?"

"Nothing's wrong. I was just thinking…"

Don't, I thought. *Don't think. Don't say anything.*

He drank and set the glass down. "We should do this more often. Get away from there."

I raised an eyebrow. The whole point of moving to The Palms was to spend time there, away from the rest of the world, with every luxury at our fingertips. "I thought you loved *there*."

"But this is nice, just the two of us."

"Right. It is nice."

I was looking for the loophole, waiting for the *but*. He twirled his glass in a small circle on the plastic tablecloth.

"What?" I asked again, torn between truth and silence. *Tell me.*

Don't tell me.

I'd been uneasy ever since the night of the mountain lion, since my discovery of the thong. I'd decided it was Kelsey's underwear, that nothing else made sense. But I was queen at making something out of nothing. The thong had still been there, wadded up in the trash can when I cleaned the bathroom at the end of that week. I'd plucked it out of the trash and examined it between two fingers. *Don't be stupid*, I'd scolded myself. *Just throw it out.* And yet I'd rolled the thong inside a clean hand towel and shoved it in the back of my dresser drawer, behind a half-slip and a strapless bra, as though I were preserving evidence for a crime I wasn't sure had been committed.

No, I was sure.

Phil took my hand across the table, twisting my wedding band around my finger, the diamond appearing and disappearing. I had the feeling there was something he wanted to say, one of the deep and important things that had to be said in a marriage, in any fleeting moment of time alone. But then he smiled and asked, "Should we box up the rest?"

It *was* nothing.

And if it wasn't, maybe I didn't want to know.

We ended up wandering through the outdoor mall in Pleasanton, an area of big-box stores swamped with shoppers on a weekend night. This was the sort of thing we used to do, back in our old life—drool over an area rug or linger in front of a sectional, wondering if it would fit our tight rental space. But there wasn't really a point to it anymore. We had everything we needed; we had plenty of things we didn't need at all.

The sidewalks were crowded, and sometimes Phil and I broke apart to pass a slow-moving couple, but we always found each other again, even if our hold was as tenuous as the touch of two pinky fingers.

Phil's phone started buzzing at six thirty the next morning, its hard case rattling against his nightstand.

"Ignore it," I murmured, throwing one of my legs over his. "It's Saturday."

He groaned. "There's that golf tournament, though."

"Oh, right." I'd successfully avoided Myriam's pleas to

work at the tournament, a fund-raiser for the Leukemia & Lymphoma Society. She already had Phil wrapped up in every stage as an unofficial project manager. His role, as far as I could tell, was to be on hand for the inevitable complaints, the patrons who had one too many shots at the bar after the first nine holes and needed to be discreetly plied with coffee. I ran the length of my leg against the length of his. "Well, Myriam can make do without you for a few minutes."

Phil laughed, wrapping an arm around me, his hand cupping a breast. Then his phone buzzed again, and he sighed, reaching over his shoulder.

"A sprinkler head malfunction," I guessed. "A dead bird on the course. A trash can that wasn't emptied."

Phil struggled to a sitting position, began scrolling through the texts. "Shit," he said finally.

"Did the landscapers forget to blow a leaf off the parking lot?"

He hopped out of bed, pulling on the clothes he'd shed the night before—the boxers, the jeans. He held up the shirt he'd worn on our pizza date, decided it was too wrinkled and went to the closet for one of a dozen Parker-Lane logo polo shirts. I watched him, propped up on my elbows, the comforter pulled up over my breasts.

"What is it?"

"The bathrooms. Some kind of vandalism."

"Oh, my God. Do you want me to—"

But Phil was already putting on his shoes. He hustled down the stairs, and a few seconds later, the front door slammed behind him.

I showered in a rush, toweled off my hair and threw on yesterday's jeans and a sweatshirt before heading over to the clubhouse. It was just after seven, and golfers had already started to arrive. About a dozen people in white pants and pastel polo shirts were milling around the clubhouse.

Helen Zhang and Daisy Asbill were standing near the entrance, wearing crisp white shirts and black pants, name tags affixed to their pockets. Helen gave me an unsubtle up-and-down look, taking in my jeans and tennis shoes.

"What's going on?" I asked. "Phil said something about the bathrooms—"

"Liz, for God's sake." Helen took me firmly by the elbow, leading me a few steps away. "We need to keep our voices down."

"Of course. I'm sorry. I just—"

Up close, Helen's eyes were almost black, flecked with bits of yellow. "They're making a decision now, I guess. Myriam's beside herself, as you can imagine, and what with people arriving..."

Daisy put in, "It's horrible. I mean, thank God I had an extra cup of coffee this morning and had to pee, or else we might not have discovered it until later. If one of the donors had discovered it, can you imagine?"

"So, it's that bad, then?"

"Well, the toilets were flooded, for one thing, and someone had spray-painted these horrible things all over the walls and stall doors..." Daisy began.

I inhaled sharply, thinking of Phil, the hours of work this crisis would demand. "What are they going to do?"

"What is your husband going to do, you mean," Helen corrected. "Parker-Lane needs to get on this, *pronto*."

The doors to the clubhouse opened, and Myriam was there in a white shirtdress and sandals, a clipboard in one hand. She greeted the guests, ushering them toward the bar for mimosas, her voice friendly and confident. "A little issue with the plumbing in the restrooms, but we're going to have that sorted in no time," she reported to the group. "If everyone just wants to head around to the back patio, we've got a drink stand set up there to get us started."

Then she was in front of us, a pinched line of worry between her eyebrows. "Parker-Lane is delivering two portapotties in half an hour," she said through clenched teeth. "*Porta-potties.* For two-hundred-fifty-dollar rounds of golf. Will someone please wake me up from this hell?"

"When did it happen?" I asked.

Myriam turned to me, frowning. "Well, I walked the course yesterday afternoon, and went through every inch of the clubhouse with your husband. Everything was in perfect shape last night at six."

"So someone must have—"

"It's that *fucking* gate," Myriam hissed. "I told Phil that leaving the gate open was a *huge* mistake, a *major* security risk. Anyone could have come in here, anyone with a bone to pick."

Helen stopped her with a hand on her arm. "I didn't realize the gate was open. When was this?"

"All week long, when those cement mixers and God-knows-what were coming through, the gates were deprogrammed."

Daisy shuddered. "Any of those workers could have done this, then."

"Surely they must do some kind of background checks," Helen said. "I certainly hope we don't have people coming in here with criminal records."

"Oh, please!" Myriam laughed. "It's a business like anything else, with a bottom line. There are no background checks, clearly. And we're reaping the results of that right now."

The parking lot was beginning to fill with BMWs and Mercedes and Infinitis, with men and women hoisting golf bags over their shoulders, calling hellos to each other. I felt myself detaching, the air growing thin. I remembered what Fran Blevins had told me about the vandalism at our house, the fixtures missing, the holes kicked in walls. That had been blamed on workers, too—on the riffraff that would drive twelve miles down the winding access road just to find an empty home to vandalize. There was no use in pointing out that the workers had been done by five, the trucks loaded and back through the security gates by the time Danielle had left for Kelsey's house, and Phil and I had headed into town for dinner. This was how it was at The Palms, how it had been with the mountain lion and how it would be with this: suggestion was truth, and truth was incontrovertible.

"The thing to do is to keep this quiet," Myriam was saying, switching back into organizational mode. "If anyone asks, it's a plumbing problem that came up overnight. We're going to do some kind of free drinks at the bar and just eat the cost..."

A silver Lexus pulled into the clubhouse parking lot, coming to an abrupt stop near us. "Ladies," Sonia Jorgensen said, stepping out in a gray dress and heels. "I thought I'd check in, see how everything was going."

"Someone vandalized the bathrooms," Daisy told her. "You should see them—filthy things written on the walls. It's a disaster."

"*Not* a disaster," Myriam corrected her. "A problem, yes. But I've got it under control."

Sonia shook her head. "My God. We can't even be safe from that, out here."

Someone called for Myriam, and she turned away, her face set in that smooth mask of efficiency and control. Daisy and Helen trailed her, and Sonia and I were left staring at each other.

"It's horrible, isn't it?" she asked.

"Horrible," I agreed.

She glanced down at the watch on her wrist. "I wish I could stay to help them out, I really do. I have this big meeting with a client in San Jose today, and I'd better get on the road."

"Are the girls still sleeping, then?" I asked. "I hope they didn't keep you up too late."

Sonia's forehead wrinkled, two parallel lines forming at the bridge of her nose. She spoke slowly, as if I were a simpleton. "The girls are at your house. They spent the night with you."

"What? No. Danielle asked if she could spend the night with you."

We stared at each other.

"Well, they aren't at *my* house. Kelsey sent me a message late last night saying she was with you." She opened her car door and reached across the driver's seat for her cell phone. While she tapped a few buttons, she told me, "I didn't think to call you. I just assumed..."

No, why would you? I thought. *When have you ever?*

"Danielle said she was spending the night at your house," I repeated. "She left around...I don't know, seven?"

"Kelsey, you need to pick up this minute," Sonia barked into the phone. "You call me back right now or there will be hell to pay."

"Maybe they're at Hannah's," I offered.

Sonia scoffed. "I don't think so."

"Can I borrow your phone? Mine's back at the house." I took Sonia's phone, punching in carefully the digits of Danielle's number. It rang four times before her voice came on the machine. *Hi, you've reached Dani…* "Danielle," I said at the beep. "This is your mother. You need to come home ASAP."

Sonia held out her hand impatiently and I returned her phone.

"But where—? I don't understand where they could be," I said. "Neither one of them can drive. Maybe I should go find Phil…" But I glanced in the direction of the clubhouse and knew this was a bad idea. He had enough on his hands.

I felt a sudden cramp, a fresh wave of nausea. Our girls were unaccounted for, and the bathrooms of the clubhouse were vandalized. The two things must be unconnected, they *had to be*. This was how my mind worked when it came to Danielle. I went for the worst-case scenarios: Danielle was missing for twelve hours, so she must have been abducted. Or she'd done something unthinkable, and she'd run away.

Sonia swore, hopping into her car. "They're at the Sieverts'. I'd bet on it. Are you coming?"

Wordlessly, I went around to the passenger side, motivated by Sonia's confidence. She turned around in the parking lot and took the corner quickly, coming to a stop when we'd reached the Sieverts' driveway. Mac's gigantic truck was parked diagonally, blocking two of their four garage bays.

It was as if we were playing a game, but I didn't know the rules. "Why would they be here?"

Sonia was out of the car, faster in her heels than I was in my tennis shoes. "Deanna told me they were doing this wine-tasting tour, two nights in Napa."

"But why would they—" I tried again, but Sonia was already ringing the doorbell, once, twice, her thumb jamming against the button. When that didn't produce an immediate result, she pounded against the door with the flat of her palm. "I do not have time for this," she muttered.

I pressed my face against the pane of glass to the right of the Sieverts' door, taking in the dark flooring, the mail on the entry table. The doorbell chimes reverberated through the house. "Someone's coming," I said. It was a shirtless Mac Sievert, a pair of athletic shorts slung low on his hips. He spotted me looking through the glass and hesitated before moving toward the door.

As soon as the lock was unlatched, Sonia pushed against the door, sending Mac hopping backward to get out of the way.

"Hey! Look, it's not my fault. Before you get all upset—"

Sonia was already inside their house, looking around. I followed her, noting the huge expanses of open space, the tasteful clutches of furniture. One of Mac's T-shirts was draped over the back of a chair. By the staircase I spotted a pair of turquoise Converse, laces still tied. Danielle's shoes.

"Where's Danielle?" I asked.

Mac ran a hand through sleep-rumpled hair. "I just wanna say, it's not a big deal. They were here last night, watching a movie, and then it got late, so…"

Sonia was racing up the stairs, another impressive feat in her heels.

"Hey, are you just allowed to… I mean, I'm not a lawyer or anything, but—"

"My husband is a lawyer," Sonia told him. "You're eighteen, right? And our daughters are underage."

Danielle's backpack was at the top of the stairs, and I picked it up tenderly, as if I were holding on to a lost relic from childhood. I gave the zipper a tug and looked inside—her school binder, fat with papers; a pair of pajamas; a Ziploc bag with her toothbrush. I felt a whoosh of relief. She was here, she was alive. She wasn't smuggling drugs in her backpack, or, for that matter, cans of spray paint. I could deal with the rest.

Mac's bedroom was on the right, through a set of double doors. The room was dark, and it took me a moment to get my bearings. It was larger than the master suite in my home, larger than some of the apartments I'd lived in when it was just Danielle and me and a load of baby paraphernalia. Mac's room had a billiards table, heaped with pool cues and balls, discarded clothes, a row of empty Corona bottles. On one side of the room, a big-screen TV was bolted to the wall, and asleep in front of it on a futon was Danielle, her knees tucked to her chest inside an oversize 49ers hoodie. On the other side of the room, Sonia was yanking Kelsey out of a king-size bed by her elbow. In her jeans and skimpy tank top, blond hair matted to one side, Kelsey might have been an embarrassed starlet, her image caught by waiting paparazzi.

I stood over Danielle and put a hand on her shoulder. She opened her eyes and stared at me, then sat up. Yesterday's mascara was a dark smear across her cheekbones, like war paint. "Mom," she croaked. "I'm so sorry."

I held up a hand, silencing her. "We're leaving. Now."

"What did I tell you?" Sonia was asking Kelsey. "No more messing around, no more getting into trouble. Six months without trouble, and we would buy you that car. Now the clock resets."

"Nooooo," Kelsey whined. "It wasn't even my fault."

From the doorway, Mac said, "It was nothing. They were

just hanging out here and then everyone got sleepy, and I said they could stay. It was no big deal."

"Were they drinking?" I asked.

"No, those are mine. Seriously, it was just—"

"You're not twenty-one, either," I reminded him.

"Yeah, but..." His smile was sheepish.

Sonia stormed past us, jerking Kelsey along like a marionette. "I don't have time to deal with this now, but believe me, your parents are going to hear about this."

Danielle was on her hands and knees, digging underneath Mac's couch. She pulled out a textbook, one that Mac had probably shoved under there during the first week of school and never looked at again. She looked up at me. "I can't find my shoes."

"They're downstairs," I said.

She pulled the 49ers sweatshirt over her head, pulling her own T-shirt up in the process and revealing a knobby ridge of spine. I fought the urge to help her disentangle herself. "Thanks," she said, handing the sweatshirt to Mac.

"No problem."

Downstairs, Danielle stuffed her feet into her Converse, and we did the walk of shame down the Sieverts' sidewalk, into the bright sunlight. Sonia and Kelsey were already backing out of the driveway, the Lexus pointed in the direction of the white house with its marble columns. Down the street, cars filled the clubhouse lot.

It was only once we were inside our house that we spoke—Danielle first, the beginning of a dozen apologies I would hear over the next few weeks. *I thought we were going to spend the night at Kelsey's house* and *Mac invited us over to watch a movie* and *It was just a bad decision* and *I'm sorry, I'm sorry, I'm sorry.*

I doubled over, resting my hands on my thighs to steady

myself. I didn't realize until that moment that I'd been shaking, anxiety rendering me breathless.

"Mom?" Danielle's voice was wobbly with tears. "I didn't
mean to—"

But the panic seeped out, like water through a colander,
leaving only anger.

I'd trusted her, and she'd lied. She'd come close to getting away with it, too. If she'd come home and hopped in
the shower, I might never have known.

"Sit down," I told her. "You're going to start again, from
the beginning."

PHIL

It had been wishful thinking, that day in the upstairs hallway. Give her a little shake, utter a little threat and hope it would all just go away.

But that would have been too simple, and nothing with Kelsey Jorgensen would ever be simple.

I suspected Kelsey from the moment I received Myriam's text, before I even saw the damage. She was capable of it. She was probably capable of anything.

Myriam met me just inside the clubhouse, near the fancy chairs and the sofa where no one ever sat. She was pacing, her pupils dilated. Panic was her drug. "How could this happen? I don't understand. I expect a certain amount of security at The Palms—"

"I need to see it," I said, brushing past her. The clubhouse was a sprawling building, with administration offices and community mailboxes on the right, dining and conference rooms on the left. Down the middle was a long hallway with public restrooms, each branching off to men's and women's locker rooms. Halfway down the hall, my shoes sank into the wet carpet.

Myriam stopped, probably not wanting to damage her fancy shoes. "I figured it must have been a plumbing problem, a burst pipe or that kind of thing..."

I pushed open the women's door first, regretting that I wasn't wearing waders. By this time my shoes were soaked, the hems of my jeans dripping.

Myriam called, "What happened to the alarm, anyway? Aren't you in charge of that?"

I ignored her.

The bathrooms had always struck me as clean and warm, spa-like. The walls were white bead-board panels, the floors a wood-grain porcelain laid on the diagonal, creating a seamless line into the locker room. Now the bathroom was a nightmare—blue spray paint crisscrossed the walls, *FUCK* and *PUSSY* and *SUCK MY DICK* sprayed on the wood panels, the mirrors, the stall doors. One of the toilets was still running, water still gushing onto the floor. I splashed into that stall and reached behind the toilet for the lever that shut off the water. The culprit was a clogged toilet, a dozen rolls of toilet paper crammed into the bowl. The inside of that stall had been sprayed, too—a blue blur of paint that stretched around three panels. Stepping back to get the bigger picture, I read *YOU HAD YOUR CHANCE*.

No matter what Myriam said, this wasn't the random work of vandals, people with too much time and a general bone to pick. This was a message.

For me.

"What are you going to do?" Myriam demanded, when I squished past her in the hallway, my soles heavy. "Where are you going?"

"I've got to make some phone calls." I rounded the corner and stopped in front of my office. I tried the handle, expecting to find the door unlocked, my files trashed, blue spray paint on the walls. But the door was locked, and when I swung the door open, leaving my key in the door, the room was just as I'd left it yesterday.

"Well, what am I supposed to do? People are arriving. We can't have them coming in here, and without any bathrooms—" Her voice rose to a shriek.

"Myriam, it's okay. I'll take care of it right now. We'll say there was a burst pipe, and we'll get some portable toilets down here."

"I hardly think that people who pay for this kind of experience—"

"Excuse me." I turned my back on her, reaching for the desk phone. When I turned around, she was gone. I had some personal phone numbers for Parker-Lane executives, and over the next half hour I worked my way from the bottom up the chain, repeating *vandalism* and *water damage* until the porta-potties were on their way, as well as an emergency restoration-and-cleaning service, an impressive team that arrived in econo-sized vans loaded with pumps and hoses and fans and guys in white hazmat suits.

While I waited for them to arrive, I took my phone and snapped photos of the damage, of the message I figured had been left specifically for me. *YOU HAD YOUR CHANCE.* It had been a mistake, I saw now, to delete the picture Kelsey had sent me. I'd been seeing headlines in my mind: *Phil McGinnis, a thirty-seven-year-old pedophile from the Livermore area...* I'd been thinking of the implications of being caught with it, like a sicko with his kiddie porn. But it had been evidence, hadn't it? I could have shown it to Liz, explained the situation. I could have it now, to pair with her taunt in the bathroom. It would have formed a narrative, a trail of proof.

But even as I had the thought, I knew it wasn't true. I'd wanted to say something to Liz last night. I'd had my chance, even with that damned arcade music beeping in the background. And I couldn't get the words out, afraid in my attempt to prove my innocence I would only sound guilty. It would be the same now, if I tried to explain the vandalism, the *YOU HAD YOUR CHANCE*. How would I do that, exactly? *There's this fifteen-year-old girl who's obsessed with me, and she wrote me this message because I didn't take her up on her offer...*

I slogged back down the hallway to the maintenance closet, where I knew there was a can of beige spray paint, one used for quick fixes in the dining room to cover scrapes and gouges made by chairs and table legs. By the time the crew arrived, I'd covered the message completely with quick spritzes.

"I already took some pictures," I explained, giving the crew a show-around. "I didn't want any of our residents to get upset by the graffiti."

Jeff Parker himself met me at the clubhouse at eleven while the tournament was in full swing, guests gamely using the portable toilets in the parking lot. Due to the noise of vacuums and high-powered fans, lunch was moved out to the patio area overlooking the putting green. My phone buzzed relentlessly with messages from Myriam and a few from Liz. She was probably worried about me, wondering how she could help.

While Jeff Parker surveyed the scene, conversation impossible over the high pitch of machinery, it occurred to me that I'd known it was coming—this or something like this—from that first day when she'd settled into the chair across my desk and told me that she was bored. I'd heard the warning bell then, that sign that something was off-kilter, that something about this girl was just not right. Jeff made a note on a pad he'd pulled from his shirt pocket, and I allowed myself to play out an alternate ending, one in which I'd flirted back, let her hand linger on my arm, not pulled away when she brushed her leg against my mine. But there was no way to entertain the thought and not take it all the way, to sex in my office late at night, the door locked, carpet burns on our knees and elbows. There was no way it didn't become the nightmare it had threatened to become all along.

I didn't have to hear Jeff's words to understand what he was saying when he turned to me, finally.

A fucking mess.

JUNE 19, 2015

6:02 P.M.

LIZ

It was the most beautiful sound I'd ever heard—first a whine like squealing brakes, then, coming closer, the looping wail of a siren. Danielle screamed, "I hear it!"

"Go," I gasped, coming back to myself, to the present. "Flag them down on the street."

Danielle turned and ran.

I blinked sweat from my eyes, trying to visualize the ambulance darting through The Palms, slowing for the speed bumps or dodging them or taking them full strength. Everyone must be hearing the sirens—the Jorgensens, too, if they were home. Not likely, considering their track record. Where was Hannah? Why hadn't she come back?

The ambulance would come to a stop in front of our house, with its grass that needed to be mowed, the overgrown flower beds—things Parker-Lane wasn't doing for us anymore, things I'd stopped caring about. The attendants would pass our front porch, heaped with unopened newspapers, push through the massive double doors that were too grand, too pretentious, that told a lie: *wealth and privilege live here. A good life is lived here.* Then they would scan the boxes

I'd stacked shoulder-high to the right of the entryway—
Bathroom, Books, Movies, Goodwill—and wonder how
we'd screwed it all up.

It seemed like only a second later that a woman was leaning over me, a hand on my shoulder. "Ma'am, we're going
to take it from here."

I crab-walked clumsily out of the way, collapsing back
onto my elbows.

A man was there, too, her partner. "What's her name?"

My tongue stuck in my mouth, thick and unfamiliar.
"Kelsey. Kelsey Jorgensen."

"All right, Kelsey," the woman said, feeling for a pulse.
"You just hang in there. We're going to help you out."

It's too late, I thought. But I clung to her words like an
anchor that would stop the world from moving, just for the
moment.

The female paramedic identified herself as Moreno, the
male as Richards. She might have been my age, a few wrinkles creasing her face, her hair pulled into an unyielding
braid. He seemed impossibly young, his shirtsleeves bulg-
ing with muscle. I followed their movements dumbly—the
duffel bags unzipped, the machines unloaded and activated.

"We've got a head wound here," Moreno said, taking over
the compressions. "She hit her head and went in the pool?"

It took me a moment to realize this was a question. "I
don't know. I was inside. But we pulled her out and she was
bleeding." My body had gone from aching to numb, my
arms heavy at my sides.

Moreno paused to allow Richards to slice open Kelsey's
shirt from hem to neck. Beneath it she wore a lacy pink bra,
and beneath that her chest was still, only springing to life
when the compressions resumed.

"Is that her blood leading to the house?" Moreno asked.

I stared stupidly at a thin trail of red drops leading back to the sliding door. "I don't know," I said. And then I remembered banging my big toe in my rush to get outside. Now, as if on cue, it began to throb. And it was a mess—the nail dangling crookedly, bubbles of blood rising from the bed. "No—that's not her blood. I tore my toenail."

She glanced at my foot, dismissing it. "Okay. Tell me what happened here. Who saw her go into the pool?"

I looked around and found Danielle in the oblong shadow of the roofline. She was shivering, arms clasped over her skinny chest. Just below her jutting hip bone I spotted the tattoo. From this distance, it looked like a smear of dirt. "Danielle, come here. Tell us what happened."

Her voice was small, nervous. "I don't know. Hannah and I were upstairs, and then we came down and she was just... floating there."

"Did you let her in the house?" I demanded.

"No! I didn't even know she was back here, until..."

Moreno looked back and forth between us. "So how long could she have been in the pool? A few minutes? Five? Ten?"

"Maybe five minutes?" Danielle's voice rose at the end, as if she were in fact making a guess, or asking a question she hoped I would answer for her. She smelled of chlorine and suntan lotion, of salt and coconut and sweat. I squinted into the dark interior of the house, but there was no sign of Hannah.

"Eighteen minutes," Richards said, as if he were answering the question for us. I held the number in my head, turning it around, trying to understand its importance. Then I realized: that was the length of the 911 call, the spell during which I'd leaned over Kelsey, breathing, pushing, pleading, praying. It had seemed like forever. Still—eighteen minutes was way too long, a colossus of a number.

"Do you know if she was drinking? Did she take anything?"

Danielle shook her head.

"She was on some kind of medication," I offered. "For depression, I guess. But I don't know what, or if she was still taking it."

Moreno glanced quickly from me to Kelsey, and I understood what she was thinking. How in the world could this girl be depressed? But when I looked down at Kelsey, she didn't look like any version of herself now. She was a patient, a *victim*. The cut on her head had been covered with stretchy pink gauze that crisscrossed her forehead in a giant X. Her chest had suddenly sprouted leads and tubes, the wires leading back to a defibrillator. An oxygen mask covered her mouth.

I bent at the waist, suddenly dizzy. The afternoon was coming back to me, hard and fast. I'd had too much wine, and I'd thrown it up in the upstairs bathroom. What had happened before that? I remembered yelling at Kelsey, remembered the shocked look on her face. But then what?

I'd fallen asleep, leaving Danielle and Hannah the house to themselves.

LIZ

I let Danielle cry it out, tracks of mascara trailing down her cheeks. I let her plead her innocence, her sobs uncontrollable, hands over her face so that it was difficult to tell what she was saying. She'd gone to Kelsey's house first—that part, apparently, had been true—but then they'd eventually drifted over to Mac's to watch a movie, and once they were there, they'd just decided to spend the night.

"What about Kelsey's parents?" I demanded.

Danielle shrugged. "They weren't home yet when we left."

"What movie?"

"Um, I don't know. Three guys on a road trip?"

I stared at her. "And you were drinking."

Danielle leaned forward, the heels of her hands gouging at her eyes. "One. One beer, I swear. It wasn't even good. I was just drinking it because—"

"You're fourteen, Danielle," I reminded her. "*Fourteen.* There is no excuse."

She spoke into her hands. "I know."

"Is there anything else you want to tell me?"

She looked up at me, shaking her head. Huddled on the couch, clutching a throw pillow to her chest, she looked skinny and helpless, like the fourteen-year-old girl I'd almost forgotten she was.

I remembered the distinctive smell of pot, ripe as cologne. "What about drugs? Did you smoke pot?"

"*Mom*. No."

"What about sex?"

She sat back. "Mom!"

It was a relief to read her shock. "Did you go anywhere else?"

"No. What do you mean? Where would we have gone?"

"To the clubhouse," I said, watching her carefully, alert to any sign that she was being dishonest. I'd always been able to tell when Danielle was lying, because she wouldn't look directly at me. Her glance might shift down or to the right, as if she were buying time before she could confront me head-on.

But she held my gaze now. "Why would we go to the clubhouse? It would have been closed, anyway."

"What about Kelsey?"

"What about her?"

I let this sit, let her words hang in the air.

She looked around suddenly. "Is something going on? Where's Phil?"

I told her what I knew about the vandalism, stressing the thousands of dollars in damage, the disruption to the morning's tournament.

"That's horrible," she said, wiping her face on the hem of her T-shirt. "Why would someone do that? I mean...you can't think that I would have anything to do with that."

I sighed, watching her. A day ago I wouldn't have dreamed

of finding her on a futon in Mac Sievert's bedroom, mascara streaked across her face. It had come—the official world of teenagerdom, the world of bad decisions and half-truths. The ironic thing was, I spent my days counseling students who had messed up in one way or another—failing grades, pregnancies, STDs, drug use. I'd wondered, time and again, how the parents had been so clueless, how they could not know what was happening in their own child's life. But it turned out not to be that difficult. You took your eye off the ball for a minute and it was your own kid.

"I know you have to punish me," she said. "I deserve to be punished. You could ground me. Two weeks."

I laughed despite myself. Danielle had always negotiated her own punishments. She'd been an incredibly easy kid, responsible and trustworthy and helpful, a single mother's dream. At nights when I tucked her into bed, she would confess her transgressions to me, as if I were a priest or God. And she was always ready with her own punishment, too—*I won't watch television for a week. I'll apologize to my teacher. I'll wash the dishes every night for a month.* But she'd missed the mark on this one. "Two weeks? You lied to me, you snuck around, you drank…"

She closed her eyes, steeling herself.

"One month," I said. "You go to and from school only. No one spends the night."

Danielle moaned. "For a *month*?"

I shrugged. "We could make it six weeks if you like." This had been my dad's type of bargaining, where a complaint would get me a worse punishment. It was something I promised myself never to do as a parent, but it slipped out so easily, like a reflex.

Danielle stood up, defeated. "No, I'll take the month."

★ ★ ★

Phil came home around noon, spotted with tan spray paint. He entered through the garage and undressed in the kitchen, kicking off his shoes, peeling off his shirt and pants and socks. He tossed the socks in the direction of the trash can. One missed, sliding wetly to the floor.

"So you ended up repainting?" I asked carefully. I'd sent him a half-dozen text messages, none of which he'd returned.

"A professional's going to come out on Monday morning," he grunted, making his way up the stairs. I followed several steps behind. "I just wanted to cover up some of the worst of it. Then we had to get the water stopped and things mopped up—it's a nightmare."

We passed Danielle's door, which was closed. I'd looked in on her after her shower and found her asleep again, worn-out from all her crying and pleading, and from whatever else she'd done the night before, I suppose.

"I talked to Myriam," I said. "I guess it's good it was found by someone here, rather than one of the guests."

Phil grunted. He shed his boxers a foot inside the bedroom and headed directly to the shower, shoulders down. He looked a decade older than the man who had tossed me onto the bed last night, beating his chest mock caveman-style.

I sat on the edge of the bathtub, steam from the shower stirring the air and settling on the mirrors. "Any idea who it was?"

"That's above my pay grade."

"I mean, I thought maybe from the graffiti…"

"You think they signed their names? It was all swearwords. 'Fuck this, fuck that.' Just your average senseless crime."

"Myriam says it's someone from outside The Palms," I said.

Phil's laugh was bitter. "*Myriam says.* Of course she does. That's the only way the world makes sense to her."

The water stopped abruptly and I passed Phil a fresh bath towel, watching through the frosted glass as he ran the towel over his hair and then down his body. When he stepped out a moment later, the towel was tied around his hips. Water beaded on his chest. "What?" he asked, realizing I was waiting.

I told him about finding Danielle at the Sieverts' house, about grounding her for a month.

He swore. "And the one night she's unaccounted for, there's vandalism in the clubhouse?"

I shook my head. "I was thinking the same thing, but it couldn't have anything to do with her. You should have seen how surprised she was when I told her about it. Besides, there was no paint on her, she wasn't wet or dirty..." I followed him back into the bedroom, sitting on the bed while he pulled on clean clothes.

"And I suppose it had nothing to do with Kelsey Jorgensen or Mac Sievert." His face was away from me, but I heard the disgust in his voice, the splatter as their names hit the air.

"Danielle says they watched a movie and fell asleep." I thought of the beer bottles in Mac's bedroom, lined up on the billiards table, the lazy way he'd come down the stairs in his shorts, bare-chested. "Yes, they're overprivileged and entitled, but that doesn't mean..."

Phil looked at me. "It doesn't?"

I stopped, hearing myself. It was what everyone here told themselves, as if it were written into the HOA agreement, a credo for membership at The Palms. Other people, always, were the bad ones—the *bad influences* at Ashbury, the drywallers and cement pourers and bricklayers and roofers with questionable backgrounds. Even at Miles Landers, when the locker rooms were vandalized, when someone sprayed *LOSERS* in Roundup on the football field, we assumed it to be the work of the crosstown rival—an assumption that never proved true. Always, inevitably, it was one of our own students. But it was the same thinking at work: Why would we do this to ourselves?

Phil shut the door of his armoire, hard, and I winced from the sound of wood hitting wood. "If you don't mind," he said, "I'm going to lie down. I've had enough hell for one day."

Kelsey was waiting in front of her house as usual on Monday morning, wearing a short black dress and silver earrings that fell to her shoulders—as if it were a Saturday night date instead of another day at school. She said hello to me and exchanged a knowing look with Danielle as she slid into the backseat. It had been a relief to have a break from her for the weekend, to lounge around the house in yoga pants and not bump into her every time I rounded a corner.

The mood was more subdued than usual, and I turned up *Morning Edition* loud enough to drown out the silence. There were other things going on in the world. Syria. The end of the embargo on Cuba. Real, important things. It took me half the drive to realize Danielle and Kelsey were texting each other, that their thumbs were saying the things they didn't want me to hear. In fact, they'd no doubt been texting all weekend—that's what Danielle had been doing in her room, when I assumed she was being conciliatory, submitting mildly to her punishment.

Shit.

This was the sort of thing I would know if I'd bonded with the moms of Danielle's classmates in the drop-off lane, if I'd kept up with them over the years, meeting for moms' night pedicures and margaritas. Instead I'd waved and headed to work; at the end of the day, I'd stayed in the car when it was time to pick Danielle up, too tired to engage. *Take note, Liz*, I told myself. Next time, grounding includes the cell phone. It includes the internet.

At school, I watched them walk off together, laughing and chatting as soon as they were out of my earshot. Well—I thought. At least I had a month without Kelsey in my home. That would feel like a minivacation in itself.

But it was a short-lived vacation. That afternoon, following a tedious administrative meeting and an hour of posting scholarship notifications to the school's website, Kelsey appeared in the doorway of my office.

For a moment I stared at her blankly, filled with the strange sense of two worlds colliding, school and home, business and personal. There were too many Kelseys: the girl in the backseat of my car, sprawled across my daughter's unmade bed, stumbling to her feet in Mac Sievert's bedroom. But Kelsey fell into my section of the alphabet—at this moment, she was just another student, and this was just another meeting.

"Is this a bad time?" she asked, leaning against the door frame. Her hair was somehow as perfectly styled as it had been this morning, the ends still holding their loose curls. It was a feat I'd never been able to manage, despite two more decades of styling experience.

I glanced up at the clock on my wall. Two thirty. "Not at all. Is everything okay?"

She shrugged. "Can we talk for a minute?"

"Of course, let me just…" I made a few clicks and saved my work before turning back to her.

My office was just large enough for three chairs, four filing cabinets, two bookshelves crammed with yearbooks, binders on testing protocol and thick catalogs from college admission departments. Kelsey stood in the middle of the room, looking around as if she had been asked to give an appraisal. "This is cute," she said, picking up a framed photo of Danielle in a plastic kiddie pool, her brown hair hanging in wet pigtails. She set it down and picked up the other frame from my desk, a photo of Phil, Danielle and me at Disneyland three summers ago, wearing matching hats with mouse ears. Danielle's mouth was ringed with the red stain of a sugary drink, and she looked heartbreakingly happy.

"We used to go to Disneyland every year," Kelsey said, sloughing her tote bag from her shoulder and letting it drop to the ground. "My parents hated the long lines."

I smiled, imagining the Jorgensens waiting in line with the tourists in khaki shorts and sweatshirts, only Tim would be in a dark suit and Sonia in a patterned dress and heels, both checking their phones every thirty seconds. "We haven't been back since we took that picture, either."

She approached the chair across from my desk. "Now my parents think I'm old enough for serious travel. Last year we went to Italy for two weeks, and before that my dad took me on a tour of all these Ivy League campuses. I was only *thirteen*, but I guess he was trying to make a point."

"Sounds like a smart dad," I said lightly. *Oh, please*, I would tell Allie later. *Thirteen years old?* I remembered Danielle telling me about the Jorgensens' trip to Italy last year, sounding awed. *They went to Italy for Christmas. Just because.*

Kelsey's gaze had gone over my shoulder, to the various

things tacked to the wall behind my desk. I half turned, seeing what she was seeing. A picture of Aaron and me, dressed up as Thing 1 and Thing 2 for a school spirit day, a Mother's Day card Danielle made me in second grade, my framed diploma from San Jose State. "Was I supposed to make an appointment to see you?" she asked suddenly. "I don't know how this works. At Ass Bury there weren't that many students, and we could just pop in whenever the door was open."

"Usually students make an appointment, but I'm free now," I said, gesturing to the chair across from my desk. I tried to keep my voice friendly but professional, neutral. Kelsey settled into the chair, her black dress rising up as she sat, exposing a long line of thigh. I turned back to my monitor. "Let me do one little thing," I murmured, typing her name into the student database. Only six weeks into the school year, there weren't any official grades on file. Although MLHS teachers were required to maintain an up-to-date online grade book, there were some liberal interpretations of "up-to-date" that resulted in the tool being only somewhat effective. Still, at a glance, I saw that Kelsey had four As, with Bs in world history and geology. Solid enough—although a bit lower than what I would expect from an Ashbury student.

I minimized the screen and glanced back at Kelsey. "What can I help you with today?"

She tilted her head to one side, twirling one of her long earrings back and forth between her fingers. "It's not, um, an academic thing. It's— I guess it's personal."

I shifted in my chair, studying her.

"But that's okay, right? I mean, counselors here handle personal issues, too."

Right there, I could have walked across the lobby to Aaron's office, rapped on his door, checked if he were available. We'd done that before, for one reason or another—a simple trade: this student for that one. He'd had a female student with an unrelenting crush on him; I'd had a parent accuse me of ruining her daughter's life, never mind the seventeen missed assignments in English that meant she would have to take summer school. I could easily have handed Kelsey off to Aaron, citing a conflict of interests. On the other hand, knowing Kelsey personally might make me the best one to advise her. I remembered what Sonia Jorgensen had said at the Mesbahs', her cool hand on my arm. It was wonderful to have another responsible adult in her daughter's life.

"Of course," I said finally. "I work with a lot of students on personal issues." My glance went to the organizer bolted to my office wall, to the crisp, bright pamphlets with their bold headings: Overcoming Anorexia. Understanding Sexually Transmitted Diseases. Dealing with Loss.

She took a deep breath, exhaling through her tiny, perfect nose. "So...is this the same as talking to a priest?"

I blinked, laughing reflexively. "Well, no. I'm not here to give religious advice, of course."

"But it's still completely confidential?"

I considered her question, choosing my words. "I like to explain it this way, Kelsey. I'm not going to repeat what you tell me unless you give me permission to do that, or unless I become concerned for your health and safety."

"So if I told you I had an eating disorder, you would have to tell a doctor?"

I smiled, thinking of all the meals Kelsey had eaten at our house, all the devoured Klondike bars and bags of Doritos. "That's a good example. Yes—I would need to get other people who can help involved. Your parents, for example, so they could make decisions about your health."

Kelsey went quiet. Finally, when I was about to prompt her, she said, "Actually, it's not just about me. It's about Danielle, too."

I stiffened, trying to keep my voice even. "Okay."

She chewed on her lower lip, working it back and forth between her lower teeth. "It's about last weekend. Saturday. I don't know if I should be telling you this, but I'm worried, because she's my best friend, you know?"

My heart was galloping, as if it were one of those mechanical rabbits being chased by a stampede of racing greyhounds. "What—"

"Well, I feel bad because I'm the one who suggested that we go over to Mac's house. There's never anything good to eat at my house, and we were bored...so yeah. We just thought we'd hang out at Mac's for a bit."

"You watched a movie," I prompted, as though I were reading from a script.

"Yeah, some dumb road-trip movie. Mac was already watching it, so we didn't even get to see it from the beginning. Anyway, we went down to his garage, where his dad has his poker nights, and they had this refrigerator full of beer—" Kelsey hesitated for a moment, glancing at my office door, open about a foot. My particular "open-door policy" meant that the door stayed open while I chatted with students, unless their parents were in the room or it was absolutely necessary to close it. You couldn't be too careful, I'd always reasoned—although now that we were talking about my daughter I wanted to stand up and give the door a tidy, careful push.

I kept my voice low. "It's okay, keep going."

"Well, we had a few beers each, and I was starting to feel kind of sick. I mean, I've barely ever had any alcohol in my life. And then Mac had some weed—I mean, I don't want to get him in any trouble, either—"

I didn't realize I was holding a pen until I saw the blob of ink on my desk calendar, bleeding through to October. A *few* beers, not one. *Some weed.*

"So, yeah. We smoked a joint, and then we went back upstairs to finish the movie, and I was feeling so sleepy, I just crawled into Mac's bed. I guess I must have fallen asleep, because at one point I woke up and the TV was off and they weren't there anymore." She stopped, giving her dress a modest tug to cover a half inch more of her thighs.

"Where were they?" I breathed.

"I don't know. I mean, I went through the whole house looking for them. I was getting worried—Mac's kind of a player, you know? I didn't want anything to happen to Danielle. So eventually I went out into the backyard, thinking they might be in the pool house, and that's when I saw them coming in through the side gate."

"Coming in through the side gate," I repeated.

"Yeah. Danielle told me they had gone for a walk. They were being kind of weird, and I didn't really want to ask about it. But then on Saturday night my mom told me about what happened in the clubhouse, and all I could think was— you know. But it's probably nothing. I just wanted to tell you…"

Blood thrummed in my ears. "I'm glad you told me," I said, the words coming although I wasn't aware of forming them. Across the desk, Kelsey gave me a sad I-hate-to-do-this smile and adjusted her dress again.

She's acting, I thought suddenly. She's rehearsed these

words. She's practiced the look she's giving me. "Did you—did you tell this to your mom?"

Kelsey looked horrified. "No! I didn't want us to get in any more trouble, and my mom would have killed me if she knew about the pot."

"But you're telling me."

"Right, because I feel so bad. It's my fault, isn't it? If I hadn't suggested that we go over to Mac's house…and, I don't know. I'm older. I should have known better. Danielle—she's kind of naive and all…"

I straightened the stack of scholarship forms on my desk, the ones I'd been posting online when Kelsey came in, buying myself a moment. What in the world would possess her to come in here, to throw her friend under the bus? Even if her story was true, how could she justify the insinuation, the implied accusation, the resulting trouble it would mean for Danielle—all while excusing her own behavior?

"And also," she continued, her words sliding smoothly into my thoughts, "I knew I could trust you, as a counselor and all."

I raised my eyes to hers. "Property was damaged, Kelsey. We're talking a lot of money—enough for it to be a felony. If I know anything about this, I need to come forward."

She sat back, eyes wide. "But you don't know anything for sure. I'm only telling you what I saw."

The bell rang, a short beep followed by a long one, Morse code for the end of the period, the end of the day. I glanced at the clock—2:57 p.m. It felt like the longest conversation of my life. I stood, and Kelsey stumbled to her feet. It was the first time I'd ever seen her less than graceful, not in control.

"You did the right thing, telling me. I think you should let me take it from here, though."

"I just don't want Danielle to get into trouble," she sniffed. "And she would know that I was the one who told on her. But I thought you should, like, keep an eye on her."

I reached past her for the door, giving it the little push that was needed to open it the rest of the way, wide enough to usher her out of the room. "You're a good friend, Kelsey," I said, and watched her walk through the lobby and out the main entrance to the counseling office, one long leg in front of the other.

I drooped into my chair, feeling weak in the knees, sick to the stomach. On my monitor, Kelsey's file was still open, minimized on the bottom of my screen. I clicked on it, bringing to life her As and Bs for this semester, and then I navigated to the tab for her 2013–2014 grades. She hadn't been at Miles Landers last year, but her freshman grades from Ashbury were in the system. This was the kind of thing I did all the time, the kind of thing it was my job to do, and yet I felt uneasy. It was the Kelsey effect, the result of knowing her in so many facets and not really knowing her at all.

During her freshman year, Kelsey had a string of As and Bs: algebra I, honors English, biology, Spanish I, world religions, advanced computers. But in her second semester of honors English, she had an I, for Incomplete. My eyes automatically went to the bottom of the screen, where a note had been added: *Incomplete due to medical leave of absence.*

I stared at that note for a long time. The Kelsey I knew, in all her types and mutations, was physically healthy. She ran around our pool with ease, ate what she wanted, didn't pause to take medication or catch her breath. I'd seen enough of her body to know there were no major scars spanning her abdomen or crossing her wrists. And yet she'd had a medical

reason serious enough not to finish a course? I remembered
Sonia Jorgensen telling me that Kelsey's friends at Ashbury
had been bad influences—though what exactly they'd in-
fluenced her to do wasn't clear. Was that what she was doing
now, setting Danielle up as the bad influence while she could
be the innocent but unlucky friend, the good girl who was
sadly misled?

Half an hour later, they were waiting at my car in the staff
lot. Danielle was complaining about a project for biology,
something that would require floral foam and toothpicks.
The complaining was for Kelsey's benefit, I realized. It was
part of the new Danielle. This was a project she would have
thrown herself into wholeheartedly last year, putting in ten
hours or twenty at the kitchen table, competing for the high-
est grade in the class.

I couldn't believe, not for a second, that Danielle had gone
to the clubhouse in the middle of the night and sprayed obscenities on the bathroom walls while Kelsey snoozed, innocent and oblivious. And even if I could let myself believe that
it was true, or even possible—which would mean forgetting
everything I thought I knew about my daughter, every moment accumulated over fifteen years—then I couldn't understand Kelsey's agenda. Was she a clueless kid? A scheming
psychopath? Was she somehow, backhandedly, confessing her
own involvement, wanting me to call her bluff?

It was a relief to drop her off at her house, to watch her
disappear between the towering marble columns and let herself in, a lonely latchkey kid.

At home, Danielle went up to her room and I paced downstairs, eager for Phil to come home. I wanted to tell him
about Kelsey's visit and my growing certainty that it was

Kelsey who had vandalized the bathrooms and was now, for a reason I couldn't figure, throwing Danielle under the bus. Of course, we would have to sort it out, make a plan of action. We'd have to talk to the Jorgensens and the Sieverts, plan a sit-down meeting between the concerned parties, laying all our cards on the table. Whoever was responsible—even, yes, if that was Danielle—would be punished.

I checked my cell phone, intending to call Phil, and saw his text.

HOA meeting tonight at 7. Probably won't come home for dinner.

The meeting could only be about the vandalism; it would be Myriam expounding on the general untrustworthiness of the construction crews, the background checks needed for gardeners and caddies and waitstaff. I'd been to one of the monthly meetings over the summer, at Myriam's needling, acutely aware that I wasn't a homeowner at all and deeply suspicious that I'd been targeted as some sort of personal improvement project. That meeting had centered around the adoption of "community-wide holiday decoration standards"—a plan to ensure that The Palms was not despoiled with inflatable reindeer or Santas, which would inevitably deflate into a plastic puddle during the daytime. After a spirited discussion, the verdict was in: only white lights, nonblinking, would be allowed, and door wreaths were encouraged. They had succeeded in stealing Christmas.

This meeting promised to be more interesting, although just as nauseating.

I called a goodbye to Danielle and headed out the door. In the clubhouse parking lot, I passed Ana, the Asbills' nanny—a Colombian girl with wide hips and acne scars. *Just unattractive enough to be safe in the home*, I'd heard Janet Neimeyer quip. She was walking slowly, steering the double-wide stroller with one hand, texting with the other. Beneath their umbrella awning, the twins dozed, fat and blond. "Hello," I called, and Ana looked up, startled. Maybe she had begun to think of herself as invisible in The Palms, like the gardeners, the men who stalked the parking lot with leaf blowers strapped to their backs. They were invisible until something went wrong, and then they were suspects.

Lindsey, one of the club's afternoon part-timers, passed me in the hallway with a clipboard. Her hair was pulled back in a ponytail so tight the skin around her eyes was stretched along with it. "I think he's got someone in there," she said, gesturing to Phil's office. "It's been crazy today, one meeting after the other."

I groaned sympathetically. "I don't mind waiting for a bit."

She smiled, edging past me.

I paused outside Phil's office. As bad as my day had been, plagued by doubts and the unwanted sight of Kelsey Jorgensen in my office, his had no doubt been worse. Parker-Lane, I knew, would be livid that the alarm hadn't been set; our neighbors would have been in here all day long, complaining and seeking reassurance. I pressed an ear against his door and heard, "I'm trying to figure out what I can do here to fix this situation."

I backed away. Past Phil's office, the hallway was roped off, a sign tactfully informing visitors that the bathrooms were under construction and temporary facilities were located in the parking lot. A crew had been scheduled to come in today to rip out the wainscoting, bloated and damaged from the flooding. It would be at least a week before the bathrooms could be reopened.

I wandered back toward the main entrance, pausing in front of the notices on the community bulletin board. There were bright, cheerful invitations to jewelry and candle parties, notices for the rival book clubs led by Helen and Janet and a men's prayer breakfast led by Jeremy Bergland. Marja Browers's "buddy walk" list was there, although the enthusiasm for it had petered out—a few weeks after the mountain lion scare, people had gone back to their solitary routines.

Beneath the bulletin board was a round table with a display of brochures and two comfortable chairs. I sank into one and thumbed through a brochure for The Palms. It was the sort of thing Myriam had no doubt shown the Leukemia & Lymphoma Society when she was planning the golf tournament. It was the sort of thing visitors picked up after a round of golf, enchanted by the view of the community from the greens, charmed by the hospitality of the waitstaff in the dining room. The pictures were glossy, no doubt altered and airbrushed to perfection. The home on the front of the brochure wasn't even a photograph, but an artist's rendition in subtle watercolors. Still, the message came across loud and clear: if you live here, you'll be happy.

Wasn't that the grand promise? Wasn't that the huge lie?

I glanced at my watch again. It was five o'clock already, and if at all possible, I wanted to catch the Jorgensens and the Sieverts before tonight's meeting. Maybe Phil could call them from his office. I passed his door again, pausing when I caught the thin scrap of a woman's laugh. Then there was Phil's voice, rising at the end of his sentence. *Whatever I can do.* The door opened, and Kelsey Jorgensen backed into the hallway, still wearing the black dress, hiked unevenly across her thighs.

"Oh, I'll take you up on that," she said, facing away from me. "I think there's a lot more you can do for me."

I was frozen a few feet behind her, considering the physical impossibility that my heart could plunge into my stomach. *There's an explanation*, I thought, mind spinning. *She only sounds flirtatious because she always sounds flirtatious. She visited him with the same story she told me, and he's humoring her, the way I humored her in my office.*

But then Phil said, "We're not going to tell anyone about this."

"Oh, I promise," she purred. "It's our little secret."

Phil closed his door with a decisive click, and Kelsey turned, eyes widening at the sight of me. She hesitated, as if she might try to explain, but in the end, she simply smiled.

For the second time that day, she'd left me unsteady on my feet. In the lobby, I dropped into one of the club chairs, the leather settling with a soft hiss while I got ahold of myself. Through the floor-to-ceiling glass windows, I saw her walking away, cutting a path between the parked cars, and I wondered if Phil was watching her, too, through the slatted blinds of his office.

Around six thirty, the front door clattered open and Phil hurried up the stairs. He spotted me in the den and called, "HOA meeting at seven. You want to come?"

I didn't answer. I was sitting cross-legged on the couch, a pillow clutched to my waist. On the table in front of me, my laptop screen had gone black. I'd been browsing Kelsey's Facebook page, scrolling through an endless string of selfies. Had Phil done the same thing, looked at Kelsey in her bikini, in her never-ending assortment of tank tops and short skirts? Had it started with this, a peek at her cleavage, a glance at her bare midriff, at the low rise of her bikini bottoms? Of course, he could have that in person, at any time. It had probably started right here, in my own house. It had probably been going on for months.

He came downstairs, tightening the knot of his tie. "I could use your support, Liz," he said. I took in the effect, top to bottom—thick, sandy-colored hair that I knew up close was flecked with gray, a broad chest, slightly fleshier than it had been four years ago, arms that stayed strong from occasional bursts of push-ups during commercial breaks. He looked just like my husband. He didn't look like a man fresh off his rendezvous with a fifteen-year-old girl from the neighborhood. But then, clearly, I didn't know what that looked like.

"Okay, well," he said, patting his pockets absently. "I'd better..." He left, the other Other Woman calling "front door open" in his wake.

I closed my laptop when Danielle came downstairs and wandered in the direction of the kitchen.

She looked around the room accusingly. "What's for dinner?"

"We're just going to grab whatever tonight," I said.

She frowned. "Where's Phil?"

"There's a meeting in the clubhouse."

"About the vandalism and stuff?"

I nodded. *The vandalism and stuff.*

She rooted around in the refrigerator and came up with a pack of frozen burritos. Two of them were stuck together by the skin of the tortillas, a few shiny ice crystals glittering between them. I watched as she put the burritos on a plate and put the plate in the microwave. She studied her reflection for a moment in the window and then turned. "What?"

I shook my head, remembering what Kelsey had told me about the beer, the pot, Danielle's walk with Mac around the time of the vandalism. But that was tainted information, considering the source. One thing seemed to be linked to the other; there was no way of broaching one subject without it all coming out. *Kelsey said you were out walking that night. But then, she might have been lying to throw me off the scent because she's having a relationship with my husband.* The thought produced a visceral reaction, a gag reflex, like those moments at the dentist's office when too many things were cluttered in the back of your mouth at once. A *relationship.* With *my husband.*

"Where are you going?" Danielle asked.

Until her question, I hadn't realized that I was shoving my feet into my shoes, reaching for the cardigan I'd draped over the back of a bar stool. "The meeting," I said, as if I'd planned to do that all along.

The clubhouse was teeming by the time I arrived, raised voices echoing through the lobby. Instead of using the smaller conference room, site of the previous HOA meeting I'd attended, the kitchen had been closed early, and extra chairs had been added around the periphery of the dining hall. The waitstaff had left a giant tray of cookies on a long side table, as well as pitchers of lemon water and goblets, but these were mostly ignored.

I paused in the back of the room, behind a cluster of potted Ficus trees. Myriam was standing near the front, reading from a piece of paper. Helen was sitting at a table next to her, taking notes. Her dog was parked at her feet, his button eyes looking out at the group. Myriam had to raise her voice to be heard over the commotion of two of the younger Berglands, playing with a stack of blocks. Carly sat in a chair next to them, hands folded across her ballooning midsection. There were a few families from the Phase 2 side of the community. I wondered if the ones I didn't recognize were our soon-to-be neighbors from the homes under construction in Phase 3.

Phil was in the front row, a yellow legal pad balanced on his lap. I watched as he scribbled something, a comment to be taken care of, an item of rebuttal?

How could he think now, how could he focus? How could he go from flirting with Kelsey to home for a fresh shirt to back to business? Directly behind him sat Sonia Jorgensen and Deanna Sievert. From the back, they might have been sisters, their hair pulled into high ponytails, their phones strapped into armbands as thick as blood pressure cuffs. I'd been worried about Phil with those women, the ones who were more or less my age. I didn't know I had to worry about the next generation, a girl the same age as my own daughter.

"There are certain expectations that come along with an investment like this," Myriam was saying, her perfectly threaded eyebrows narrowed. "Chief among those expectations is the safety of our families. As you may know, I was the organizer of an annual fund-raiser for the Leukemia & Lymphoma Society this past weekend…"

I leaned against the wall as she related the horror of the soaked carpet, the vandalized bathrooms, the shock, the shame of having a subpar facility for her guests, the mad scramble to save The Palms' reputation. Not to mention the danger—if it could happen in the clubhouse, it could happen to any one of our homes, at any time.

Deanna waved her hand impatiently until Myriam ac-

THE DROWNING GIRLS
151

knowledged her, with the pinched expression of a teacher calling on the worst student in the class. Turning to face the people behind her, Deanna said, "It's horrible what happened, but I think Myriam should be acknowledged for all her hard work on this, and for bringing us all together. We need someone to take a leadership role here. Thank you, Myriam."

There was a smattering of applause. Phil joined in, pen clutched in one fist.

Sonia echoed, "Yes, well done, Myriam."

It's your daughter! I wanted to say, stepping into the room like a detective about to reveal the murderer in front of the assembled party of guests. It was Kelsey. I didn't know how or why, but I knew Kelsey was at the heart of it, the way she'd been at the heart of everything going wrong—my sweet daughter, the strain I'd felt in our marriage, how distant Phil seemed when he held me, when he rolled off me and turned away, falling asleep.

"Hiding out?" someone asked, and I turned to see Fran Blevins behind me. She put a finger to her lips and gestured for me to follow her back through the lobby to the night air.

"You've got the right idea," Fran said. "It's all a bunch of ridiculousness, anyway."

"I think I'm done," I told her.

She unfastened her falling-down ponytail and shook out her curls. "Sometimes I tell Doug it's like living inside someone's papier-mâché creation. At its core, it's just a bunch of air."

I nodded, attempting a smile. I couldn't help it—a tear dribbled down my face.

"Oh, honey," she said, refastening her ponytail and enveloping me in a sturdy two-armed hug. I leaned against her, breathing in her smell—like baby formula and medicine and sanitary wipes. It was like being comforted by a medical professional, someone adept at handling precarious situations. "Don't let them get to you," she said into my ear. "You have your own life, your family. Everything else is survivable."

I pulled away, releasing myself from her grasp. She didn't know why I was crying—she couldn't—but her words made sense, anyway. I did have my own life, an education and a steady job, a daughter I loved more than anything. A day ago—a few hours ago—I would have included Phil in that list of assets.

We walked back in the direction of our homes, Fran's arm around my shoulder. I imagined my neighbors watching this display, wondering about poor Liz who couldn't seem to get her life together. At my house, Fran stopped, apologetic. "I really should go. I told Doug I'd be back to help him with bath time."

We hugged again.

"Thanks," I whispered.

"Just take care of yourself, okay?" she asked.

I watched her walk away, her white tennis shoes disappearing into the darkness.

Take care of myself, I thought. *Everything else is survivable.*

PHIL

I'd been sick since the discovery of the vandalism—a deep-down sick, rooted in my bones. The afternoon of the golf tournament, I'd listened from the darkness of my bedroom to Myriam's voice on the PA system, announcing prize drawings and silent auction winners. She would have complained even without the vandalism—the dining room wouldn't have been set up properly, or the parking lot would have been inadequate—but I knew enough to brace myself for the real complaints, the ways that Parker-Lane had failed generally and I had failed personally.

I remembered how Jeff Parker had stood, eyeing the damage, subtly not eyeing me. He hadn't said it directly, but he didn't need to—doubt was written all over his face. Maybe I wasn't the right person for the job. Maybe it just wasn't working out.

Adding together the costs of portable toilet rentals, emergency cleaning, new carpet and wood paneling and paint, the repairs would be in the thousands. Chump change for people at The Palms, maybe; but then, they would never have to pay. I would be the one to pay, one way or another.

Keep them happy, Jeff Parker had instructed me. At the time, it had seemed like the simplest task in the world.

I hadn't figured on Kelsey Jorgensen—the variable on which so many things suddenly hinged.

That afternoon in bed, I toyed briefly and halfheartedly with the idea of calling the police. Parker-Lane wanted to keep it a private matter, because a police report would generate a crime statistic, and crime statistics were matters of public record. Even if I ignored their wishes, there was no way to make the call anonymously and have it carry weight. What would I say? *I know something about the vandalism at The Palms over the weekend.* If I revealed my name, I'd have to reveal the full circumstances. *Well, there's this girl who's been following me around, harassing me. This was her revenge, because I wasn't interested.*

Would they look from me to Kelsey Jorgensen and laugh themselves silly? And what would I give for proof? The message I'd photographed before painting over, one that only made sense to me?

If I made the phone call, I'd have to tell Liz and Danielle, too. Liz—maybe, *maybe*—would understand. She worked with troubled kids; she'd seen just about everything come walking through her office door. It was the idea of telling Danielle that broke my heart—sweet, funny, naive Danielle. *Your friend is only using you to get to me.* No—I wouldn't use those words, even though that was how she would hear them. It now seemed likely that their entire relationship, all those hours of YouTube surfing and texting and trying on clothes and makeup, was based on Kelsey having a juvenile crush on me.

And of course—Kelsey would deny everything, from her obsessive behavior to involvement with the vandalism. She would throw the blame on Danielle or me, and in the end, I wasn't sure I could prove anything. Calling the police would be like flinging a boomerang of trouble and not being able to duck when it zoomed back toward me.

I shivered, remembering that day on the stairs. I could still feel the skin above her elbow, pinched hard between my thumb and forefinger. I could still see her shocked blue irises. But clearly, threatening Kelsey hadn't worked. She'd simply fired a shot, knowing I couldn't fire back.

That afternoon, Liz brought me aspirin and crackers to wash down with a 7Up: the food of the sick. I didn't look at my phone again until that evening, not wanting to see the texts from Myriam and the missed calls from various higher-ups at Parker-Lane. Those were there, but so was a notification of an email from kelseybelle98@gmail.com, sent at 10:37 a.m. this morning. The subject line was blank, and I steadied my-self before opening the message, not sure what I would find. If it was a picture—another suggestive shot, or an incriminat-ing one of her with a can of spray paint, for example—I was going to keep it this time. It would be evidence.

But her message held only a single question.

Did you like it?

I stared at the screen for a long time, the words burning into my retinas, before replying.

We need to talk.

It felt, even to me, like a last-ditch effort. End this— whatever this was—now, before anything else happened, before anyone else found out. The ship was taking on water too fast, and all I had to bail us out was a paper Dixie Cup. But it was a shot worth taking—if only because I had no other shots to take.

I would start with flattery.

You're a beautiful girl.

Believe me, if circumstances were different...

If I were a younger man...

If I didn't have a family...

If you weren't such good friends with my stepdaughter...

Maybe that was what she really wanted, deep down. She was a teenage girl, after all, and I knew something about flattering women. I'd sold homes this way, following a basic principle: make the wife happy, and the husband would be happy, too. It was sexist, sure, but that was the way the world operated. Whenever I turned on the TV, women had their noses buried in fresh-smelling laundry, were marveling at the capacity of paper towels. Liz scorned that crap, citing Betty Friedan and the sexual sell, but I was banking on Kelsey to have a shred of naïveté. Either that, or a kernel of goodness, buried deep down. I could sell this to her.

If that didn't work—and I was prepared for it not to—I would show her the letter I'd spent Saturday night drafting and Sunday refining. It was a record of everything that had transpired between Kelsey and me, dating back to June, that first day she'd plopped herself down in the chair in my office. It was a formal request—stop now before I seek legal action. If I had to, I would send the letter (to her parents, to Parker-Lane), although it would come at a high cost. At the very least, I'd have to leave The Palms, and I hadn't been with Parker-Lane long enough for them to see me as anything but a liability. But there were other jobs. There were other homes.

I'd have to show the letter to Liz, of course. That, too, felt like a risk. I'd waited too long, kept things from her that she should have known up front. But if I showed her the letter, let her read the words I'd carefully crafted, it might be better than the chance of ad-libbing it, watching the emotions play over her face. Disgust. Anger. Distrust. But we could talk it through, work it out, get ahead of it. Together we could talk to Danielle, a united front, a team.

Kelsey's reply didn't come until Monday, when she was at school. I felt dizzy thinking of her on her cell phone in class, a teacher droning away at the front of the room and Kelsey sitting in a standard-issue student desk, flirting away with her married, imaginary lover.

Your wish is my command, master.

She came right after school, fresh out of Liz's car, minutes from saying goodbye to Danielle. I'd been waiting for her soft knock, for the doorknob to turn and for Kelsey to slip inside my office, closing the door behind her. It was as if she'd dressed for dinner and a movie—tight black dress, silver jewelry, red lipstick.

I didn't stand. "Kelsey, I'm glad you could come. Have a seat." I was trying for a fatherly tone—grandfatherly, even. It was time to establish the relationship that should have been there from the beginning.

She took the chair across from my desk, crossing her legs. Seated, the bottom half of her dress almost disappeared, leaving only the long line of her legs visible.

I made sure to keep my gaze up, on her face. "I think you know why I asked to see you today."

Cocking her head to one side, she played with a dangling earring. Looking at her face was dangerous, too.

I pressed on. "Kelsey, you're a beautiful girl, and I'm flattered, believe me."

She smiled. "How beautiful?"

"If we were the same age—if I were one of the boys in your class, say..." I stopped, disconcerted by her smile. It had gone well in my head, the dozen times I'd rehearsed it. But the reality of Kelsey sitting in front of me was a different story.

"What? What would you do then, Mr. McGinnis? Would we be boyfriend and girlfriend?"

The words were innocent enough, but somehow, it was like being in a porno, something with a hideous title like *Boning the Boss* or *Office Sex*. I'd been growing more nervous all afternoon, but now my shirt was sticking to my back, sweat puddling at my armpits. It occurred to me suddenly that she might be recording our conversation, a microphone taped close to her skin. And if someone walked into the room—Lindsey, or one of the kitchen staff—they would take one look at my sweaty face and Kelsey's naked legs and jump to all the wrong conclusions.

I took a deep breath and pushed the letter across the table to her.

She picked up the paper and read for a minute, frowning. "What is this?"

"It's a letter I hope never to send, Kelsey. I'm only showing you because I want you to understand what a serious situation we're in. Like I mentioned, I've been very flattered by your attention, but I'm going to have to stop it right here. It can't go any further." I could smell my own fear now, rising sour from my armpits.

She read to the bottom of the page, then pushed the paper back to me. "I don't understand why you would say these things."

"So far no one else has seen this letter, Kelsey. Only you and me. And no one has to see it. I could slip it right in there—" I gestured to the shredder against the wall. "It's to protect both of us, the way I see it."

She stared at me. "I mean, if you're going to write it all down, you should be accurate. You're missing some things."

My heartbeat picked up the pace, a canter to a gallop. "What am I missing?"

"Well, let's see." She frowned, as if she were trying to re-member. "What about that time you exposed yourself to me in your backyard? Or the picture you sent me. Or the time we kissed in your office."

I sat back hard, cracking my spine against the chair. Talk about a colossal misjudgment. This wasn't just a prank. It might not even be a criminal matter. Kelsey was delusional. She needed a doctor's care, psychotropic drugs. Shock ther-apy. "I think we're done here, Kelsey. If that's the way you want it to be, I'll send the letter out tomorrow. I'll hand-deliver it to your parents, if that's what I need to do."

Anyone else—a kid, a teenager, an adult—would crack, I thought. Kelsey wasn't *normal*. She just shook her head, a smile still playing on her lips. "I saved that email you sent me. I look at it every day."

"The game is over," I told her, more forcefully. "It's done."

"You're the one who started the game. If you didn't want me, why would you send me that picture? And from your work email, too. That wasn't very smart."

I stared at her and then glanced, reflexively, at my com-puter screen. "You were the one who emailed me, Kelsey.

You sent me that picture from school, and I told you to knock it off."

Kelsey looked up at the ceiling, as if she were trying to remember something. "It was August 10, I think. I was at your house, hanging out with Danielle, and all of a sudden my phone beeped. That was pretty gutsy, with your family right there. But don't worry, I didn't tell anyone. I knew you wanted it to be our little secret."

I was already navigating the icons on my computer screen, my fingers clumsy, impatient. I clicked on my outbox, scrolling through the list of emails I'd sent to Parker-Lane, to Myriam and the HOA committee, to contractors and suppliers. There it was: an email to kelseybelle98@gmail.com on August 10 at 10:55 a.m. I had no recollection of the day, six weeks ago now. "You hacked into my email," I said.

"I did?"

"You must have." I clicked on the message and it opened, the photo slowly appearing, top to bottom. I recognized the backdrop of my house, light tan and darker brown, and then my own head, shoulders, chest, my own naked and erect penis.

I grabbed the wastebasket under my desk and retched drily into it.

"It's a lovely picture," Kelsey said over my shoulder. "Impressive."

I remembered the night, of course. The Mesbahs' party. Liz and I had both been tipsy, elated to have our new house entirely to ourselves. I remembered undressing and standing at the edge of the pool, watching Liz on her back, floating, her breasts bobbing and ebbing with the water. But Liz wasn't part of this image. This was just me, grinning and aroused.

My mind spooled back, as if it were going through an

old film. The party had been in June, after Kelsey had visited my office. Had she been camped out on the golf course, spying on us? On me? Was she plotting, even then, how she would get inside our house, how she would worm her way into our lives?

That had been months ago. Naively, I'd thought I could get ahead of this today with my letter, but she'd been planning for ages. She'd been on checkmate before I'd made a move. She must have taken the picture and then bided her time, waited for an opportunity to get into my office. What had I been doing on August 10 at 10:55 a.m.? Had I stepped into the bathroom? Stopped by the kitchen to chat with someone on staff? Was there anyone who could vouch for me, give me an alibi? Maybe there would be someone who had seen Kelsey in my office? Not that this was unusual—she'd stopped by a dozen times before then, a dozen times since.

I closed the photo, not wanting to see it for another second. "This was a private moment with my wife. There has to be some kind of law against taking a photo of a person at his own home—"

"I'm sure there are sexting laws, too. Aren't there? I know someone who got in big trouble for sending a naked picture."

I could smell her behind me, her lotion flowery and overpowering.

"Aren't you going to delete it? Of course, I don't think that matters. Obviously I have a copy of it."

I whirled around in my chair, knocking my knees against hers and causing her to take a step back. It took a great effort to keep my voice calm. "I'm trying to figure out what I can do here, to fix this situation. But I don't understand what you want, except for something you can't have."

She lowered herself onto the corner of my desk, spread her thighs slightly, teasing me.

I almost retched again, fighting off a horrible creeping feeling of arousal and a sick disgust at her. *Imagine someone coming in*, I told myself. Lindsey. One of the contractors working on the bathrooms. *Liz*, for God's sake. "You need to leave. You need to leave now."

"I'll let you off the hook," she said. "One kiss."

I shrank back, buying myself a few inches of safety. "It's not going to happen."

"One tiny kiss," she said.

"I can't do this, Kelsey. I'm a married man."

"Please. That's such a cop-out. One kiss and I keep quiet."

It was blackmail, plain and simple. You couldn't give in to blackmail—everyone knew that. It started small and it grew. It built into this untenable thing, unsustainable. You were pinched, put into a tight spot. The proverbial rock and a hard place. Blood out of a turnip. How had it come to this?

Her eyes grew watery, her lip wavered. "Don't you even find me pretty at all?"

Of course I did. She was beautiful and hideous, fascinating and repulsive. She was every middle-aged guy's fantasy, heroine and villain at once.

"Kelsey," I said, softening. I was trying to find my way back to the script, back to *I'm so flattered* and *if only*, but she slipped off the edge of my desk, her bare knee parting my thighs. I put my hands on her arms to stop her from moving forward, and her mouth was on mine for the briefest of moments before I shifted her away, her lips grazing my neck.

She pulled back, patting her hair into place. "It was nice," she said. "Tell me it wasn't nice."

"Kelsey, we can't. Look, whatever I can do to convince you—"

She opened the door, still facing me. "Oh, I'll take you up on that. I think there's a lot more you can do for me."

I was coming back to my senses, the life I'd been living flashing before my eyes. It was less of a kiss than a near-death experience. "We're not going to tell anyone about this."

She stepped into the hallway. "Oh, I promise. It's our little secret."

I locked my office door behind her, ready to burst out of my skin. *Delete the photo.* Yes. No. Obviously I hadn't taken it—someone had taken it of me. Could I prove that I hadn't sent it, either?

I fumbled in my desk drawer and came up with a flash drive, a cheap promotional trinket that Parker-Lane gave out to visiting guests. I took a screen shot of the email and saved it. It was hard to look at my grinning face without seeing what a parent would see, or a prosecutor. It was hard not to imagine it plastered across Twitter and the evening news, maybe with a little black censor bar across my genitals. *Fuck.*

I stashed the flash drive and went back to my email where I deleted the picture, deleted the deleted picture, emptied my trash can. I deleted the email Kelsey had sent me earlier that day—*Your wish is my command*—and wished I had the IT skills to wipe it from the hard drive. Then I scanned the rest of my emails, my inbox and my sent folder and my saved mail and my drafts and my deleted mail before being satisfied that there was nothing else.

But of course, there was something else.

Or there would be. It was coming.

I wouldn't be able to solve this, and it was too late to get ahead of it.

I wiped off my mouth with a tissue, rinsed and spit into a trash can and popped a piece of gum into my mouth. Get rid of her taste—strawberry lip gloss? Get rid of the feeling of her thigh, her chest leaning over mine.

It never happened. *Deny, deny, deny.*

There was a knock on my door, a jiggle on the handle. "Mr. McGinnis?"

I made it to the door on unsteady legs and opened it to find Lindsey holding her ubiquitous clipboard.

"Sorry," I said, gesturing to the door. "Figured I'd grab a moment to myself to get ready for the meeting."

"No worries! I just needed to check on something, actually. I'm thinking you might want to use the dining room rather than the regular conference room. That way we can pull in some extra chairs—"

"That's a good idea."

"Okay. I can let Myriam know about the change, if you'd like."

"Perfect. Thanks, Lindsey."

She smiled at me. "One more suggestion, though."

I leaned against the door frame, exhausted. "Shoot."

"You might want to change your shirt."

I rushed home, my collar turned inward to hide the pink smear of lipstick. I remembered Kelsey's lips brushing my neck, a deliberate action. And she'd simply left me to explain myself. What if I'd gone to the HOA meeting like that, or run into Liz?

Thankfully, Liz was sitting on the couch in the den and didn't look up as I rushed up the stairs, pulling my shirt over my head. In our bathroom, I squirted some hand soap onto the collar of my shirt and worked the fabric back and forth under the faucet. I only succeeded in smearing the color, in creating an even bigger pink stain. I would have to get it downstairs to the laundry room, where there was bound to be a gallon of bleach and a dozen other laundry-related products, none of which I'd ever used. Or I could bring it back to the clubhouse later, toss it in the trash. Maybe it was safer that way. For now, I stashed it underneath the bed.

From the doorway, I asked Liz if she was coming to the meeting. "I could use your support, Liz," I said. She looked up at me but didn't reply. Something was going on—a bad day at school, a fight with Danielle. But I didn't dare to come closer, not with my heart thudding in my chest. In the bathroom mirror, my face had looked normal, the same old Phil. But would it be visible to Liz—an illicit kiss, horrible and thrilling in its own way? Would she take one look at me and see how guilty I felt about something I'd never intended?

The meeting was a blur of faces and complaints—Myriam and Deanna and Helen and Sonia, yes, Sonia, sitting so close behind me that I could hear her phone vibrate. Was it Kelsey, texting her mother that she'd been assaulted by Phil, the creepy community relations specialist? I hardly dared to turn around, for fear that Kelsey would be in the audience herself, sitting in a folding chair with her legs parted invitingly. A quick scan of the room revealed that she wasn't there—but neither was Liz.

I couldn't find my focus. I nodded along with everything they were saying, all but accepting responsibility myself for something I knew Kelsey Jorgensen had done. They might have been calling for my resignation, and I would have accepted it with the same bland acquiescence. Someone might have suggested that I be brought outside and stoned, sacrificed for the good of the community, and I would have gone willingly.

It had just been a kiss, one I hadn't solicited and couldn't have prevented. Or, no—I could have been more forceful. I could have pushed her backward. I could have dodged her, run out of the room, let her do what she wanted with the picture I hadn't sent her. Instead, I'd held her arms and she'd leaned over me, perfectly comfortable with the role of aggressor. Her hair had fallen across my face. Her lips had been soft. The worst—and I would take it to my grave, I knew that already—the worst was that it had excited me, that my body had responded even while my brain was telling me no, no, *no*.

Stoning was the least I deserved.

I knew something was wrong the second I entered the house. It wasn't ten, but the first floor was dark. Upstairs, I flicked on the light in our bedroom, expecting to see Liz curled beneath the comforter, but the bed was empty, still haphazardly made from that morning. In her room, Danielle was sprawled across the bed, talking on her cell phone. She gave me a little wave.

"Where's your mom?" I asked.

She frowned, cupping her hand over the phone. "Downstairs, I guess."

I found Liz on the patio, shivering in a blanket. The night had turned cold.

"There you are," I said. "Jesus, it's cold. What's going on?"

She turned, staring at me. Her mouth was red-rimmed,

and I glanced at the bottle of cabernet on the table. When I picked up the bottle, an inch of wine sloshed at the bottom.

"Did you open this tonight?" I asked.

"Oh, there you go. It's all my fault. Shift the blame," she said.

Liz wasn't a good drinker—one glass made her happy, two made her punchy, three brought her to a place outside herself, where her mouth and body no longer moved in sync. She was there already, eyes glazed, words slurred.

I set the bottle carefully on the ground next to her. "What blame? I don't know what you're talking about. Why didn't you come to the meeting?"

She shifted in the chair, her legs pinioned by the blanket. "Why? Were you lonely? Didn't Kelsey come to comfort you?"

I took a step backward, my mind reeling. Kelsey must have talked to her. They'd probably been out here, the two of them, while I'd endured Myriam's litany of complaints. Or maybe she'd found the shirt where I'd wadded it up beneath the bed, made the leap between lipstick and infidelity. There were things to tell her—there was a kiss to confess—but her mind had gone beyond that already, to planning and plotting, to stolen moments and half-clothed sex, not unlike the trashy scenarios that had flitted through my mind.

It wasn't fair.

"What are you saying, Liz? What are you accusing me of, exactly?"

"I heard you," she spat. "In the clubhouse. I saw her coming out of your office."

I fought for control. What had she seen, exactly? What had she heard? I'd been protesting. I'd been saying no and warding her off. "That's right. I wanted to talk to her about the vandalism—"

"You asked her to keep it between the two of you. She said it would be your little secret. Her dress was hiked up—"

I took a deep breath. "Liz. You're thinking about this all wrong. I asked her what she knew about the vandalism. I was trying to get a few answers before tonight's meeting. I can't prove anything, but I have this gut feeling she was involved."

"I heard you. I saw the two of you together."

"Of course we were together. We were talking in my office. I asked her to keep the conversation between the two of us. What do you think, Liz? That I'm some kind of pedophile? Our neighbor? Our daughter's friend?"

She had worked her legs free of the blanket and was trying to stand, supporting herself with one arm against the deck chair. In the process, her foot hit the wine bottle, which toppled with a clank and rolled away, the last of the cabernet dribbling onto the concrete.

"Liz, for fuck's sake—"

She fumbled free of the blanket and pulled something from her pocket, black and silky. "I saved this," she said, holding it out to me. "I didn't know why at the time, but I kept it. And now I'm glad I did, because it proves how long this has been going on. It proves how stupid I've been."

I stared at her outstretched hand. "What is that?"

"You tell me." She flung it at me, the fabric hitting my chest with a soft slap.

I snagged it with one finger on its way down and lifted it, a triangle of fabric. "Is this someone's underwear?"

"Like you don't know. It's Kelsey's. I found it in our bedroom the night of Deanna's mountain lion crisis. Were you interrupted, and she didn't have time to get her panties back on?"

I dropped the underwear, and it floated to the concrete, wispy as a ribbon. "I don't know what's going on here, Liz. I've never seen this before. You found this in our room, two months ago? And for two months you've been thinking that..." My voice trailed off, my thoughts spinning in an exhausted loop. That next day, after the mountain lion crisis, Kelsey asked me if she'd found her little present. I hadn't, but apparently Liz had.

"I was with you, Liz," I reminded her. "That night, out here. We heard Deanna scream. And then that idiot Victor convinced me to ride around like a vigilante with him. I have no idea why this was in our bedroom, but it doesn't have anything to do with me."

"I heard you," she repeated. "And I've known something was going on—I just knew it. All these women, hanging on your every word, and you at their beck and call. Deanna with her big boobs. Even Janet—every silicone inch of her. Was that why you moved us out here, so you could be around the beautiful people?"

It was that, more than anything else, that put me over the edge. I felt trapped, and this was what happened when you felt trapped—you did illogical things. I laughed. "Deanna Sievert, that bimbo? Janet? She's probably old enough to be my mother. Who else, Liz? Maybe I've been seeing one of the waitresses in the dining hall? Maybe I've been entertaining the nannies during my lunch hour?"

"Keep your voice down," she said, rising unsteadily out of the chair. She grabbed my shirtsleeve, and I pushed her back. I'd never done anything like this—never laid a hand on Liz or anyone, other than a kid on the playground when I was in grade five, and that kid had deserved it. This push was harder than I intended—at least, that's what I would tell myself later—and it caught her off balance, drove her back until she crash-landed against the arm of the deck chair.

I swore and stepped toward the pool, glimmering in the moonlight like a living thing, and wound one foot back as if I were going for a penalty kick. My loafer connected with one of the giant terra-cotta pots along the edge and soil spilled onto the concrete.

"Stop—" Liz said, her voice laced with pain. "Let's just stop."

But this was what happened when you were trapped—you pushed your wife, you took out your anger on a potted plant. You denied, denied, denied, and even though it was true what you were denying, you found yourself doubting your own denial. On the second swing, my foot connected more forcefully, the pot cracking down the middle, splitting into heavy chunks.

"Don't! People can hear you, Phil."

On the third kick, the pot splintered apart, the topiary falling free, its roots a tangled ball.

Liz was on her feet again, her fist clutching the hem of my shirt, where it had come untucked. "Okay, okay. We'll talk about this. Just tell me it's nothing. Tell me nothing happened, that nothing's ever happened, that nothing ever will happen."

I pulled free of her grasp and a final kick sent the whole thing—the shards of pottery, the bewildered plant—sailing into the water. My foot was numb with pain.

Liz joined me at the edge of the pool and together we watched the aftermath. The pottery itself was surprisingly porous, sinking briefly and bobbing to the surface, the remains of a small wreck. Dirt fanned out across the water like black mold, pulled by the gravitational edge.

My voice caught in my throat. "Did I hurt you?"

She shook her head, then said, "A little."

"We're not ourselves," I said. "We can talk about this later, when we've calmed down."

"We're not ourselves," she repeated.

The last of the terra-cotta pot was sinking below the surface.

"Should we clean it up?" Liz asked.

I shook my head. I felt exposed suddenly, as if I were naked again, and Kelsey Jorgensen was lurking in the darkness, snapping pictures and rejoicing in the havoc she'd wreaked.

We turned to the house, the fight gone out of both of us. I think we noticed Danielle at the same time on the other side of the slider—her face pale, hands to her mouth, eyes wide. When I took a step toward the door, wanting to explain— but how could I? How could I even begin?—she turned and ran for the stairs.

JUNE 19, 2015

6:14 P.M.

LIZ

Time was going too fast; it was going too slow.

I watched the paramedics busy themselves with Kelsey, heard the crackle of a radio at Moreno's hip.

Stop, I thought. *Go back.*

I was aware of Danielle's sobs, low, whimpering sounds. She was still holding her cell phone, clutched in one hand. With the back of the other, she wiped her nose, a shiny trail of snot smearing her skin.

Oh, Danielle. What did you do?

Suddenly Richards, who had been talking into the little clip on his ear, said distinctly, "I've got a pulse."

"Oh, thank you, thank you," I whispered.

"Let's get her loaded up," Moreno said, and there was a flurry of movement as Kelsey, limp as a sack of sand, was heaved onto the stretcher.

"Dispatch has her parents on the phone," Richards said. "They're en route to the hospital."

I hobbled behind them through the house, my leg throbbing from knee to toe. What did it matter anyway, a little bit of blood, a torn nail? Kelsey was alive. "What hospital? We'll follow you."

"Memorial," Richards said.

They crossed the lawn and loaded Kelsey into the back. Our last glimpse, as the ambulance rounded the corner, siren screaming, was of Moreno crouched next to Kelsey. *Déjà vu.*

"Mom."

I'd been so rooted to the lawn, listening to the siren fade into a faint whine, that everything else had gone out of focus. Something in Danielle's voice made the rest of the world come back—the noise of a bird overhead, the asphalt shiny under the sun. I turned, looking down the street.

All the way down the block, our neighbors stood at their curbs, watching us.

LIZ

After the fight, I called in sick for three days, summoning a cough each time I spoke to the school secretary. Phil took Danielle to school in the morning and dutifully returned to pick her up in the afternoon, when I'd barely moved from the bed. I *was* sick in a way—hungover at first, then exhausted and finally ashamed. Phil and I hardly looked at each other.

I'd been so sure that night, piecing two and two together— her flirty voice, ripe with promise, her underwear on our bedroom floor. But Phil's explanations were logical; they made more sense than what I'd been formulating. Maybe I was wrong about everything. Maybe what I thought I heard wasn't what was said at all. I'd gone too far, out there by the pool. It was like one of those nightmares where you sense things are going badly and you try to turn them around, but you can't. I couldn't stop myself, even when I'd seen the hurt and confusion on his face.

The bruise on my hip went from red to purple before fading slowly to greenish-yellow, but that was the only physical sign of our fight. On Tuesday afternoon, a man in a white pickup truck came to clean out the pool. Phil had called him. I watched from our bedroom window as he fished out chunks of pottery and the remains of the topiary with his long-handled skimmer. He didn't ask questions; maybe he'd fished stranger things out of pools. An hour later, the water was sparkling, with no trace of the previous night's destruction. I didn't ask what happened to the thong, but that was gone, too.

The only other person I talked to was Sonia Jorgensen. I was hoping to reach her voice mail and was surprised when she answered my call. "Something's come up," I began, and told her I wasn't going to be able to bring Kelsey to school for a while.

"I see," Sonia said, her voice considerably cooler than when she'd greeted me.

I didn't think she could possibly see, but I hung up without offering an explanation or an apology for the last-minute inconvenience. Let her think what she wanted. Let her dispatch another one of her minions to handle the task.

Phil and I found ways to talk to each other without really talking, to apologize without really apologizing. He said *it's all a misunderstanding* and I said *sometimes I jump to conclusions* and we managed to never mention her name. I wished we could laugh it off, find a way to give it instant inside-joke status. *That time you kicked the plant into the pool. That time you thought I was sleeping with the neighbor girl.* But it didn't happen. It wasn't easy to forget the smile Kelsey had given me coming out of his office, the scraps of their conversation that lingered in my mind. Phil had explained, and I had chosen to believe him, but that didn't mean I'd silenced my doubts completely.

What was that expression? *Trust, but verify.*

So we moved on. It helped that we were busy, Phil with the video cameras Parker-Lane had decided to install throughout the community, me with quarterly grades and the resulting flurry of parent conferences. We threw ourselves into our work, and our conversations began to center around it. *How was your meeting? How is the construction coming along?* We became polite roommates, carefully avoiding each other, dealing only with essentials like food and money. We avoided each other in bed, too—or at least I did. If I brushed against him, even in sleep, I pulled back. If I woke to his hand on my thigh, I slid quietly out from under it, rolling away.

It would just take time, I figured.

And life at The Palms was better without Kelsey in our house, the perpetual visitor, the daily guest. Of course, I still saw her at Miles Landers, walking hip to hip with Danielle toward the cafeteria, and sometimes, at the end of the day, I saw her waiting on the curb in front of the school, her fingers working furiously on her phone. I wondered how long she would have to wait before one of her parents arrived, but I didn't waver. Once the cancer was gone, you didn't invite it back into your life.

I never knew what Danielle saw that night, what she heard or thought she heard. When I tried to talk to her, she went so far as to plug her ears, like she'd done as a kid, faced with the possibility of bad news. "Leave me out of it," she said, over and over. "It's between you and Phil. It doesn't involve me."

She submitted to the weeks of her grounding with stony glares and silence. At dinner, she pushed the food around her plate. Afterward, she all but barricaded herself in her bedroom for the night.

Our longest conversation turned into a fight, with Danielle pounding up the steps and slamming her bedroom door so hard my ears rang. I'd told her that Phil and I didn't want her hanging around Kelsey, that while we couldn't stop them from seeing each other at school, I would prefer if she didn't invite Kelsey to our house, even when her grounding was finished.

"You know it was you who forced us together in the first place!" she yelled on her way up the stairs. "Why did you tear me away from my old life, anyway?"

It was the right thing to do, the only thing to do, if Phil and I were going to save our marriage. The suspicion and scrutiny would be there every time Kelsey stepped through our door, every time she tossed her hair over her shoulder, or dived into the pool. But the change in my relationship with Danielle felt seismic, foundational. Even when we were in the same room, she barely looked at me. There was no witty banter, there were no silly jokes. On our drives to and from school, she slumped in the passenger seat of the Camry, headphones on her ears, staring sullenly out the window. From time to time, I expected to catch a glimpse of Kelsey in the backseat, smirking at me.

In November, Kelsey celebrated her sweet sixteen. Since the party was held at the clubhouse and it would have created all sorts of awkwardness if she didn't attend, I sent Danielle off, teetering in a pair of my heels. Sonia had hired a band, a gourmet pizza chef and a "cake artist" who had appeared on Food Network. All night, cars passed our house, driven by well-coiffed kids, their parents or, in a few cases, dark-suited chauffeurs.

Phil spent the evening at the clubhouse, too, keeping an eye on the newly renovated bathrooms. Myriam had pro-

nounced them a *huge improvement*, due to the light gray porcelain tile and sunny yellow paint. We had short memories
at The Palms, it seemed—while everyone had swooned over
the improvements, we had conveniently and collectively forgotten the vandalism.

For my part, I watched the whole thing unfold on Facebook and Instagram, where Kelsey was tagged in dozens of
photos, being "liked" and "favorited" by hundreds of followers. She looked very *Real Housewives of Beverly Hills*—
large, tumbling curls; a shiny sheath dress; heels that could
have doubled as weapons in a pinch. In each photo she was
surrounded by people, laughing, teasing the camera, opening gifts, sipping from one of the nonalcoholic beverages on
the menu at the bar. I even spotted Hannah, awkward in a
floral dress that was more Sunday school than sweet sixteen,
hovering at Danielle's shoulder.

And then at some point I caught what I was doing, and I
slammed the lip of the laptop shut.

No more Kelsey, I promised myself.

At the time, I thought it was a promise I would be able
to keep.

The video camera installation was scheduled for the week
of Thanksgiving, when most of the residents of The Palms
would be out of town and the clubhouse dining room was
closed. Phil planned to stay to oversee its completion, and I
put up only the weakest of protests.

It had been a tradition for all of my adult life to have
Thanksgiving with my family in Riverside. I'd come home
even when Danielle was young and money was so tight I
could pay the gas only one way, and had to beg money from
my parents for the return to San Jose. When my dad died,

the trip became something of an annual pilgrimage. For the past four years, Phil had come, too, the three of us crowding into my mother's house, overwhelming her kitchen, eating too much of everything and talking through the Macy's parade and marathons of *Law & Order* and *NCIS*. Most years, Allie could come; this year, with her new job in Chicago, she was only flying out for Christmas.

Still—I was looking forward to the trip, even though it would be only the three of us. It was four full days away from The Palms—a vacation from the vacation, as it were. Was this how my neighbors felt when they headed off to Aruba for a week, to Napa for the weekend?

And yes, it was a vacation from Phil, too. Maybe distance was what we needed, an unofficial, short-lived break to put us back on course. I told myself that anyway, as he loaded our suitcases into my trunk on Tuesday morning in a T-shirt and a pair of old sweatpants. He leaned against the driver's window, double-checking that I had our boarding passes and, for emergencies, the lone credit card we hadn't maxed out.

"What will you do without us?" I asked.

"Miss you horribly." He leaned in, giving me a quick kiss on the cheek. It was the closest we'd been in a month.

He waved at Danielle, who was digging her earphones out of her backpack. "Have a good time, Danielle."

"Yup," she said, not looking at either of us.

Somehow, while I mocked the amenities at The Palms, I'd grown used to them. It was a shock to drive down Mom's street in Riverside, where the front lawns were set close to the street, the lampposts covered with graffiti. She still lived in the bungalow where I'd grown up, although more and more the house seemed to be caving in on itself, the linoleum curving at its edges, cobwebs blooming in the corners. How much longer could she live here, and where would she go when she couldn't? Since our move to The Palms, I'd been trying to envision Mom there, sunning herself on our deck, walking arm in arm with me on the trail. But I knew she wouldn't go willingly.

Over the years, Allie and I had offered to move Mom into our various apartments and rentals, but she had always insisted on her independence. She had a once-a-week housekeeper, but the walls were smudged with fingerprints and the windows streaked from a sloppy effort. Six years since Dad's heart attack, the walls still smelled like his nicotine.

Beneath her black tunic, Mom's body seemed more frail, her collarbone and cheekbones more prominent. With the busyness of our move, Danielle and I had skipped our summer visit, so the ordinary changes of aging were less subtle. We hugged and kissed, and then Mom turned her attention to Danielle. "Very chic," she pronounced, running her fingers over Danielle's hair. And then, making us laugh, "But why are you wearing so much makeup?"

We took Mom to a Mexican restaurant just around the corner, a place where she had a particular booth and a waitress who knew her order. Halfway through the meal I realized I was exhausted, the tension of the past weeks catching up to me. Between the drive to the airport, the shuttle ride, the flight and the hassle of picking up a rental car, it had been a sixteen-hour day. Back at Mom's house, Danielle and I collapsed into the twin beds in the room I'd shared with Allie. We'd long ago removed our posters and books and knickknacks, but the space held the same creaky furniture, the same plaid comforters. It wasn't until we'd turned out

the light that I realized I'd never called Phil to tell him we
arrived, and he'd never called me to check.

On Wednesday we went grocery shopping and baked
pumpkin bread in Mom's galley kitchen, bumping into each
other and apologizing and backing out of each other's way.
Her kitchen made me feel nostalgic for the one Phil and I had
left behind in Livermore, where we'd brushed against each
other constantly, where he'd stood behind me, humming
some off-key tune, arms around my waist while I chopped
a pepper. At The Palms, there was no need to bump into
each other, ever.

Once the bread was in the oven, Danielle excused herself
to lie on the couch in the living room, where the cushions
were indented from Mom's daily use, the corduroy worn
shiny.

Mom poured me a cup of coffee, expertly gathering cream
and sugar and a little tray of cookies. "Does Danielle want
something to drink?"

"Let me see." I peeked into the living room again and reported that Danielle was napping—mouth open, one arm
draped over her head.

"She didn't even get up until nine thirty," Mom commented. "It must be rough being a teenager."

I laughed. "I bet she could sleep for twelve hours at a
stretch, every day."

Mom smiled, wetting a cloth in the sink. "You were like
that, too."

"I was?"

"Of course. You and Allie both, always in your bedroom
after school, napping before dinner."

I closed my eyes, instantly gutted. It was impossible to
remember my own teenage years without a guilty lurch.

Payback's a bitch, Allie had written to me after Danielle's grounding—and I agreed. If there was any what-comes-around-goes-around karmic fairness, I had more coming to me.

"It was like you'd run a marathon each day," Mom continued now, and I remembered all the times she'd stood in the doorway of our bedroom, whispering, "Allie? Lizzie?" It was easier to pretend I was asleep than to explain that I was reading or scribbling in my journal, guarding my thoughts from her as if they were possessions that could be snatched away at any time.

Still, I reminded myself as Mom bustled around the kitchen, wiping off countertops and door handles, it had been surprisingly difficult to keep secrets from her. Since she couldn't see what we were up to, her other senses were on constant overload. By smelling one of Allie's shirts, she deduced there was a boyfriend; hearing me laugh late at night, she somehow figured out my plans for an upcoming party. And then there were her hands—roving, finding, assessing, on a persistent search to find evidence about our lives.

It was uncanny how she knew that something was wrong, even now, when I was standing still next to her. Maybe there was the scent of failure about me, an aura of sadness. I hadn't intended to tell her anything about Phil. Where would I have started? Mom loved Phil; she'd seen him as a sort of savior, appearing out of the blue with his charming accent to rescue her single daughter. It would break her heart to hear that we were having trouble; it would shatter her to learn what I suspected and what still lingered as a nagging doubt.

I saw that her head was cocked, as if she were listening to all the things I wasn't saying. "Well," she said, "are you going to tell me?"

I took a sip of coffee and cleared my throat. "Tell you what?"

"Oh, honey," she said, with the voice that could always make me melt, even at thirty-four. "Aren't you going to tell me what's wrong?"

"What do you mean? There's nothing..." But my voice cracked, and I set down the mug with a clank. Of course there was. Since we'd moved to The Palms, everything had been sliding away, the ground continually shifting beneath my feet.

She wiped her hands on the dish towel hanging from the oven door and came to me, touching my forearms first and working her way up, until her thumbs were tracing over my cheeks, gently tapping away my tears.

Our flight was delayed on its return, and it had taken a while for our suitcases to come tumbling down the baggage claim, so it was dark when Danielle and I pulled up to the entrance of The Palms on Friday. After the coziness of real life with my mom, The Palms felt impersonal as a movie set. Beyond the giant security gates, there was hardly a leaf on a front lawn or a weed that dared to poke itself through the mulch in a flower bed.

Maybe because The Palms always looked perfect, it was easy to spot the fliers affixed to the lampposts, their edges fluttering, like one of those "What's Wrong?" picture pairs Danielle and I used to look at together on the back of *Highlights for Children*. I knew the HOA had a rule about posting fliers, like they did about lemonade stands and garage sales and inflatable Santas.

"Grab one of those for me," I said, pulling in front of the Browerses' house.

Danielle unfastened her seat belt and hopped out. Down the street, I spotted Phil's SUV in our driveway and felt the uneasiness return. In four days, we had exchanged a few texts, but only one phone call, made postfeast, while I was stuffed with turkey and buttery yams. *You can work it out*, Mom had told me, knowing only the barest of details. *Everything can be worked out when you love each other.*

She almost had me convinced.

"Here," Danielle said, handing me the flier as she got back into the car. "It's that dog."

MISSING
Virgil Zhang
Virgil is a three-year-old Bedlington Terrier, white, 18 pounds, with a recently groomed and trimmed coat.
He was last seen on Thanksgiving Day in our backyard at approximately 8:30 p.m.
$1,000 reward

The bottom half of the flier was dominated by a picture of Virgil, a fussy, expensive-looking animal, more lamb than dog, and four different contact numbers for the Zhangs. They had doted on Virgil, taking him for walks twice a day and to the groomer every other week.

"Maybe it got out the back," Danielle said. The Zhangs' house was another one on the fairway; a low fence separated their property from the golf course, same as ours. "It could be anywhere, poor thing."

We parked in the driveway and hauled our suitcases up the path, using the front door. For a moment, sliding the key into the lock, it felt as if we were visitors, here with our luggage for a night at a colossal B and B.

Phil was on the couch in the den, a few empty beers on the coffee table in front of him, an open bag of chips. I recognized Marlon Brando as Don Corleone on the TV, paused midsentence. Phil was wearing the same sweatpants from earlier in the week, and his patchy beard suggested that he hadn't shaved since then, either.

"Hey," he said.

"Hey." I bent over the back of the couch and planted a soft kiss on his cheek. And then I joined him, putting my feet up on the table in front of us, not caring if my shoes scuffed the finish. On the flight home, I imagined telling him every little detail of the trip—the expired cans I'd tossed from Mom's pantry, the game of Trivial Pursuit we'd played, Danielle and me no match for Mom. It had been so long since we'd really talked, since we'd been the real Liz and the real Phil. I'd been packing my head with a mantra about new beginnings, about all great relationships being tested, about not throwing out the baby with the bathwater.

But we didn't reach for each other. We didn't talk about how much we'd missed each other or the minutiae that had filled our time apart. For a long time we said nothing, and then I commented, "It looks like Virgil Zhang got out."

Phil took a sip of beer and said only, "That stupid dog."

PHIL

I stayed behind over Thanksgiving, telling Liz that Parker-Lane wanted me to remain on-site for the installation of the cameras. This was true, although I'd been the one to suggest it to them in the first place. The main reason was that I needed a bit of time alone.

I made sure Liz and Danielle wouldn't be coming back for something they'd forgotten, and then I got in my SUV and drove to San Francisco to meet with an attorney. I had a folder with the letter I'd written and revised, the flash drive with Kelsey's emails and tucked away in the bottom of my old briefcase, a Ziploc bag with the underwear I'd rescued from the backyard the morning after my fight with Liz.

I had three appointments lined up, and I went from one to the next, telling my story. These were free consultations, but I had two thousand dollars in cash with me, filched from our slim savings account. If there was a bottom line to sign, I would sign it.

One cut me off with a raised hand and said he didn't want anything to do with a case involving a minor and sexual harassment. Another looked from Kelsey's thong to me, disgusted. He was probably ready to report me to CPS then and there. The third only cringed and commented that he was glad it wasn't happening to him.

"What do you recommend that I do?" I asked.

"Are you serious about this? Go to the police. File a report."

I shook my head. Did he think I hadn't considered this a thousand times over? "She'll deny it and claim that I'm the one harassing her."

He looked thoughtful. "I have a buddy from law school who handled a case like this. Lives in Atlanta, though."

I jotted down the buddy's name and contact information, but tossed it into the trash on the way past the receptionist's desk. Atlanta? That would never work.

At first, residents at The Palms were divided over the video cameras. Rich Sievert wondered if the feed could be hacked by the NSA, if the private comings and goings of residents would be a matter of public record. Myriam wanted to know who *exactly* would be monitoring the cameras, as she had done some research and objected to a number of companies who had received poor customer service ratings.

Until that issue was settled, I was the only one with access to the footage. The software had been installed on my office computer and on my personal laptop, and when I activated it, the screen sprang to life with the live feed from dozens of cameras, each visible through tiny rectangular boxes.

"No one expects you to spend much time on that," Jeff Parker had assured me. "Just installing the cameras goes a long way toward easing anxiety. If something happens, we can look back on the record. That's probably enough to deter most of the crime around here, anyway."

I found the video feed to be strangely addictive, my own private reality show.

Until their lives were on display for me, I hadn't been interested in the comings and goings of my neighbors. Most of them had cleared out for the Thanksgiving holiday, but I watched the rest of them go about their daily lives—the joggers, the yoga enthusiasts, the tennis players, the golfers, the retired couples, the nannies taking kids to the play structure. Video cameras had been installed in conspicuous areas, and at first the residents were aware of them, sometimes glancing in the direction of the camera or even waving. But after the initial interest, they resumed their regular lives. I caught husbands and wives arguing or kissing; I caught joggers stopping to adjust their bras or pluck a twisted piece of fabric out of a crotch. Brock Asbill patted his nanny on the ass and outside the clubhouse, Mac Sievert smoked a joint with a friend.

I watched for evidence of Kelsey, since the Jorgensens had stayed home for the holiday. They were hosting Sonia's side of the family, blond and blue-eyed, the lot of them. There was a camera trained on the hallway outside my office; if Kelsey passed by, it would catch her. Another camera was trained on the walking trail behind our house, and if she decided to play Peeping Tom again, it would catch her then, too.

The night before Thanksgiving, I went to bed with a biography of John Adams that I'd been trying to read since before we moved to The Palms. When I woke, the room was quiet, the moon a sliver outside the window. Then I heard it again, the sound that must have woken me in the first place. It was a slight ping against the window and as I waited, it came again, then again.

I flicked on the bedside light and stumbled toward the

window, yanking back the sash. Kelsey was down below, standing next to the pool in her black bikini. I shook my head, ordering myself to wake up.

She waved and stepped onto the diving board. It was a dream, I thought—I'm dreaming of that first day she came to the house. I watched as she took a little hop and did an easy swan dive into the water, which barely rippled. I held my breath, counting, but she didn't surface. Ten seconds, twenty. I was about to charge down the stairs, dive into the water and get her, when she emerged from the far end of the pool, naked.

She must have been freezing, but it didn't seem as if she were in any hurry. Looking up at my window, she twisted her hair behind her head, wringing it free of water.

Stop, I ordered myself. *Look away.*

Before, it had been a glance at her cleavage, a kiss full on the mouth—things I hadn't asked for, things I had to keep reminding myself I didn't want. Now there was the full sight of her—firm breasts, a narrow waist, the dark V of her crotch. Too late, I remembered I was collecting evidence and grabbed for my phone. She had on a pair of sweatpants by the time I snapped her picture. A moment later, she had pulled a sweatshirt over her head and slipped her feet into a pair of shoes. Without looking in my direction again, she exited through the back gates and disappeared.

I raced downstairs to grab my laptop and looked back through the feed. There she was, passing the camera in her sweats; there, less than ten minutes later, she passed in the opposite direction, her hair hanging wet on her back. After leaving my house, she'd taken the walking trail past the clubhouse and disappeared onto the Jorgensens' street. How had she explained her absence, then her reappearance a short time later dripping wet, in the middle of a house of relatives?

She was sick. That was the only word for it.

It had come to the point where things could only end badly.

Still, I couldn't help it; I dreamed about her all night long—hair blond and wet, body young and sleek. I didn't want to think about her. I wanted not to think about her at all, ever, but she wasn't going to let me.

It wasn't until the following afternoon that I thought about her swimsuit, and I rushed out to the pool. The pieces of black fabric were floating separately, the trunks near the deep end, the top near the steps. Not knowing what else to do, I brought them inside to dry and added them to my bag of evidence. What if Liz had come home and spotted the bikini in the pool—what then? We were on shaky footing as it was; there was no way I could explain this.

In the garage, I found a yard of twine and tied it tight around the latch on the inside of the gate. The fence was only four feet high, though, intended for an unobstructed view of the course. It was low enough for Kelsey to climb over, but for that matter, she might appear next at the front door, naked beneath a trench coat.

When Liz called, I realized I'd forgotten completely about Thanksgiving; I'd heated a frozen pizza and worked my way through it, piece after cold piece, scanning the laptop footage for any other sign of Kelsey. If she had a sickness, it was rubbing off on me.

Liz had stocked the bottom drawer of the fridge with beer before she left. Had she envisioned me sitting on the couch in the dark, downing one drink after another? I watched the live feed until my eyes grew bleary, empty bottles accumulating on the coffee table in front of me. Had my neighbors at The Palms envisioned this, when they'd voted in favor of video surveillance?

It was dusk when I saw a bit of movement on one of the live feeds, from a camera on the walking trail beyond the Mesbahs' house. My eyes were so tired by then and my mind so clouded by what I thought I would see—Kelsey, shirtless, her nipples high and hard—that I almost convinced myself I'd seen nothing at all. It had merely been a shadow, a white blur on a gray background. The sun had set; the sky was a deep purple sliding into black. I leaned forward, almost off the edge of the couch, my face close to the screen. And there it was again.

This time it was definitely real.

This time it couldn't be dismissed as a figment of Deanna Sievert's imagination.

The mountain lion was more muscular than I would have expected, its body meaty, haunches rolling with each step. All along I'd been imagining a starving thing, nothing but ribs and bone and luminescent eyes. This cat was massive— its paws thick, tail swinging, alert. I was seeing it from behind, watching as it passed from one camera's range to the next. First the back of its head, a neck that was more like a torso, then the rippling back and its powerful hind legs. Something was hanging from its mouth—a rag doll, a child's stuffed animal. Its limbs dangled limp.

Shit.

It was Virgil, the Zhangs' pet. Helen took that dog everywhere she went, including into the dining room at mealtimes, where I'd seen her slip it scraps under the table. Of course it was against the rules to have a dog—any animal—in the dining room, but that rule didn't seem to apply to the Zhangs. Myriam was the only one who complained, but she was too close to Helen to do it publicly. Besides, it had been well natured, watching the rest of us quietly from wide-set eyes.

But now it was, plainly, dead.

The mountain lion disappeared from the last frame on the walking trail, just beyond the Berglands' house. I got to my feet, slipping on my shoes. Beer sloshed in my stomach. If I had a rifle, or Victor's handgun, maybe I could go after it, take it down. Not that I was a trained marksman, especially at the range I would need for safety, and in the growing dark.

The Zhangs were home; earlier, I'd seen the twins walking past with their tennis rackets. I could call Helen, speak to her calmly. Say I'd seen something suspicious on the video feed and ask her if Virgil was in the backyard. But of course, he wasn't.

I grabbed a flashlight from the garage and slipped out the sliding door. "Back door open," the Other Woman warned me. In the backyard, the water lapped hungrily against the edge of the pool. The gate was padlocked, but it was easy enough to get one leg up and hop over the fence. The mountain lion must have done the same thing in the Zhangs' backyard, helpless Virgil dangling from its jaws.

I kept my back to the line of houses and swung the beam of the flashlight across the fairway, alert for any sign of movement. Farther out, the flashlight beam alighted on a small red-and-white bundle, like a discarded wooly sweater. I swung the light in wider circles, trying to spot the mountain lion. Was it still out there, lurking in the dark, or had it returned to wherever it was from, sated?

I approached the little hump on the greens, moving slowly, as if my legs were waterlogged. If the mountain lion returned, I was dead, anyway. Even sober, I would lose at a footrace.

What was left barely resembled Virgil. Helen had once explained to me that Bedlingtons had their ears and the sides of their heads shaved, leaving the top fuzzy.

That part of Virgil was visible now, but the rest of him

was a mess of blood and fur and entrails. I took a step away, heaved once and brought up a six-pack of Corona.

I was my own worst enemy, really. If I hadn't been looking at the video feed in the first place... Jeff Parker had said, *You have better things to do than stare at some grainy surveillance footage all day long.* But apparently I didn't. I'd spent Thanksgiving alone, and that was the best I could come up with. If I'd been with Liz and Danielle, we would have been eating pumpkin or apple pie by now, telling stories about Liz's childhood. Someone else would have discovered Virgil's mangled body, either late that night or early the following morning, and I would have learned about it from a message on my voice mail. "What is it?" Liz would have asked, seeing my grimace.

But I wasn't at a safe remove—I didn't have objectivity or distance. I had a mind clouded with the slow, impending horror of Kelsey, the estrangement from Liz, the secrets upon secrets I was keeping for what seemed, now, no discernible purpose. This would be the beginning of a new nightmare, involving everyone at The Palms in one way or another. It would make the news; Deanna, prophet of doom, would return to remind us of her close encounter in August. Myriam would call an emergency HOA meeting; Victor would return to his nightly patrols, and we would be lucky if he didn't pluck off a jogger or two on his quest to rid the neighborhood of danger. There would be a wine-and-cheese fund-raiser at someone's house, the monies designated for a memorial bench to Virgil Zhang.

And I was just so sick of it all.

I was sick of this place. I was sick of the life I'd wanted for us. All that happiness and security had only been a mirage, evaporating as soon as we approached.

I stripped off my T-shirt and laid it next to Virgil's body, then rolled him over with a nudge of my foot until he was completely on top of the cloth. The smell coming off his body was foul, and I retched again, bringing up beer and pizza. Still, I managed to tie the corners of the shirt together in a makeshift bundle and carry Virgil back to my house, his body swaying next to me.

For once Kelsey Jorgensen was nowhere to be found, not hiding in some bushes, giggling and waiting to pop out at me, not naked in my pool. I worked as quietly and quickly as I could, retrieving a shovel from the garage. The far corner of our lot, next to the fence, was the best place. The dirt was thick and wet, having been hit by the sprinklers that morning, but it was harder work than I could have imagined. My body was weak and heavy by the time I'd buried Virgil and tamped down the soil, evening it out over the general area.

I didn't sleep much that night. It was like that Poe story with the dead man's heart beating in the other room. Only with Virgil, what I kept hearing was the bark that Myriam had pronounced so irritating. What I kept seeing were the dark button eyes, open and staring, wondering what the hell I was going to do about the situation. I worked on the laptop until early morning, carefully deleting and splicing the digital file until it showed nothing at all—no mountain lion carrying a pet in its jaws, and no man sneaking out onto the golf course and returning ten minutes later shirtless, holding a bloody sac in front of him.

It was surprisingly easy to do—a few snips, and I'd rewritten history. I'd removed myself from the story of Virgil Zhang, and for that matter, I'd removed his story, too.

JUNE 19, 2015

6:21 P.M.

LIZ

The ambulance gone, I closed the front door behind us and leaned against it, my heart racing. Danielle and I stared at each other.

"You need to tell me," I said. "Right now, before we get in that car, before we—"

"What do you mean? I already said—"

I grabbed her by the arm. "You're going to tell me now."

"I told you!"

"From the beginning." I shook her arm and she pulled away.

"Fine. We were upstairs in my room. I was looking for a CD. And then we came back downstairs and I saw Kelsey in our pool. I had no idea she was out there. I thought—"

"What?"

Danielle was a messy crier, a trait she'd inherited from me. Her face was instantly blotchy, red patches appearing like a rash of poison ivy. "I thought it was some kind of joke. You know, something dumb, like she was pretending she'd fallen into the pool. So at first I didn't do anything. And then I saw the blood."

I was struck by how small she was, how young. With everything that had happened in the past few months, I'd managed to forget she was still a teenager, not even old enough for a driver's license.

"Did you invite her here?"

"No! Why would I do that?"

"I don't know, Danielle. I'm trying to figure out why she was in our backyard in the first place, and how she ended up unconscious in our pool with a gash on her head."

She turned away, but I caught her words. "Maybe if you hadn't been so drunk, you would know why."

"Excuse me?"

"I smelled it on you, Mom! When you came downstairs."

"I had *a* glass of wine."

She snorted.

"There's no messing around here, Danielle. We're going to the hospital, and there will be all kinds of questions for us. The Jorgensens will demand answers. The police—"

"I told you. I don't know anything!" She wiped her nose with the back of her hand. "Anyway, she's going to be okay, isn't she? They said there was a pulse."

"I don't know."

Danielle sobbed, "But she had a pulse!"

I reached out, touching her on the shoulder. For once she didn't pull away. "I don't know," I repeated. I couldn't shake the feeling of Kelsey's body beneath my hands, settling like a dead weight between compressions. "Come on, we have to get going."

Instead of moving, she pointed at my foot.

I was bleeding all over the floor.

In the master bathroom, I sat on the edge of the tub, wincing while Danielle made tentative dabs at my foot with a wet washcloth. She was still wearing her blue bikini, and when she bent over, the bony ridge of her spine was exposed.

My toenail was only attached to one side, where it hung on like a little red flag, bearing the remnants of an old strip of polish. I bit my knuckle, forcing down the pain. When Danielle got up to rinse out the washcloth I asked, "Can you find some gauze for me? I think it's in one of the boxes in the hallway."

She complied wordlessly, discarding several other packages—tampons, a tube of bath salts, unopened bars of soap—before coming up with a package of large gauze strips. I helped her unpeel the wrapping and she applied the strips to my foot.

I stood, testing it out. "Okay, put some clothes on and meet me at the car."

"No 'thanks'? I did just bandage your disgusting toe."

"Thanks." I pointed. "There's blood on your shoulder."

She rinsed the washcloth in the sink and dabbed at her shoulder, erasing the stain.

Too late I wondered if I should have said anything about the blood, if it might have been, somehow, evidence.

I limped past her and took a right turn to the closet I'd planned to pack earlier in the day, a lifetime ago. It was painful even to slip into a pair of open-toed sandals.

Danielle followed me to the doorway. "I didn't do anything, you know. Even if she deserved for horrible things to happen to her, it had nothing to do with me."

"Get your shoes," I told her. "We're following them to the hospital."

I'd started the car before I realized that I didn't have my cell phone. I left Danielle in the car and hobbled back into the house. I would have to call someone, once I figured out what was going on—Allie or Phil, or, God help me, the Jorgensens. My phone was resting on the table in the foyer, and when I touched the screen, I saw three missed calls from Phil, all from earlier in the afternoon. On my way back through the house, I spotted another phone on the kitchen peninsula, one in a black-and-red ladybug case. Was it Hannah's? I brought the phone to life. There was no password screen, and I hesitated for only a second before clicking on the icon for her text messages. Her last exchange had been with Kelsey at 4:30 p.m.

I thought you were coming over.

Her mom wouldn't let me.

Well, you need to come over. We have a surprise for you.

I'm supposed to stay home.

Yeah, and you always do what yr supposed to, right?

I'll come around the back.

I dropped her phone, and it clattered onto the counter.

NOVEMBER 2014
LIZ

By the Sunday after Thanksgiving, our laundry done and the house relatively clean, I felt antsy. Danielle had two chapters to outline for her history class and had left them until the last minute. Phil had spent the day on his laptop, looking at the new video surveillance software that had been installed there.

I couldn't get my mind off Virgil Zhang or the tearful panic of his owners. Earlier that day, I'd joined a search party to walk the golf course, even though Phil insisted it was a futile exercise.

"They probably left the gate open and he wandered away," he protested. "It was days ago. He could be miles from here by now."

"But wouldn't he have shown up on a camera?"

He shook his head. "Not necessarily. I've gone over and over that footage."

"Dogs don't just vanish," Helen had wailed, making me wonder what kind of world she lived in. Had she never seen the classified section of a newspaper before? Vanishing was one of the things dogs did best. She had upped the reward to $5,000 by Sunday night, and I wondered if I should take a day off work to continue the search myself. We could use the money.

On Monday, there were the typical after-holiday tasks to attend to at work—wilting plants to be watered and a dried-out piece of pumpkin pie to be split with Jenn while we contemplated an impressive stack of mail.

"How was your Thanksgiving?" I asked, forking a bite of stale crust.

She made a little seesawing motion with her head. "Oh, it was great. Ate too much, of course, vowed to go to the gym in the morning, but then I ended up getting sucked into one of those Black Friday sales..."

I only half listened, smiling. It was good to be back at work, good to slip again into the routine of things. I stabbed at the last of the pie crumbs with my fork.

"...and the best part," Jenn was saying, "is that Christmas is right around the corner. Two weeks of class, a week of finals and then, *bliss.*"

"Can't wait," I said.

"Oh, that's right. Your sister's coming, isn't she?"

"Yep." I grinned. "My mom, too. For a week."

"Hey—" Aaron stuck his head into the break room. "Got a minute, Liz?"

"Sure." I tossed the paper plate in the trash and the fork in the sink and joined Aaron in his office. He was at his computer, his face grim. I closed the door behind me. "What's up?"

"Our little friend is back," he said, adjusting the monitor so I could read the screen over his shoulder. His browser was open to a Twitter account called MLHS Stories.

"Shit," I said.

"Yeah. Looks like it went live again over the weekend, so I spent most of yesterday reading this junk." He shifted to one side so I could get a better look.

MLHS Stories was a gossip account that had first flared up a year ago to report on the more salacious exploits of Miles Landers students—and occasionally, staff members. Like most things that fell under the category of trolling or cyberbullying, the account worked on a basis of anonymous reporting. People sent in private messages, which the account owner would then post verbatim. It wasn't exactly a fact-based reporting system, although many regarded it that way. A year ago, the account had accused an unnamed teacher of having a relationship with a student, and the rumor mill had gone wild for a few weeks, until the feed had suddenly disappeared. Without fuel to add to the fire, the rumors had eventually died down as well, but not before several teachers had been hauled before administrators.

"Here's everything since it went live," he said, scrolling up from the bottom.

"I hate this junk," I complained. It was the exact way I didn't want to see our students—as sex- and drug-obsessed, petty and vicious. I would rather exist in a state of blissful ignorance where students' out-of-school lives were concerned, except that what happened online had a way of spilling over into our actual lives, producing a stream of crying, hysterical students, their worried/angry/clueless parents and occasional verbal exchanges that culminated in pulled hair or thrown punches. Last spring, an incident of cyberbullying had led a fifteen-year-old in a neighboring district to commit suicide, and our counseling staff had been told, in no uncertain terms, that monitoring social media sites was in fact our business. The senior counselor on staff, Dale Streeter, claimed he couldn't navigate the internet. I was officially in charge of the beast that was state testing; and that left Aaron to the more unsavory side of student life.

"The first ones are just the usual crap," Aaron said.

MLHS Stories @ Miles Stories—39d
Where all of ur friends turn on you for ur mistakes.

MLHS Stories @ Miles Stories—3d
Where the Asian girls disappoint their fathers.

"It's the grammar that offends me most," I murmured—although that wasn't true. It offended me that this site existed, that someone spent their time spreading such useless and hurtful things.

"So, it goes on..." Aaron scrolled through the posts, about five a day. "Oh, yeah, and there's this one."

MLHS Stories @ Miles Stories—9h
Where a girl gets fingered at lunch everyday and thinks no one sees.

"That's it," I told Aaron, over his shoulder. "We're never eating in that cafeteria again. Promise me."

"Keep reading," he said grimly.

MLHS Stories @ Miles Stories—9h
Where a freshman "accidentally" sends a nude pic to her brother.

MLHS Stories @ Miles Stories—8h
Where the hottest girls have the most messed-up teeth.

MLHS Stories @ Miles Stories—8h
Where the seniors smoke pot in their cars and spray this nasty-
ass lemon scent to cover it but everybody knows.

I kept reading, wincing. It was like verbal diarrhea, a constant spewing of hate and gossip. And then I came to the one
he'd wanted me to see.

MLHS Stories @ Miles Stories—7h
Where a sophomore hottie has sex with her 37yo neighbor and
wants more.

I steadied myself with a hand on Aaron's desk.

"Yeah, so there's that little gem to worry about," Aaron
said, tilting the screen away from me. "That's really the high-
light. Or—lowlight, I guess."

I cleared my throat, which was suddenly parched, my
tongue coated with pumpkin pie. "What are you going to
do?"

Aaron said he had already emailed Sanjay Gopal, the assistant principal in charge of discipline, and Gopal had told
the other APs by now. Dick Blaine, our principal, had been
briefed via email. "'Course, I don't know what we can do
about any of it. Twitter isn't going to shut down the account
over a few anonymous rumors, and whoever this yahoo account owner is, he's probably protected by the press shield
act or something."

I nodded, trying to recover. It felt as if I'd been punched
in the face. "Any idea who it's talking about? The sophomore, I mean."

Aaron shook his head. "Please. As much as I like to think
I have my finger on the pulse of this place…it's pretty vague.

Disturbing as hell, but vague. Plus there are plenty of hot sophomores."

I mock-punched his shoulder.

He laughed. "Well—seriously. I bet ninety percent of this stuff is just posturing, anyway. At least, that's what I tell myself. Otherwise, I wouldn't be able to keep my faith in humanity."

I stood up, heading for the door.

"Hey," he called after me. "You're sticking around for that AP Bio meeting after school, right?"

"Yeah. Unless Streeter volunteers to go in my place."

"Are you kidding me? He's in the home stretch now. Probably planning to hibernate until May 22."

I gave him a weak smile. Dale Streeter had been threatening to retire every fall for years, but by spring he always backed out. Somehow, this entitled him to "mailing it in" for as long as I could remember.

I paused in the lobby, steadying myself. Near my office door, a senior was hovering, binder clutched to her chest.

"Mrs. McGinnis?" she asked, the final syllable of my name rising into a question. "I heard there was a new Ag department scholarship?"

I summoned a smile, ushering her inside my office. I had the scholarship form on my desk, and while we chatted about the qualifications, I tried to force down my thoughts, the *nononono* racing through my brain. *The sophomore hottie, the 37yo neighbor.*

All day, beneath the in and out, the rush and flow, there was a heaviness in my stomach, as solid as a mass. Aaron was right—there were other hot sophomores. There were surely other neighbors. But we'd celebrated Phil's thirty-seventh birthday the week of our move to The Palms, and the specificity was unnerving. A *neighbor.*

He'd denied knowing anything about the underwear. He'd told me that I'd misunderstood what I'd heard outside his office door. Those things were both plausible. Yet it had been weeks since Kelsey had been in our house, and my suspicions had never fully disappeared. The mere suggestion had proved too strong.

It was like that old party game: *try not to think about the pink elephant. Think about anything except a pink elephant. Don't even concern yourself with the pink elephant.* And then inevitably all you could think about was the pink elephant.

I couldn't *not* think of my husband and Kelsey Jorgensen.

Phil had stayed home over Thanksgiving, the house to himself. He'd been surly with me over the weekend, withdrawn and moody. Something must have happened.

Had Kelsey been around for Thanksgiving, too? Had she been in our house, in my bed? A picture came, unbidden—Kelsey's fingers spreading through his chest hair, Phil's grunts in her ear. If she'd been in my bed, she'd been in my bathroom, too. She'd sat on my toilet, bathed in my tub, dried herself off with my towels. She'd pawed through the odds and ends of my makeup drawer. She'd used my hand lotion, laughed at the jar of my wrinkle cream.

I'd seen her getting out of Tim's car this morning, just before the tardy bell, wearing her standard tiny skirt over black leggings. I hadn't thought to ask her if she'd had a nice Thanksgiving, if she'd had a good time fucking my husband.

It was like an itch that needed to be scratched, a facial tic I couldn't control. Spend five minutes helping a student, check the Twitter feed. Answer a phone call, pop back on to Twitter. Reply to an email... MLHS Stories hadn't posted anything new, but more and more users had favorited and retweeted the post, presumably students from their class-rooms, the bathroom, the lunch line, the hallways. MLHS loved its scandals. The replies were typically callous. Haha your mom, one said. Another read kiss my 37yo ass. The most popular comment had been retweeted a dozen times: Did you slip him a Viagra first? Lol. The words burned in my brain, an endless loop. The *sophomore hottie*. The *37yo neighbor*.

I decided to leave as soon as school was over. Phil was in San Jose for a meeting at Parker-Lane, and I could search the house without him there, looking for evidence. That was what I needed—proof. A stain on the sheets, another piece of clothing left behind. Without proof I would look as stu-pid as I had the night of our fight by the pool, my accusa-tions easily dismissed and defended. *I don't understand*, Phil would say, looking at the Twitter feed. *This is supposed to be me? Where does it say my name?*

Jenn spotted me packing up my tote bag and poked her head into my office. "Did you forget about the AP Bio meet-ing? It's starting in five minutes."

I groaned, dropping my bag. With my thoughts in such a jumble, I had forgotten my promise to Aaron. "No, I'll be right there."

The meeting ran long—AP teachers tended to be long-winded, and AP parents vocal complainers. For the next hour, I sneaked glances at the overhead clock, a sturdy, in-dustrial piece of equipment that was nonetheless an hour off six months out of the year. Danielle was waiting in my of-fice when I returned, and I hurried her out to the car. Traf-fic on 580 was backed up, a nightmare of commuters all trying to get home to their families. As we inched along, I kept thinking about how this would go, what it would mean if it were true.

For one, Danielle and I couldn't stay at The Palms. We couldn't stay with Phil. It would be back to the single life— a condo, if we were lucky something with a patch of grass. We'd done it before. It was our normal, actually—The Palms and everything that came with it had been an aberration. But Danielle and I would be okay. We'd been here before. We'd squeak by financially. I'd make sure she kept her grades up, applied for every scholarship.

"Mom!" Danielle squawked, snapping me back to reality. I'd nearly missed our exit. I braked, my blinker on, waiting to merge into an oncoming stream of traffic.

"What is up with you?" Danielle demanded.

"Nothing," I croaked.

"So you're just acting crazy for no reason?"

I didn't answer.

"Fantastic," she muttered.

We made it home by six—not enough time for a thorough search. Danielle closed her bedroom door, and I preheated the oven for a frozen lasagna before racing upstairs. I pulled back the covers to study the sheets, then got on my knees to peer under the bed. *Nothing.* There was nothing out of place in the bathroom, but then there wouldn't be—I'd given it a good scrubbing yesterday, wiping away all signs of Phil's bachelor life, and all evidence, if there was any.

Maybe downstairs, then. I studied the couch cushions, the rug in front of the fireplace we'd never used. What was this, *CSI*? I had to laugh at the ridiculousness of it, of *me* on my hands and knees, searching for a blond hair that might have been left anytime during the summer. Then, as if pulled by a magnet, I approached the dining room. Phil had been using it as his makeshift office, since we ate all our meals in the informal nook off the kitchen or at the peninsula itself, our elbows on the granite. Back in July, I'd scoured the internet for something the right scale (seating eight to ten people) at a decent price (impossible), and we'd ended up putting a folding table from Costco in there instead. That table was spread with papers, which I thumbed through now—a report from a contractor, a bill for a cement mixer. There was a map of The Palms, marked precisely with little red Xs at the locations of the security cameras. He'd been monitoring those cameras ever since Danielle and I returned, as if he were a prison guard watching for unusual activity from the inmates. Then I spotted his laptop, slim and silver, in the middle of the desk. Why hadn't he taken it with him? It seemed like the sort of thing that would be needed for an all-day meeting.

I sat in his chair—a folding chair, temporary, like everything else about our lives—and lifted the lid.

This was where the proof would be. There would be emails, photos, a chat room history. The internet was where people lived their lives, where they kept their secrets. Somehow, people always thought they could keep their dark deeds hidden, that they were smarter than the others who had failed before them. They were clichés, the Tiger Woodses and Arnold Schwarzeneggers, the men who thought they could keep it all under wraps.

I took a deep breath and entered Phil's password: SFGiants#14. The Giants were his adopted team, rewarding him in the past decade with three World Series titles. His password, updated each year, reflected that allegiance. I hesitated before hitting the enter key, but I needed the proof.

The display jiggled, notifying me of an incorrect login.

I tried again, varying the strokes. No capital letters. All

capital letters. Maybe he'd needed to change a password for one reason or another, so I tried some variations of his favorite players with their jersey numbers. Passwords had become ridiculously complicated lately, with about seven different requirements that made them almost impossible to remember, let alone guess.

Still, I tried it—variations of Kelsey's name, of Phil and Kelsey's names together. It felt like proof on its own. He knew my password, but suddenly his was a mystery?

I didn't hear Danielle come down the stairs, and I didn't see her until she was right in front of me.

"What are you doing on Phil's laptop?"

"I'm trying to pull up a file I need," I said, brushing off her accusatory tone.

She came around the side of the table, and I assumed she was going to cut through the dining room to the butler's pantry we only used as a passageway to the kitchen. But instead, she swung around the end of the table and said, *"Mom."*

I followed her gaze to the laptop, to the screen that notified me of an incorrect password. I closed the lid. "It's not what you think."

She said, "I don't even know what to think," and left the room.

I went to bed early that night and pretended to be asleep when Phil came in. He read for a while next to me, turning pages slowly and deliberately. It was a biography of John Adams, and he'd been reading it halfheartedly for months, a page or two a night, but it disgusted me now. It felt like an act—a child molester pretending to be a normal human being.

Molester.

I'd been dancing around the word, not allowing my mind to go there.

Because there was another piece to the puzzle, too. I was an employee of a public school in California and therefore a mandated reporter. The law didn't require proof; it required reasonable suspicion. If you suspected a minor was being harmed (even, yes, a minor like Kelsey, who was aggressively sexual and quite possibly a willing participant), it had to be reported. And as a mandated reporter, I couldn't do so anonymously. I couldn't put their names out there and stand behind vague details. I would have to give my name.

Try it out, Liz, I told myself. Imagine saying *I'm Liz McGinnis and I'd like to report an inappropriate relationship between a thirty-seven-year-old man and a sixteen-year-old student at my school. His name? Phil McGinnis.*

I would have to say what I suspected and why. I'd be criminally liable if I had even the faintest suggestion and didn't report it. The procedure was a phone call to the county welfare department or the police, followed by a written report within thirty-six hours. I'd made those phone calls before and filled out the forms; we had a stack of them at work, and each year I'd conducted a brief professional development training for the rest of the staff on the process. Last year, I had a junior girl in my office, and when she'd bent over to pick up a piece of paper, I'd spotted a bruise on her back where her shirt rose above her jeans. Something about it had nagged at me, and I'd made the phone call. It turned out that she had an abusive older boyfriend, one who served a few months in jail as a result.

But this was my husband.

You don't know anything for sure, I reminded myself. *It's all rumor and innuendo. It looks bad, but it can't be true. Phil would never.*

Then, just as fast, the pendulum swung back, and I remembered that first day Kelsey had come over, when her bikini top had become twisted in the pool.

Of course he would.

But there was no way I was going to make that phone call and put our lives in jeopardy without absolute proof.

I began to watch Phil closely, tracking his movements the way he was tracking the movements of everyone else in The Palms. I left school as soon as I could each afternoon, drove faster on the way home, and popped into his office unannounced. Kelsey was never there, but somehow he always looked guilty, as if one of his hands had been pinched in the cookie jar. He was traveling to San Jose more often for meetings with Parker-Lane, sometimes leaving his laptop at home. I kept track of his mileage, and it roughly checked out.

"Why all the meetings?" I asked.

"Oh, we're in an expansion phase," he said, an answer too vague to be useful.

We occupied the same space, but I'd begun to think of us as separate entities, roommates for the sake of splitting expenses. In the first week of December, the three of us went to pick out a Christmas tree and we carted it home, where it stood in a bucket of water, leaning against the back of the house. A week later, Danielle asked when we were going to decorate the tree, and Phil and I looked at each other. Apparently both of us had other things on our minds.

We were waging a cold war, our sole battle over Danielle's plans to attend Winter Formal the Saturday before the end of the semester. Danielle had made plans to go with a large group that was splitting the cost of a limo, a group that in-cluded Kelsey Jorgensen. I was inclined to allow it, since I would be chaperoning the dance anyway, and would be able to keep an eye on her. Weirdly, it was Phil who was adamant that she was too young, that she didn't need to be out so late.

"It's a high school dance," I reminded him. "She is a high school student, after all."

"I don't like it," he said, but I overrode him, as I'd done only a few times before. It was part of a new pattern of dis-missing his opinions, discounting his advice.

The week before Winter Formal, I drove Danielle to the mall in Pleasanton and lurked outside the fitting room while she tried on dress after dress. She wanted a picture of herself in each one, and I dutifully obliged, snapping shots while she posed with a price tag dangling from her underarm. An-other girl from a different high school was in the dressing room at the same time, and I struck up a conversation with her mother while we waited for our daughters, bemoaning the cost of the dance tickets, the dinner beforehand, the dress and shoes and hair and nails.

Meanwhile the other girl emerged from her dressing room in a white dress with strands of beaded fringe. Even under the fluorescent lighting she was stunning, the fringe shim-mering like liquid metal. While she tried to convince her mother of the price tag, Danielle settled on a sleeveless black dress with a low back, one everyone else had passed over on the sales rack. "You look beautiful," I told her, and she rolled her eyes but smiled at her appearance in the mirror. I snapped her picture, getting into the spirit of it now. She *was* beautiful, even wearing a pair of socks, her hair pulled back by a headband.

And she was beautiful the night of the dance, too, her hair

sprayed in a dramatic faux-hawk, gold earrings dangling from her lobes. She looked as if she'd stepped off an album cover.

Phil whistled when she came down the stairs, heels dangling from one hand.

"Gross." Danielle mock-swatted him. "Stepdads aren't supposed to whistle."

"Maybe I should come along with you," Phil said. "Ward off attack, keep young men from dancing with you, that sort of thing."

"Creepy, but no thanks." She turned to me.

"Gorgeous," I pronounced.

She grinned. "Really?"

I gave her an air kiss, careful not to smear her makeup. She would be picked up in the limo by seven, have dinner with her friends and be at the Miles Landers multipurpose room by no later than nine thirty, when the doors closed. I reminded her, "No alcohol, no drugs, call me if anything makes you feel uncomfortable and I'll come pick you up."

Danielle sighed. "Right, I know."

"Or call me," Phil said, puffing out his chest, Tarzan-style. "I'll beat them away with my club."

As chaperones, Aaron and I were stationed at different doors, giant orange plugs protruding from our ears like the knobs on Frankenstein's monster. Even with the earplugs, the music thumped and my teeth vibrated. It was my favorite dance to chaperone—if *favorite* was the right word for a compulsory situation—because the students had put so much effort into their hair and clothes that they generally stayed out of too much trouble.

The multipurpose room was essentially the school's cafeteria by day, the site of board meetings and choir concerts and fund-raisers by night. For the dance, the walls had been papered in black, and thousands of white Christmas lights glittered from the ceiling and floor, illuminating the perimeters of the space. The only other lights came flashing from the stage, where the DJ stood behind a massive set. In the pulse of these lights, hundreds of students were exposed in staccato flashes of dresses and tuxedos and corsages and boutonnieres, their arms over their heads, bodies close together.

There was a photo booth behind the curtain on the stage, and at first the line was long, populated by groups of girls and couples holding hands. In the crush of students I noticed the clock—nine, then nine fifteen, nine twenty. The cafeteria was filling up, a large cluster of students dancing in the middle of the floor, couples scattered here and there. On the chairs around the perimeter, girls were perched on their dates' laps. I left my post at the door and wandered around the room, looking for a sign of Danielle. At one point, in flashes of the strobe light, I saw Kelsey. The lighting gave her an almost magical quality, her pulsing, jerky movements accompanied by the swinging of her blond hair.

I met up with Aaron at his post. He shouted something that sounded like *Kill me now.*

"Have you seen Danielle?" I shouted back.

He shook his head.

I wandered toward the main entrance, pulling my cell phone from my pocket. There were five missed calls, all in the past half hour, all from Danielle's number. With the noise, I hadn't heard it ring. She'd left me one voice mail, but I had no hope of hearing it inside the building. I pushed through the double doors of the lobby, trying to get away from the music. "I'll be right back," I told the staff members minding the cash box.

I had to take about twenty steps away from the building before I could hear anything other than the relentless, booming bass. My heart racing, I popped the foam earplug out of one ear and listened to the message. Danielle was sobbing so hard, I had to play it twice to understand. *Mom… you have to take me home. Something horrible has happened. I'm in the bathroom.*

I raced back inside, brushing past Sharon Hegarty, the home ec teacher.

"Liz?" she called after me, but I couldn't stop to explain myself. I was thinking of a million horrible scenarios at once. Danielle never asked me to bail her out of situations. I'd never picked her up from a sleepover or summer camp. Once, in elementary school, she'd scraped her knee on the playground, ripping her jeans and requiring her to change into a pair of too-big shorts from the school's clothes bin. But still—she hadn't called for me. When I'd picked her up at the end of the day, she'd simply handed me the ruined jeans in a plastic bag.

Maybe she was sick now. Appendicitis, food poisoning, cramps, any one of a hundred things that could go wrong with a person's body. Or she was hurt. Someone had hurt her. One of the boys from the limo ride, from dinner.

I had to fight my way through a group of girls clustered around the bathroom door. A few of them gave me uncertain, wavering smiles and quickly scattered. In their sparkling dresses and painful heels, I barely recognized them. I pushed open the door, stepping over coats and bags stacked on the floor. Six stalls gaped, empty, but the last one was locked.

"Danielle?" I asked softly. "It's me."

She threw the latch and peered at me from behind the stall door as if I were a stranger on her doorstep. She'd been crying; mascara ringed her eyes, and her cheeks were streaked with the remains of her glittery eye shadow.

"Oh, honey." I pulled a few yards of toilet paper from the dispenser, wetted them in the sink and returned, locking the stall door behind me. As I dabbed at her makeup stains, I felt her body shaking, shoulders rising and falling in silent, thrashing heaves.

"Sweetie, what's wrong?"

"It's—it's too—horrible."

I pulled out another stream of toilet paper and held it to Danielle's nose. She blew obediently, and I tossed the soggy mess into the open toilet.

"Whatever it is, you can tell me, Danielle. You know you can." I drew her close, but at the same time I allowed my glance to rove over the rest of her body. Her hair was slightly flatter than it had been when she'd left the house, but it wasn't mussed. Her dress was the same—not ripped or wrinkled. She had kicked off her shoes and was standing barefoot on a bathroom floor that had seen cleaner days.

I pulled back to look her in the face. "Dani—tell me."

"They're saying that I—"

The outside door opened then, music that had been a dull throb in the background becoming, briefly, a full roar. Danielle shrank back against the wall, bumping her shin against the toilet. More girls had entered. Through a gap where the door locked, I saw them huddle in front of the dingy mirrors and I stepped back to tuck my feet out of view.

"Are you kidding me? It has, like, four hundred favorites already."

"Oh, my God. Let me see."

"I would so die if this were me."

Danielle closed her eyes and leaned against the stall wall, tears streaking down her cheeks.

"I know she's only a freshman, but doesn't she know that—"

"Please. Some bitches are just stupid."

I grabbed Danielle's hand and felt her grip in return, sweaty and desperate, as if she would fall if I let go.

"What happened to her, anyway?"

"I wouldn't show my face if that were me."

There was some laughter, then the sound of water running in the sink, a towel being ripped off the automatic dispenser, and we were alone.

I looked at Danielle's tear-streaked face and said, "Let's go home."

"I thought you had to stay," she sobbed.

I shook my head. "This is an emergency. They'll understand."

She yanked my arm, frantic. "I can't go out there!"

"Well, we're not going to wait in here for two more hours." I looked around. "You don't have a coat?"

"No."

I unlocked the stall door and grabbed a black peacoat from the pile near the doorway.

She looked at me. "I can't just steal someone's coat."

"I'll bring it back to school next week and put it in the Lost and Found. Come on." I helped her into the sleeves, pulling the collar high around her face. I went first, peering out the door. After the fluorescent brightness of the bathroom, I blinked, my eyes adjusting. The area around the exit was clear because the dance floor was crowded, writhing with bodies. It took me a moment to place the song as "Billie Jean." Really? Michael Jackson in 2014?

I jerked my head, and Danielle slipped her shoes on, one hand against the bathroom wall for balance.

She kept her head down as we went through the lobby. I mimed an apology at Sharon Hegarty and we headed into the cool night. On the sidewalk, Danielle stopped to take off her heels as we rounded the corner in the direction of the staff parking lot.

"Dani—"

"Let's just go," she moaned. In the passenger seat, she bent double, head in her hands.

"Hold on a second." I dug my phone out of my jeans and sent Aaron a text. Emergency. Had to leave. Tell the others for me? I shoved my phone back into my pocket, not waiting for a reply.

Danielle bent forward, head in her hands, until we were on the freeway, cars zooming past us in the left lanes. Finally, I asked, "Can you tell me what's going on?"

She didn't look at me. "I don't even know how to say it."

"So just say it, then."

She took a deep breath, and her voice came out as a whisper, almost lost in the exhalation of the heating vents. "Someone started a rumor that I'm gay."

"Oh." I steadied myself, aware of my own breath, my hands on the wheel. The thing to do...the thing to do was to be supportive and encouraging, to be a listening ear. I'd been witness to a few of these conversations in my office over the years, and I knew how badly they could go wrong. "I'm glad we're talking about this, Danielle. It's absolutely okay if—"

"Mom!" Danielle shook her head. "Hello? I'm not gay. It's a stupid rumor started by stupid small-minded..." Her voice trailed off. I watched as she pinched her eyes shut, catching the tears with her index fingers.

"Why don't you start from the beginning? What happened after you left the house?" The words were out of my mouth before I realized they were coming, as if by rote. I'd questioned students this way before—reluctant girls who wanted to talk but didn't know how.

"Well, we went to dinner. It was that Italian place in Pleasanton, the one with the striped awning and the big statue out front."

"And what happened then?"

Danielle shook her head, her gold earrings flashing. "That's what I don't get. Everything was fine. We were just laughing and eating and I went to the bathroom, and when I came back they were all talking about me. And one of the guys, Josh—the one who's a senior?—said he didn't know I was a dyke."

"Do you know why he said that?"

She was less hurt now, more angry. "Yeah, one of the girls showed me something that had been posted on that stupid Twitter account. You know, that gossip account?"

I nodded, heart sinking. I knew it all too well, and so I knew what Danielle was up against, gay or not—the nasty rumors, the slurs and innuendos. That was what the girls in the bathroom had been talking about; the favorites and comments and shares meant it was already all over the internet. I tried to keep my voice even. "What did it say?"

"That's the stupid thing. It was that picture you took of me, in the dressing room, remember? I posted it on my Instagram, and someone made a meme out of it."

"That picture was completely innocent," I said. "How in the world—"

"Because that other girl was in there, trying on her dress.

It looks like I'm checking her out. So someone wrote this nasty comment—" She wiped her eyes again.

I swallowed. This was the great trick that social media had played on us. Take any image, pair it with any language, and the two were linked. Taken out of context, everything was titillating, ridiculous, revisionist history.

"The worst part was Kelsey," Danielle continued, and I froze, my arms stiff against the wheel. "I know I'm not gay, so—whatever. But she was just laughing, like it was the funniest thing she'd ever heard. She said that must be why I invited her to spend the night, so I could sleep in the same bed as her. She said that she was flattered, but we weren't playing for the same team." Danielle stared out the window. We were nearing the end of the access road, the last turn where the road widened and split. I slowed down, sensing there was more to the story.

"And then, the guys wanted us to kiss. They kept, like, saying it. I tried to just laugh about it, but it was awful. And Kelsey said she was up for it, just once, but I wouldn't do it. I don't know. It just wasn't funny anymore." She cupped her face with her hands.

At the entrance to The Palms, the gates rolled back, slowly. I had a mad urge not to wait for them to finish, but to take out the gates and the post with the front of my car, to drive and not care who or what got smashed in my path. Instead, I rolled slowly down the street, pulled into our driveway and shut off the engine. Neither of us moved.

Finally, I said, "I'm so sorry, honey. She's not a good friend, to treat you like that."

"I know. You were right." Danielle got out of the car, picking her way across the slate landscaping path in her bare feet.

A moment later, still seething, I followed her.

★ ★ ★

Phil met us in the entryway, looking at his watch. "I thought you were…" He stopped, seeing Danielle's blotchy, tear-streaked face.

I shook my head and his thought dangled, unfinished. Upstairs, Danielle's door closed with a quiet click.

"I need to use your laptop," I said.

"What? Why?"

"I need to look something up, right now."

"And you can't use your laptop?"

I stared at him.

"All right, fine," he said, moving past me. His laptop was open on his makeshift desk, facing away. "Let me just—"

When I came around the side of the folding table, he was closing out his open tabs. I watched as a screen with a scales-of-justice logo and a multipart name disappeared. Someone, someone and Fitch. What the hell was that? A law firm?

He shifted out of my way and gestured to the keyboard with a flourish. "Are you going to tell me what's going on?"

My fingers unsteady, I navigated to Twitter, then to the MLHS Stories feed.

Danielle's picture was the most recent post on the page, with 537 favorites and more than a hundred retweets. It was the picture I'd taken in the dressing room, with Danielle in front of the mirror. Next to her was the other girl in the white dress, the fringe a blur. It was just an accident of timing, a trick of the camera, but it looked as if Danielle was checking out the girl's backside. On top of the picture, in heavy white font, it read Watch your booty girls. The thought was finished beneath the picture: Babydyke is coming for you.

Phil leaned in to get a better look. "What the hell is that? That's supposed to be Danielle?"

"That *is* Danielle."

"Oh, my God. Who posted that?" He reached in front of me, navigating on the mouse pad. He clicked on the replies—a stream of them, littered with *dyke* and *queer* and the ubiquitous *lol*. One read *Hey, I went to science camp with that girl. No idea she was a lesbo.* Another said *I heard she put the moves on her best friend.* Phil barely got his fingers out of the way before I slammed the laptop shut.

I dug in my pocket for my cell phone.

"Who are you calling?"

"Gopal—he's the assistant principal. Maybe he can get the picture taken down. I know it's too late—it's everywhere by now. But at least it's a start." I left a message on Gopal's voice mail, telling him to look at MLHS Stories and call me back.

Phil had opened his laptop again. "These comments are awful. Who did this?"

"Who do you think?"

He stared at me, his face a mask. "I don't know. That's why I'm asking."

"It had to have been Kelsey. And if it wasn't, then she didn't do anything to make it better. Danielle said she was laughing along with everyone else."

"Why would she—"

"I don't know, Phil," I said, my voice a sheet of ice. "Why don't you ask her?"

Danielle's room was completely dark, and she was face-down on her bed. "Go away," she mumbled.

I pushed the comforter to one side and lay down next to her.

"Mom, come on. I just want to be alone."

"Me, too. Let's just be alone together."

Danielle groaned. She was still wearing the black dress, bunched now around her thighs.

"You want to change out of that? You'd feel more comfortable."

"Why, sure, Mom. That would make everything better."

We lay side by side in the dark. A phone buzzed, and I reached reflexively into my pocket, hoping it was Gopal.

"It's my phone," Danielle said. She was holding it in her hand, facedown. "It's Kelsey again."

"She's texting you from the dance?"

"Only a hundred times. You want to see? Here." She passed me her phone. The screen was stacked with lines of green text bubbles, all from kelseybelle.

Saturday 9:21 PM
You think I had something to do with this? That's crazy I was just playing along. Stupid joke but I'm sorry.

Saturday 9:38 PM
Come on I'll tell them it was a stupid joke.

Saturday 9:45 PM
It's just a joke, srsly. Let it go.

Saturday 9:56 PM
Did you go home? WTF?

Saturday 10:14 PM
Omg text me.

Saturday 10:29 PM
Can't believe you left me.

"What am I supposed to do?" Danielle asked.

"You don't have to do anything. You didn't do anything wrong."

"I mean—I have *finals* next week. How can I go back there? Everyone thinks I have a crush on Kelsey. I'm going to fail all my classes and be a freshman dropout."

I smiled in spite of myself, but I gave her a little nudge. "You have to go back, you know."

"Keep my head up, you mean? Take the high road, and all that crap?" She sighed. "I don't want to see her again."

"You don't have to see her again. You don't have to text her back. You don't have to do anything you don't want to do."

Between us, her phone buzzed again, a line of text lighting up the screen.

Saturday 10:35 PM
Are you just never going to talk to me or what?

Danielle ignored the phone, turning it facedown.

"Besides, you have other friends."

She snorted. "Last year I had other friends. Now I don't anymore."

"They're still there, I bet."

"I don't know." After a moment, she spoke again, her words muddled against her pillow.

"What?"

She rolled onto her back. "One of the guys said he knew I was gay because of my haircut."

"One of the guys is an idiot, then," I told her. "Actually, you look great with your hair this short. I like it."

"Really?"

I kissed her on the cheek. "Don't reply to her messages.

Don't do anything. Just get a good night's sleep, and in the morning, we'll see how you're feeling about it. Is that okay?"

Danielle sighed, too emotionally exhausted to argue with my platitudes. I suppose she'd lived long enough to know that sometimes it wasn't better in the morning. Sometimes, in fact, it was worse.

Sanjay Gopal worked quickly and Danielle's picture was down by noon on Sunday. I know because I kept checking on my laptop, refreshing the page every few moments.

"I took screenshots of all the comments, too," Gopal told me. "Some of them are clearly recognizable as our students, and I could call them in, make things a bit difficult."

As a parent—as a *human*—I wanted to punish every kid who had written *dyke* and *queer* and some slurs I'd had to look up online to understand. But I had bigger concerns. "Can you call in Kelsey Jorgensen, too? She's a sophomore, new this year."

"Why? Is she involved somehow?"

"She was part of the group Danielle was with, and she was laughing and basically encouraging the rumor. She might have posted the picture, too."

Gopal was silent for a moment. "Look, I know this has upset you, Liz, but there's really no way to know where the meme came from. Your daughter posted the picture, and just about anyone could access it. You might want to consider changing her privacy settings."

"I know Kelsey's involved, Sanjay. Can't you just call her into your office and talk to her? Put a little pressure on her and see what she says? Or at least give her a warning, let her know someone is paying attention?"

I could feel his hesitation, the weight of things he wasn't saying. Most APs came and went, moving their way up the ladder,
but Gopal had been at Miles Landers for five years now, and he
was good at the job. The staff thought he was conscientious,
and for the most part, students thought he was fair. This was
the first time we'd connected on a personal level, and I knew
he was thinking that I was just another crazy parent, making unreasonable demands and expecting impossible results.

"Okay," he said finally. "Monday. I'll call her in and see
what she has to say."

"I appreciate it, Sanjay," I said.

Danielle did go back to school on Monday, but it was a
different Danielle, her hair less styled, with only a bit of mascara and lip gloss. She wore a long sweater over her jeans and
her beat-up pair of turquoise Converse.

"I'm proud of you," I told her in the car. And I was—
almost to bursting. It felt like a movie scene, minus the swell
of uplifting music.

She shrugged. "I may as well get it over with."

"You can come to my office anytime," I offered. "If anything happens that you don't like, if anyone says anything to
you, then you can come right to me."

"I'm not sure it would help my social status if I ran right
to my mommy," she said. "But anyway, thanks."

Aaron came into my office at the beginning of fifth period lunch, the sleeves of his yellow Oxford rolled up to his
elbow. He held one hand behind his back.

"So," he said.

"So."

"It's a shitty thing, Liz. How is she?"

"I think the worst of it is over by now." I gestured to

his arm. "What's behind your back? A bottle of Johnnie Walker?"

"Next best thing." He brought his arm around, producing a cafeteria tray heaped high with the daily special. "I present to you, faux chicken."

I grimaced.

"These nuggets represent your tax dollars at work, Liz. And personally, I hate the thought of my tax dollars ending up in a trash bin at the end of the day."

I scooted a few loose pens and papers out of the way, and Aaron set the tray on the desk in between us. He'd brought a half-dozen sauce containers and proceeded to open them one by one, peeling back the thin plastic strips carefully, like a solicitous waiter.

I picked up a nugget, holding it to the light. "Do the kids actually eat these?"

"No, and that's my point."

We ate in silence. I hadn't realized how hungry I was until the first nuggets passed my lips. They were surprisingly good for food that was far removed from any kind of natural state. We ate in silence, picking apart the breading, chewing with great concentration.

"So, let's hear it," Aaron said.

I swallowed and took a swig from my water bottle. "Well, the worst part is that she's convinced her friend Kelsey—the one you met at registration?—was behind the whole thing."

"Some friend, huh?" Aaron sighed. "I'll never understand girls. Guys, we punch it out and that's the end of it. Girls go for the jugular. Look, I know this probably isn't helpful, but it could have been worse."

"I know. It'll die down, like any other rumor. The weird thing is, even though people are more accepting than ever, being gay is still the low-hanging fruit. I mean, this can't be helping kids who actually are gay."

"Right." Aaron grabbed a tissue and took a swipe at his chin. "Now, I have zero experience with the whole parenting thing. My cat causes me very little trouble, as you know. But, Liz, if there's anything I can do…"

"There is, actually."

"Really? Because that was just a standard consolation phrase."

I laughed. "Jerk. I was just thinking—maybe you could call Danielle in sometime, just to see how she's doing."

He nodded. "Sounds like a plan."

There was a short rap on my door and Jenn popped her head in a few inches. "Liz? There's someone who wants to talk to you. A Mrs. Jorgensen? She doesn't have an appointment, so if you want me to tell her—"

"No, it's fine," I said. "Give me just a minute."

Aaron tipped the rest of the chicken nuggets and the empty sauce containers into the trash can, and I straightened the top of my desk. Sonia Jorgensen was *here*? For the first months of the year, she hadn't even taken a turn bringing Kelsey to school. She'd been in Raleigh for a convention on Back-to-School night, and to my knowledge she'd only set foot on campus for registration. *Gopal*, I thought.

"Excuse me," Sonia said, passing through the doorway at the same time as Aaron, who left with a sympathetic smile. Instantly, I felt like I always did when I saw Sonia—horribly underdressed. She wore a silk blouse and pencil skirt, smart three-inch heels. She held a buttery leather briefcase by its handle. Her gaze swept over my room—dusty binders, stacks of memos that should have been tossed a month ago, Post-it notes affixed to half the surfaces—before coming to rest on me. I had the feeling that what I'd seen of her at The

Palms had only been a polite veneer, but that pretense was gone now.

Sonia dropped her briefcase onto the chair Aaron had vacated. "You accused my daughter of spreading rumors on Twitter?"

I stepped behind her to shut the door. In the lobby, I caught Jenn's raised eyebrows. "Did Mr. Gopal call you?"

"No, Liz, my daughter called me. In tears. Apparently she was called into the assistant principal's office for cyberbullying. I was on my way to the city, but I had to cancel my appointments and drive all the way back." This, clearly, was what she found most upsetting about the entire situation.

I stared at her. "I never used the word *bullying*, but yes, I do believe she knows something about what happened. It concerns our students, so that's why the assistant principal is involved."

"Our students?" Sonia repeated. "We're talking about our *daughters*. This could have been kept between you and me, and we could have chatted it out over coffee."

I cleared my throat. "Actually, it doesn't involve you and me. It mainly involves Danielle. Did you see the comments on that Twitter account?"

Sonia shook her head. "I only just learned about this. But Kelsey told me there were some horrible comments. I'm very sorry about that. I don't know why you would think Kelsey had something to do with this, though."

I had to plant my hands firmly on my desk to steady myself. "She mocked Danielle. That night, in front of the other kids in their group. She was humiliated. I found her crying in the bathroom."

"I'm sure Kelsey didn't mean anything by it. After all the things she's been through…"

I waited, but she dropped the thought.

"Try to see this from my daughter's perspective, Liz. If everyone thinks her best friend is gay…"

My throat felt tight, as though I were in the throes of an allergy attack.

There was an incredible pettiness to her, I saw now, a lack of empathy, a myopic shortsightedness. The world began and ended with Kelsey. It was a fitting attitude for The Palms; maybe it was written into a homeowner's manual somewhere, like a commandment: Thou shalt look out for thyself first.

That's not the worst of it, I wanted to tell her. *That's only the beginning of what your daughter has done to my family.*

I remembered what Sonia had said about the other students at Ashbury. She would never be convinced that her daughter had been in the wrong. She would always be the victim. I gave her the fake smile I'd perfected at The Palms, the smile-through-it-all, the smile down my nose. "Maybe you're right, Sonia. Maybe my daughter just has too many issues. It's probably best that they don't see each other anymore. I wouldn't want Danielle to be a bad influence on her."

Sonia was quiet. Her posture had gone rigid, her face red.

I stood again and moved around the desk, opening the door for her. "I'll be sure to let Danielle know," I told her. And then in a voice loud enough to attract Jenn's attention on the other side of the foyer, I added, "Thank you so much for coming in, Sonia."

I thought I detected a slight flinch, a small crack in the armor that was Sonia Jorgensen before she turned and walked toward the outside door, the points of her heels smacking against the tile.

PHIL

After Thanksgiving, Kelsey was everywhere—hitting balls on the tennis court early in the morning, her short white skirt billowing up to the tops of her thighs. She was driving herself to school now, so sometimes she skipped first period to have breakfast in the clubhouse. If she could touch me, she did—her leg grazing mine, her arm brushing against me. She straightened my collar, fixed my hair. Once, she bent down to tie my shoe.

Close-up, there was something repulsive about Kelsey Jorgensen. It was only at a safe remove—when she was stripping in my backyard, or flouncing past my window—that she was exciting.

I'd begun to dream about her, too. When Liz rolled over in bed, I woke in a cold sweat, sure it was Kelsey next to me. If the house made a creaking noise, I thought it was Kelsey coming up the stairs. It helped if I took a sleeping pill, bringing myself to a numb state, almost incapable of dreams. But I would wake up with a memory of her lips on mine, my fist around a clump of her hair. I punished myself by throwing on jogging clothes and running fierce early-morning laps on the walking trail. As if I thought I could sweat her out.

I widened my search for attorneys—Palo Alto, San Jose, Santa Rosa. One of the lawyers I met was an ethics professor at Stanford. He seemed almost delighted by my problem; mine would probably be a case study for a future course. He steepled his fingers in front of his face, delivering a summation. "So it's a clear case of obsession, then. The subject being a minor and the object being a—well—virile adult male. It's an interesting predicament to be sure. And you've never so much as touched her, never done anything that could be construed...?"

I shook my head, forcing down the memory of grabbing her by the arms in the hallway outside Danielle's bedroom, not mentioning the touch of her lips on mine in my office. I'd told him about her appearance in the backyard over Thanksgiving, leaving out the fact that I hadn't wanted to look away. I cleared my throat, driving out the image. "My concern is that if I come forward, everything I say can be interpreted another way. Kelsey's smart. She's—calculating. She knows how to work things to her advantage."

He smiled. "Well, that is the worry, isn't it?" When he didn't call after two weeks, I knew he wouldn't take the case.

I met with two other attorneys and one, Jacob Fitch, accepted me on a two-thousand-dollar retainer. Every time we spoke, I imagined him calculating the minutes in quarter-of-an-hour increments—fifty dollars here, a hundred dollars there. I sent him all my files, downloading everything onto a flash drive and delivering it in person to his office in Moraga. Yet I couldn't be sure he wasn't just a huge sleaze-ball. He didn't seem to believe in my innocence—but then, I didn't, either, not since the moment Kelsey had kissed me inside my office. He replayed our conversations with a smile on his lips and a sort of delighted twinkle in his eye.

"What do you want to do with this?" he asked me in the beginning. "Press charges of your own? File a restraining order?"

"I just want it to go away," I told him.

He nodded. He alluded to a previous career in corporate law; he knew what a scandal like this could do. When he said *out-of-court settlement* and *gag order*, I heard *hush money* and *guilty, guilty, guilty.*

Jacob advised me to avoid her, then—to stop gathering evidence, to stop giving her opportunities. But I found it was easier to play along, to let her sit in my office one afternoon rather than be ambushed by her the next. I could control the situation that way.

In early December, she told me about Winter Formal. I'd already heard about it at home from Danielle, and I'd voiced a concern that Liz had ignored. Once the decision had been made without me, the rest was only detail. All that was required of me was to open my wallet.

"Here's my dress," Kelsey said, showing me a picture on her phone. It was red, emblazoned with thousands of tiny sequins and skintight, but of course, it was chaste compared to what I'd seen of her.

"Do you have a date for the dance?" I asked, trying not to let too much hope into my voice.

She had to stand to slide her phone into the pocket of her jeans, revealing a flat stomach still tanned from the summer, the tiny elliptical sphere of her navel. "Are you volunteering?"

"Not at all."

"Really? It would be fun. A limo ride, a fancy dinner, slow dancing. We could get a hotel room at the end of the night."

I shook my head. What she was describing was a high school boy's dream, an all-American experience. Why was she here, when she could have been hanging out with a boyfriend after school, making out on her bed and pretending to complete math homework? "So you don't have a date? Why not?"

She rolled her eyes. "With one of the idiots at my school?"

"They can't all be idiots."

"Yes, they can."

"Isn't there a—I don't know—captain of the football team or a class president or just some cool guy with a guitar?"

She leaned forward. For once she didn't look sexy, just angry. "They're just boys. They haven't been anywhere and they don't know anything. And the sex?" She let the question dangle in the air before answering it. "Boring."

I dodged the bait. "But eventually, that's what you'll want. Isn't it? Those guys will grow up. They'll mature. I was the same way in high school."

She didn't answer.

"I mean, you'll go off to college—"

"Stop it," she said.

"No, really. You're an attractive girl. Some guy is going to spot you walking across campus, and before you know it—"

"I said stop. I'm not going to college. I'm not interested in any college boys."

"Not now, maybe."

She stood up. "What don't you get? I practically throw myself at you."

Not *practically*. "But seriously, Kelsey, long-term. This is just a—"

"Don't you tell me this is a phase." Her voice was dangerously shrill.

I glanced at my closed door.

"I can't believe this," she said. "After everything I've done for you. In the end, you're still picking that bitch over me."

I flinched. "Don't you ever say that. There was never any picking. She's my wife. And you're—"

She slammed the door behind her.

And so I waited. She would get her revenge, of course. She would flood another toilet or spray-paint something on a wall—maybe on the outside of my house. She would send me a picture or show up naked in my kitchen one morning, slicing a bagel with a carving knife. *Bring it on*, I thought. She was bound to screw up, to get the attention of others.

"Maybe you should call the police," Jacob Fitch said. "Or I can. I've got an old friend who's a retired detective. I could pay him a visit, run some hypotheticals past him to get the lay of the land."

I added up that cost in my head—visit to a friend, lunch on my dime. "If you think that's necessary."

"Don't you? And, man. I think I'd watch out, if I were you."

"I'm getting out of there," I told him. I hadn't worked out the specifics, but I understood it needed to happen.

His laugh was wistful. "How soon?"

But I'd miscalculated. I saw that the minute Danielle came through the front door on the night of the dance. Only Kelsey could be responsible for those tears. I'd been wary of their friendship all along, but I thought there was a line she wouldn't cross, a hallowed ground of friendship.

I didn't tell Jacob Fitch about the rumor Kelsey had started about Danielle, or how that discovery had made me read back through the feed on MLHS Stories, my eyes burning with each new post. Forget what the experts say about kids today being just like kids of previous generations—it's simply not true. That was where I found, dated two days after her naked swim in my pool, this post: **Where a sophomore hottie has sex with her 37yo neighbor and wants more.** It had been sitting there for weeks, presumably seen by all the account's followers. The entire student body at Miles Landers must have gagged over it; Liz must have seen it, too, which explained her growing distance, the suspicious look she gave me at each turn.

I'd begun to question how much good Jacob Fitch was doing me anyway, now that I'd thrown the money his way. It was like talking to a therapist; it had been good to unburden myself, but somewhere between his office and The Palms, that relief always dissipated. What could a lawyer do in the real world, the next time Kelsey Jorgensen struck?

I didn't want to tell him, either, about the card I was holding. This had come to me late at night, an idea so diabolical that it was finally a match for Kelsey. I asked her to meet me one afternoon in an empty house in Phase 3, where I knew no one would overhear our conversation.

I'd brought a basket of wine and cheese with me, tucking a note in the raffia between two bottles. *Happy holidays from the McGinnises.* If anyone asked, it was my alibi.

I was waiting in the kitchen when she entered, looking around the cavernous emptiness of the house. Work would be finished by Christmas; the owners would take up residency January 1.

She shivered in her short black dress and knee-high black boots. "Why is it so cold in here?"

"Heat's not on yet."

"Why are we here, then?"

I gestured to the basket on the counter. "I was hoping you could deliver this to your parents. It's from Liz and me."

She glared at me. "Seriously?"

"And I thought we could have a little talk."

She narrowed her eyes. We hadn't spoken since she'd stormed out of my office, since before she'd started the rumor about Danielle.

"Here's the thing," I told her. "I've been afraid of you. I've been afraid of what you might do to me. Maybe you would accuse me of something, and then I'd be known as this rapist or a pedophile. And I figured that would be the worst thing."

She folded her arms across her chest. "I could call rape right now. I could scream and people would come running."

"You could," I said evenly. "But then after what you did to Danielle, I realized that I could take it. I could fight it. But my daughter? She's just a kid."

She didn't bother to deny anything. "She's your stepdaughter. And she's not a kid."

I kept going, as if she hadn't spoken. "So, I figured that two could play at this game. I have a story of my own ready."

She laughed. "You're going to say I raped you?"

"No. I'm going to say you confided in me. You kept coming to my office after school just to talk, and then one day you finally told me that your father has been molesting you, and I knew I had to report it."

Her mouth went slack. "That's sick."

"Authorities take those sorts of accusations very seriously."

"But it's not true. And you don't have any proof!"

"No, of course not. But it'll take a while for it all to get sorted out. In the meantime, I'll probably get hauled in for questioning. And that's bad, yes, but I've had time to get used to the idea. I've been making other plans, anyway. But your poor father, Kelsey. Think of him. This would destroy him—even the suggestion of it. He's a lawyer, right? Job, gone. Your poor mother. Trust, gone. Marriage, gone. Believe me, I know how easily that can happen." I hadn't meant to say the last part—it just slipped out.

"You wouldn't do that to me."

"But I would, if that's what I had to do. If you post something on social media, if you hurt my daughter or my wife, if you do something to hurt me one more time, that would be it."

"No one would ever believe it. Not for a minute."

I nodded. "That may be true, Kelsey. But I've been getting some legal advice of my own, so I have an understanding of just how bad it would be for your father. Poor man. He'd probably make bail after a night in jail, but the community would crucify him. Imagine what the papers would say. Imagine the jokes on social media. Even if he's cleared—years later, when the investigation is finally closed—there will always be that question, won't there? Did he or didn't he?"

She was trembling, her irises moving frantically, as if she couldn't figure out where to look. It was the first time I'd ever unsettled her. And I'd unsettled myself, too. It was terrifying to actually play the trump card. Terrifying and sickening—Tim Jorgensen didn't seem like father of the year, but his only real crime, as far as I knew, was being far too permissive in his parenting.

"I hate you," she whispered.

"I understand, Kelsey. But that won't stop me."

She practically ran to the front door, forgetting the basket of wine.

★ ★ ★

I actually thought, for a delirious, happy moment, that it might work. That we might be rid of Kelsey for good. Oh, I still had another plan, in the form of two job interviews scheduled for the beginning of January. If one of them panned out, I'd be faced with giving Liz the inverse of the speech I'd given her last spring, when I brought her to The Palms for the first time.

But I figured at the very least, I'd bought myself some time.

What I didn't expect was that Kelsey would burn down the fucking house.

JUNE 19, 2015
6:32 P.M.

LIZ

When we backed out of the driveway, I saw them immediately—our neighbors were now circled in a clump under one of the palm trees in front of the Mesbahs' house. All of their heads turned at once. Deanna took a step forward uncertainly and stopped.

Only Fran was on her side of the street, the sunlight catching her unruly curls and the silver spokes of Elijah's wheelchair. I rolled down my window and leaned across Danielle's lap.

"Liz, my God. What happened?" Fran asked. Elijah's wheelchair was between us, and in it he sat wide-eyed and alert.

"There was an accident with Kelsey Jorgensen," I told her. "I don't know how it happened, but she fell in the pool."

"Dear Lord. I saw her earlier today, just wandering around in front of your house. I wondered what she was doing."

"We're going to the hospital now. Will you—tell the others?"

"You mean the vultures? Sure."

And then I pressed down on the gas, gunning the engine

through the winding streets of The Palms while Danielle clutched the door handle, leaning in to the turns. I remembered Phil's explanation for why there were no straight lines in the community, how it made for an interesting streetscape and a sense of seclusion and privacy.

Phil. However irrational, it would be nice to lay this blame at his feet. At the very least, he'd brought us here in the first place, almost a year to the day. No matter what, he should have been here to see us out.

We turned to the west, the sun an angry orb sinking lower in the sky. I half expected to see the ambulance in front of us, just around the corner. Stupid, of course—we'd lost time bandaging my foot and then more time as I'd looked through Hannah's cell phone. It felt as though my car understood the rush and was propelled forward by sheer adrenaline. I had to brake hard to stop myself from taking the curves too fast.

Halfway to the freeway there was a turnout in one of the driveways leading to a ranch, and I slowed down, then came to a stop. Here the land was a brown-brown, the result of a drought that seemed endless. White stalks of weeds cropped up here and there, impervious. In the spring, this had been a pretty drive, green as far as the eye could see, the white wind turbines on the distant Altamont as lovely as children's pinwheels. Now, only a few days into the official grip of summer, the hills were a rolling brown, and in the rearview mirror, only a single windmill turned listlessly on the horizon.

Danielle gaped at me. "Why'd you stop?"

"Because you're going to tell me the truth. What was the surprise? What were you going to do to Kelsey?"

"What do you mean?"

All I had to do was stare at her, and she caved.

DECEMBER 2014
LIZ

On the first days of our winter break, Danielle and I finally decorated the tree, which was considerably flattened on one side from leaning against the back of the house, and we'd baked a dozen different kinds of treats, working mostly in silence side by side.

That last week at school had been difficult for Danielle, I knew—anonymous notes had been passed to her in class, a used tampon placed in her PE locker. The Gay-Straight Alliance had taken up Danielle's cause, actively campaigning against hate speech. Well-meaning students had conducted class visits preaching tolerance and calling for a stop to the shaming. Although the message was a good one, it kept implicitly reflecting back on Danielle and the crush she didn't have on Kelsey Jorgensen.

All she needed was two weeks off, I figured. In January, the silly rumor from Winter Formal would be yesterday's news, replaced by some new drama. That was the way scandals worked in the adult world, too. Politicians banked on our short memories.

In the meantime, she'd struck up a friendship with Hannah Bergland, who'd brought over some of her mom's homemade peanut brittle. The two of them ate the entire plateful watching a movie in our den.

Allie and Mom arrived the Tuesday before Christmas. The previous day, Allie had flown to SoCal, renting a car at the airport and reversing the route in the morning with Mom for their trip north. I'd been waiting for them all afternoon, calculating the time it would take for them to get off the plane, visit the bathroom, retrieve luggage, pick up the rental car and follow the route prescribed by GPS all the way to our front door.

I was already halfway down the sidewalk when Allie stepped out of the rented white Hyundai.

"What is this place, Xanadu?" she called.

"Wasn't that an island?"

"No idea," she admitted, collapsing into my hug. "I refuse to watch movies everyone else insists I must watch."

"God, you're skinny," I commented, pulling back. Allie's hip bones had dug into my hips with the ferocity of her hug. "Don't they feed you in Chicago? Isn't that the home of the deep dish pizza?"

"She's too skinny. I said the same thing," Mom said, opening the passenger door. I came around the side of the car to help her, but not before she'd already found the curb with her foot.

Allie grinned. "I'm going to take Mom with me every time I travel from now on. Priority seating for the plane, plus we got to ride around in one of those little carts with the driver honking at everyone to get out of our way. It was great, wasn't it, Mom?"

"Not so much for me," Mom said. She gripped my arm tightly as we headed up the walkway.

"Where's your cane?" I asked. "Didn't you bring it?"

"And let everyone know I'm blind?" she sniffed. Over her head, Allie and I rolled our eyes. Mom's ever-present dark glasses, perched on her nose day and night, were as obvious as any white cane, and a lot less practical for getting around.

"Don't worry. I packed it in her suitcase when she wasn't looking," Allie said. She'd thrown open the trunk and was stacking bags on the curb.

"Grandma! Aunt Allie!" Danielle ran out of the house in her socks. Allie grabbed her in a tight hug and rocked her side to side.

"When did you get taller than me?" Allie demanded, holding her back for a closer look.

Mom reached a hand, feeling the air around herself as if she were looking for something. "Where's Phil?"

Allie glanced at me quickly, and I shook my head, meaning that nothing was settled, that things were just as bad as I'd hinted. Worse, if you considered that we were no longer talking, and that twice in the past week, Phil hadn't come to bed at all. I'd found him asleep on the couch in the den when I went downstairs.

"He's over at his office. I'll take you there later, on the grand tour."

"The grand tour," Allie repeated. "Mom, you remember that show, right? *Lifestyles of the Rich and Famous*?"

"'Champagne wishes and caviar dreams,'" Mom said, not missing a beat.

It felt like the first time I'd laughed in months.

Danielle carted suitcases—to the downstairs suite for Mom, furnished with the full-sized bed that had come from our house in Livermore, and to an upstairs room I'd hastily thrown together for Allie, complete with a blow-up mattress and an old IKEA nightstand retrieved from the stack of furniture in the garage.

"Holy wow," Allie commented, entering the house. "There really is an echo."

"What does it look like?" Mom asked.

Allie jumped in before I could say anything. "Well, there's lots of beige. Or is that not the right word? *Neutral*, then. It's very...neutral. Also, huge. If you moved this place to Chicago, you could rent it for about nine thousand a month."

"So, cheaper than here," I commented.

Allie laughed. "Touché."

I had coffee and pumpkin bread waiting in the kitchen, which Allie pronounced "bigger than my entire apartment."

I fetched the creamer from the refrigerator. "Mom? Can I pour you a cup?"

Mom was feeling her way around the kitchen, bumping against the bar stools, opening drawers and cabinets. She ran her hands over the granite counters. "It's beautiful, Liz. Such a beautiful home."

I thanked her, then busied myself with the mundane details of plates and napkins, cups and saucers. It was beautiful, but that had little to do with me. And I'd come to think of it as an ugly beauty, contradicting itself over and over, too expensive, too cold—impossible to love.

Outside, Allie pulled off her socks and boots and insisted on putting her feet in the pool. The automated cover was in place, but I rolled it back so she could get up to her calves, her jeans bunched high on her legs. "I can't believe it's so warm," she said. "Can we go swimming later?"

"If you want. I haven't been in for a month." Phil had put

the cover up after Thanksgiving, and we hadn't bothered to move it since.

"Not me," Mom said. I'd held her arm, walking her between the house and the pool several times, so she could get a sense of the distance. She'd been a vigorous swimmer when she was younger. There were even pictures of her as a teenager with her dark hair in one of those old rubber swimming caps, festooned with dozens of white petals. Blind, she worried that she wouldn't be able to find the edge, that she would become entangled in something beneath the surface of the water, that she would lose a sense of which direction was up.

"It's cold out here, anyway," she announced. "I think I'll head inside."

"It's fifty-five degrees," Allie said. "This is like late spring in Chicago."

We did throw on heavier coats for the walk around the exterior of The Palms. Mom insisted she didn't need her cane, so Allie and I each took an arm and the three of us walked close together, laughing at how out of sync we were, like kids in a six-legged race.

Phil was finishing up in his office when we arrived, and he hugged Allie and Mom as if everything were fine. Allie looked between the two of us and back at me. I'd been vague in our weekly phone calls—*stress, problems, fighting*, as if our biggest issues were over who was going to do the dishes and whose turn it was to take out the trash.

Phil shut down his computer, waiting until the screen went black to leave his desk. "I was just about to lock up and check out the progress on a few homes in Phase 3 on my way. Would you ladies like to join me?"

I looked at Allie, who shrugged.

But Mom smiled; she was charmed by Phil's accent, the formal, almost courtly way he treated her. "Of course."

He locked the door behind us and took Mom's arm, walking her through the clubhouse toward the main exit.

Allie pointed to a flier on the community billboard. An Un-Christmas Party. "Is that like an ugly sweater party? We had one of those for the PoliSci department. Of course, most of those guys had a dozen sweaters they could have worn from their regular rotation."

I sighed. "No. This is Janet Neimeyer's big thing. She's one of our neighbors. I guess the basic idea is that everyone gets together the day after Christmas in party clothes, and brings some kind of ugly gift they received."

"Like a white elephant party?" Mom asked.

"Right. Also known as another excuse to dress up and drink."

"Sounds like fun. I'll wear my best jeans," Allie said.

"No, don't worry. We don't have to go."

Phil turned around. "I told Janet we would come. I figured after a couple of days together, you'd be dying to get out of the house."

Allie laughed. "Really? We practically have a thousand square feet each. It's not exactly a chicken coop."

"No, you kids should go," Mom said, smiling up at Phil. "I'm no good in those types of situations. I never have any idea who's talking to me."

Allie said, "Well, why not? I can borrow something of yours, can't I?" We were crossing the parking lot at this point. It was empty, save for a few cars on the far end that belonged to Parker-Lane employees.

"Please. Whatever I have would fit you like a tent."

"I guess I could borrow something from Danielle, then."

"You're killing me right now, you know that? You're actually killing me."

Allie and I slowed our pace, falling behind Phil and Mom. He was pointing out the features of the communal area, as if Mom were a potential buyer who would be making use of the tennis courts and the putting green. Allie and I linked arms, leaning against each other.

"I can't believe you're here," I said.

"I can't believe you're here," she countered. "I mean— look at this place. It's amazing. Your thousands of snarky comments didn't really do it justice."

A golf cart was coming off the last hole, rounding the little path around the clubhouse to the parking lot. We stopped for a moment, watching the twosome in their khakis and windbreakers.

"I have a confession to make," I blurted.

"Do tell."

"I've always thought that golf is a stupid sport."

Allie threw back her head and laughed so loudly that the men in the cart turned, spotting us. "I knew it. I *knew* it."

"Phil doesn't play, either—not really. He's been talking about taking lessons."

"I could see him in a lime-green polo."

I smiled weakly. "Don't forget the checkered pants."

Allie wheezed with laughter. "Stop, or I'm going to commit a public act of urination in your beautiful community."

I pulled her along. "Better not. They'll put you in the stocks."

Six of the homes in Phase 3, an entire cul-de-sac's worth, were in the final stages of completion, and two of the owners were planning to move in on New Year's Day. There was a general contractor who provided specific oversight, but Phil had taken an active role in monitoring progress and finessing the details. It had been his ongoing project for months, far more rewarding than listening to petty complaints about the club's dining room or monitoring surveillance cameras that captured grainy images of our neighbors driving by, jogging by or walking by.

The contractor was waiting for him at the first home, and the two of them splintered off to check out the tile work in an upstairs bathroom. It was a huge house, made larger by the absence of furniture and the reverberation of our voices off the mahogany floors. A strip of plastic had been taped down the middle of the hallway to serve as a walkway.

"Don't worry, Mom," Allie said. "You're not going to hit anything. You've literally got fifty feet before you run into the back wall. Just stay on the plastic."

"High ceilings," Mom commented, listening to the echo.

We stopped in the kitchen. Concrete countertops had been poured, and the white cabinets were still encased in plastic wrap.

"Very eco-chic," Allie commented, running a hand over the concrete. "Who buys one of these places, anyway? Doctors and lawyers? Who else can afford this?"

"You can't throw a stone without hitting a doctor or a lawyer around here. But also investment bankers, wealthy ex-wives, people who own real estate. And don't forget," I said, raising a finger, "high school counselors."

There were footsteps on the stairs, and we heard Phil saying, "Well, the decorator is coming in on Monday. So before we get to the actual furniture stage..."

"No, absolutely," the contractor said. "I'll get someone to come in here on Friday. That's got to be taken care of."

"Ready to hit the next one?" Phil asked, taking Mom's arm. I'd gotten so used to him not looking at me that it was strange to see him actually paying attention to other people.

"Where's the below-market-rate section?" Allie wanted to know.

The contractor laughed. "There's a three-hundred-square-foot shed you might be interested in."

"Lead the way," she said.

What amazed me during those days was how normal our lives were. We were like any other family getting together for the holidays, eating our way through a bag of red and green M&Ms one afternoon, slurping up eggnog at night. We opened gifts—a telescope for Danielle, black sweaters and tunics for Mom. Allie and I exchanged books, as we always did—our favorites from throughout the year. Phil had asked for new dress shoes, and he modeled them with his jeans rolled to his knees, making us silly with laughter. Phil's present to me was a silver necklace with tiny onyx beads, as well as a folded note, wedged in the top of the jewelry box. I unfolded it to read: *IOU. Anywhere in the world you want to go, it's on me.* I refolded the paper along its precise creases and tucked it away.

For Christmas dinner, Phil smoked a turkey outside, Mom made a pecan pie and Allie and Danielle mashed a five-pound bag of potatoes while I tackled the green vegetables. Phil moved his office junk, and we covered the folding table in the dining room with a fancy tablecloth and ate until we felt sick, the adults telling stories about our childhoods. Mom told an oldie but a goodie—the time Allie had handcuffed herself to the cafeteria service line, protesting the poor food selection. "She'd been reading about Gandhi and civil disobedience," Mom sighed. "And that was her big social stand."

"My *first* social stand," Allie corrected. "I was only four-teen, for Pete's sake. I couldn't very well protest the state of health care or trickle-down economics. I had to work with what I had."

"Oh, here we go," Phil said, refilling our glasses for the second time. He proclaimed himself a "political agnostic," but he had no problems pointing out the flaws in American systems when it suited his purpose.

Danielle reached for another helping of mashed potatoes. "Tell me a story about my mom. Did she ever do anything crazy like that?"

I held my breath, half expecting my mom to launch into the story of me arriving on their front porch at nineteen, five months pregnant. Instead, she told the story about how I'd passed high school chemistry by finding a loophole in the syllabus. Since there was no specified limit on extra credit points, I'd simply written a hundred summaries on science articles, and I'd received a B without ever passing a test or quiz.

Danielle gasped. "Mom! Why didn't you just do the as-signments?"

"Your grandmother forgot to mention that this class was ridiculously hard. It was the first time in my life I was actu-ally in danger of failing. I just found the loophole, that's all."

"A loophole that was immediately closed by the teacher," Mom said. "I was furious with Liz when he called me, but your grandfather was fine with it. He said we all have to learn to get by in the world, one way or another."

"Hear, hear," Allie said, holding out her glass for a toast.

★ ★ ★

That night, Allie and I bundled up and sat out by the pool. She told me about her courses and her students, the landlady at her crappy apartment, the guy she dated three times who turned out to be unemployed and spending his days at Starbucks for the free Wi-Fi. "And that wasn't even the deal breaker," she said over my groaning laughter. "I'd felt this immense compulsion to help him out, you know? Help him polish his résumé. Connect him with someone at the university for an interview. I would have done all of that, but when he took me back to his place, it turned out his place was shared by his ex-girlfriend, who was letting him live there rent-free. He saw absolutely nothing wrong with the situation."

"Awkward," I said.

"Extremely awkward. I'm going to put that on my next dating profile: 'I prefer only to date men with serious issues who will introduce me to uncomfortable situations.' Not a bad idea, actually. I'd get more hits, I'm sure."

"And more unemployed guys."

"I'm not getting any younger," she pointed out, unwrapping and rewrapping the blanket so that it was pulled up around the side of her head. Only her eyes and nose were visible.

I'd learned, over the years, not to say things like *Your time will come. The right guy is out there.* Those were Mom's phrases, stock sayings that rang less and less true as time went on. For a long time, Mom had complained that she'd done something wrong, having two girls who couldn't find decent men. Allie was attractive, but in a "hard edges" kind of way—a sharp gaze, a loud voice, a closet full of button-down Oxfords. She hadn't met the man who was her match. I'd always felt Mom was more relieved than happy for me when I'd introduced her to Phil. It was a validation of a normal life—no longer the single, unmarried daughter, but the family that could be displayed on a holiday card and stuck to the fridge. It made me sick to think that I might still disappoint her.

Allie could always read my mind. Her voice came from within the blanket, but I heard her clearly. Maybe I'd simply been waiting for her to ask.

"So, spill. You told me there were problems, but that seems like a bit of an understatement. Something's changed between you two. I saw how you looked when you opened his gift. And you didn't even try on the necklace. You put it right back in the box."

I shook my head.

"Come on," she said. "Haven't we always told each other everything? If you want me to hate him, I'll hate him. Say the word."

I didn't say anything. I couldn't, because the minute she'd started talking, the tears had come. And come.

"Scoot over," Allie said, and the two of us crammed into a single deck chair, hip to hip. She held me, and I cried until my lips went blubbery and numb. This was what I'd come to, then—give me a few minutes alone with Mom or Allie, and I was a wreck.

"Let it out, kid," Allie said, her hand on top of my head.

At some point, the slider opened and then, after a moment of hesitation, closed. No one had come out, and I didn't know if it was Mom or Phil or Danielle who'd come to check on us.

Janet's party was in full swing by the time we arrived. Phil wore dress pants and a gray shirt with the new tie he'd received from Danielle. I wore black pants with a silky shirt and the necklace from Phil. If he noticed the gesture, he didn't say anything. Allie had borrowed a dress from me, after all, and Danielle had tied a complicated wrap belt around her waist, gathering the excess fabric in a way that made it look less maternity and more Grecian.

Myriam's voice greeted us before we were ten steps inside the clubhouse. "Oh, Phil, I was wondering if you would…"

I took Allie's arm and steered her toward the bar. "You'll need some liquid courage to get through all the introductions."

Allie laughed. "Fill her up. You're driving, right?"

They were all there, standing in little clusters: Rich and Deanna, who had a neckline that plunged nearly to her waist; Janet and her newest boyfriend, Michael; even Jeremy and Carly Bergland, who had left the baby home with a sitter. I pointed them out sotto voce while Allie marveled.

"It's like a collection of the world's most beautiful people."

I groaned. "Please don't tell them that. They don't need any more encouragement."

Allie got a few curious stares herself, especially at the snake tattoo that wrapped its way around her wiry upper arm.

At the bar, Charlie Zhang was refilling Helen's glass.

"How is everyone, Charlie?" I asked.

He shrugged. "I thought it would be a good idea to get the kids a new dog for Christmas. Who are we kidding, anyway? It's been a month. Virgil isn't coming back. But Helen's taken it pretty badly. That dog was her life."

"It's so strange," I said, accepting my glass from the bartender. "I would have thought there would have been some sign of him by now."

"The best-case scenario is that he ran off and one of the ranchers took him in, although of course Helen canvassed that whole area with fliers. Still, that's the hope." He shoved a twenty in the tip jar and walked away.

"Their dog went missing," I explained to Allie.

"I gathered as much."

Janet Neimeyer was behind us suddenly, dripping with jewels. "Liz, dear. Who's this?"

"My sister, Allie, from Chicago."

Allie held out a hand, and Janet hugged her instead, bracelets jingling off her leathery arms. "We're all family here, you know. All family. And we keep things in the family, too."

Allie and I exchanged smiles. It was her own party, so why not get hammered if she wanted to?

Janet leaned forward. "I'm talking about the Asbills, of course. Didn't you hear?"

I shook my head.

"It turns out that Brock has been—how can I put this delicately—shtupping the nanny. Oh, my dears. The plates that were thrown, the names that were called. Be happy you're over on your end of the cul-de-sac, let me tell you." She set down an empty glass of wine and picked up a full one.

"How is that even possible?" I asked. "Daisy was always there. I thought she wasn't working anymore."

Janet raised an eyebrow. "A girl has to go to town sometimes."

"But they're here." We'd just passed them talking to Deanna, and nothing had seemed amiss.

"Well, it's yesterday's news by now. The girl's on a plane back to Colombia, of course, and Daisy's beginning to wonder if she can't just take care of those kids on her own. Never trust the help, I say. Not that I think Brock's a catch, mind you, but the things that Brock's money can buy, now, that's another story." She took a half step away, stumbling and catching herself on Allie's arm. "Now where's that yummy husband of yours?"

"He was talking to Myriam."

She patted me on the arm. "Don't you worry. I'll go rescue him."

Allie laughed into her gin and tonic. "I don't even know where to start with all that. The *nanny*. Isn't that so stereotypical?"

I laughed, too, but I couldn't take any joy in the ridiculousness of it. I felt bad for Daisy. Did she feel trapped now, mother to twins who were barely walking, wife to a man who'd gone for the low-hanging fruit? In the end, I hadn't told Allie anything about Phil, the gut suspicions I hadn't been able to prove. That would be a stereotype, too—the younger neighbor, akin to the babysitter, the subordinate, the secretary. It would be the kind of thing people laughed about at parties like this one. The Janet Neimeyers of the world wouldn't be able to stop themselves from spreading it, ear to ear.

"Well, hello, stranger," someone said, and I turned around to see Fran grinning at me. "Doug's home with Elijah for the night, so I figured…"

I gave her a one-armed hug, careful not to slosh her with my drink. I'd never seen Fran wearing anything other than cargo pants with a zillion pockets and her sturdy white shoes. "You look fantastic."

She beamed and twirled, her burgundy dress fanning out like a flamenco dancer's. "Every now and then, I guess."

"This is my sister, Allie."

They shook hands, and Fran leaned in close. "I'm not doing that ridiculous gift exchange. I'm here for the entertainment aspect only. Last year there was some sort of scuffle

between Deanna and Janet that almost ended in hair pulling. Although if that happens again, Doug will be sorry to
miss it."

"It is just like the *Real Housewives*," Allie marveled when
Fran moved along to greet Carly Bergland. "I feel like an an-
thropology student trying to figure out the cultural norms."

"That's how I felt at first. But it's far less rewarding than
you might think."

"I can see how it would get old."

We clinked glasses and moved toward the dance floor.
Deanna and Rich were the only ones dancing. She had her
head on his shoulder, and he was holding a tumbler of whis-
key in one hand, his other hand on her back. They were
laughing.

Tim and Sonia Jorgensen passed by, their heads above the
crowd. Sonia gave me a cool nod, and I told Allie, "The tall
couple? Heading toward the bar? Those are Kelsey's parents."

"Want me to beat them up?"

"Could you please?"

Allie took a mock step in their direction and wobbled on
her borrowed shoes, a half size too big. She grabbed my arm.
"Actually, can we sit somewhere? The last time I wore a pair
of heels, I was interviewing for my job."

We found two club chairs next to the Browerses, who
looked less than enchanted with the whole scene. I asked
about their Christmas, and Marja told me they were leaving
in the morning for a cruise with her sister and brother-in-
law. "I'm planning to walk the deck a hundred times a day,"
she told me. "And that will be my justification for eating
everything at the buffet."

"It sounds like an excellent plan," I told her. "Although if
it were me, I'd probably just skip the walking."

Marja smiled. "You're young. You can still do that."

A few more couples were dancing—the Berglands, the Roche-Edwardses, two men I recognized from Phase 2. I got up to refresh our drinks and when I returned, found Victor Mesbah in my seat, leaning in close to Allie. When he saw me, he excused himself.

I handed Allie her drink. "What was that?"

She grinned. "Apparently, he heard I was an *intellectual*. That was his word. He said he's always interested in meeting other *intellectuals*."

"He likes to ride around in a golf cart with a shotgun," I told her.

"A Renaissance man, then."

"You should be flattered. He certainly doesn't consider me his intellectual equal."

We were laughing when the commotion started. The music was loud near the dance floor, so at first it didn't sound like more than voices raised to hear each other over the beat. Then Myriam raced by, cell phone in her hand.

Allie set her drink on the carpet and braced herself against the chair to get to her feet. "We're missing the fight, I think."

Rich called, "What now? Haven't we had enough excitement for a while?"

I looked around for Phil. Carly Bergland was on her phone, too, saying, "Just keep the kids inside, no matter how much they beg..." Our eyes met. "What do you mean, Hannah isn't there?"

Allie was right behind me as we made our way out the clubhouse doors, skirting around the Browerses. Fran Blevins was suddenly beside us, moving efficiently even without her tennis shoes. "It's a house fire," she said, breathless.

But by that point, we could smell it—a bitterness that

hung in the air, scorching our nostrils. In the dark, people were milling around, shadowy shapes in fancy, impractical shoes. Allie and I shed our heels halfway across the parking lot. Wordless, I pointed at an orange flame, its tongue licking the night sky. Black smoke had blocked out the stars.

"Oh, my God," Allie said. "It's one of the new houses."

My throat went tight.

"Isn't it? That's where we were yesterday."

I couldn't answer. I was running by now, panting, smoke searing my lungs. We crossed one block, then another, cutting across the Asbills' lawn, through the Jorgensens' driveway. It seemed like half the residents of The Palms were there already. They stood in the middle of the cul-de-sac, flames crackling fifty yards away.

The entire house was engulfed, red flames leaping inside the windows.

Someone was screaming. Around us, everyone was talking, their words coming in snatches over the popping of wooden beams.

"Get a hose! Buckets, something!"

"The water hasn't been turned on out here."

"At least no one's living there. They were supposed to—"

"Who called 911?"

"It's going to take twenty minutes for a fire engine to get out here."

"At least it's not windy. The Asbills have their pool house right behind the fence."

Allie was gripping my arm, her short nails digging into my flesh. We hadn't brought our coats, but the air was warm, as though we were roasting ourselves over a spit. She pointed through the crowd. "There's Phil."

He was standing off to the side by himself, hands in his pockets. His face reflected the flickering light.

Someone said, "The Zhang boys called 911. They were playing tennis and smelled the smoke."

"Probably some kind of wiring problem."

"There's been people working on this house all week. I thought it was almost done."

Allie asked if I had my phone. I shook my head.

"We should go check on Mom," she said. "She's going to freak out if she hears those sirens."

I nodded. "Let me tell Phil we're going."

He didn't see me until I was right next to him, waving my hand in his line of vision.

"Allie and I are going home," I said. "We're going to tell Mom and Danielle what's going on."

He stared at me blankly.

"There's nothing you can do, Phil. The fire department will be here soon."

"There was nothing I could do," he repeated.

I touched him on the arm. It was the most intimate gesture that had passed between us in weeks. "Don't do anything stupid." I meant it as a joke, but when he didn't react, I shook him by the shirtsleeve. "Seriously. Let the firefighters do their jobs, and come home. Okay?"

There was a crashing sound, and I turned to see that the roof over the front of the house had collapsed, wood and materials splintering. Black smoke poured through the hole. It was impossible to look away.

Allie was calling for me, and I joined her. My upper body was flushed, but my feet were freezing in my black tights. More people were pouring into the cul-de-sac as we left.

The Jorgensens, with Kelsey behind them, Brock and Daisy, Janet. We were on our lawn when we heard the sirens.

Mom was waiting at the front door. "What's going on?"

"There's a house fire," I said. "Where's Danielle?"

"I'm here," Danielle called from the top of the stairs. "Whose house is it?

"One of the empty ones," Allie called. "Mom, it's the one we walked through yesterday. It's so bizarre."

"Horrible," Mom said. "That beautiful house? What a waste."

The four of us walked back to the fire a few minutes later, after Allie and I had changed clothes. Two engines had arrived by then, and the cul-de-sac was crawling with firefighters in yellow reflective suits. They'd pushed the crowd back to the other side of the street. Most of the onlookers were still in their party clothes, the women shivering now that they were away from the warmth. The general consensus was that it was horrible, another example of shoddy workmanship at Parker-Lane.

Not spotting Phil, I walked through the crowd. Victor was shooting a video with his phone. "Have you seen my husband?"

He jerked his head slightly in the direction of the clubhouse. "On the phone with his boss, I'm guessing."

When I rejoined Allie and Mom, Danielle was standing off to one side, watching water pour onto the flames with Hannah Bergland. I gripped Mom's arm tightly, and she reached up with her other hand, feeling along my face.

"I want to tell you something," she said into my ear.

I leaned down so I could hear her better.

"Danielle left the house for a while," she said.

I froze. "What do you mean? I thought the two of you were watching TV."

"I wasn't following the story, so I went into my bedroom to listen to a book on CD. But I heard your alarm, the one that tells you what door is open."

"It told you a door was open?"

"Right. It said, 'Front door open.' And I called for Danielle, but she didn't come. Then about ten minutes later she was back, because I heard the alarm again."

I didn't say anything.

"Oh, I know I'm an old fuddy-duddy. I just thought I'd tell you."

"Tell you what?" Allie asked. "What are you two whispering about?"

I shook my head. To Mom I said, "You don't have to worry about it. She has friends here, Mom."

"I was only surprised," she said. "I figured she would have told me if she was going to leave."

It's nothing, it's nothing, it's nothing. I repeated the words to myself, tears smarting my eyes. It wasn't just the smoke, of course. It was everything in my life falling apart, more of a slow burn than this fire, but a wreck nonetheless. The nightmare that was Phil, a horror I kept myself from fully imagining. Then there was Danielle, absent twice now during disasters in the community. I spotted her with Hannah, the two of them turned away from the fire. A cell phone screen glowed between them, and they were laughing.

Of course not.

But then again, maybe.

PHIL

Jacob Fitch laughed at first, thinking it must be a joke. He hadn't been getting it all along. And then he saw my face and he asked, "What, she actually burned down a house?"

"She burned down a house," I repeated.

"And you know it was her? You can prove it?"

I hadn't told him about meeting her at that house, about my threat relating to her father. It was the best move I had, but she'd called my bluff. "Of course not," I said. "She's too smart for that."

"Come on, she's what? Sixteen. A sixteen-year-old isn't smart enough to get away with arson."

He didn't understand. He hadn't understood from the start. Kelsey Jorgensen got away with everything, based on the premise that someone so young, so entitled and so attractive would never do the things she did.

"If this is true, man—if it's true—" He leaned back in his chair, shaking his head.

"It's true," I told him. I hadn't seen Kelsey since the night of the fire, when she'd stood in the flickering glow between her parents. I'd been waiting for my email to ping, delivering the selfie she'd snapped with the burning house as a back-drop. I'd scanned the video feed a thousand times, looking for her, before turning it over to investigators. Worried that she'd left a message inside the house, I'd donned a hard hat and walked through the damage with the inspector, half expecting to see my name sprayed across the wall in giant blue letters. PHIL McGINNIS IS A PEDOPHILE. But there had been nothing. Half the neighborhood turned out for the demolition and debris removal, but Kelsey wasn't there.

The thing was—I no longer needed physical evidence. I knew, deep down, that she was capable.

But I could see Fitch's hesitation, his appraising glance. He'd been willing to go along with a lot of things—the photos, the vandalism, the skinny-dipping in my pool, but I could sense him reevaluating the situation now. Was I really so special that a teenager would become obsessed with me, that she would commit a felony that could land her in jail?

No, of course I wasn't. But that was part of her sickness.

"If it's true, you have to call the police," he said.

"Better yet," I told him, "I'm getting out of there. I'm getting the three of us out of there. I have a plan."

Fitch shook his head, almost admiringly. "This is just so wild. You know what it's like? That movie, the one where Glenn Close shows up in the bathroom with that knife. What's it—"

"Fatal Attraction," I supplied.

"Right." He considered this. "And all because the guy had this meaningless affair."

I stood up. It would be my last visit to Jacob Fitch. He'd never been interested in supplying me with legal advice. He'd listened to my story like it was a weekly podcast, on edge for the next titillating detail. He was a voyeur of my personal hell. "Except the difference is, I didn't have an affair," I reminded him.

On the way home, I thought about that movie, too. Glenn Close had been robbed of that Oscar—the thought of her in those final scenes terrified me even now, more than twenty years later. Of course, that movie hadn't ended with Glenn Close's character killing anyone. She'd ended up dead herself, shot in the heart.

After the fire, the *Contra-Costa Times* ran an article about The Palms. The newspaper was delivered each morning by a mother-son team in a falling-apart green Civic, but that morning the paper seemed to have arrived by divine circumstance. The photo accompanying the article showed the temporary orange cyclone fence that had been installed around the perimeter of the home's blackened remains, a sort of modern-day House of Usher. It looked like a biohazard site rather than a community where the homes started at a million-five.

I flattened the paper against the kitchen counter and read:

Community on Alert after Renewed Safety Concerns at The Palms

A series of problems at The Palms, a luxury home development on the outskirts of Livermore, has residents on edge. Last fall, reports of a mountain lion in the area, followed by rumors of vandalism in the community clubhouse, prompted San Jose–based builder Parker-Lane Homes to invest in state-of-the-art video surveillance.

Now a recent fire has destroyed a new home in the

community, and residents are speaking out against the builder.

"We've got security gates and cameras, but more and more, when I walk through this community, I don't know that I feel safe at all," said resident Helen Zhang, whose dog, an elite-bred Bedlington Terrier, went missing from her fenced backyard in November.

"There's a certain amount of expectation you have, moving into a home like this in a place like this," said Rich Sievert, one of the first residents of The Palms. "Now I find myself wondering if it's all just a myth."

Sievert's residence is not far from the site of the new home that burned on December 26, shortly before its owners were set to move in. That owner, Mark Hassan, has since vacated his arrangement with Parker-Lane Homes. Hassan said that the "overall quality of workmanship was not as promised" and that he believed the "integrity of the building process was compromised." The Hassans are now looking at a home in a gated community near Pleasanton, offered by a rival luxury home builder.

Early indications do point to a cause of faulty electrical wiring, but that hasn't stopped residents from speculating. Janet Neimeyer, who walks past the ravaged home site daily, believes that lax security has allowed too many nonresidents into the community. "It's horrible to look at people and wonder, does someone have a bone to pick with us? Is my house going to be next?"

Jeff Parker, vice president of development for Parker-Lane, is taking steps to reassure residents, beginning with a series of town-hall-style meetings to address specific concerns. "We've already installed state-of-the-art video surveillance equipment, and this spring we'll be offering a series of safety workshops to our residents and focusing on improving our on-site emergency equipment."

Myriam Mesbah, chairman of the homeowners' association, believes this is not enough. "People are disgruntled. We pay thousands a month in fees, and it's hard not to wonder if we're throwing that money down the drain."

Asked if he believes a home in The Palms is still a good investment, Parker noted rising home values in the area, including the lot recently damaged by fire. As early as the end of the month, that lot will be back on the market for a higher premium than before.

The article was written by someone named Andrea Piccola, and I looked hard at the thumbnail of her picture—a white face overwhelmed by thick, dark hair. She must have been out here, going door-to-door, interviewing the neighbors. Somehow she'd missed talking to me. It was just as well—I knew nothing about the planned town hall meetings or the safety workshops.

Parker-Lane wanted me out, and fast. When I asked Jeff Parker for a letter of recommendation, he didn't hesitate. His praise was effusive, the letter full of statements he might have thought about me six months ago but had now been seriously called into doubt. His message was clear—get out, and get out soon.

I intended to do just that.

I'd made it through the first round of phone interviews with a builder in Los Angeles and knew I was a shoo-in for the job. The company vice president had ended up chatting with me for forty-five minutes after the official conference call. When I'd mentioned that I'd lived on Corfu—emphasizing myself as less of a co-owner of my brother's bar and more of an entrepreneur—he'd told me a story of his gap year, a crazy weekend on the island. I could picture him there, blond and tanned, alcohol leaking through his pores. I might have made his dinner. I might have sprayed his vomit off the bathroom floor. Life was funny like that.

The second interview would be in LA. My plan was to drive to Oakland, take a midmorning flight, interview in the early afternoon, allow myself to be wined and dined around town and fly back the next morning. I told Liz only that I had a meeting in San Jose with Parker-Lane, and that if it went late, I would spend the night. She didn't need to know anything about the new job until it was officially mine. And if I was lucky, I wouldn't have to tell her everything—but it was all there, the files I'd saved on my laptop, the Kelsey Jorgensen saga, *A* to *Z*.

Allie and Liz's mom were leaving that same morning as my interview, so my plan was to beat them out the door. We said our goodbyes the night before—a stiff, formal hug from Allie, while Liz's mom held me as if it were the last time we would ever see each other. I nearly blurted that we would be seeing her soon—a perk of moving to Southern California that Liz couldn't deny.

I was walking out the front door with my briefcase in hand when Kelsey pulled up in her silver Acura, a gift for her sixteenth birthday. Oversize sunglasses shielded her face even though it was only 7:00 a.m., the sun a thin wisp breaking through gray clouds. She stopped her car behind mine and rolled down the passenger window. "Where are you going?"

"Meeting," I said.

"Meeting where?"

"I'm running a bit late, Kelsey, if you don't mind." I opened the car door and set the briefcase on the passenger seat, hoping she would take the hint and leave.

"Meeting where?" she called again.

I sighed. "Seattle." Why did she deserve the truth? *Get away from me*, I thought, *you crazy, crazy bitch.*

She waited, car idling. What would she do when I was gone, when Liz and Danielle and I packed up our belongings and left her, once and for all? I had a horrible fleeting certainty that she would find me there, too, wherever I ended up—that one day I would step out of our new place and Kelsey would be waiting.

"Move your car," I ordered.

She didn't respond. It was unnerving to see the hard set of my jaw reflected in her sunglasses.

I looked around—no one was out. The early runners were already back home, drinking their wheat-grass smoothies. The ladies who brunched wouldn't appear for hours.

"When are you coming back?" she asked.

I jingled my keys. "Maybe never, if I like it." I admit—I loved watching her eyes widen, her mouth go slack.

"You wouldn't leave," she said, like a dare. "Not for good."

I walked closer to her car, leaned one arm against the roof as if we were having a friendly chat. If Deanna looked out her window right now, that was what she would see. "I don't have a lot of choice anymore," I told her. "Not after the house fire, you see. It seems I'm not the right person for this job."

Her face was blank, her eyes unreadable behind the sunglasses.

"Now get away from my fucking driveway before I back into you," I said, straightening. By the time I'd started my car and glanced at the rearview mirror, she was gone.

JUNE 19, 2015

6:57 P.M.

LIZ

"It was a stupid idea," Danielle said. She wasn't looking at me, but down at her hands resting nervously on her skinny knees.

But I already knew that. How could it be anything other than a stupid idea, when we'd all but signed our lives away to the Jorgensens, when my name had been in the paper, accusations whispered from the lips of everyone I knew?

Danielle sighed. "We made this fake Twitter page. Well, Hannah did. She's really good at that. She took some kind of independent study in computers and she can do all the back-end stuff, you know?"

I asked what was on the page, although I was fairly sure I knew—at least the tenor, the tone. It had been months since Danielle's humiliation at Winter Formal, but of course that hurt wasn't gone. It had just been dormant, waiting for the right moment.

"So, Hannah made a mock MLHS Stories page, and we put up this fake picture of Kelsey. It was pretty bad."

"What picture?"

Danielle closed her eyes. "It was Kelsey's face on this naked woman. She was really fat and—just, unattractive."

"That's horrible. No matter what she did, that's horrible."

"It was just a fake page! But we made up all these accounts with comments under it. We were going to show it to her, like it was real. We just wanted to freak her out. I mean, after everything she did to us..."

"So you invited her over?"

"Hannah did. Yeah."

"I saw Kelsey earlier today. She came up to me when I was working in the garage, and I sent her away."

Danielle ran her palms over her legs. She was sweating, I realized, even though I was blasting the air conditioner. "I guess she went around to the back. But we didn't know! She was supposed to text when she was there and I was going to let her in. We were waiting for her upstairs and Hannah was adding this animated thing to the site."

I massaged my temple with my right hand. "Who else knew about this?"

"No one. Me and Hannah."

"It's on your laptop?"

"Yeah. Hannah's parents check hers like crazy. She can't even—"

"When we get home," I told her, "you're going to delete it. Do you understand? You need to erase it off your hard drive."

"But it has nothing to do with—"

"Danielle! You're going to delete it."

"Okay," she said, chastened. "Fine."

I pulled back onto the road, the headache that had been a fine pulsation beginning to throb, as if it were keeping time with my heartbeat.

JANUARY 2015
LIZ

The stench from the fire lingered for days—sharp and acrid, stinging my nostrils. Even the omnipresent sprinklers couldn't quench it. All but the most hard-core runners took a few days off; the Zhang boys didn't even go near the tennis courts. But still, we kept visiting the sight of the burned home, singly and in pairs, gathering in little clumps to marvel at what was left.

Allie and Mom left the day after New Year's. It had been the plan all along, but when their bags and odds and ends were placed by the front door, it felt way too soon, as if circumstances had ripped us apart. "I want to drive by that house one more time on our way out of here," Allie told Mom, and I understood—there was something magnetic about it, something that demanded a mute, compulsive obedience. Mom was still shaking her head at the waste of it— the beautiful home she'd never seen, reduced to beams and pieces.

"All it takes is a bit of faulty wiring, I guess," she said. "One bad connection."

I didn't believe in the electrical wiring theory that was circulating. A burning house was just a more extreme manifestation of a vandalized bathroom or holes kicked in walls. I'd waited until after Allie and Mom had been gone half an hour, long enough to ensure that they wouldn't come racing back inside for something left behind, a phone charger or a pair of shoes. Phil had left early that morning, too, briefcase in hand, off for an emergency meeting with Parker-Lane. I wondered if he would come home without a job, if Parker-Lane would give us at least a month to get settled somewhere else. When Danielle came out of the shower, a towel wrapped around her body, I was waiting on her bed.

She froze when she saw me, her hair flicking water droplets onto her shoulders. "What?"

"I know you left the house the night of the fire."

"Yeah, with you. Remember?"

"Before that," I said.

She turned her back to me, carefully sliding on a T-shirt and shimmying into a pair of underpants behind the modesty of her towel. "I was home with Gram. We were watching TV."

"She went to her room, and she heard you leave the house and come back about ten minutes later."

Danielle whirled around. "And she told you that?"

"She was worried."

She yanked open a dresser drawer to grab a pair of jeans and jammed it closed unevenly. "I didn't realize I was still under house arrest. Okay, I left for a few minutes. I was at an orgy across the street."

"Very funny."

She sighed, exasperated. "Hannah left her iPod here, and I brought it back."

"Except Hannah was gone, too," I said, remembering the snatch of Carly Bergland's conversation that I'd heard on my way out of the clubhouse.

"Yeah, I met her outside her house. It's too noisy to talk in there." She pulled on her jeans, the fabric sliding easily over her slim hips and turned, watching me watch her. "What is this? Now you think I'm an arsonist or something? First it was the bathrooms, and now this?"

"I didn't say anything about arson. I asked where you went," I said evenly. "And at first you lied and said you didn't go anywhere."

"What do you want—my alibi? Okay. Hannah was there, and her million brothers and sisters, and some babysitter for the little ones. They were watching *A Christmas Story*, you know, that stupid movie with the little kid with the big glasses. Maybe you can dust their doorbell for my fingerprints. Go ahead, start the investigation!"

I picked up a sweatshirt from the pile on the floor, the one she'd been wearing that night. It smelled vaguely like smoke—although to be fair, everything smelled like smoke, beginning with the inside of my nostrils. "It seems like a bit of a coincidence, that's all."

"That doesn't even make sense. You were gone, too, and Aunt Allie and Phil. Maybe one of you set the fire."

"Danielle."

"This is unbelievable! I don't even understand you. It's like you think the worst of me, all the time. One time I made a mistake. I was grounded and everything, but it's like you want me to keep paying for it. And it's not like you've never made a mistake. I know that. I'm here, aren't I?"

"Stop. Stop it right now." I was on my feet, and she was dodging my approach. "You were not a mistake."

Her laugh was more like a shriek. "What's the politically correct term, then? A blessing in disguise?"

"Come on," I said. "I asked you a simple question—"

"It wasn't a simple question! And I had to lie, because if I didn't, you would think what you were already thinking, anyway."

"Danielle. Come on, let's talk," I said, but she sidestepped me and ran into the bathroom, locking the door behind her.

I waited outside her bathroom door for a long time, growing worried at the silence behind it. "Open up, so I know you're okay," I ordered her. "I'm not kidding. I'll break the door down if I have to."

The lock turned and she was there, glaring at me. "Fine. As you can see, I'm just peachy."

I was downstairs, staring at a pile of last night's dishes, when I heard the sirens. Danielle met me in the hallway, and we stared at each other.

My God, I thought. Whose house was it this time?

We made it to the front lawn by the time the ambulance passed, its red strobe light bouncing off surfaces, catching us in its glare. Deanna was on the sidewalk in a bathrobe, her hair flat and lifeless. Helen Zhang, dogless, hurried past. We exchanged wordless glances. *What now?*

The ambulance had stopped in front of the Jorgensens' house. A crowd was assembling on their curb, like mourners at a prayer vigil. The Zhang boys joined us. Carly Bergland was there, her baby slung around her neck in a sort of miniature hammock. Behind us, the soft whirr of wheels on the asphalt announced the arrival of Fran, pushing Elijah.

The paramedics hurried into the Jorgensens' house, leaving the door gaping open. It was funny, but after all the open houses and jewelry parties, after all the mornings I'd picked up Kelsey and all the afternoons I'd dropped her off, this was my furthest glance into the Jorgensens' lives.

"Maybe I should go in there," Deanna said, next to me. "To see if they need anything. It's just that I'm feeling so sick. I have this awful cold…"

We ignored her. What did she think she could do, exactly? What services could she offer?

"Whose car is that in the driveway, next to Tim's?" Helen asked.

Danielle whispered, "Kelsey's." No one else heard her.

"We don't know anything," I told her. "It could just be…" But I couldn't find a satisfactory way to finish the thought, and my voice trailed off.

Deanna said, "This is killing me. I need to find out what's going on." She had just started down the sidewalk despite our feeble protests when the paramedics came out, a stretcher rolling between them. There was a collective moan—we recognized that blond hair hanging over the side, even if the face was obscured by an oxygen bag, quick puffs of air being dispensed into her mouth.

Danielle and I looked at each other, and she grabbed my arm with a clammy hand. Tears pooled in her eyes.

Sonia was right behind them, wearing jeans and slip-on tennis shoes, her face tear-streaked. I took a half step back. It was the closest we'd been since the day she stormed into my office.

Deanna ran toward her. "What happened?"

"We found her that way," Sonia sobbed into Deanna's bathrobe.

Tim came out of the house then, holding Sonia's giant shoulder bag and a set of keys. "Come on, let's go now. We don't have time to stand here talking." He took Sonia by the elbow and they exchanged a few words with the paramedics before getting into his sedan.

We watched stupidly, silently, as the ambulance did a three-point turn in the cul-de-sac, lights flashing. Through the back windows, we could see the paramedic bending over Kelsey, her bare feet upright. The siren resumed as the ambulance rounded the corner, the Jorgensens on their tail. I imagined the gates opening slowly, so slowly, the way they always did, before the ambulance could emerge into the outside world. No one said anything until the siren faded completely, not even a strand of sound floating back to us.

Helen said, "It's just like last year."

I turned. "What do you mean? What happened last year?"

She pursed her lips. "I shouldn't say."

I stared at her. I'd never noticed before how pinched Helen's face was, how tight and disapproving. "Why shouldn't you say?"

Carly adjusted the baby in its sling. "Helen, for goodness' sakes. Last year, Kelsey took some pills—"

Deanna stepped in front of Carly. "Sonia wouldn't want us talking about this! She told us these things in confidence."

"She didn't tell *me* in confidence," Carly said. "It was all over Ashbury."

"Did you know about this?" I asked Danielle.

"A little bit," she said.

"She took some pills, and she made some crazy claims, and they yanked her right out of that school," Carly said. To me she added, "That's why I don't like Hannah hanging around her."

Deanna said, "Carly! She was a friend of your daughter's. And we don't even know what's happened now. She could be dead. How would you feel if you were standing here spouting off these things and it turned out she was dead?"

Next to me Danielle began crying in earnest. Her hand was gummy in mine.

"That's enough," someone said. It was Fran, on the outside of the group, the voice of reason. "It's no good to stand here speculating. Deanna, why don't you give Sonia a call in a while and see what you can find out, if there's anything they need. We should be thinking about how we can help them, not stirring up trouble."

At home, Danielle went straight upstairs, slamming her bedroom door behind her. I stood inside our entryway for a long moment, listening to the silence, before heading over to Fran's house. She talked to me while she fed Elijah, a giant navy bib tucked to cover his entire torso. He submitted to the spoon reluctantly, looking off to the side.

"I don't know all the specifics," Fran said when I asked about the incident Carly had referred to. "Something about Kelsey and a teacher at her school. It would have been a big scandal, but the Jorgensens are good at keeping things hushed up. Must be all his training as a lawyer."

"Are you talking about an inappropriate relationship?"

"That's a nice way to say it. I don't know the details, mind you. Just that it got pretty ugly, and it ended with Kelsey swallowing a bottle of pills. It was like déjà vu all over again, hearing those sirens and seeing her get wheeled away. The weird thing is, Elijah doesn't mind the sound. Maybe it's the lights—I don't know." She swiped the edge of the spoon against Elijah's mouth, scraping off the excess. "I wonder if something like that is going on again. An older guy, taking advantage. But I guess you'd know if that was happening at her school."

I inhaled sharply.

Straightening, she looked up at me. "Are you feeling okay?"

I shook my head. "I think just...the shock of everything. I should go."

Outside, I steadied myself with my hands on my knees, ready to lean over and retch into the low bushes that marked the division of our properties.

Kelsey's suicide attempt was the talk of The Palms that weekend. Deanna got in touch with Sonia, then spread the news of Kelsey's near-tragedy throughout the community with her customary indiscretion. Apparently Kelsey had taken a bottle of over-the-counter sleeping pills sometime that morning, and Sonia and Tim had found her in the bathroom, passed out next to the toilet. She'd vomited some of the pills, which meant that she was out of the woods by the time the paramedics arrived. By Monday, Kelsey would be transferred to a "private hospital," Deanna told me, putting air quotes around the words. "Of course," she concluded, "I'm only telling this to the people who know Kelsey and care about her."

I wasn't sure I fit both of those conditions, but I said, "Of course."

Deanna shuddered. "And right after New Year's. I mean, just the *symbolism* of it."

"I think the reality is somewhat worse than the symbolism," I commented.

She took a step back, as if I'd slapped her. "Well, obviously, Liz. I only meant... Never mind. Just, never mind, then."

I watched her walk down the sidewalk, heading not back to her own home, but in the direction of the Zhangs and the Mesbahs, no doubt reveling in her privileged position of knowledge. There was a dark, horrible part of me that wanted to slip some crushed sleeping pills into whatever it was that Deanna drank—some mango or acai berry concoction, a pomegranate margarita.

And maybe I'd fix one for myself, too. Phil hadn't come home the night before, calling late to say that his meeting would be continued in the morning. At least I knew he wasn't with Kelsey; the two of them weren't holed up together in a love nest. Was that still an expression? I thought again of the website for the law firm he'd been looking at, the brief flash that was there and gone when he'd closed the screen, and suddenly I doubted very much that he'd been chatting with Parker-Lane.

When he called from wherever he was, I told him the news about Kelsey Jorgensen. He was quiet for so long that I thought maybe he had hung up.

"Did you hear me? She took some sleeping pills. They had to pump her stomach."

"This morning?" he asked.

"Yeah, this morning."

"It's horrible," he said finally. "It's absolutely horrible."

After that, neither of us had anything to say.

Danielle kept to herself that weekend. On Sunday night, I found her sitting next to her bed with the lights out, listening to the ukulele version of "Over the Rainbow." A few years ago, she'd burned a CD with the song playing on an endless loop, but now it struck me as so sad—a desperate yearning for trouble to melt like lemon drops.

At one point I put a blanket around her shoulders and found her glassy-eyed, tears melted on her cheeks.

"Is it because of me?" she asked.

"Why would you say that?"

"I mean, I just stopped talking to her after what happened at Winter Formal. And I was her friend. Maybe I could have helped her. Maybe she just needed someone to talk to."

"No," I said, kneading Danielle's shoulders with my thumb. "No, baby. Don't think that way. We don't know what she was thinking. Maybe it was completely unrelated to all of that."

"But I never even answered her texts."

I remembered what Fran had told me about Kelsey—the inappropriate relationship, the sleeping pills. I'd been turning it over in my mind since that conversation. Had another "inappropriate relationship" ended, causing her to attempt suicide again?

"She told me that she took some pills last spring, but she said it was no big deal, that she wasn't trying to hurt herself," Danielle said. "It was all over some guy, I guess. Her boyfriend."

The song wound down, the plaintive question dying out: *Why, oh, why, can't I?* The final chords faded, the room was quiet and then there was a faint buzz of static before the song began again.

Danielle's voice came thick with tears. "I just feel so horrible…"

I rubbed her shoulder through the blanket. "It sounds like she's had problems for a long time, and now she can get some professional help."

I felt pretty horrible myself. I was a counselor, for God's sake—I was trained to see when there was something wrong, to recognize a person in a fragile state. I'd dismissed Kelsey

Jorgensen as manipulative at best, a home wrecker at worst. But she was only sixteen, still a kid in many ways and a troubled one at that.

Over the years, I'd counseled a number of traumatized students. At first, they'd been hesitant to tell me what was wrong, but after a few minutes, the floodgates usually opened and it all came spilling out—the abusive boyfriends, the unemployed parents, the threats and bullying. My first year at MLHS, I'd had a girl come in—Cassie, a name that still weighed on me—and I hadn't asked the right questions. She'd wanted to know how to prevent a pregnancy, and I'd given her a pamphlet and information for a local clinic and sent her on her way. I still wondered: if I'd called her in every week, if I'd talked to her parents, would she have ended up pregnant at fourteen, the father a nineteen-year-old friend of her older brother?

In the same way, I couldn't stop thinking about Kelsey. Had I missed the signs that Kelsey was crying for help, dismissing them as the silly behavior of a self-absorbed teenage girl? I didn't have all the facts, of course—until she was being loaded into the ambulance, I'd never heard about a previous suicide attempt or a relationship with a teacher. And I'd never been able to prove a relationship with Phil, although I believed it, deep down.

Still, as a counselor—I'd failed.

I'd struck out with his laptop months before, but I'd never tried his phone. As soon as he was asleep, I tiptoed around to his side of the bed and took the phone off his nightstand. I was quiet on the stairs, and I sat on the couch in the den in the dark, startled by the outline of my reflection in the wall of windows. That other Liz, the shadow one, would have been shocked to see what I was doing.

Phil hadn't changed the password to his phone—it was the street address of our old house, our first house together. When I keyed in 1-5-2-7, the phone came to life. He'd configured his phone to receive his work emails, and I went there first. It was horrible, like peeking inside his personnel file. As I worked my way backward, I saw emails that were short and snappish, that all but blamed Phil himself for the house fire and the vandalism in the clubhouse, that ordered him to keep everyone calm about the mountain lion. When he'd been hired last summer, the tone had been more friendly. It wasn't hard to see that he was on his way out, that the bloom was off the rose. He would need more than the old Aussie charm to buy him more time.

His personal email account was there, too. It was a shitty thing to do, but not hard to rationalize. Sure, I would have been upset if he went through my email—but I had nothing to hide other than the odd credit card receipt for a new pair of shoes that he never would have noticed on his own. No, this was the noncheating spouse's prerogative, to find the evidence and be able to plan an action, or to be reassured that nothing was going on, after all. His inbox was a collection of emails from his brother, Zeke, in Corfu—mostly chitchat. There were a few mentions in his recent emails about looking for another job, or as he put it, keeping his options open. What options were those, and did they include Danielle and me?

Scrolling through his folders, I found one called "Legal." I clicked on it, heart pounding. The messages were all from Montgomery, Lahovary & Fitch—the website he'd been browsing in December, when he hadn't been able to minimize the screen fast enough. I opened each of the emails, but they were all administrative—appointment reminders and receipts. Apparently Phil had been meeting an attorney every other week for months, tossing down three and four hundred dollars each time.

A divorce attorney. What else could it be?

I clicked on the icon for his texts. They were mostly from me, quick, impersonal notes about dinner and groceries and reminders, the to-do lists that comprised the backbone of a marriage. They were just short bursts of language, but I could read the coolness in my voice, in my "picking up pizza" and "almost home." There were texts between him and Danielle, and those were more personable—smiley-face emoticons and inside jokes.

I saved the pictures for last. He was horrible at organizing his photos, never deleting or moving them, so there was always a continual, chronological roll of images. The most recent ones were of the burned house, then the fire itself, flames shooting above the roofline. There were dozens of Christmas photos—Allie and me side by side in the kitchen, Danielle and Mom hugging, Danielle opening her gifts. My throat clogged seeing them. What I wouldn't give to have Allie next to me right now, telling me that I was crazy or urging me to get to the bottom of it. I scrolled past random shots of The Palms—repairs that needed to be made, mostly, a few shots of the homes in Phase 3 in their nearly final stages.

There's nothing here, I told myself.

And then I saw it—in thumbnail, a dark photo with a white blur in the middle. When I clicked on it, the image became Kelsey Jorgensen in a pair of sweatpants, her chest naked, wet hair gleaming. A pool—*our* pool—glistened in the background.

Fuck.

I dropped the phone, which bounced off my thigh and thumped onto the rug.

There would be no talking his way out of this one. I could march upstairs, flip on the light switch and hold the phone in front of his face. *Here she is, your girlfriend.* What in the world was his plan—to divorce me and take up with Kelsey, maybe waiting until she turned eighteen to declare his love publicly? Or had it been a fling, something he'd ended, leaving Kelsey to swallow a bottle of pills?

I picked up his phone again, bringing the screen to life. Chronologically, it fit into the week of Thanksgiving break, when Danielle and I had been in Riverside. It fit into the timing of that horrible Tweet: *Where a sophomore hottie has sex with her 37yo neighbor and wants more.* Had he been replaying our little pool scene from last June, with a younger and more willing companion?

I'd made huge decisions before. When I found out I was pregnant the spring of my freshman year in college, I'd told my boyfriend. He'd held my hand when I cried, promising that he would come up with the money for an abortion. I'd decided to have the baby on my own, to be a single mother working odd jobs and taking classes part-time, so I could give us a better life down the road. Every single decision I'd made then seemed difficult, monumental. Take Danielle to the emergency room when she had a high fever in the middle of the night? Call in sick when she had a cold and risk losing the shitty job that was keeping us afloat? Buy the more expensive diapers and skip the fresh produce, or load up on fruits and veggies and treat the diaper rash?

In comparison, this wasn't a huge decision at all. I didn't need a massive list of pros and cons. In the morning, I'd find a lawyer of my own. Danielle and I would move out, move on. "I'm getting a divorce," I said to the quiet of the den, and what surprised me was how *not* scary it was. They were just words like any other words, an oral confirmation of the thoughts I'd been having for weeks.

What I did next didn't take much thinking, either. That would come later, when I was crawling back into bed, shivering so hard I had to clamp a hand over my mouth to keep my teeth from chattering.

This was about getting rid of evidence.

This was about getting, in my own way, revenge.

I grabbed one of Phil's sweatshirts, a massive hooded thing that he'd draped over a chair in the den, and I slid his phone into the pocket. It was going to be a trick to disable the alarm without waking anyone. I played around with the options on the keypad, finally finding a button for volume control. No one would be able to hear the Other Woman announce "Garage door open" and "Back door open." In the garage, I slipped my feet into an old pair of Phil's boots, dried mud caked into the treads. When I walked, they left crenellated trails of dirt, like Hansel and Gretel's bread crumbs.

I took a flashlight off the workbench and used it to light up Phil's tool chest, which was disorganized at best. Still, it was easy enough to find a hammer in the mess—the sturdy wooden handle, the cold steel head.

I exited through the back of the garage, a door we rarely used. Again, no mechanical voice stopped me—and no human voice, either. When we'd lived in Livermore, there was always some kind of noise, even late at night or early in the morning—a trash can being dragged to the curb, a dog barking, someone's stereo thumping, blocks away. Noises at The Palms had always seemed primitive to me, the sounds of water and grass and wind, of insects and animals. I crossed our backyard in this near-silence, the hem of my pajama pants whisking moisture off the lawn. I had to use the flashlight to open the gate. There was a simple locking mechanism, just a latch and a hook, but at some point Phil had tied it with a bit of twine, maybe to keep the gate from blowing open. Once I was through, I glanced back at the house, expecting to see Phil at our bedroom window, his outline filling the frame. But the house was dark.

Mindful of the surveillance cameras, I kept my head down as I crossed the walking trail, the hood covering my face. I didn't feel recognizable, even to myself. On the security footage, I would only be a person taking a late walk, there and gone. Halfway across the fairway, I turned around to look at The Palms. I'd be leaving it soon enough, for good, and I almost felt a nostalgia for the orderliness of it, the quiet dignity of the homes facing the golf course. If I only had to worry about myself, I could keep walking right now, past the ranch land and out onto the main road and on and on. It was just a grown-up manifestation of the fantasy I'd had as a child—that a better life was just around the bend, and I could find it if I tried.

I stopped at the far end of the golf course, where the greens ended abruptly, cut off by a low fence and the sparse, weed-choked grass of neighboring ranch land. The rain hadn't come, but a general dampness had, allowing weeds to sprout, full of new life. If there was a mountain lion, I was firmly in its territory and too far away for my scream to be heard. Life was funny like that sometimes—ironically funny, the kind that presents as terrifying in the actual moment.

I removed the case from Phil's phone—it was too soft, too flexible to be damaged—and flung it like a Frisbee over the fence, off the official grounds of The Palms. I had to get onto my hands and knees to get the right amount of leverage, and then I made the first strike with the hammer, the screen splintering like a spider's web. It made more noise than I would have thought, but even if the sound carried in the dark, it would have been unidentifiable. It was best to be quick, sure. I brought the hammer down repeatedly, breaking apart the phone's innards. Somewhere in the mess of innards that came spilling out, there was a GPS tracker, and I didn't want Phil to be able to track it out here. I raised the hammer and brought it down, smashing and battering and pummeling. What was that movie Phil loved so much, he could watch it any time it was on television? I could picture the trio of men in their shirtsleeves and ties and khakis, beating the crap out of a faulty printer. With each motion I told myself I was getting rid of something, and I was taking back something that belonged to me.

In the yellow beam of the flashlight, the results looked like a miniature plane wreck, the parts littered across a field. I gathered them in the hem of Phil's sweatshirt and then walked up and down the fence line, scattering them like apple seeds—the little metal bits, the jagged pieces of plastic.

I was careful, retracing my steps, the hammer hanging low in the double pocket of the hoodie. I kept my head down on the walking trail, hands balled in my pockets. I was a person finishing my walk, looping back. I retied the twine around the latch as I passed through the gate and retraced my steps around the pool shed, into the garage. I stepped out of Phil's boots, kicking them under the utility sink out of sight. In the morning, I'd toss his hoodie in the wash with a load of towels. I returned the hammer to the yellow toolbox and the flashlight to its spot on the workbench and entered the darkened kitchen. At the alarm pad, I reactivated the sound.

Upstairs, I passed Danielle's darkened room and slid into the bed next to Phil. The hems of my pajama pants were wet, and I thought about slipping them off and tossing them onto the floor. I was about to do that when Phil rolled over with a groan, his arm landing on my hip.

Get your hands off me, I thought, but my heart was thumping too loud for me to move.

"Were you downstairs?" he asked.

"I was thirsty," I said into the darkness. I glanced over at him, but he was already asleep.

PHIL

On Sunday morning I woke up to the sun already streaming through the windows. I must not have set an alarm on
my phone, or I'd slept through it. My dreams had been like
nightmarish movie trailers, little flashes of Kelsey unconscious, inert, her icy blue eyes staring up at me. I'd had such
good news, too—a job offer with salary and full benefits,
not to mention moving expenses. I'd been a different version of myself in that interview, a better one. I was the old
confident Phil, talking about the future as if success were a
guarantee, not simply one of a roster of options.

They wanted me to start in one month.

On the flight home, I'd rehearsed all the things I would
say to Liz. There were about a million schools in the greater
Los Angeles area. Once she got a job, we could settle close
to where she worked, and I would do the commuting. We
wouldn't be that far from Riverside—an hour or so on a
Saturday morning, every weekend, if she wanted. *Please*,
I would say. I would get on my knees if I had to. I would
throw myself at her feet. *Please, let's get out of here. We need to
do this.* Kelsey's suicide attempt was proof of this—the longer I stayed, the worse it would get.

But when I'd arrived home on Saturday night, Danielle was in tears and Liz had snapped into full mother mode. I caught her going into Danielle's bedroom, a cup of tea balanced in her hand.

"Not now, Phil," she said, but I put a hand on her arm, and she looked at my hand as if it belonged to a stranger, a man who had grabbed her on the street.

"It's really important, Liz. I know that things between us—"

She pulled away. "Seriously, Phil. There's no way I can possibly have this conversation with you now. Can you try to understand that? Kelsey could have killed herself."

I'd gone to bed resolving to have the conversation in the morning, to sit Liz down and tell her that I'd accepted the job, that we would have to start figuring out things, fast. She would want to finish out the year at Miles Landers, and that would probably be best for Danielle, too. In the meantime, I had to find a place for myself, and we'd have to figure out where Liz and Danielle could stay. It would only be four months, and I could come up every weekend once I was settled in.

I reached over to Liz's side of the bed, but it was cold; she was already up for the day. I fumbled for my phone to check the time. It was usually on the nightstand, but I couldn't find it now. I leaned down and felt around the bed skirt, sweeping my arm blindly under the nightstand. Nothing.

I looked in the pockets of yesterday's pants, then in the bathroom. I headed downstairs to peek between couch cushions, beneath catalogs and magazines. It wasn't in the kitchen; it wasn't plugged in and charging in the dining room next to my laptop. I figured Liz was outside with a cup of coffee and a book, but she was gone, too, the Toyota missing from the garage. Desperate, I knocked once on Danielle's door and stuck my head in.

She sat up in bed, alarmed. Her eyes were still red-rimmed from the night before. "What's going on?"

"Sorry. I can't find my phone. Can you call it with yours?"

We did this for ten minutes, Danielle calling and me searching high and low. I usually turned the ringer off before going to bed, but I should still have heard a vibration. Maybe the battery was dead; it had been at 40 percent last night, when I'd last checked my email.

"It's probably in your office," Danielle said, but I knew it wasn't. I hadn't been back to my office since the interview, and I'd used my phone last night—I even remembered setting my alarm for seven thirty, thinking I'd get up early to make breakfast for the three of us, to butter up Liz for a talk.

Danielle thought for a minute. "Don't you have that app, the one that you can look up on your computer to find the phone's GPS coordinates?"

"I don't think so," I said. But I booted up my laptop anyway and tried various websites, none of which worked.

And then I thought: *Liz.*

"Where did your mom go?"

Danielle shrugged. "I don't know. Maybe to get groceries?"

"Can I use your phone? I want to call her."

Danielle sighed elaborately, as if it were a huge imposition to let the person who paid for her phone actually touch it, but she handed it over without further complaint.

I dialed Liz's number and got her voice mail. "Hey," I said to the recording. "It's me. Can you give me a call—or Danielle, since this is her phone?" I waited, but she didn't call back.

"She never picks up when she's driving," Danielle pointed out.

I waited another half hour, but she didn't return the call. Eventually, I took a shower, retracing my steps through the bedroom one more time looking for my phone. Had Liz taken it for some reason? Was she looking for something, or maybe checking up on me? She'd seemed suspicious about my overnight trip, and I was eager to tell her the truth. At least she wouldn't find anything from Kelsey on my phone. All those files were on a flash drive tucked away in my briefcase. I had this thought while I was in the shower, and then I hurried to rinse and throw on clothes and rush downstairs to check the inside zippered pocket of my briefcase, but the flash drive was still there, as well as the Ziploc bag with Kelsey's thong and bikini. I laughed, stupid with relief—I'd carried this briefcase onto the plane, into my interview and never thought about it once. Kelsey had been out of my mind as soon as she was out of my sight.

But at least Liz hadn't found that. I could only imagine her disgust if she knew that I'd kept Kelsey's underwear. And if she did have my phone, there was nothing incriminating there.

Except—

Shit. *Shit.*

I'd copied the picture of Kelsey, half-naked and pulling on her clothes, onto the flash drive. But had I ever deleted it from my phone? I tried dialing Liz and got her voice mail again. *Hi, you've reached Liz McGinnis...*

Assuming she had seen Kelsey's picture, what had she done with my phone? Had she taken it as evidence to show someone—Kelsey's parents? The police, even? And then I remembered last night, waking up to Liz's movements in the bedroom, afraid as always that it was Kelsey climbing into bed next to me. She'd been cold, shivering as if she'd been outside.

Because she had been outside.

I practically raced back to my laptop. The video surveillance software was still loaded on there, although I hadn't checked it once since I'd reviewed the fire footage. What was the point?

It took me a while to find her, but she was there. The clock in the upper right corner of the screen read 2:19 a.m., and she was just a flash on the screen—a hoodie pulled up around her face, the hem hanging to her lower thighs. *My* hoodie. She must have left through our back gate and crossed the walking trail, heading out to the golf course. I slowed down the feed and waited. It was 2:42 a.m. before she reappeared, head down, carrying a flashlight in one hand, the light off.

Liz came home late that afternoon with a bag of groceries. The leafy ends of a head of romaine poked out of a brown bag like an alibi. I was sitting in the den, my laptop open in front of me.

"Hey," she said, and then called upstairs, "Danielle! Come on down to help me with dinner."

"She's not here," I said, loud enough so that she turned to look at me, really look at me. She was wearing black pants and a button-up blouse, several steps up from her usual weekend clothes. "I sent her to Hannah's."

"Why?"

I said, "You would know the answer to that if you listened to the messages on your phone."

Liz froze, looking at the kitchen peninsula, where she'd dumped her purse.

"Don't bother anymore. The messages are all from me, and I can tell you in person now." I'd told Danielle that there was an important conversation I needed to have with her mother, and she'd protested, insisting that she should probably be there, too. *You can't be*, I told her and finally, she'd accepted it. Now I said, "We need to talk, Liz."

"Let me put these groceries away first."

"Forget the groceries," I said.

Maybe she heard it in my voice this time, because she came into the den and sat in one of the club chairs perpendicular to me.

I told her, "We're going to talk," and she let out a long sigh, as if she were completely deflating her lungs. On my lap, the monitor displayed the surveillance footage, the screen split into twelve different views. One camera covered the tennis courts, where the Zhang brothers were engaged in a fierce volley of shots from the baseline. It had been a beautiful, cloudless day, but The Palms felt deserted now. I took a deep breath. "You went out last night. In my sweatshirt."

She didn't say anything.

"Do you want to see the footage? I have it all cued up. I found my sweatshirt in the dryer. And you came to bed with your pants wet. They're dry now, but there's some mud along the hems."

She looked at me, waiting.

"You did something with my phone. I have no idea what. I walked all around the walking trail and the golf course with Danielle's phone, dialing my number."

Her face crumpled. "I found the picture! You bastard, you sick, opportunistic bastard. While we were gone for Thanksgiving! And all along, the two of you..."

I leaned forward. "There was no two of us. She's sick. Did you look at that picture? I took it from our bedroom window because she came over to the house, jumped in our pool and took off her suit. She knew you were gone, she knew I was home by myself."

"No." She closed her eyes, shaking her head. "You're not going to convince me this time that you're this innocent husband and I'm the crazy jealous wife. You had that picture on your phone. A naked teenager, on your phone, since November."

"That's what I wanted to talk to you about, Liz. I've wanted to tell you for months, only you wouldn't listen. You had these crazy accusations…" I pulled the flash drive out of my pocket and loaded it into my laptop. "There's more, too. I've been gathering evidence because I thought I might need it, in case she accused me of anything. Here." I clicked on my own photo, the one I'd allegedly emailed to Kelsey.

Liz recoiled when she saw the picture. "What the hell? You go walking around our backyard naked?"

"That was the night of the Mesbahs' party. Remember? We were drinking, and we got into the pool…"

She snatched the laptop from me and held the screen six inches from her face. "How do I know it was that night?"

"I can prove it. Zoom in a little more, to the right. See it, on the grass?"

"It's your shoe," she said.

"Yeah, remember? I kicked off my shoes and one of them went flying—"

"And I found it on the grass the next morning."

I leaned back. "We heard someone out there, remember? Someone was at the gate, and you got out of the pool."

Liz sat back in the chair, pulling her legs to her chest. "What are you saying? Kelsey Jorgensen took this picture? She was trying to humiliate us or something?"

Not *us*, I thought. *Me.* "I didn't know she was out there, obviously. I had no idea. But she'd been hanging around my office, being kind of flirty. Well, you know how she is. I didn't think anything of it at first."

She raised an eyebrow. "At first?"

"Liz, she became obsessed with me. There's the underwear—well, you know about that. She told me she'd left me something in our bedroom, but you found it before I did. And she sent me this picture of herself. She wasn't naked, but it was revealing, and—"

Liz put a hand to her temple, as if she were fingering out a knot. I was the knot.

"Anyway, I deleted the picture, and right after that, the clubhouse was vandalized." I set the laptop on the coffee table and clicked on the folder labeled "Bathroom." Liz tilted her head to the side, trying to understand the spray-painted messages, the taunts on the walls. She looked at the laptop and then back up at me. "See? This was why I was talking to her that day, because I knew that she was responsible for what happened."

Liz's head jerked back. "But I asked you. I confronted you about all of this in October. You had a chance to tell me everything, and you denied it. You lied to me."

"I know. I know. Because—you had it all wrong. You were thinking I was the one—"

"No, you were innocent all along. Is that what you're saying?"

Not completely. I hadn't moved out of the way when she kissed me, and I hadn't looked away when she stood in front of me, naked. I'd threatened her—twice. But yes, I was innocent in that I hadn't sought it out, any of it. That had to count for something, didn't it? "Liz, believe me—"

She cut me off with a laugh. "You had to think about the question?"

I leaned forward, putting a hand on her knee. "I wanted to tell you, but I didn't want to involve you or Danielle. But it's gotten to be a huge mess. She might have taken the pills because of me. I saw her that morning, before I left. I told her I was going to Seattle, but—that was a lie, because I didn't want her to know—"

Liz put her hands to her temples. "I don't understand what you're saying. It's like you're speaking another language. Why would you tell her anything? Why would you talk to her at all, when you wouldn't even talk to me? I'm your wife, Phil. Doesn't that count for anything?"

"Listen. *Listen.* Of course it does. I was going to tell you, I just didn't know how—I knew you would assume I was some kind of pervy weirdo for suggesting it. So I went to a lawyer." Her eyes grew wide. "Yeah, I talked to someone who could give me legal advice. That was a mistake, I realize now. I had to take money out of our savings, but it's okay. It's okay now, because—"

"What was his name?"

"What, the lawyer? Jacob Fitch. But I'm not going back there. I'm trying to tell you, there's a way out. I've found us a way out."

"You've found us a way out," she repeated. "You had this problem you didn't tell me anything about that you suddenly expect me to believe, but you and your lawyer figured it out."

"No—forget him. This whole thing was my mistake. I handled it wrong. I see that now. Back in the beginning, I should have put my foot down with her. When you invited her to the house, I should have told you that she was bad news. I should have called the police on the vandalism. And then the house—my God. I should have called the police then. I still could."

"The house that burned?"

"Yes, but I don't think that matters anymore. I mean, it does, but it's Parker-Lane's problem now, not ours. That's what I want to tell you, Liz—" I had slid off the couch and was on the floor in front of her, balanced on my knees. It was almost like I imagined it, except the words weren't coming out right, and I couldn't read Liz's expression. "This whole thing—it was this beautiful, stupid dream. I wanted to give you everything. Look how hard you work, how long you did it all on your own." She let me take her hands, although they were unresponsive in mine.

I pressed forward, going all in. I told her about the job, about the condo I'd found online, with the lease starting the second week of February. For a few months, it would be rough financially, but it was a higher salary than Parker-Lane paid, and our money wouldn't be trapped in a four-thousand-square-foot home. Eventually, we'd find a small house. A manageable one, something that made sense for our lives.

She stared at me.

"This condo I found, it's close to the water—"

"You had an interview down there?"

"That's where I went Friday. Until it was set in stone, I didn't want—"

She yanked her hands away from mine, and I leaned back, wincing as my spine caught the corner of the coffee table. "I can't believe this," she said. "I can't believe it."

I wondered what part—the photos, my explanations, the job, the move. Probably all of it.

"I didn't have any illusions when we got married. I wasn't this starry-eyed twenty-year-old who thought marriage was forever. I knew it would be hard. I knew there would be times…" She stood, moving to the other side of the couch, as if she were putting a barrier between us. "Do you remember what we promised each other? To be honest. To just always be fucking honest."

"I know." I remembered everything about that day: Liz's lavender dress, my tan suit. We didn't want any of the pomp and pageantry that came with a wedding, all the showiness of it. We wanted the part that was real. "And maybe it's too late, but that's what I'm trying to do now. I'm telling you the truth, and I'm asking you to trust me."

She made a sound as if she were laughing, but it turned quickly into an ugly sob, her words battling through tears. "You made a decision about our lives without even telling me. What am I supposed to do, just walk away from the job I love and start all over? And what are we supposed to do until the end of the year? I'm assuming Danielle and I can't stay here."

"I don't know, but I can talk about all of this with Jeff Parker on Monday. We'll figure something out. It's only for a few—"

She swore.

"Liz, come on." I was standing across from her now, and I reached out toward her. My hand hung heavy between us. "We can work this out, can't we?"

She shook her head slowly. When she spoke, it was almost as if she were speaking to herself, asking the rhetorical questions her mind could answer. "Would this have happened if we hadn't moved out here? I mean, maybe it would have happened anywhere, in our crappy little rental, too. Maybe it was inevitable that things would fall apart. Doesn't it happen to about every other couple, anyway?"

"We're not so fallen apart that we can't come back together, Liz."

"How could we ever trust each other? Look what we've come to. You have this entire other life I don't know anything about. And me—I snooped on your phone. I read all your emails and I looked at all your pictures, and then I took your phone out onto the golf course and I smashed it with a hammer."

It was—almost—funny. "With a hammer?"

"I wanted to get rid of the picture."

"I have a copy of it, though. It's on the flash drive."

She shook her head. "I wanted to hurt you, at least a little bit."

That was fair enough. "I understand that we'll have to rebuild trust—"

"If there's anything else, I need to know right now. Not six months down the road, when you think it's the right time—now."

I hesitated, and that was my fatal flaw.

Because one of the truths about a marriage—I knew that then, and I know it now—was that there should be some secrets. Small things, inconsequential things. I didn't believe a person could ever know another person wholly, inside out, and I was okay with that. Because inside, there were some ugly things, the blood and guts, the things that were better buried, better unsaid.

"Tell me you didn't ever sleep with her," Liz said, her face white. "Tell me you didn't let it get that far."

I flinched. "How could you think that, after everything I just told you? No, there was nothing like that. I was just under so much stress. But there is something else." I put my head in my hands, palms meeting on my forehead, and I told her about Thanksgiving night, about the image on the surveillance video.

She gasped. "You killed the Zhangs' dog?"

"No, of course not. I *buried* it. A mountain lion got it. It was the most terrifying thing ever, and it was just taking these big, easy strides with that dog, with Virgil, just clasped in its jaws. I went out there later, and I found it on the golf course mauled to bits. There was fur everywhere. It was—so horrible. I just didn't want it to be this huge mess," I explained.

Liz had both hands over her mouth as if she were holding in a scream.

"It was already dead, Liz. And I was under so much pressure about the mountain lion and the vandalism—"

"Those poor people," she breathed. "They organized search parties! They've been offering a reward. Charlie told me that Helen practically cries herself to sleep every night. And all along, you knew."

"It was better that they didn't see it," I protested. "It didn't even look like their dog anymore."

"And you never told anyone about the mountain lion," she marveled. "There's been a vicious animal on the loose, and you've never said anything. Think about all the joggers! Think about Fran, pushing Elijah. All those Bergland kids..."

"I know. I do know. But once it was done, it wasn't something I could exactly undo, was it?"

She stared at me. "I don't even know what to say. It's like a horror movie."

"We can get through it."

"And Kelsey—she could have killed herself. Twisted and messed up and whatever else she is—you needed to do *some*-thing instead of just hiding it."

"We've both been hiding things," I pointed out. "We're the same kind of awful."

"I don't know," she said, backing toward the stairs. "I think we're different kinds of awful."

JUNE 19, 2015

7:09 P.M.

LIZ

We waited in the hospital parking structure, six floors up, the exit sign a bright red flash in the dim interior. Danielle peeked at me from time to time, trying to figure out what I was going to do next. The motor was still running, and I held my hand on the key in the ignition.

It had been so easy for Phil to run off, to shed his old life and put on a new one. Maybe he'd been doing that all along—leaving Australia for Greece, leaving Greece for the United States, leaving bachelorhood for married life and leaving us behind, too.

Maybe that was the freedom that came with being a man. Wives and children could be shucked off, because the woman would stay with her daughter, would do her best and see it through. Danielle had been his pal, but not fully his responsibility. What if I did call him, if I dropped all this at his feet? Would he say, *Shit, Liz. What are you going to do?* Would he hang up, glad he'd dodged this bullet?

"Mom," Danielle said sharply.

"I'm thinking," I snapped.

She made a small movement with her forefinger, and I

followed the gesture. Sonia Jorgensen had passed our car, moving toward the exit. She looked disheveled, her blouse hanging out of her skirt, one of her purse straps flopped to the side.

Maybe in some ways we were the same. We'd each had one daughter, and we'd had years to watch that daughter grow and mature. We'd had the same fears about broken bones on the playground or our girls running into the street, oblivious to oncoming traffic. It was easy for me to judge Sonia Jorgensen, to believe that she had failed as a mother because she'd produced a monster of a daughter.

But was I any better?

I turned the key in the ignition, the car falling silent.

"Come on," I told Danielle. "We're going in."

FEBRUARY 2015
LIZ

The news of Kelsey's suicide attempt was all over MLHS that January, spawning memos to parents and extended hours in the counseling office and a #prayforkelseyj hashtag on Twitter. It was the talk of The Palms, too. Sonia had backed out of a women's conference she was supposed to be planning for later in the month, and she was staying near the private treatment center in Carmel where Kelsey was a patient. I heard this from Carly, who'd heard it from Janet, who'd heard it from Deanna, who had spent long hours on the phone with Sonia, offering advice.

To me, Carly said, "It's just like last time, then. She just wanted to get everyone's attention."

I turned this comment over in my mind, looking at it from every angle.

And I began to think.

On my next quiet afternoon in the office, I searched the Ashbury Prep website, clicking on the individual pages of staff members, scrolling down their biographies and links to publications and their syllabi and homework assignments. I

PAULA TREICK DeBOARD

remembered the Incomplete notification on Kelsey's transcript for her English class and clicked on a dozen dead ends before I found her: Megan Cummings, Honors Freshman English and Classical Mythology. Her biography said that she held a master's degree in English from Berkeley, but her picture told me she looked too young to have been teaching for very long. She had brown hair cut in a severe chin-length bob, glasses instead of contacts. Her navy blazer, embellished with the school crest, was tight through the shoulders. Young, earnest, helpful, self-conscious—yes, she was the one I needed.

I called the main phone number for Ashbury from my office phone and asked to be put through to her.

"You've called at just the right time," the secretary told me. "Ms. Cummings is on her preparatory period now and should be in her classroom. I'll put you through."

Preparatory period, I thought. Not *prep period*, not at Ass Bury. Aaron would get a kick out of that, if I ever told him about this conversation—which I would not.

After a series of beeps, Megan Cummings answered in a timid voice that made her sound like a high school student herself. Telemarketers probably asked if they could speak to her mother.

I introduced myself as a behavioral counselor with the county. "I was wondering, Ms. Cummings, if I could speak to you privately for a moment."

"Yes, I…suppose. I'm not sure what this is about. You said you were from…where?"

"The Alameda County Behavioral Health Services," I repeated. "I'm calling about a confidential matter concerning a student who attended Ashbury last year."

"Oh. I think you would want to speak to one of our administrators, then?" Her voice rose uncertainly, a question for me as much as herself.

I plowed ahead, the fake title bestowing me with a strange power. "I intend to do that, Ms. Cummings. But in my position, I've worked with a number of school personnel, including teachers and administrators. It's been my experience that administrators know a few of the bare-bone facts, but the teachers are always more knowledgeable about situations regarding students. After all, you spend so much time with them on a daily basis, and administrators barely know their names."

"Well, that's true." She laughed a bit nervously, as if there were an administrator lurking on the line, waiting to catch her in a trap.

"The student I'm calling about now attends Miles Landers High School in Livermore, and there have been some concerns. Her name is Kelsey Jorgensen."

Megan Cummings inhaled sharply.

"I'm not sure if you're aware, Ms. Cummings, but Kelsey was recently involved in a serious incident, and I've been working with the staff at Miles Landers to see how we can best handle the situation. Whatever you tell me is completely confidential, of course, but I'm trying to develop a whole picture of Kelsey at the moment."

"An incident," she repeated.

"I'm sure you understand that I have to speak a bit obliquely, as there are some concerns about privacy. I think it's enough to say that we're concerned with treating both Kelsey's physical health as well as her mental health."

"Um, okay. I— What is it you need to know?"

"The staff here is very concerned about how to look out for Kelsey's best interest, as well as the interest of other students and staff members. It would be very helpful if you could shine a light on some of her past behavior, so we can be informed about how to proceed."

"The thing is—" Megan hesitated, and I thought for a moment that I'd lost her. She might insist that I speak to an administrator, and then that would be the end of my charade. "Her parents had us sign these papers. What do you call them? Nondisclosure agreements."

Ah—that explained why nothing had popped up on Google. "I know about the nondisclosure agreements," I said, thinking fast. "As you know, those papers are legally binding, but they don't apply to situations where the person is at medical risk. I'll be blunt, Ms. Cummings. Kelsey Jorgensen attempted suicide right after the first of the year."

"That's horrible. I mean, again? You know that's what happened last year." Her voice was raw. I could imagine how she'd felt last year, learning that one of her students had attempted suicide. Shock, disbelief, guilt.

"You see why this is so important," I prodded.

It was all I needed to say. Megan exhaled deeply, then launched into the story. Kelsey had come to Ashbury in seventh grade, the year the Jorgensens moved to their house in The Palms. She'd been popular with the other students, elected as a class representative. There had been some minor problems with a few of the girls—rumors of jealousy and sniping and on-again, off-again friendships. "Typical adolescent stuff," Megan said, dismissing this. The real trouble had started at the beginning of her ninth grade year, when she'd become obsessed with her history teacher.

"Yes?" I urged, my pulse racing.

"Well, it was a crush at first—that's how he explained it. She just started hanging around, trying to get his attention,

doing extra credit work and volunteering to clean his classroom after school. He didn't take it very seriously, but then…"

Then things had turned ugly—he was finding notes she'd
left in his classroom, in his car. She got his cell phone number and called him at all hours. "He had a fiancée when all of
this started," Megan said, "but then, I guess she intercepted
one of Kelsey's calls, and she'd had enough. And that wasn't
even the worst of it."

The worst came at the beginning of March, when Kelsey
went to the administration and said that she had been forced
to give her teacher oral sex in the bathroom on a class field
trip. "There was no way to prove it," Megan told me. "I
mean, I'm not saying that we should doubt women who
come forward with stories of rape and abuse, but—this had
supposedly happened months before, and one day it was like
she just woke up and decided to ruin his life."

Kelsey's parents had called for the teacher's dismissal, but
they'd wanted to keep what happened out of the news. In
the end, the board agreed to dismiss the teacher (but with
glowing letters of recommendation). In exchange for the
staff's silence on the matter, Kelsey's parents wouldn't bring
a lawsuit against the school. The teacher didn't even finish
out the year. Once he was gone, Kelsey swallowed a bunch
of Advil, and she finished the year on independent study.

That was last spring, right before we moved to The Palms,
before Sonia Jorgensen told me the students at Ashbury had
been bad influences, before she suggested that our daughters could be friends.

"I was just so appalled that something like that could happen here, at Ashbury," Megan said. "I mean, you hear of
these things…"

"What I've learned over the years," I said drily, "is that a thing like that can happen almost anywhere."

"I feel bad saying this, because she was one of my students, but when she left, it was like we all let out a sigh of relief. I mean, if she could do that to one of us, who was next? We were all sitting ducks."

I thanked Megan Cummings very sincerely on behalf of the Alameda County Behavioral Health Department, telling her she had been very helpful and assuring her that I would not be mentioning her name in my report.

"It was my pleasure, Ms.— What did you say your—"

I repeated, "Thank you so very much," and hung up.

It wasn't until I hung up the phone that I started shaking— literally shaking, my hands wobbly, my knees too soft to stand. Kelsey had been obsessed with an older man, one with a fiancée, and she'd come close to ruining his life. I hadn't fully believed Phil when he told me; it was too much to absorb, all at once, and too conveniently packaged.

But now I could see her hand in it—the underwear left behind, like an animal marking its territory; the vandalism in the bathrooms, retribution for something that hadn't gone her way. She could have sent the message to MLHS Stories herself, intending to blackmail him or drive a wedge between us—or maybe even because she believed it had happened. I was already convinced that she'd started the rumor about Danielle, and now that made a kind of sense, too. Had she only been interested in Danielle's friendship for the chance to get inside our house, to get closer to Phil? He was sure that the fire was all about getting his attention, too. I remembered the way he'd stood there, hands in his pockets, his face a shiny canvas reflecting the flames. And when she couldn't have him, she'd swallowed a bottle of pills—just like she had with the history teacher.

It made, in its own nightmarish way, a kind of sense.

But even then, I wasn't sure it excused anything.

Since Phil's confession, it was as if I were split in two, entertaining both possibilities. Phil was telling the truth, and our marriage could be saved, so I would look for jobs near LA and begin planning our move. Or Phil couldn't be trusted, and Danielle and I were going to stay. That Sunday after smashing his phone, I'd driven to school, deactivated the alarm and locked myself in the counseling office while I surfed information on divorce laws in California and rentals around Livermore. More and more, the idea was growing on me. If nothing else, it would buy me time to think.

Phil moved out on a Monday in February, while Danielle and I were at school. He had to—his job in LA started that week, and Parker-Lane had already cleaned out his office, rekeying the locks. I knew it was coming; since our talk, the clock had been ticking. Still, it was horrible to come home and find his SUV gone, his laptop and files out of the dining room. Upstairs, Phil's side of the closet was empty, the coats and shirts and ties, the hanging dress pants. His dresser drawers had been emptied, too, even of the musty, heavy sweaters he would never need in Southern California. Staring into the closet, it felt like half my life was gone.

We'd talked to Danielle the Saturday before he left. She'd been watching TV, and Phil hit the mute button, prompting her protests. I wished he would have turned it off; through the entire conversation, the actors distracted me with their exaggerated facial expressions, their behind-each-other's-backs gestures.

He told her about his new job, and I explained that we would be staying through the end of the school year. Parker-Lane wanted us out, but Jeff had assured Phil that as long as we were completely gone by the end of June, they wouldn't raise a fuss.

"I knew there was something going on," Danielle spluttered. "How long have you known about this?"

"Not long," I said, at the same time Phil said, "A few weeks."

She glared at us. "What does this mean? What's going to happen to us?"

"At the end of the school year, we'll pack up the house and you'll move down south. We'll be living in Laguna Niguel. You'll love it there," Phil said.

Danielle was watching me. "Mom?"

"We'll see, honey. We'll just have to see." I didn't look at Phil.

We slept side by side the next two nights, not touching, but somehow companionable. I was too tired of hostility. I was too tired of it all.

And then he was gone.

After Phil left, I received a letter from Parker-Lane. It had clearly gone out to all residents of The Palms, and had been delivered to us, too—either as an act of spite or an administrative oversight.

Dear Homeowner,
Due to some recent changes in personnel at The Palms, Phil McGinnis is no longer employed as our community relations specialist. A new member of our team will take up residence at The Palms later this spring. In the meantime, residents are encouraged to call...

* * *

Our neighbors must have noticed Phil's car was missing from our driveway, and I was sure the note set off a vicious round of gossip, to which I was no longer privy. I could read their bewilderment each time I passed through in my Toyota.

What the hell is she still doing here?

Does she think she can afford this place on her own?

Someone from Parker-Lane came to inventory Phil's office, and he left a message for me when Phil wouldn't return his calls. Did I know if my husband had made backup copies of any of the files, any of the video surveillance? For all he could see, the hard drive had been completely wiped clean, and there was some kind of bug that prevented the software from recording.

One day Deanna called my name when I was getting out of the car, and she came across the street in slightly teetering steps, four inches taller in her wedge heels. "I just want you to know that I don't blame you, not one bit."

I wondered what exactly she didn't blame me for, and I decided to ask. "For what?"

"Oh, you know," she said, embarrassed. Her hand went to her hair, probably checking to see if her walk across the street had displaced some strands in an unforgivable way. "Everything that happened here under Phil."

A car passed, slowing in front of our house to gawk. Deanna gave me a little wave and scuttled back to her own driveway as if she were afraid to be seen talking to me.

School was the one constant in our lives. As busy as the fall and winter seemed, spring was a marathon of state testing, schedule requests for the fall and the typical issues of failing seniors and approaching graduation. We left earlier in the morning and stayed later at night, picking up dinner on the way home, carrying inside paper bags with limp fries and cold hamburgers, pizzas with grease stains seeping through the boxes. We ate in front of the TV, not talking, and then Danielle would disappear upstairs. She'd been slowly finding her place at Miles Landers without Kelsey, although her closest friend, surprisingly enough, was now Hannah Bergland. They spent a lot of time together at night, watching TV in the den or talking quietly in Danielle's room. Hearing their voices through the walls, the earnest confessions and muted sounds of laughter, I felt incredibly alone.

At the beginning of April, I was in the lobby of the counseling office with Jenn, sorting through testing materials, when a dark sedan passed the window once, then circled the visitor lot and returned. I stood up.

Jenn squinted into the parking lot, following my gaze. "Who is that?"

I couldn't form the words, although of course I knew the car. I'd seen it threading through the streets of The Palms, parked in the Jorgensens' driveway. I'd seen it follow the ambulance that day Kelsey was taken away. Tim stepped out of the sedan, his navy suit coat unbuttoned, tie flapping in the slight breeze. He held a briefcase in his right hand.

"Is he from the district office or something?" Jenn asked, noting the suit.

I shook my head and moved trancelike toward the door. Tim looked up, surprised to see me right there, watching him. I pushed open the door, and the bell overhead gave its customary merry jingle.

He nodded at me, oddly formal. "Do you have a few minutes, Liz?"

"Of course." I gestured to my office and he led the way,

settling himself instantly into the chair across from my desk. Jenn looked at me with a puzzled smile, her head cocked. My armpits were already damp when I pulled the door shut. This was the third member of the Jorgensen family to visit me at work, and I wasn't expecting anything pleasant.

Tim set his briefcase on his knees, popped the latches and removed a slim manila folder. My mouth went dry. I was standing at the door, and it occurred to me that I could still escape this somehow. Slip outside, get into my car, drive away from my life. No—I'd have to grab Danielle first. I could almost imagine myself bursting into her classroom and dragging her out by the arm, being chased by Tim Jorgensen in his long strides. But he was looking up at me expectantly, so I came around my desk and lowered myself into my chair.

"I hope Kelsey's doing okay," I blurted, fumbling for words, as if I could set the course of our conversation. "I heard she was back home." I hadn't so much heard this as I'd seen her in the passenger seat of Sonia's car, rounding the corner at the end of our street. Tim didn't say anything, and I kept babbling, coming out next with a bald-faced lie. "Danielle and I thought we would visit her someday, when it's a good time for everyone."

He finally spoke. "She's not okay, Liz. She's not remotely okay. And you're not coming anywhere near our house." He tapped the folder in his hand significantly and set it on the edge of my desk.

It felt like an absurd game where I had to guess the contents of the folder. Maybe he would give me three chances before I lost. But whatever was inside there, it was bad news.

He cleared his throat. "Kelsey's been seeing a therapist. We're trying to get to the bottom of some of her issues. She's been— Unfortunately, she's been easy prey for some of the adults in her life. For a long time, she didn't want to tell us anything. She would just start crying every time we tried to talk to her. And then finally, yesterday, we had a breakthrough, and she told us about what's been going on with your husband."

The cup of coffee I'd gulped down half an hour ago was suddenly there again, threatening to rise in the back of my throat. I whispered, "What do you mean?"

Tim flipped open the folder, and there was Phil, standing naked at the edge of our pool in a glossy eight-by-ten. "He sent her this picture," he snapped. "I saw the email. A grown man sent this to a teenage girl. How would you feel if this were your daughter, Liz? If your sweet, innocent girl opened up her email and had this waiting for her, from the creepy neighbor next door?"

"But—no," I said. "He explained it to me. Kelsey got into his email. She sent him that photo—"

Tim shook his head, as if he were disappointed with me. "You can explain it however you want, Liz. The bottom line is, he took advantage of her. She told us all the things he made her do, right there in his office."

My face was hot. "Nothing happened," I protested. "She was the one who came on to him. She—had a chance to stay away from him, but she came over to our house... My husband had nothing to do with her. He told me it was all one-sided, an obsession."

"And you believed him?"

"Of course." I thought of the picture on Phil's phone, the one I'd been so bent on destroying that night with the hammer. If I had it now, that would have proved something. Or would it? It might have only proved he was indeed a pervert, for snapping a photo of a naked girl and storing it for all these months. Suddenly, too late, I understood why Phil had kept quiet. It didn't matter what the truth was, because there was only one version that everyone would see.

I looked at the picture again. Phil, naked and beautiful and lost to me now. "Tim, Phil didn't take this picture, obviously. Your daughter took it. She was outside our house that night, out on the trail, spying on us."

Tim closed his eyes and again shook his head. "I wanted to believe this had nothing to do with you, Liz. I really did. I always liked you. You seemed smarter than the other ladies, like someone who wouldn't let anyone boss her around. I liked that. But clearly you'll do anything you can to protect him—and yourself. You took this picture, didn't you? Maybe you meant it as a private thing, but your husband must have liked how he looked in it, because he passed it along to my daughter."

"I didn't..."

He gave me a look of disgust. "The worst part, Liz, is that she tried to confide in you. She came in here to talk to you about what was happening with your husband, and you made excuses for his behavior, just like you're doing with me now."

"No," I whispered.

"She came in here to talk to you, didn't she? Back in September? Eight months ago. She told you that she was uncomfortable around your husband—"

"No! She never mentioned anything like that. She's the one— She left her underwear in my bedroom, she vandalized the bathrooms in the clubhouse."

"Your husband forced her to strip in his bedroom. He tried to frame her for the vandalism in the clubhouse, which he did himself."

"That's ridiculous!" I heard the desperation in my voice. "I know about your daughter. I know that she tried this before, only a year ago, with one of her teachers at Ashbury."

"Any information relating to that case was sealed via a court order," Tim said. He pinched the photo of Phil between his thumb and forefinger and placed it back into the folder. "And if there's any connection, it's that my daughter continues to be taken advantage of by men in her life who are in positions of trust. Although it's not just the men, is it? If you'd done your job when she came to you, if you'd taken her concerns seriously, this whole thing could have been prevented."

Stop, I wanted to say. He was going too fast, spinning my mind around with his dizzying logic. Everything was wrong. It was like seeing an old film negative, where the white should be black and the black should be white.

He stood, shaking out the creases in his suit. "As mad as I am, Liz, it's nothing compared to Sonia. She trusted you, and you had information that we needed to know in order to keep Kelsey safe. I'm pretty sure that that's your job as a guidance counselor, Liz. To guide. To counsel." He picked up the folder with the photo and slid it into his briefcase.

My voice came out as a croak. "What are you going to do?"

"I think my daughter has been through enough, frankly. I know I could call the police and have your husband arrested, but I'm not sure if that would benefit Kelsey at this point. She's so fragile right now—to have to relive it would be a nightmare. Plus, from what I understand, your husband is now living in Southern California. As long as he doesn't come near The Palms or near our daughter, I won't have him arrested."

I waited, knowing that more was coming. Tim looked too satisfied to be finished. He was a lawyer, I reminded myself. He was enjoying the spectacle.

"But my next stop today is your principal's office, to explain to him that the person who counseled my daughter was woefully deficient, which may have contributed to her suicide attempt. It's unconscionable to me that you can sit in here and dispense advice to frightened and worried kids, when my daughter spent a month in a hospital as a result of your incompetence."

I understood then why Ashbury had caved, why the teacher had agreed to a dismissal, why everyone kept their mouths shut about Kelsey Jorgensen.

I understood, finally, why Phil had been running in circles trying to keep a secret even when he was innocent. And I believed that, finally. He was innocent of everything except bad judgment. Without thinking, I was out of my chair, my body sliding between Tim and the door. I was close enough to see the veins in his sclera, red and angry, like little forks of lightning.

"She's a liar," I told him. "She's manipulative and destructive, and it's obvious where she gets it from. What are you going to say when she does this again next year, with someone else? Who will you blame then? How many lives will you let her ruin?"

It might have been an accident—or it might not, I thought later—but as Tim grabbed the door handle, his briefcase connected with my knee, and I fell back, gasping with pain.

"What in the world...?" Jenn asked as I hobbled through the lobby. Tim strode across the parking lot, where Sonia was waiting next to his sedan in a dark suit. I almost did a double take when Kelsey came out of the backseat. I'd only seen her in bikinis, tank tops with skinny straps, short skirts, deeply plunging V-necks. Today she wore a gray sweater dress that fell past her knees. A pink scarf was wrapped around her neck. The three of them walked toward the main administrative entrance, Tim and Sonia flanking Kelsey like bodyguards.

Jenn asked, "Liz? What's going on? Do you need me to—"

I hurried back to my office, my knee still smarting. "No, it's okay. I just have to..." But there were no more words, no means of finishing the sentence. Inside my office, I bent at the waist, my breath coming in ragged gasps.

Kelsey had played her trump card. Right now, she was sitting in Blaine's office, summoning the requisite tears and the appropriate shame. I remembered her that day in my office, so earnestly trying to tell me that my daughter had trashed the clubhouse bathrooms.

She would make an excellent victim.

I'd been at MLHS for seven years. I'd worked with Blaine long enough to know the date of his anniversary and the names of his grandchildren. I'd outlasted a revolving door of assistant principals, most using MLHS as a stepping stone on their way up and out. It was impossible to be a counselor, to deal with sensitive student information and unhappy parents and not receive a complaint or two each school year. None of these had been serious—just the standard woes about class placement and grade notifications that had slipped through the cracks. No matter who the parent was, no matter how hard they pushed, those complaints amounted to nothing. This was because I documented everything. I crossed my t's and dotted my i's, keeping the paperwork, making notes in my files. I had a good reputation. I had a track record of helping students and communicating with parents. I took work home; when I needed to, I came in early and stayed late. I responded to all emails before I left work for the day. No matter what Tim and Sonia and Kelsey were telling

Blaine right now, I had nine years of a good service record
going for me, too.

I glanced at the clock. How long would the Jorgensens
be in Blaine's office? How long until he called me in, demanding answers? There were twenty minutes left in fourth
period. I consulted the staff phone list and punched in the
number of Taryn Edwards, Danielle's fourth period geometry teacher.

"Hi, it's Liz McGinnis," I said, surprised by how normal
I sounded, how clearheaded. "I hope it's not too inconvenient, but I was wondering if you would send Danielle up
to my office before she heads to lunch?"

Danielle knocked once and opened the door, clutching
her fat binder to her chest with one arm. Her backpack slung
low off her shoulder, weighted down by books. "Did you
call for me?"

I shut the door behind her with a quiet click. "Sit down."

She did, too stunned to remove her backpack. "What's—"

I sat on the top of my desk, directly in front of Danielle.
"I need you to listen to me."

Her eyes went wide. "What happened? Is it Grandma?"

I softened. "No—no, it's not Grandma. She's fine. But I
need to tell you something, before you hear it from someone else."

"Hear what?"

"There are some rumors going around that there was a
relationship between Kelsey and Phil."

Her eyes went wider. "Oh, my God."

I knew I had to explain fast, before we were interrupted.
"It isn't true, Danielle. Kelsey's made up the whole thing.
I've been doing some digging, and she's sick—she's seriously

disturbed. She made up lies like this at Ashbury, too. Her teacher was engaged, and his fiancée ended up calling off the wedding."

"Is that why Phil left?"

"He needed to get away from the situation. She'd been sending him emails and bothering him at his office. When we were gone for Thanksgiving, she got into our backyard and went swimming in our pool, naked. She was obsessed."

"Eww."

"I know this is a hard thing to hear about your friend. And I'm sure she has some very nice qualities, but the bottom line is that she's sick and she needs to get some help."

"She's not my friend. We haven't even talked in months."

"The thing is, right now she's in Blaine's office with her parents, and she's telling them that I knew about the relationship and that I should be fired."

I hated what that did to Danielle. She'd acted so casual about Phil leaving, so defiantly nonchalant, as if whatever was going on with us wasn't possibly going to affect her. And now I'd as good as pulled the rug out from under her feet. I could almost feel her mind spinning, the gears shifting. No more Phil. Mom losing her job.

"She's vindictive, Danielle. You know that. When she couldn't get her way with Phil, she decided to bring me down, too."

"And me," Danielle added.

"And you. That's right. And whatever she's saying right now is going to affect your life, too. That's why I'm going to ask you something. It's very important. Do you understand?"

She stared at me.

I lowered my voice. "If Mr. Blaine or Mr. Gopal, or if any adult asks you, you're going to say that Kelsey told you she had a crush on Phil, and that she was starting to creep you out, because she was always asking you questions about him and wanting to get closer to him. Do you understand?"

"That's disgusting," Danielle said. "I'm not going to lie. She never told me anything like that."

"You're not understanding the whole picture, Danielle. She's telling lies that we can't prove. We have to do something. I'm going to go to Blaine and tell him that she made it all up, that her parents are protecting her because she's mentally unstable. But you have to back me on this, too."

"There was nothing going on, then? For sure?"

"Danielle! Of course there wasn't." I could see her wavering, processing. She was sorting the evidence, same as I'd done, trying to remember when she'd seen them together, if they'd ever exchanged a significant glance.

There was a knock on my door.

"Just a second," I called.

"Why do I have to lie about it?" Danielle asked. "Why can't I just say I didn't know anything? That's the truth. I *didn't* know anything."

"Because that's not going to be good enough. Listen, I need you to do this. You have to do this. Everything is on the line here."

"Liz?" Jenn called. She opened the door an inch. "Blaine's calling for you. He says he needs to see you right away."

I came around to Danielle, leaning down to kiss her on top of the head. And I whispered in her ear, "I'm counting on you."

I felt like a chastened student in Blaine's office, where I'd sat a hundred times before and been treated like a professional. A thin manila folder sat on his desk, probably the same one Tim had been holding when he came into my office. I shuddered to think of the picture inside—my husband, naked and grinning.

I argued my side of things, but he only listened with a tired expression, the lines on his face so deep they might have been etched in with an X-Acto knife. When I finished, he pointed out the obvious. I'd disappointed him, I'd kept things hidden—things that were my responsibility as a counselor to report—for my own self-interested reasons. He'd have to disclose this whole mess to the superintendent, and that would likely mean facing these allegations in front of the school board.

I didn't say anything—because of course he was right. I'd circled wagons. I'd been focused on how their possible relationship might affect me, not about the health and well-being of a student under my charge.

Danielle didn't talk to me on the way home from school. She sat stone-faced, staring out the window when I asked how it had gone with Blaine. When she didn't look at me, I banged the flat of my palm against the steering wheel. "This is serious. I don't think you understand how this could affect us. What did you tell him?"

In response, she unzipped the small pocket at the front of her backpack. I watched carefully, thinking she was going to hand me something, some piece of evidence that related to what we were discussing. But she was untangling the cords of her earbuds from the pens and pencils.

"You're not going to put those on," I snapped. "You're going to listen to me. You're going to talk to me."

She didn't look at me as she fitted the buds into her ears, left first, then right, and plugged the cord into her phone.

"Hey," I said, louder, my eyes darting between the road

and her blank expression. "You're going to talk to me. This isn't some kind of game."

She fiddled with her phone, adjusting the volume.

I reached across the console and yanked on the cord, and the earbud came flying.

Danielle flinched, hand going to her ear. "Mom! That seriously hurt."

"I'll throw it out the window," I said, still holding on to the cord. It wouldn't have been hard—one more yank and it would be in my hand. It was strange—I heard my voice, but didn't believe it was me talking. It was like a nightmare, a daylong waking dream in which everything was real and not real, in which nothing was solid, everything was just outside my grasp.

"Fine," she said. "I did it. I lied for you. There, now you can go ahead and award yourself mother of the year."

I let the cord go—not sailing out the window, the earbuds flailing through the air like a flimsy stethoscope, but simply falling into her lap. I kept driving, not seeing the foothills or the still-green brush or the wind generators in the distance, although I knew they were there, turning and turning, slicing the air like a knife.

That night I finally told Allie everything, in a three-hour phone call that was mostly questions on her end and sobbing on mine. "You have to fight this," she told me. "Don't let them ruin your life."

When I told Phil, he was silent for a long time on the other end of the phone before letting out a string of curses. "I'll come up there," he said. "I'll handle it."

Instead, I asked him to send me the letter he'd written,

the one that he'd told me about during his wild confession about Kelsey. It might be better if he was heard, not seen.

My meeting with the superintendent, Gerald Fiedler, might have been an inquisition. Fiedler sat on one side of a table with the assistant superintendent, the district lawyer and Blaine. I sat on the other side with Vicki, my CTA rep. Aaron had offered to come, too, if only to walk back and forth in front of the office with a picket sign.

Fiedler was dressed in a three-piece suit, as if he had a meeting at the bank later in the day. It was warm for April, and I wanted to get up and crack a window. It was hard to focus on his words. "...a position that comes with certain expectations and responsibilities..."

"They cannot possibly fire you," Vicki had told me in advance. "You have grounds for an appeal if they do. It might be ugly, because they'd have to examine all kinds of evidence. But you're entitled to a private session before the board..."

Now I just wanted Fiedler to get it over with, like pulling off a Band-Aid in a single, stinging motion.

"...imperative that we have the full trust of the students we serve, not to mention parents and the wider community of stakeholders..." Fiedler was good at this, very professional. There was an almost apologetic tone to his voice. *Believe me, I don't want this. If it were up to me...* But I knew he'd talked to the Jorgensens, and I was sure he'd used the same tone then.

Blaine, beside him, was watching me. Over the years I'd spoken up dozens of times at staff meetings, arguing a point, correcting a wrong. He was expecting me to speak up now, too—maybe he'd even been counting on it.

"No one wants this to become an issue for the entire district," Fiedler said, and I heard *an embarrassment.*

"I understand," I said.

Vicki swiveled in her chair to face me head-on. "What they're saying, Liz, is that they don't have a bit of real evidence, just conjecture. And you have a sworn affidavit and the witness of your daughter. You don't have to accept any type of punishment."

Blaine cleared his throat pointedly, and I knew it was my last chance.

The thing was—somewhere along the line, I'd stopped believing that I was in the right. I'd made mistakes, and maybe it was time to take my punishment and move on. Danielle had already lied for me once, and I didn't want her to have to repeat the lie again at a board hearing, or a civil trial.

When I didn't say anything, Fiedler continued, "What we think might be best, Mrs. McGinnis, is if you were to transfer to another position in our district. We feel the Jorgensens would be satisfied with this response. I know this might seem as though the district doesn't support you, or that I don't value the work that you've done at Miles Landers, but I hope you see it instead as a chance to move on from what could potentially be an ugly situation."

"Liz?" Vicki asked. She was like a gnat hovering by my ear. "You don't have to say anything right now. This is absolutely not something you have to accept without discussion. Why don't we think about this a bit and schedule another meeting?"

But I shook my head. It was better than I'd hoped for. I said simply, "I'll take it."

The following afternoon, there was a burgundy Mazda in front of our house, parked with one wheel up on the curb. Judging by the dusty exterior and sagging rear bumper, the car didn't belong to a resident of The Palms.

I parked in the driveway and handed Danielle my keys. "Leave the door unlocked for me," I said.

The young woman who stepped out of the car looked familiar—pale face, thick hair held back by a clip. I recognized her as the reporter who had written about the house fire. She looked younger than she had in the tiny head shot that accompanied her article. "She's home now. Let me call you back," she said into her phone.

"How did you get in here?" I asked.

She shrugged. "I followed someone in."

"Security around here really is going to hell," I commented.

She laughed and held out a hand. "I'm Andrea Piccola from the *Contra-Costa Times*. And you're Liz McGinnis, right?"

I shook her hand and found myself assessing her against The Palms standard—eyebrows too thick, fingernails too ragged, shirt too boxy. The bag slung over her shoulder looked old rather than *vintage*. In other words, she looked more like a Liz McGinnis than a Deanna Sievert.

"I don't have anything to say to you," I told her.

"It's my understanding that there have been some issues recently at Miles Landers, some allegations of incompetence." This was the rumor mill at work, then—I'd already been hit with a sheath of papers from the Jorgensens' attorney. There was a nondisclosure form, too, old hat for the Jorgensens.

"I'm sorry," I told her. "I really don't have anything I can say to you."

She followed me halfway up the sidewalk, asking questions about my job and the unspecified scandal.

I kept walking.

"I'm just trying to get all the facts," she called after me as

I opened the front door. "If it were me, I would want to be represented fairly and accurately in the media."

I leaned against the closed door and waited for her to get back into her car, finish a phone call and drive away. Easy enough to say, but it wasn't Andrea Piccola in the situation. It was me, and it was a horrible, lonely place to be.

Andrea Piccola wrote her article without me, Phil or the Jorgensens. It ended up as just a blurb: Incompetence Alleged Against Miles Landers Counselor. She'd talked to Fiedler, who made vague references to the expectations for guidance counselors, and to Blaine, who would only state that I'd been a counselor in good standing for seven years, and had helped many students. She'd reached Aaron, who said that I was an asset to the school and would absolutely be missed. The Jorgensens were silent, not wanting to open that can of worms. My official reappointment happened during a closed session of the school board. In the fall, I would be counseling junior high students at two schools, twenty minutes apart.

On the day the article appeared, I packed up my desk and told Blaine I would be taking sick leave for the next thirty days, through the end of the school year and into summer. I'd only taken a day or two a year on average throughout the years, and I had more than enough days left. Jenn gave me a long hug, Aaron kissed me on the forehead and said he refused to believe it was happening, and even Dale Streeter stuck his head out of his office to say it was a shame. He'd agreed to stay on for another year, to give some continuity to the department.

Aaron carried one of the boxes to my car, and while I re-arranged things in the trunk to make more room, he said, "I'm worried about you—both of you. I've been talking with

Danielle, you know. She's told me a bit of what happened with you and Phil."

Ah, so that was it. "Keep talking to her, will you? She's not talking to me at all."

We hugged once more at my car, and I drove away. When I returned later that day to pick up Danielle, I avoided the staff parking lot and queued in the long line of parents in front of the school.

It was an understatement that Danielle wasn't speaking to me. She spent her afternoons and evenings in her room, sometimes with Hannah; she rode next to me on the way to and from school with tinny music seeping out of her headphones.

I yelled, I pleaded, I cajoled and then I stopped. When I was a kid, we'd had a cat that was a finicky eater, and Dad always said it would eat when it was hungry. I applied the same logic here. Danielle would talk when she was ready. She couldn't be silent forever.

In the meantime, she communicated by Post-it notes left next to the front door: *I need $10 for the BBQ* or *We're out of Popsicles.*

By the end of May, I had enough money for a deposit and first and last month's rent on an apartment not far from the freeway, near the proposed extension for the commuter train, still a few years away. The entire complex was built on that hope, on the idea of what might be coming around the bend. It seemed fitting. Danielle and I took a tour after school one day, although it took a great deal of coercion to get her out of the car. The general manager pointed out the laundry areas, the fitness center and the communal green space. The laundry room consisted of four washers and dryers, and the fitness center was a row of treadmills and a stack of hand weights in the corner. I smiled encouragingly as he spoke, wondering how long it would take to get The Palms out of my head, to stop comparing everything else in life to its lavishness.

Phil was still convinced that I would come to my senses, that by the end of June we would be joining him at the condo in Laguna Niguel. "You can't just throw it all away, Liz," he said. But the more I thought about it, the more I realized that I could.

My mom didn't understand, either. To be fair, I'd skirted all the nuances of the situation and focused only on Phil's new job. She gave me her standard speech about things happening in a marriage, about putting in the effort to work things out. Was that what she had done with Dad, when she found out about his woman on the side? Or had she just accepted it, turning her blind eye, because there was nothing else she could have done?

In May, we marked Danielle's fifteenth birthday with a gourmet pizza split three ways with Hannah. I offered to take the two of them somewhere—a day trip to the city, a visit to the new IMAX. Danielle glared at me stonily, shaking her head. What gift do you give your daughter when you're in the process of ripping her life apart? In the end I settled for a stack of crisp, impersonal gift cards, a note that said I loved her. The gift cards disappeared into her wallet; the following week, I spotted my note in her trash can.

We lived out the rest of the school year and the beginning of the summer like hermits. Since Phil no longer worked for Parker-Lane, we avoided the clubhouse and the communal areas and made our brief forays into the real world by car.

There was something ominous about the way the access gates closed behind us each time, I realized. One day I wondered if they simply wouldn't open to readmit us.

"We'll make the most of it," I told Danielle. I'd hoped to be able to send her to camp for one more summer, as a volunteer-counselor-in-training, but the fee was too steep. "It's only until the end of June. You can still go swimming every day, you can hang out with Hannah…"

For once she acknowledged that I had spoken, giving me the fake, patronizing smile that had appeared out of nowhere these past few weeks. "Sounds like paradise," she said.

It didn't occur to me until later that she was quoting Phil. That was what he'd told us the first time he'd brought us to The Palms, into the cavernous empty house. We'd looked out the row of windows on to the back deck, and he'd put an arm around each of our shoulders. *It'll be like living in paradise.*

Hannah Bergland was the only person in The Palms who was going to miss us. She took the place in Danielle's life that had been vacated by Kelsey; it was now Hannah's shoes I tripped over in the entryway, Hannah's sweatshirts that got mixed in with our laundry. Her sixteenth birthday this spring had been marked with much less fanfare than Kelsey's had last fall, but she ended up with a sporty Ford Focus and a prepaid gas card.

"We can go anywhere," she told Danielle, dangling the keys from a braided leather rope embossed with her name.

Danielle raised an eyebrow. "Anywhere?"

I wondered just how far away she wanted to be, just how far she would go if she had the chance. Technically, Hannah wasn't allowed to have a minor in the car without another adult present, but the Berglands didn't seem to be aware of this rule, and I was too exhausted to enforce it. Besides, Hannah was a meticulous driver, even putting on her turn signal to round the curve of our cul-de-sac.

"Just be home before dark," I told them, and they always were—returning with giant Slurpee cups, talking about their round of Putt-Putt or the movie they'd just seen. Sometimes, at night, their talk turned to Kelsey Jorgensen—she was the common denominator in their lives, the low-hanging fruit. "...such a bitch," Hannah would say, and Danielle would respond, "I can't believe I let her use me like that." They reported Kelsey sightings: "I saw that whore riding in Mac's truck" and "My mom saw her outside the pharmacy, probably loading up on her anti-psycho meds." Once, I heard them picking out men for her—a guy they'd seen in the mall, checking them out while he waited for his wife to finish in the dressing room. "We should have given him Kelsey's number," Danielle said, and Hannah shrieked with laughter.

I should have stopped them—I knew that. I'd come to the point where I realized that Kelsey Jorgensen was a tragic figure, really, almost Shakespearean, ruled by an obsession she couldn't conquer. The Jorgensens had insisted that we cease all contact and communication with Kelsey, which wasn't hard to comply with, except that she often walked past on the sidewalk in front of our house, her face shielded by massive sunglasses. I saw her when I was loading the car with junk to take to Goodwill, when I was unloading groceries, when I was backing up and pulling in. Without Danielle and Phil, she must have been as lonely as she'd been last summer, when I'd spotted her doing the same thing. Did even a small part of her regret what she'd done?

No, I couldn't blame Danielle for her anger, even when it spilled into mocking bitterness. Kelsey had come through our lives like a tornado, catching us all up in her swath of destruction.

Sometimes, days went by where I saw only flashes of Danielle—down the stairs and out the door, through the den to the refrigerator, out to the pool, where her body was a shimmery flash two feet beneath the surface.

This was what it would be like next year—she'd be at Miles Landers, and I'd be splitting my time between junior highs, and I'd know less and less about her life every day. This was what it would be like when she went to college—she'd be a weekly phone call home, a visit on Christmas.

The distance was allowing me to see her from a new perspective. She would be driving within a year; she wasn't just a kid, not the cardboard cutout of my own hopes and plans. She was already far more complicated than I could understand.

One night she came home with a tattoo on her hip, a Chinese symbol visible just below the hem of her bikini. She wasn't trying to hide it—she walked right past me on her way to the refrigerator.

"What's that?" I asked, grabbing her arm. I ran my finger over the raised puff of skin. "How did you get this? You're not eighteen. You needed parental permission."

She pulled away, as if I were toxic. "I told them I was an orphan."

"I hope it came with some kind of insurance policy," I shot back. "Maybe a treatment plan for your hepatitis C."

She rolled her eyes.

I was furious, of course, demanding to know why she'd done it and where. I threatened to ground her for the rest of the summer or the rest of high school.

"Why not?" she shrugged. "You've already ruined the rest of my life."

Later, I looked up the character online—it was like a fancy lower-case *h* and I found it under a list of Most Popular Chinese Tattoos. It meant *strength*. I wondered if that was how she saw herself, as someone who had overcome great challenges. Or if she meant she needed strength for whatever was coming next.

I hated the tattoo—even when it wasn't visible, I knew it was there, just beneath her waistband. But I hated, too, the thought that a stranger had touched her while she waited in her underwear, wincing, biting her lip, trusting herself completely with her own stupid decisions.

My job that summer was to pack. It was a massive downsize—4,000 square feet to 750. I'd grown ruthless with my decision-making. At each pass through the house, I was calculating what we needed and how we could get rid of the rest. We wouldn't need the linens I'd purchased for the dining table that had never materialized, or the dozens of towels and washcloths scattered between the home's five bathrooms. I listed the bar stools and the club chairs on Craigslist, as well as the king-size bed that wouldn't fit in my new bedroom. Phil and I had paid over two thousand for it—were still paying, probably, the finance charges climbing monthly—but I found a buyer for six hundred who would also carry it downstairs for me, out to his waiting truck and away. While he strapped it down with bungee cords, Helen Zhang walked past with the family's new dog, a narrow-faced whippet. She didn't acknowledge me.

Good riddance, I thought.

Goodbye to all that.

★ ★ ★

The third Friday in June was hot and still. I'd spent the morning in the garage, sorting through the boxes we'd never unpacked last summer. I'd been inclined to toss it all, but then I opened one box and found Danielle's papers from elementary school—her stiff watercolors, poems written in faded color pencil, an essay on dinosaurs and their habitats.

Danielle came in with a box labeled Sweaters and dropped it in the keep pile.

"What are your plans for today?" I asked, wiping sweat from my forehead.

She shrugged. "Hannah's coming over to swim."

"I made chicken salad, if you want to have sandwiches," I called after her retreating figure. I'd vowed not to buy any more groceries before our move, so I'd been thawing meat from the freezer and working our way through cans in the pantry. I was also tackling the wine Phil and I had accumulated over the past year and had a bottle of Riesling chilling in the refrigerator for later. We wouldn't have room in our new kitchen, and it seemed a shame to leave it behind.

On the other hand—maybe the new owners would need it. I certainly had.

I ate lunch on a paper plate, since I'd already packed most of the dishes. I'd packed the wineglasses, too, so I ended up drinking a few swigs of Riesling straight from the bottle, a tragic figure in my own kitchen.

Later that afternoon, I braved the heat of the garage again in a tank top and shorts, opening the bays to allow for at least a little air movement. Why should I care what Deanna thought, pausing on her walkway, purse dangling from her wrist? Did it matter what Victor observed, jogging past bare-chested, his shirt hanging from the waistband of his shorts?

I was on my knees, elbow-deep in a box of Christmas things, ornaments and tangled strings of lights and cinnamon-scented sachets, when I saw Kelsey Jorgensen in our driveway. She was looking down at her phone in its bright magenta case. I stared at her. It seemed impossible, with everything that had happened, but Kelsey had somehow thrived. She looked healthy, her skin a glowing tan, her body strong and beautiful in a T-shirt and shorts.

I struggled to my feet, moving toward the open garage door. "You can't be here," I yelled. "You need to get off my property."

She looked down at her phone and back at me. "I just wanted—"

"No." I shooed her away with an angry hand. "It doesn't matter what you want. Your parents don't want you here, and I don't want you here. You need to leave now." She didn't move. I retreated to the wall-mounted controls and hit one of the buttons, sending the first door down in front of her. She stepped into view in the next door as it was closing.

"Can I just say—"

"No!" I shouted, hitting the third button. For a moment I thought she would duck under the door as it lowered, come rolling ninja-like into the space. But I watched her disappear, chunk by chunk—head and shoulders, chest and torso, her long, long legs, until the garage was fully dark.

I was shaking when I went into the house. I should call the Jorgensens, tell them to come get their daughter. Or the police, to tell them I was being harassed. *No.* In a week, Danielle and I would drive away, and I planned to be fully done with Kelsey Jorgensen. She wouldn't be at our apartment complex; she wouldn't stop by my office.

Done. *Finito.*

It was cold in the house, but sweat was still streaming into my eyes, into the V of my bra. I took the Riesling out of the fridge, uncorked it and let it slide cool down my throat. Why not? Maybe it would even help to get a little drunk. It might go faster if my senses were dulled, if I couldn't deliberate over every little thing. After a few glasses, maybe I would forget where things had come from, what they had once meant.

For a long time, I stood by the slider, watching Hannah and Danielle in the pool. It was a beautiful day, the sky cloudless, the sun a flaming ball heading slowly west. Hannah had lugged over her stereo and the whole house seemed to throb, the windows pulsing like a heartbeat. I thought about stepping outside, discreetly turning down the volume while I reminded them to put on sunscreen. But they looked happy, and I didn't want to spoil the moment.

I raised a hand to my reflection, pressing my palm against the glass. It had never been more than a fantasy, this place. We'd had only a tenuous toehold on this life, and it was easy enough to take ourselves away from it. Maybe it was all anyone had, after all. The bank accounts and the big houses might have been a buffer from the rest of the world, but they couldn't keep you safe. They couldn't make you happy.

Once we were no longer here—not just Phil and Liz and Danielle McGinnis, but everyone else, too, the Zhangs and the Mesbahs, the Sieverts and yes, the Jorgensens—how long would it take for the earth to come back and claim its own? How long until the critters found their way inside—the ants and snails and spiders and moles? How long until they burrowed into, tunneled through, nested in? How long before weeds took over the yard, before shrubs and trees grew tall enough to hide the evidence of our lives?

Tipsy, I took the bottle upstairs and sprawled on top of

the sheets. Even up there, I could still hear the music pulsing, pulsing. Occasionally, the mechanical voice of the Other
Woman interrupted my thoughts: "Back door open" and
"Back door open" as the girls entered and exited, hunting
for a can of soda or hurrying to the bathroom.

   Phil should be here, I thought, staring up at the ceiling fan.
Not just to help with the packing, but to see it through to
the end. We'd never had the life he'd envisioned here, not
the backyard barbecues, the nights in the den with all the
guys watching a game. It hadn't been that grand of a wish,
now that I thought about it. I'd resented him for bringing
us out here, for leaving while everything crumbled around
us. But when it came down to it, all he'd really wanted was
happiness. That was all he'd been asking for.

   In the bathroom it all came up—the wine, the remains of the
chicken salad sandwich I'd had for lunch. I sat hunched forward
on my knees, shoulders shaking. Downstairs, I heard Danielle and Hannah laughing. She would bounce back from this.
Maybe Phil and I would, too—separate or together. In a few
years, maybe, we would laugh about all of it, as in *whew, look at
the bullet we dodged there*. Maybe a time would even come when
we forgot her name, when down the road we would look at each
other and say, *What was that girl's name again? Kelsey something?*

   I got to my feet uneasily. At the sink, I splashed water on
my face, rinsed and spat. *One more week*, I promised myself,
sliding between the cool sheets. I closed my eyes against the
dizzying circles of the ceiling fan. The faint overhead whir
reminded me of something—an airplane, a helicopter, a boat
with an outboard motor. Or maybe it reminded me of a movie
scene, one of those images that isn't real but feels like it could
be—so close, so tangible, so personal. Almost like a dream.

PHIL

The new job was going well. It was a relief to be away from The Palms, to have the shame of failure behind me. I was part of the builder's marketing team, tasked with making million-plus-dollar homes look attractive to buyers. It wasn't that hard; once you were committed to living in a certain zip code, the rest was just details. The difference was that I wasn't one of them, not this time. I wore my suits and I flashed cheerful smiles and I shook hands with a hearty confidence, and I left them at the end of the day to drive to the condo where I ate a TV dinner on a lawn chair in the living room and fell asleep on a mattress on the floor. I hadn't taken a vow of poverty; I was waiting for Liz to say she was coming, too. I pictured the three of us renting a U-Haul and driving it south on I-5, over the Grapevine, into the smog that was LA.

I was right to get out when I did—I knew that. It wouldn't have ended with Kelsey Jorgensen otherwise. She would have found new ways to worm herself into my life, the way she'd wormed herself into my thoughts. It took at least a month before I stopped waking up in the middle of the night in a cold sweat, ashamed of what I'd been dreaming.

I begged Liz to come down, even for a visit, but was met with her stubborn silence, even when the Jorgensens came for her job. That was my moment, I figured. If she had to leave the school she loved, she might as well start completely over with me. I sent her links to job postings all over LA, but she never replied. I talked to her about the school I'd found for Danielle, a science magnet not far from my condo, and she gave me only a noncommittal grunt. When she stopped taking my calls, I sent her text messages. I miss you. I love you. I want the two of us to start over together. Her responses were chilling, they were so practical. What do you want me to do with that old Greek rug?

She told me she planned to be out of The Palms by the end of June, but wouldn't give me any specifics about where they were going. I couldn't handle the idea of her going wherever it was without me.

And so, one Friday at the end of June, I rented a car for the six-hour drive to The Palms. I wasn't concerned about the wear and tear on my SUV, but I didn't particularly want to be recognized by my former neighbors. I imagined Myriam calling the police, the Jorgensens arriving with stones and pitchforks. I stopped on the way for lunch, then at a Trader Joe's in Pleasanton for a bouquet of flowers.

The Palms looked the same, the lawns bottle green despite the fact that the drought was a real thing now, not just a worrisome theory. Helen's white BMW was parked in her driveway; Mac's ridiculous truck was parked at the Sieverts'. Even the guest access code had been the same—I'd simply punched in the four digits and the gates had rolled back for me, although I wasn't exactly the prodigal son.

When I passed Liz's house—*our* house—all three of the garage doors were open, and I caught a glimpse of Liz bending over a cardboard box, dark hair falling into her face. I could have parked right there, but something told me to keep going, to take my time with the approach. I ended up at the far end of the clubhouse parking lot, shaking life back into my muscles. I was wearing khaki shorts and a white polo, the leather flip-flops I'd bought since moving south. I didn't recognize any of the golfers who came zipping past in their carts, but I put on a floppy fisherman's hat just in case, a relic from my years in Corfu.

I rounded the corner on the side of the Berglands' house, their front yard littered with giant plastic toys. I would stand in the driveway until Liz looked up. She would be glad to see me, relieved. I could almost feel her in my arms. *It'll be a new start*, I would promise her.

But I stopped short on the sidewalk when I recognized who was standing in the driveway, who had beat me to my own punch. I'd managed to forget about her for the most part, although it had been difficult in Southern California, where every girl had her same long blond hair, her golden tan.

I couldn't hear what Kelsey was saying, but Liz was practically screaming. *You need to leave now.* I heard the garage bays closing, one after the other, over Kelsey's protests.

I turned, heading back in the direction of the clubhouse. *Don't run*, I told myself. A man in a floppy hat with a bouquet of flowers running down the sidewalk was sure to bring attention to himself. I went back to the rental car and sat there, slumped low, watching for Kelsey. Eventually she would have to go home, and that meant she would have to pass in front of the Sieverts' house. I waited, the car baking-hot, but she didn't come. Was she still standing in front of our house, waiting for Liz to open the door? Had Liz relented, allowing her inside?

I called Liz, but her phone went right to voice mail. Typical.

The Zhang boys passed, swinging their rackets. The Asbills came by, their twins walking with the thick, trunk-like steps of toddlers.

I dialed Liz again, hanging up without leaving a message.

What if she had left the house? It was a Saturday; maybe she had errands to run in Livermore.

Eventually, I decided to go around the back, via the walking trail. I wondered if Parker-Lane had found anyone to monitor the surveillance cameras, if some poor schmo was sitting in my old office right now, flipping between surveillance screens and a game of solitaire. I heard the music before I saw our house—the bass line thumping. A stereo was sitting on the table under the giant orange umbrella that we'd barely used last summer. The back door was open, and then Hannah Bergland came out, still a bit pudgy, her reddish curls wet against her head.

From inside the house, someone—Danielle—called, "Which kind do you want?" Over her shoulder, Hannah called, "Pepsi's fine." She grabbed a beach towel off a deck chair and tied it around her hips before heading back inside the house, sliding the door shut behind her. I felt a bit dazed, maybe from the heat or the long drive. It was as though I'd stumbled into an old memory, a scene of déjà vu. Here were the people from my old life, moving right along without me.

"I knew you'd come," someone said behind me, and I dropped the flowers.

"You're not supposed to be here," I told her. "Didn't my wife just tell you that a few minutes ago?"

Kelsey smiled at me, coming closer. "I didn't know she was still your wife."

"Get away from me, Kelsey. I'll call the police."

"I live here," she said. "I'm allowed to be on the walking trail. You're the one who's not supposed to be here."

I reached for the gate latch and found the stubborn knot of twine I'd tied there months ago.

She smirked. "What's the problem? Does someone not want you here?"

It wasn't a tall fence; I hooked one foot on the lower beam and vaulted over, landing on grass higher than my ankles. Liz must have stopped the lawn service.

"Why are you running away from me?" Kelsey called. "That was your big mistake, you know. You could have been with me this whole time. I would have gone with you, wherever you went. We could have gone to Vegas and gotten married in one of those little chapels."

"You're crazy," I said over my shoulder. "You're absolutely insane."

I expected someone to spot me from the house—Hannah or Danielle, maybe, or Liz, if she wasn't in the garage anymore—but no one came. I turned around to see Kelsey climbing over the fence after me. "Wait, wait!" she called, as if we were meant to be doing this together.

I skirted around the side of the pool, where two soda cans were perched on the edge. In the long grass, I stepped on a bottle of sunscreen, nearly twisting my ankle. When I looked up, my eye caught the slight mound in the planter bed, under which I'd buried Virgil Zhang, not so expertly, after all.

"Remember that first night, when you went skinny-dipping?" Kelsey called. She was right behind me now, and I turned around, swinging my arm wildly to ward her off. She stepped out of the way, laughing. "We could do that now. We could do that together."

I looked up to my bedroom window, expecting to see Liz there staring down at us. She probably couldn't hear us over the thumping of the music. What was this music, anyway? When had Danielle started listening to rap? I just needed to make it to the back door. It would be open and I could step inside, or it would be locked and I'd have to bang to get someone's attention. Either way, I needed to get away from Kelsey.

We were on the deck when she grabbed the hem of my shirt, yanking me backward. I swung my elbow behind me and felt the crunch as it connected with her jaw. She let go and stumbled to the ground, cradling her face in her hands.

"I'm sorry," I said, kneeling beside her. My heart pounded. It was a mistake, this whole idea. *Abort, abort.* "I didn't mean to hurt you. I was just trying to get you off me. I don't need this trouble right now. Can you stand up?"

I helped her to her feet. The lower half of her face was red. I knew what was coming next. It was the same night-mare it had always been, just a different version.

She gave me that smile, the same one she'd given me a year before, when she came into my office and told me she was bored. She was so helplessly bored. Was that all it was with her? If she'd had a hobby like painting or macramé or horse-back riding, would that have done the trick? She touched me on the arm, as if she were feeling my biceps, and she said, "If you don't take me with you, I'll tell everyone you at-tacked me. I'll say I saw you sneaking into the backyard and

I tried to stop you, and you attacked me. I'll scream. Everyone will believe me."

I didn't think—I just reacted.

Later, on the long drive back, sweat pouring off my face,
I did all the thinking I couldn't do then. I told myself it was
for the best, for everyone. Kelsey would never have been
satisfied; she would have schemed and planned and ruined
everyone she came across. I thought about how easy it had
been, how miraculous that none of the nosy neighbors in
the The Palms had been passing by on the walking trail.
Liz and Danielle and Hannah must have been upstairs, the
scuffle at the pool drowned out by lyrics that were incom-
prehensible to me. I thought about how light Kelsey's body
had been in my hands, how easy she was to maneuver, like
a puppet or a rag doll. She went over the edge of the pool
headfirst, turning to face me in the middle of the motion,
her eyes surprised as her head struck the handrail, and then
she was gone, sinking into the shallow end, wisps of blood
blooming on the water like tiny, beautiful jellyfish.

JUNE 19, 2015
8:42 P.M.

LIZ

Once upon a time, I'd been a sneaky little kid hiding secrets from my blind mother. Once upon a time, I'd been nineteen years old, staring at the blue lines on the pregnancy kit, my hand rank with my own pee, knowing for certain what I'd refused to know for weeks, for months. Once upon a time, I'd had too much to drink at a hockey game and kissed a man with a sexy accent and let myself believe in a fairy tale.

Once upon a time, I'd sat in my office with a diploma on the wall behind me, host to a parade of mothers and daughters, holding my cattiness in check, biting back judgment. I'd cringed when mothers told me that their daughters were their *best friends*—a comment that had always reduced, rather than elevated, my opinion of the mother. You're in your late thirties, and your best friend is a fifteen-year-old girl? *Poor you*, I'd thought. *Poor her.*

Once upon a time, I hadn't understood those parents, the ones who had sat in my office and defended their children to me: *this is so unlike her; he's always been so responsible.* There was something fierce about that love, a wild urge to defend, to protect, to believe, to deny, deny, deny.

Once upon a time I'd been disgusted by the Texas cheer-leader mom.

I'd thought it would be so different with my own daughter when she was a teenager. I would be able to see her clearly, without being clouded by sentimentality, without pushing her to live out my own dreams. We'd survived middle school, which had a tendency to make previously lovely children into monsters, and I'd thought that we could make it the rest of the way, through tough classes and first love and heartbreak and college applications, the way we'd made it through colic and the bumps and bruises of learning to walk and day care and skinned knees on the playground.

Once upon a time, I'd told a lie and a lie and a lie, and here we were: sitting in two chairs in the waiting room, watching as people in blue scrubs and white coats hurried in and out of swinging doors marked Emergency Personnel Only. We'd checked in with the attendant at the front desk and been told to wait, and we'd sat through most of *The O'Reilly Factor* playing on an overhead screen, lip-reading the anger and indignation and scorn.

Then we were called into a windowless room within the interior of the ER and Penny Fausset, the hospital social worker, took notes on a clipboard as she listened to our re-sponses. I strained, but couldn't see what she was writing. I imagined the checked boxes as a series of appraisals of in-nocence or guilt, truth or falsehood, good mother or bad mother.

I asked if Kelsey was going to be okay.

Penny Fausset said that unfortunately she didn't have any information.

We were asked to wait in the small room, and I looked ev-erywhere but at my daughter—at the artwork on the walls, which reminded me of a cheap motel: beach scenes, a few brushstrokes meant to evoke an eternity of ocean. There was a poster that explained the risks of heart disease, and I felt Kelsey's heart again, immobile beneath the pulsing of my locked hands.

I closed my eyes.

When the door opened, a police officer was there, pausing in the doorway as if he were taking in the scene—the smear of blood on my forearm, the sunburn pinking Danielle's skin. He introduced himself as Officer Ahearn, and before he took a seat his hand went casually to the holstered weapon clipped to his belt. He thanked us for waiting. I said it wasn't a problem. We were happy to help in any way we could.

He asked what happened.

She wasn't allowed on our property, I explained. There had been some grievances. She'd come to the front of the house earlier and I'd turned her away. But she was determined to talk to us for some reason, and so she must have gone to the back gate. She'd been taking antidepressants, I told him. There had been two previous suicide attempts.

Maybe that's what this was, I suggested. Or maybe it was an accident, and she just slipped and hit her head.

It was funny the way things seemed more true the more often they were repeated. Mantras worked like that, and mission statements.

"Is that right, what your mother says? You don't have anything to add?"

Danielle shook her head, glancing over at me.

"It's true," I said. "She didn't even know Kelsey was there until they spotted her in the pool."

He left the room at one point, and in the diminishing triangle as the door closed, I recognized in the hospital corridor

Tim Jorgensen's back: his gray suit, his neatly trimmed blond hair. I didn't see her, but I heard Sonia's voice, a high-pitched wail. "But eighteen minutes? What does that mean for—"

We waited, listening to snatches of sound from the corridor—a machine beeping, a voice over the PA system. I stared straight ahead at the beach print, seeing nothing.

"Mom," Danielle began, "you know that—"

I cut her off. "Don't tell me. Don't ever tell me."

"There's nothing—we didn't—"

"I mean it," I said, my voice sharp, echoing off the tile.

Danielle whimpered, but I didn't look at her.

My little life had slipped away. There was no more Phil, no more giant house, no more twisted neighbor girl. In many ways Danielle was gone, too, no longer the daughter I could trust, no longer a girl I could recognize. I tried to imagine the two of us in our new apartment, politely side-stepping each other in the narrow hallway. I couldn't do it, not day in and day out, not for the three years before she went off to college.

Officer Ahearn returned to say that he'd been in touch with Hannah Bergland, who confirmed Danielle's version of events, and we were free to go. His face was expressionless as he told me this. His eyes held mine. "Someone from the department will likely be in touch," he said.

I asked how Kelsey was doing, if she would be okay.

He said it was too early to know for sure, but I could tell that he knew and wasn't going to say.

When I stood, I bumped my injured toe against a table leg and let out a gasp. Not understanding, Officer Ahearn put a hand on my shoulder and said, "You're to be commended for the CPR. You did the absolute best you could."

There were more people in the lobby now, the chairs

filled and people standing near the doors. A man held an ice pack to his face.

Danielle looked at me. "What are we going to do now?"

I shook my head, imagining the drive back to The Palms, the massive entry gates, the stares of our neighbors, the boxes upon boxes that held the scraps of our lives. I thought about Phil, the missed calls on my cell phone. At the very least, I could cash in on the IOU from Christmas, the promise to take me anywhere in the world.

We were ushered outside without seeing the Jorgensens. It was dark by this time, and our stomachs were growling. My foot ached, but I'd been afraid to ask the nurses for an aspirin, knowing it would lead to paperwork and another hour of waiting.

Until she spoke, I didn't recognize the woman who came up to me, even though her thick hair and falling-apart shoulder bag looked familiar. "I was wondering if that was you," she said. "I heard it on the police scanner, and I recognized the address."

"Keep walking," I told Danielle, pushing her in front of me.

"I'm just trying to gather information, Mrs. McGinnis," Andrea Piccola said, following us through the parking lot. Danielle took a few steps forward and stopped beneath a light post. She looked worried, her eyes bright with tears. She was so young, so shortsighted. Her whole life was ahead of her.

And so I turned to Andrea Piccola, and I told her that Kelsey had sneaked into our yard and hit her head when she fell into the pool. It was a horrible accident.

And it was, as far as I knew, the truth.

★ ★ ★ ★ ★

ACKNOWLEDGMENTS

Writing, for the most part, is a solitary activity. For days on end, it seems that I only see baristas at the coffee shops where I write in a dark corner, an anonymous figure with my laptop and my headphones. My conversations are polite exchanges with the regular patrons, as nameless to me as I am to them.

But when I sat down to write the acknowledgments for this book, it was overwhelming to realize just how many people have helped along the way—with research, brainstorming, reading, editing, proofing, general and specific hand-holding, designing and marketing.

A huge thanks goes to the team at MIRA, particularly my (very patient and wise) editor Michelle Meade; Sean Kapitan and Quinn Banting for a cover that still gives me chills; the marketing team of Amy Jones, Julie Forrest and Evan Brown; copy editor Tracy Wilson-Burns; proofreader Alexandra Antonel, Liz Stein and publicist Emer Flounders. Thanks always to the whip-smart Melissa Flashman with Trident Media Group, and I extend my standard wish for good karma to Alanna Garcia.

On a local level, I've been blessed to have talented friends who can turn a chat over a cup of coffee into serious art. Thanks, Melissa Martinez, for your designer's eye and behind-the-scenes tech help. Rob Brittain, I won't be able to repay you for the late-night meetings and book trailer genius. (But will chocolate chip cookies help?) Overdue thanks goes to Blake Gentry and Scott Campbell for hours behind the camera and in front of the computer. Okay—cookies to you, too. Beth Boon is not only my sister but also a talented graphic artist who creates amazing designs for me in a pinch (which is usually when I think to ask). Thanks, thanks, *thanks*.

When I set out to write this book, I didn't anticipate all the twists and turns my life would take (let alone this plot). But I'm grateful for all the technical advice I got along the way from Craig Macho (who is hopefully writing his own book at this very moment), Julie Powers, Katie (VanderWal) Bos, Patsy Hite, and my sister-in-law and fearless emergency room nurse, Christina DeBoard Young.

I'm immensely grateful for all the people who talked shop with me—my Go Deep! compatriots in yoga and word wrangling, the Tuesday night trivia crew, and of course, the Del Monte Avenue Feature Film Freaks. Love as always to my dear English Girls, to the Treicks and DeBoards, and to everyone who asked (perhaps not anticipating the long saga of my reply), "How's the writing going?"

Thanks to *The Modesto Bee* and the Stanislaus Library Foundation for supporting a writer in their community, to libraries and bookstores and book clubs, to teaching faculty and fellow writers at Stonecoast MFA, to my teaching colleagues and students past and present at San Joaquin-Delta Community College, Modesto Junior College and University of California, Merced. And thanks to my readers, nearby and far-flung, without whom my words would exist in a void. The "I owe you big-time" award goes to Kelly Jones, Beth Boon, Sara Viss, Leah Dashe and Beth Slattery, for reading early drafts.

I always save my last thanks for Will DeBoard, who might not have known what he was getting into all those years ago when he asked me out for coffee. These days he juggles his busy professional life with mine—taking on extra dog-walking duties, understanding when it's necessary for me to disappear for hours (or days) at a time, and always giving me the honest truth. I know the dedication of this book might seem odd, given the nature of this story—so let me finish by saying: Will, thank goodness for your sense of humor.

QUESTIONS FOR DISCUSSION

1. Why is Liz so concerned about fitting in with her neighbors at The Palms? How does this change, and why? Does Liz's desire to fit into this fictional world resonate with real life?

2. As a parent, Liz is torn between wanting what's best for Danielle and wanting to control (or at least influence) certain aspects of her daughter's life— such as her friends and social contacts. Compare this to the approach other parents (such as the Jorgensens and the Sieverts) take toward their children. How much control can or should parents have over their teenagers' lives, especially when it comes to technology and social media?

3. Phil begins his narration by insisting that he isn't a pedophile, and is merely trapped in a "lose-lose" situation. Do you think he has an accurate understanding of the dilemma? Would problems have been avoided if he had tried to seek legal action such

as a restraining order against Kelsey from the very beginning?

4. Kelsey is presented as deeply troubled in this book. What might be the cause of these problems? Why do her parents continue to believe and support her in the face of contrary evidence?

5. At the end of the book, Liz is unsure of the role Danielle has played in what happened to Kelsey, but seems determined to protect her daughter (and therefore her daughter's dark secrets). What motivates Liz at the end of the book? Is it the same thing that motivates the Jorgensens relating to their own daughter?

6. Phil tells Liz that he believes they're the same kind of awful, but Liz disagrees. Is Phil merely a helpless victim of circumstances brought on by his life at The Palms? Is Liz?

A CONVERSATION WITH
PAULA TREICK DeBOARD

The Drowning Girls **is an unsettling story about the dark underbelly of an idyllic neighborhood, and how one family finds themselves sucked into a world of secrets and lies just below the community's seemingly flawless surface. What was your inspiration for this novel?**

For years I was a freelance writer for a real estate publication, and once or twice a month I would visit these fantastic new home communities that were each promising the world to their clients—not only the granite countertops and the six-panel interior doors, but the implicit guarantee of happiness. Deep down, those physical things can't matter too much; they're just the circumstances of our lives. There's that saying that "wherever you go, there you are"—meaning that our problems and insecurities have a way of following us anywhere, no matter the change in location.

The Palms is a perfectly manicured, incredibly wealthy gated community—a big departure from the rural

communities and lower middle-class families that featured in your earlier novels. Why the change? What similarities and differences do you see between the people in these communities?

Ultimately, I'm interested in the many varieties of the human experience—what makes us tick, and what pushes seemingly average or happy people over the edge? In my first novel, *The Mourning Hours*, the book revolved around a small, tight-knit community in Wisconsin. *The Drowning Girls* might be set in a gated community near Livermore, California, but in many ways the main characters are facing the same pressures: the scrutiny of their neighbors, the importance of their reputations, the personal secrets of marriage and family.

All of your novels center on everyday families placed under an enormous amount of pressure from extenuating circumstances. What draws you to family dramas, and how do you decide which perspectives will narrate their experience?

I've always been interested in the dynamics of family life. That's not rooted in any deep-seated issues with my own family, but really just out of a curiosity about what makes people's lives work. When it comes down to it, most of our joys and sorrows are connected with our families—those few people on earth who know the best and worst of each other. In my first two novels, I gave the young characters a voice in the narration, but in this book, the story seemed to belong to Liz and Phil. And actually, Phil's voice didn't come into the story until after the first draft. Once I started writing from his perspective, the whole story suddenly came together.

Can you describe the writing process for this novel? How did the story evolve as you worked through it?

This story went through several twists and turns in my mind before becoming the final version of *The Drowning Girls*. When I began writing, I saw The Palms much as it would have looked on one of the builders' glossy brochures. With each draft, the place became a little darker in my mind, the characters more complicated, the stakes higher for Phil and Liz. When I look back on it now, it's almost as if I approached the story from the outside and circled it in increasingly narrow loops until I knew exactly who the characters were and where their conflicts rested. This book really wouldn't have come together without some wise advise from my beta readers, including my editor, Michelle Meade, who freed me to go further, push harder. In my mind, I needed that permission to go to the dark place where the story had to go.

Do you read other fiction while you're doing your own writing or do you find it distracting?

I read constantly, even while I'm in the middle of a draft— but I'm careful not to focus too heavily on one writer or style of writing, as that has a way of influencing my own writing voice. I love to teach Hemingway, but there's a problem when I start to sound like him. The trick for me has been to select at random from my massive "to be read" pile and approach each new book as an escape from my own writing. I've become hooked on audio books as well, which makes me pay attention to the sounds of individual words. That's something I pay attention to as the story approaches its final draft.

What was your greatest challenge in writing *The Drowning Girls*? What about your greatest pleasure?

I juggle a few different lives at once—writer, teacher, wife/daughter/sister/friend—so sometimes it gets a bit tricky. I've learned to dedicate blocks of time specifically to writing, so when I sit down at my laptop, I'm entering a period of "hyperfocus." You could stand in front of me and wave your hand in my face, and I might not notice—this has happened. I'm also learning not to feel guilty when I'm writing. There are a dozen little things demanding my attention, and just about all the time, those things can wait.

My breakthrough with *The Drowning Girls* actually came while I was on a plane, traveling approximately five hundred miles an hour and 35,000 feet above my regular life. My husband was in the seat next to me, asleep, and I opened up a notebook and wrote for about four hours straight. Normally, I'm a laptop and neatly ordered folder-and-file type of writer, but there was something that was just so *right* about this moment, that I knew I had tapped into the heart of the book. Before that, *The Drowning Girls* was just a file with a lot of words. After that, it was a story.